ART ACROSS BORDERS

Weatherhead
East Asian Institute

Studies of the Weatherhead East Asian Institute, Columbia University

The Studies of the Weatherhead East Asian Institute of Columbia University were inaugurated in 1962 to bring to a wider public the results of significant new research on modern and contemporary East Asia.

ART ACROSS BORDERS

JAPANESE ARTISTS IN THE UNITED STATES BEFORE WORLD WAR II

RAMONA HANDEL-BAJEMA

MERWIN ASIA

MerwinAsia
Portland, Maine

MerwinAsia
59 West St., Unit 3W
Portland, ME 04102
USA
www.merwinasia.com

Distributed by the University of Hawai'i Press

Library of Congress Control Number: 2021916252

ISBN 978-1-937385-81-1 (Paperback)
ISBN 978-1-937385-84-2 (Hardcover)

Printed in the United States of America

The paper used in this publication meets the minimum requirements of the American National Standard for Information Services—Permanence of Paper for Printed Library Materials, ANSI/NISO Z39/48-1992

(Front Cover): Ishigaki Eitarô, "City," (1925), oil on canvas, The Museum of Modern Art, Wakayama.

(Back Cover): Miyatake Tôyô, "Itô Michio in the Pizzacati," (1929), Collection of Toyo Miyatake Studio.

For my mother,
Jane Handel

Contents

Acknowledgments

Many historians fortunate enough to work with Carol Gluck have been quick to recognize her guidance in the first sentence of their acknowledgements. I am no exception. I have been a fan of her scholarship since my first days as a U.C. Berkeley undergraduate studying Japanese history and have been unduly honored to call her my advisor during my years at Columbia. My appreciation for her constant support, tireless rigor, and unending inspiration is boundless.

I have been one of the lucky ones to be mentored by a dream team. Harry Harootunian gave me a treasured commodity – his time – as well as challenged my intellect beyond what I thought myself capable of. I am grateful for the guidance of Kim Brandt, Marilyn Ivy, Rebecca Karl, Naoyuki Uemori, and other scholars of East Asia that insisted that my ideas need not be regionally or nationally bounded. Mae Ngai and Alexandra Munroe also generously lent their ideas and support for the dissertation that was the basis for this book. All my mentors, including Gregory Pflugfelder and Henry Smith, encouraged me to be a historian that used more than the written word as text. Other professors at Columbia University including Mark Mazower, Partha Chaterjee, Victoria de Grazia, Eugenia Lean, and Gregory Mann showed me that a scholar of Japan can thrive beyond departmental borders. I am grateful to the art historians, curators, and artists who welcomed a historian to address artists and visual culture. Jonathan Reynolds, Frish Brandt, and Karen Sinsheimer helped my writing about art. Robert Flynn Johnson facilitated access to Obata Chiura's artworks at the Fine Arts Museum of San Francisco as well as introduced me to images from his own collection. Historian Iizawa Kôtaro was also very generous with his time and guidance.

Ella Gudwin has provided me with professional opportunities to excel in humanitarian aid and international development that allowed me to understand the world in ways that benefited my academic work. Artists, writers, actors, and musicians have blessed me throughout my life with their encouragement: Lydia Lunch, Lane Nishikawa, Karma Lekshe Tsomo, René Yañez, Eric Hayashi, Robert Englund, Culture Clash (Richard Montoya, Ricardo Salinas, and Herbert Siguenza), Kelvin Han Yee, Henry Rollins, bell hooks, Sean Thackrey, Susan Thackrey, Eva Garcia, and my godmother Pamela Prince among many others have demanded that I pursue excellence in my research and work. They all taught me how artists shape our world and are important bellwethers for understanding and translating history. I am grateful to Gary Moriwaki, who shared stories about his family's experiences when incarcerated in concentration camps. Yoshizaki Masahiko deserves gratitude for being a stable and supportive friend through many career twists and turns.

My gratitude to my colleagues – Chelsea Szendi-Schieder, Adam Bronson, Nathan Shockey, Andrew B. Liu, Max Ward, Phil Kaffen, Simon Taylor, and Timothy Yang – is tremendous. They have been my intellectual and political comrades and this thesis would not exist without their questions, challenges, and humor. Hitomi Yoshio and Christophe Thouny helped me keep my foot in the academic ring while I was engaged in disaster relief work.

I am grateful to the Weatherhead East Asian Institute of Columbia University and the support of Laura Warne and Ross Yelsey. With the generous support of a fellowship from the Japan Society of the Promotion of Sciences, I was able to complete my year of research at Waseda University. I am thankful to my colleagues, who welcomed me into their seminar with open arms: Uechi Satoko, Sano Tanomori,

Matsusaka Hiroaki, Dexter Thomas Jr., Shirai Satoshi, Andrew Gebert, and Shigeta Shinji. A special thank you is due to the Tochigi Prefectural Museum of Fine Arts, Wakayama Museum of Modern Art, Crystal Bridges Museum of American Art, Tokyo Photographic Art Museum, the Miyatake family, and the Japanese American National Museum for access to the artists' works as well as archives. Kimi Kodani Hill not only allowed me to reproduce her grandfather's masterworks in this book, but she also provided me with a photograph of Obata Chiura taken at a joint- exhibition with his father, Rokuichi. Growing up in San Francisco, I have wonderful memories of roaming the Palace Legion of Honor's rooms and I am delighted to include a photograph of Obata taken there. Thanks to Douglas Merwin and Lucian Burg, this book left my computer and ventured into a wider world.

I am grateful to my family, Maria Nation and Roberto Flores, for providing dogs to cuddle with, delicious food, and a sanctuary while I was in graduate school. Their kindness and generosity provided the quiet comforts that a graduate student truly craves. Don Bajema taught me to question established narratives and to translate that skepticism into writing. A big, heart-filled thank you goes to my angel, Delilah, who made me a better person.

My mother, Jane Handel, has had the greatest role in this process: inspiring curiosity about the world, supporting me while I study, and expecting excellence. First to read everything I have written; I am blessed by her friendship and wisdom.

Note on Names and Translations

Some of the artists in this book are more commonly known in the United States by their first names followed by family names. (For example, Chiura Obata and Toyo Miyatake) For consistency, I have chosen to write all Japanese-origin names as they would be understood in Japan with their family name first. (Thus, Obata Chiura and Miyatake Tôyô) I use diacritics to indicate long Japanese vowels. For Miyatake's first name, I include diacritics, which are not always used for his name. Unless otherwise indicated, all Japanese translations are my own.

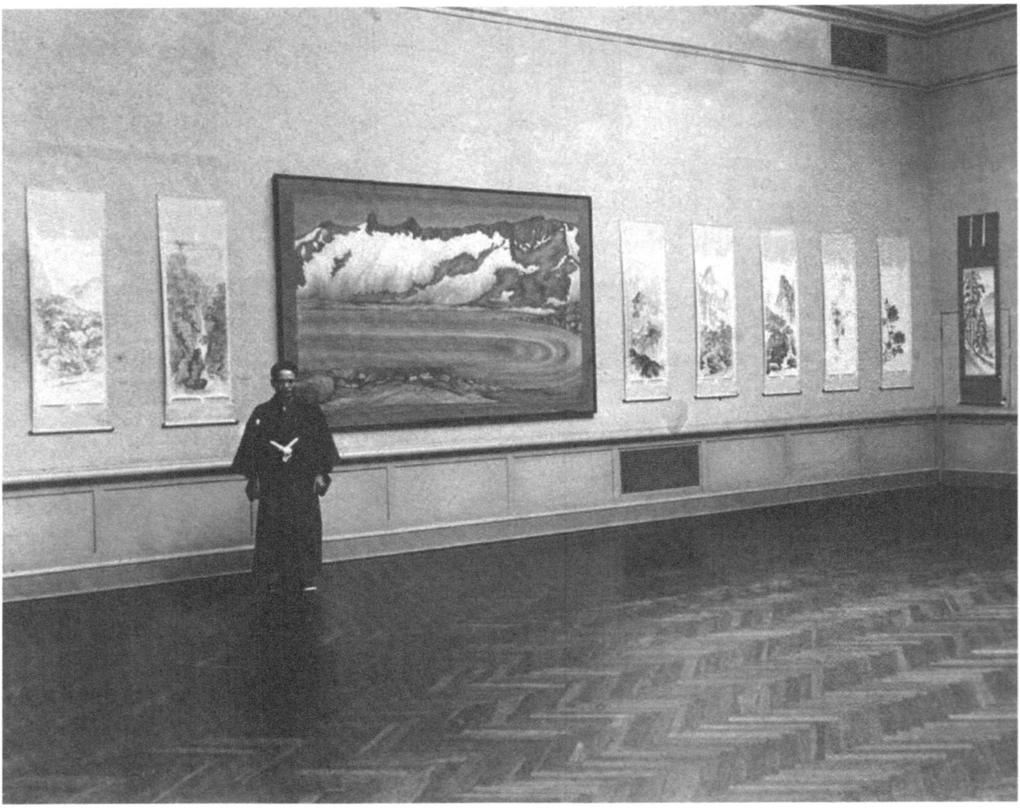

Obata Chiura at his joint exhibition of his paintings and those by his father, Rokuichi. California Palace of Legion of Honor, 1931. Courtesy of the Obata Family.

Introduction

To Be an Artist Is a Wonderful Thing

The Museum of Modern Art included five paintings by the Japanese artist Kuniyoshi Yasuo in its 1929 exhibition entitled "Paintings by Nineteen Living Americans." Born in rural Japan, Kuniyoshi was ineligible for U.S. citizenship, but the New York art world had embraced him as one of its own. He was not the only Japanese artist active in early American modernism: Shimizu Toshi won out over fellow exhibitors John Singer Sargent and Stuart Davis for the top prize at a 1921 art and sculpture exhibition held in Chicago. During the Depression, the Works Progress Administration hired Ishigaki Eitarô to paint a mural of George Washington and Abraham Lincoln on the wall of a Harlem courthouse. In California, Obata Chiura became an art professor in 1930 at the University of California, Berkeley, while photographer Miyatake Tôyô curated gallery exhibitions for his friend and mentor, Edward Weston, in Los Angeles' Little Tokyo.

Hundreds of Japanese artists traveled to the United States beginning in the late nineteenth century. Some arrived as trained artists, hoping to capitalize on American interest in Japanese arts and crafts. For others, the United States was a stepping-stone to studying in Paris, the center of the European art world. After days spent cleaning hotels or picking grapes, a few were inspired to become professional artists by way of evening drawing classes. All helped to define modern art in America, but they have since been largely forgotten in the United States. Not in Japan, however. Virtually unknown in the Japanese art world during their lifetimes, most of their paintings are now in Japanese collections after Bubble Era buying sprees. Attention to the artists' works waned in the United States after World War II, but Japanese scholars and institutions saw in the artists' cosmopolitan engagement and prewar political activism an alternative experience to Japan's fascist era when its own artists were either suppressed or actively supported its war effort.

I have selected five artists–Kuniyoshi Yasuo, Ishigaki Eitarô, Shimizu Toshi, Obata Chiura, and Miyatake Tôyô—because they represent a range of experience of Japanese artists in the United States during the first half of the twentieth century. Arriving as a laborer in California, Kuniyoshi Yasuo, the most renowned member of the group, enjoyed critical and commercial acclaim during his lifetime. A darling of the American modern art scene from the 1920s until his death in 1953, "Yas," as he was known to his friends, exhibited works throughout the country, won numerous awards, led national art associations, and taught at the Art Students League in New York City. Whereas Kuniyoshi was ambivalent about leftism, able to unite militant and moderate members of artist groups, Ishigaki Eitarô was a committed leftist throughout his life and career. Ishigaki was also a political activist, whose canvases and murals depicted social injustices and urban life. Associate of the Ashcan School and American Scene painters, Shimizu Toshi was active in New York before moving to Paris and returning to Japan in the late 1920s, when he abandoned his cosmopolitan modernism and became an illustrator for the Japanese imperial army. Obata Chiura, who unlike the others had been formally trained as a painter in Japan before moving to California, represents a community of artists—as well as tens of thousands of Japanese immigrants—who lived on the West Coast. Obata applied Japanese materials and techniques to scenes of the Western frontier, creating a fusion of East and West that appealed to Californian tastes. Finally, Miyatake Tôyô, a fine art and commercial photographer, was a pioneer of modernism in Los Angeles during the 1920s, anticipating the city's dystopian film noir works decades later.

Theirs is not only a bilateral, Japan-United States story, however. These artists navigated multinational and multiethnic art worlds that had attracted others from around the globe. Japanese artists were one of the many crosscurrents establishing American modernism as the United States grappled with how to differentiate itself from the European art world during the early twentieth century. Visiting artists faced a shared paradox: they wanted to participate in modernism as well as refer to their culture of origin, places often understood as more "primitive" and "traditional" rather than modern. Although Obata could paint with *sumi* ink, the other artists in this study had never seen an *ukiyo-e* block print until they arrived in the United States, when American colleagues suggested they incorporate Japanese stylistic devices into their work. What ultimately distinguished the American art world from the European one was its heterogeneous mixture of multiple influences.

The example of Japanese artists in the United States indicates how relegating any artist who lived across national boundaries to a single or even hybrid national category—Japanese, American, Asian-American—is to miss the intricacies and value of their experience as well as their art. Other than Obata, these artists in this study could not produce Japanese aesthetics for Americans, because they trained in the United States. They were Japanese nationals making American art. They did not feel responsible for contributing to Japan's state-building project by serving as ambassadors for its national aesthetic abroad. Nor did they lay claim in their early years to the United States as a permanent home, much less assert an American identity. For most of their lives, they occupied a liminal space, planning their next move after their United States tenure. Often vague about when (or if) they would return to Japan, they were uncertain as to how long they intended to stay in the United States or to relocate to France or somewhere else. Shimizu, for example, planned to go to Paris before returning to Japan despite decades living in the United States as a known figure in Seattle and New York's art scenes. Obata had intended to travel from California to France for further study, but marriage and children kept him in San Francisco. He moved his family back to Japan in the 1920s, but he left again for the Bay Area when his American-born children struggled to integrate into Japanese society. Miyatake also returned to Japan, setting up a photo studio, but poor business propelled him back to Los Angeles' Little Tokyo. In other words, these artists were not United States immigrants, individuals who permanently relocate to a foreign country. For those who permanently settled, it was almost accidental due to circumstances, not by their design. Hence, categorizing them within one rubric is to miss the transitional nature of their lives and how that might have affected their artwork and careers.

Kuniyoshi attempted to explain that we needed to allow that an artist and their art could occupy separate categories. Popular in New York's art world, Kuniyoshi was occasionally embraced as an "American artist," but he was always treated as a Japanese man. Kuniyoshi demurred from attempting to solve the debate whether an artist's influence was derived from "environment (or) inheritance," he said, but he asserted that "cultural assimilation" certainly affected an artist's work. "If (an) individual lives and works in a given locale for a length of time," Kuniyoshi argued, "regardless of nationality, work produced there becomes indigenous to that country."[1] Even if a person did not assimilate to a new place, their art would absorb their immediate environment. Kuniyoshi could philosophize on differences between "East" and "West," while insisting in another venue that he had no special knowledge of Japan, since he read the same newspapers as Americans. Dressed in kimono for an interview in his downtown New York studio, Ishigaki also opined about the difference between East and West art worlds, explaining that his perspective was informed by being a Japanese.[2] At the time of the 1922 interview, however,

---

1. Yasuo Kuniyoshi, quoted in Donald B. Goodall's "Introduction," in *Yasuo Kuniyoshi, 1889-1935: A Retrospective Exhibition*. Austin, TX: University Art Museum. 1975, p. 17.
2. "Young Japanese Artist Finds Strange Contrasts in American Men and Women: Eitaro Ishigaki Marvels That Women Are So Much More Cultured and Better Educated Than Opposite Sex Members," (Interview with Ishigaki Eitarô.) *Evening Telegram New York*, November 4, 1922.

Ishigaki had lived in the United States for nearly fifteen years, had never visited the Tokyo art world, and had been fully trained in San Francisco and New York art classrooms. These artists' national borders were defined by Japanese passports, European aspirations, American art schools, and the hybrid communities they occupied.

It was not until 1952, when Japanese in the United States could be legally recognized as citizens. They were denied a legal status as "Americans" despite decades spent living there. Instead, they occupied an intermediate state, never completely rooted in the United States due to their marginalization and disenfranchisement. If these artists were neither Japanese nor American, were they Japanese-American? Their artwork does not reflect any compulsion to carve out space for the "Japanese-American" immigrant experience; in fact, they were more inclined to depict injustices inflicted upon African Americans than Modesto's Japanese farmers. As Japanese nationals living in the United States, they experienced the attendant prejudices directed at all minorities in American society, but they did not self-identify as "Japanese-American." It was a category that was simply not available to them at the time.

Theirs was not exclusively a Japanese, an American, or even an Asian-American story. Rather, they were part of a creative, multinational diaspora occupied by writers, musicians, dancers, as well as visual artists. New York offered porous and accepting international community, where like-minded citizens intermingled. Even in California's insular, ethnic enclaves, artists could explore beyond those borders. By assigning these artists a hyphenated identity—Asian-American or Japanese-American—does not better serve our understanding of them. Indeed, the category marginalizes these artists by limiting them to a social category that they would not recognize, at least in the way such categories are understood today.

This is not to say that they occupied a utopian space free of categories. The art world is not a cosmopolitan utopia in which all nations are equally treated and an artist could simply be an Artist free of racism or reductionist categories. Nor is it one in which artists are free from the burdens of representing their place of origin. However, the artists in this study demonstrate how one's national label was fluid, determined not only by inherent factors like citizenship or heritage, but also by external actors: curators, critics, dealers, collectors, geopolitics, and market trends. An artist's own self-identification changed over time as well. How to ascribe national characteristics to an artist like Ishigaki Eitarô, born in Wakayama Prefecture, who spoke most comfortably in Japanese, and painted the Cuban revolution in his downtown Manhattan studio?

These artists never forgot they were from Japan, and they would on occasion refer to their cultural heritage in interviews. In that 1922 *Evening Telegram* interview, Ishigaki was nostalgic about his hometown's cherry blossoms, while also commenting on how much better educated American women were than Japanese. Obata Chiura always wore traditional Japanese dress to his exhibitions and painting demonstrations, while his wife decorated gallery spaces with *ikebana* (floral arrangements). To "nationalize" these artists after the fact, as happened following World War II, is to diminish them when they were in their prime. It also minimizes the specific political, social, and cultural contexts that enabled them to flourish in inter-war America.

Of course, national categories mattered then, and they still do today. Entering a museum gallery with an exhibit of Cubist paintings, we might approach a canvas that invites us to view it more closely—examining the artist's techniques, materials, and color choices, even understanding something of the era in which it was created. But this can change in an instant, if we see that the artist's name is Ishigaki Eitarô. At that point we might wonder which elements in the painting are Japanese. Such an assessment of a work along national lines is less likely to occur if the artist's name is Georges Braque. We would not view the painting through a French lens when we returned our gaze from the text to the canvas. One could argue that Western artists like Braque are encompassed within "isms" as nation-less styles, whereas non-Western artists cannot be interpreted without reference to their ethnic or national identification. No contemporary artist from outside the West—or even with a non-Western name—is exempt. As soon as we identify the artist as Japanese, we look at the painting with different eyes, seeking some visual sign of nationality on the canvas. This is, I suggest, a limitation, not of the artists, but of us, their audience.

Kuniyoshi, Ishigaki, Shimizu, Obata, and Miyatake give us a glimpse of a multinational world in which art, innovation, and politics mattered more than national identity, and they also represent five examples of what life in the United States was like for Japanese immigrants in the era of cosmopolitan culture and legal exclusion. The 1790 federal act that restricted naturalized U.S. citizenship to "free white males" was amended in 1870 to include African-Americans, but not Asian immigrants. No one born in Japan could become a naturalized American citizen until 1952 when the Walter-McCarran Act removed race-based restrictions to naturalization. As Japanese nationals, they would never become citizens, or be accorded any attendant rights. Relations between the United States and Japanese governments directly affected their daily lives in wartime and afterward. Their legacies —once strong in the United States, now vanished and currently housed in Japanese prefectural museums – show how deeply national categories determine artists' legacies. Perhaps viewers in 1929 of Kuniyoshi's works at the "Paintings by Nineteen Living Americans" were better prepared to understand him as an artist first and a Japanese second. But first we must remember that he was there at all.

Before World War II, the world of "modern art" was a small one: dealers, curators, critics and artists largely knew one another. Kuniyoshi, Ishigaki, and Shimizu left the West Coast to become active members of the New York art scene, part of a social fabric that included students and teachers from the Art Students League, 14th Street artists like Reginald Marsh and John Sloan, and Greenwich Village bohemians and intellectuals. The "American-ness" of the New York art world had distinct factors that made it unique. Given the diversity of its population, its Harlem Renaissance, and its Lower East Side-born Irish governor, Alfred Smith, many Americans at that time regarded New York as a foreign island on the fringe of the United States. Even as New York set the pace for the acceleration of the multiethnic population in the twentieth century, the rest of the country tended to view the city with both fascination and fear. Thus, the "America" these artists encountered was different from the one they and their predecessors had found in California.

Obata, who stayed in California throughout his career, remained outside the New York-based artists' orbit, geographically as well as stylistically. Obata stayed committed to his Japanese technical training. He collaborated with Tokyo printmakers instead of New York art associations. Obata's cherished subject was nature; his mentors included wilderness advocate John Muir rather than modern artists or the latest "ism" in New York. His landscapes of the West were in tune with the Californian Arts and Crafts movement, real estate developers' idealized versions of the West, and Pacific Rim stylistic influences that embraced East Asian and Spanish Colonial aesthetics. Miyatake, on the other hand, was a leader of Japanese photographer associations in Los Angeles that followed international modernist trends led by László Maholy-Nagy and Karl Struss. Miyatake collaborated with dancers like Itô Michio, who returned from London and Paris, where he performed Ezra Pound's interpretations of Noh theater. By way of London, Berlin, and Tokyo-based exhibitions and photography journals, Miyatake and a Los Angeles-based cohort were in tune with their global avant-garde contemporaries, though limited by Little Tokyo's borders.

Not that the New York-based Japanese artists removed themselves completely from Japanese networks. Indeed, they constituted an even smaller constellation within New York's modern art galaxy. Kuniyoshi, Ishigaki, and Shimizu were friends and colleagues: they joined the same art classes, shared meals, and exhibited together. They established groups for Japanese in New York like the Gachôkai (Painting and Sculpture Association) and organized exhibitions of Japanese resident artists. They hosted and fed Japanese artists passing through New York to Paris as well as those who were returning from Europe. In this way they learned about the Japanese art world as well as changes in the Parisian scene, while forming useful connections with people who would someday return the favor of hospitality when they were in Tokyo.

Kuniyoshi, Ishigaki, and Shimizu shared another similarity: their work did not look typically "Japanese," as such a thing was generally imagined. Their canvases did not feature bamboo, cherry blossoms, kimonos, or Mt. Fuji. Their composition, brushwork, and colors referred to John Sloan and José Clemente Orozco more than to the woodblock prints of *ukiyo-e* or the painting of the Kôrin School. (One can more easily see their links to contemporary, Western-style oil painters in Tokyo like Yorozu Tetsugorô and Umehara Ryûzaburô.) Try as they might, critics have never convincingly argued that Kuniyoshi's images carry an intrinsic Japanese-ness. Shimizu painted butchers, tennis players in Central Park, and movie ticket vendors. The only Japanese element was the occasional inclusion of his son as a subject. Ishigaki's paintings—Cuban slave rebellions, protests in Washington D.C., a lynching in the South—even more conspicuously lacked any discernable Japanese touch. Japanese art historians have not wasted their time looking for Japanese overtones in Ishigaki's work. They are content to investigate Ishigaki's actual influences–members of the Ashcan School like Robert Henri, George Bellows, and George Luks—rather than those he might have received by osmosis. These artists created oil paintings without attempting a fusion of Japanese aesthetics associated with Fujita "Leonard" Tsuguharu, who outlined his white nudes with *sumi* ink. Rather, their art teachers encouraged them to paint what they saw, so they featured flappers on 14th Street, Maine barnyards, and tenements inhabited by Ukrainians and Sicilians with laundry hanging out to dry. Kenneth Hayes Miller told his students—that included Kuniyoshi, Alexander Brook, and Reginald Marsh—to study Honoré Daumier's drawings of political scenes. He did not instruct them to study Hokusai's "Great Wave." Japanese artists in New York's modern art scene were not treated as guest members of a "Western" art movement, but as participants in the formation of a self-consciously American art, one defined by U.S. citizens, immigrants, and sojourners gathered in New York.

The paths of the New York-based artists constantly intersected, but they also diverged, often propelled by political and economic forces. Only Kuniyoshi gained enough success to enjoy a measure of financial security, including a summer home in Woodstock, New York. He was also one of the leaders of art world institutions. Long before the onset of the Great Depression, socialists like Katayama Sen, who was in exile in California in 1914, politicized Ishigaki. His commitment to leftist politics continued after he left California in 1917 for New York, where he created art that expressed his views. He hosted visiting Japanese leftists, some of whom would later establish the Japanese Communist Party in 1922, transmitted documents between the Soviet Union and Japan and helped in 1929 to found the John Reed Club, which brought together an international coterie of leftist writers and artists. Shimizu, in contrast, never wavered in his desire to return to Japan, nor did he identify as an American artist despite his years of training in Seattle and New York. He moved in New York and Parisian cosmopolitan circles, but he avoided political groups. Determined to return to Japan, he hoped to enter its art world (*gadan*) as a cosmopolite, educated in modern art by way of New York and Parisian studios. Once he did become politicized after the economic depression that hit Japan in the early 1930s, he landed on the side of Japanese militarists.

Targets of anti-Japanese violence and exclusion, Obata Chiura and Miyatake Tôyô's political and economic lives centered on survival in their Japanese communities in California. To be a Japanese national on the Pacific Coast meant their economic fates were dependent on the support of the Japanese community. Prior to World War II, Japantown and Little Tokyo were virtual outposts of Japan and their populations were treated as such by the Japanese state. Buffered by large communities of Japanese, they were more isolated in ethnic enclaves, rarely entering cosmopolitan circles.

The five interwar figures treated here followed a generation of Japanese artists who arrived in the United States only a few years earlier, but they had a radically different experience. The first wave of Japanese artists who landed on American shores in the late nineteenth century were trained painters and craftsmen, hoping to take advantage of the "Japan craze" that had delighted American bourgeois consumers. Following in the wake of the "art for export" trade, which emerged from Yokohama, these artists crossed the Pacific to offer their decorative works in San Francisco and Boston. Their selling trips to the United States were mercenary since their goal was to earn enough money to enable them to study art in Europe. Having worn tailcoats and trousers in Tokyo, they now donned kimono and served tea in Boston salons. Because they painted in a variety of styles and techniques—oil painting, watercolors, and brush painting—their flexibility enabled them to adapt their style to trends in both the Western and Japanese art markets. They understood that Americans wanted Japan (carp ponds, cherry blossoms, bamboo), but the Japanese wanted Europe (haystacks, bowls of grapes and pears, cottages). They could oblige both demands.

Members of the first wave of Japanese artists to the United States were products of a dichotomized art discourse that emerged in Japan after it opened trade with the West in the mid-nineteenth century: traditional versus modern, East versus West. During the 1870s and after, the Japanese art world divided into two forms of painting: *yôga* (Western style) and *nihonga* (Japanese style). *Yôga* was first defined in the context of state encouragement to adopt European styles, materials, and techniques as part of the enthusiasm for Western "civilization" that swept Japan. European instructors arrived in Japan carrying books of reproductions from museums and cathedrals, inspiring young Japanese to visit London, Paris, and Rome to learn firsthand from the Masters.

Enthusiasm for *yôga* was challenged in the late 1880s and early 1890s. Campaigns against teaching Western art in Japanese schools arose in the context of the rising nationalism of those years. Conservative intellectuals suggested that the wholesale adoption of Western techniques would lead to the loss of Japanese traditions, as if Japan's aesthetic heritage was about to vanish at the hands of Western-style painters. As they nurtured their own understanding (and personal collections) of Japanese art, some Americans living in Japan participated in leading the charge against *yôga*: In a lecture called the "True Meaning of Art" given in Tokyo in 1882, Ernest Fenollosa urged his Imperial University audience to value traditional Japanese art and preserve its cultural heritage, before it was crushed between Western culture and Chinese influence. During his 1882 lecture, Fenollosa also coined a new word, "*nihonga*," or, Japanese-style painting, as the antidote to Western art. Eventually, Fenollosa's term included art that was a fusion of Western techniques with Japanese themes. An artist, who did Japanese-style woodblocks, might be a *nihonga* artist, but an oil painting of a Japanese woman in kimono holding a fan was also a *nihonga* piece. By framing the Western oil painting as "Japanese-style," the *nihonga* compromise seemed to usher Japanese tradition into the realm of modern art.

Although he arrived only a few years earlier than the others, in many ways Obata Chiura can be said to belong to the first wave of Japanese artists to the United States. Though he meant to study in France and eventually return to Japan like other "first wave" Japanese artists, Obata started a family and worked as an artist in the Bay Area. Obata trained with Japanese brush painters from an early age before moving to Northern California in 1903. He never studied art in the United States, rejecting stylistic references to emerging modern art movements. This was in stark contrast to his compatriots, who moved to east from California. New York's modern artists were less interested in art that did not reflect their immediate world and did not constantly innovate new "isms.

Interest in Japanese arts and crafts in California as well as a large immigrant population with ongoing ties to Japan enabled Obata to find steady work as a set designer, department store decorator, book illustrator, and, eventually, art instructor. Obata did illustrations for Japanese-language newspapers and periodicals for the immigrant community living in California. Income from commissions for magazines afforded him time to go on sketching and hiking tours throughout California. The Western landscape continued to inspire Obata through the prewar period, prompting a series of paintings and woodblock prints of the High Sierras. It was not until his internment during World War II that he used art as social commentary, recording Tanforan Assembly Center funerals and the shooting of a Topaz camp internee, who walked his dog too close to wire fencing.

The second wave of artists differed dramatically from first wave artists like Obata. Kuniyoshi (arrived 1906), Shimizu (1907), Miyatake (1909), and Ishigaki (1910) came from modest backgrounds in rural Japan. Seeking adventure, fortune, and English skills, to better their employment prospects in Japan, they arrived as poor laborers who became artists. They were both untutored and unaffected by Japanese art, whether traditional or contemporary, except for what they encountered in primary school drawing classes. They had not participated in the *yôga* vs. *nihonga* discourse. Their nescience enabled them to contribute to a dawning era of modern art in America without feeling any impulse to make room for modern Japanese art on the global stage.

Kuniyoshi, Shimizu, and Ishigaki began their American sojourn on the West Coast and arrived in New York just as its artists were bent on overthrowing the academic traditions dedicated to realist renderings of idealized subjects, traditions already challenged by photography. Writing in 1930 about modern American art's period of development, Samuel Kootz argued that modern art had been slow to emerge compared to Europe, because early American painting had no utilitarian value to Puritan ideals, other than as a way of securing a portrait of family members.[3] During the 1910s, American artists were turning to expressionism, a broad category that included non-realist, non-abstract art. Expressionist art was meant to show the artist's emotional response to his subject rather than as strict portraiture. Kootz identified the modern painter, whom he called creators of the "art of defiance," as an individual in revolt against Romanticism both in society and in art. (Kootz included Kuniyoshi as one of these modern painters in his book entitled Modern American Artists, arguing that the Spaniard Picasso, the Russian Chagall, and the Italian de Chirico all painted in Paris, but no French nationalism was required of them. Kootz's position on the topic was unique.)[4] Influenced by social and political trends, artists also desired liberation from one version of American culture that celebrated gentility and virtue and wanted instead to depict the lives and cityscapes they observed in their daily lives. John Sloan painted bartenders at Irish pubs, George Bellows showed boxers in the ring, and Reginald Marsh

---

3. Samuel M. Kootz, *Modern American Painters* (New York: Brewer & Warren Inc. 1930), 16.
4. Ibid, 1.

chose passengers reading newspapers on subway platforms. Japanese artists of the second wave had studied drawing on the Pacific Coast and left for New York to be part of this art revolution. Their timing was impeccable, as they became pioneers, not mere participants, in early American modernism.

To become an artist is a wonderful thing, Kuniyoshi wrote in 1945, reflecting on his choice to leave Los Angeles for New York.[5] It certainly felt that way after the 1913 International Exhibition of Modern Art at the 69th Regiment Armory, known as the "Armory Show," when Americans came face to face with the transformative, modernist canvases coming from European easels. Although many pseudo-Cézannes were born in 1913 and cubism became a fashion, most New York artists—such as members of The Eight and the Ashcan school—saw the Armory Show as validation of their quest for liberation from academic realism and an invitation to join modernism. If they had felt that art was more than painting portraits of people who could afford them, works by Paul Gauguin, Henri Matisse, and Marcel Duchamp confirmed their inclination. Kuniyoshi, Shimizu, and Ishigaki were participants in a mass exodus out of uptown New York and Philadelphia art academies to the liberal Art Students League, where teachers encouraged their students to seek out new frontiers.

During the 1920s, Kuniyoshi, Shimizu, and Ishigaki explored New York as their urban playground. They locked arms with German, Romanian, Mexican, and Ukrainian artists, along with friends from Illinois and Vermont, at masquerade balls, gallery openings, summer holidays at art colonies, and drawing salons that ended with bowling competitions. Kuniyoshi married the painter Katherine Schmidt, and Ishigaki lived with Gertrude Boyle, a fellow artist who had accompanied him to New York from San Francisco. While Ishigaki lived in Harlem and associated with Emma Goldman, Shimizu haunted Chinatown, intoxicated by its nightlife. It was the Jazz Age and these Japanese artists flourished in New York's cosmopolitan

---

5. Yasuo Kuniyoshi, *Yasuo Kuniyoshi.* (New York: American Artists Group, New York, 1945), 3.

atmosphere. As Uruguayan painter and writer Joaquín Torres-García noted in 1920, "One only has to listen to New York's devilish music to glimpse that another art is possible."

They were not deaf to the siren call from Paris, which continued to be the global capital of modern art. Shimizu left for France in 1924. He understood that the Japanese art world would not validate his artist's passport without the stamp of a Paris sojourn. Kuniyoshi traveled to Paris on two occasions, but he returned to New York each time to reclaim his place in what was then the smaller pond. Ishigaki never went to Paris; his political activities in New York kept him occupied. Neither Obata, who had five children to feed, nor Miyatake, who had three, could easily leave the West Coast. However, Miyatake's voracious study of international journals featuring avant-garde photographers kept him abreast of the Bauhaus and Man Ray from his portrait studio in Little Tokyo.

Miyatake's proximity to Hollywood and the presence of passionate Little Tokyo photographers meant that he was part of a vanguard of new photographic techniques. He did not need to visit Paris to study the avant-garde; he was already a member. California's painters were captivated by its scenic landscapes, but Los Angeles' Japanese photographers captured images of oil ditches, rail yards, and the Hollywood Dam. Nineteenth century Pictorialist photographers like Alfred Stieglitz and Edward Steichen used the camera and printmaking process like painters to express beauty in still lifes, domestic scenes, and landscapes. By the 1920s, Miyatake was one of several Los Angeles-based, Japanese modernist photographers looking to Japan and Germany as sources of innovation. Modernists like Miyatake were interested in abstract forms, geometry, and bold contrasts between light and dark. Until he was interned at Manzanar, stripped of both his studio and camera equipment, Miyatake was an active leader, exhibitor, and teacher in modernist photography circles worldwide based in his 1st Street studio.

The 1929 stock market crash put an end to good times for many, no less so for artists. Ishigaki sold a painting one week before the November crash, but had not yet received payment from his now bankrupt customer. Kuniyoshi traveled to Japan to drum up business, but he sold nothing. The economic depression was global: Shimizu, back in Japan by the time of the crash, suffered from a lack of sales and commissions. Serving as a military illustrator for an army aggressively expanding into China became his income source. In the wake of the economic crisis, political fervor brought artists in the United States together in an unprecedented show of solidarity. Both Kuniyoshi and Ishigaki participated in the establishment and maintenance of the Artists Union and the American Contemporary Art Gallery (ACA Gallery), which pressured the government to financially support artists during the Depression.[6]

An international coterie of artists came together to protest fascism during the 1930s, but their efforts and those of others did nothing to stave off another World War. When he became an enemy alien on December 8, 1941, the day after the attack on Pearl Harbor, Kuniyoshi frantically wrote letters to colleagues pleading with them to confirm to authorities that he supported the United States war effort. Ishigaki and his second wife, writer Ishigaki Ayako, were in the middle of giving a speech about the terror the Japanese military was inflicting on Chinese civilians when they were escorted back to their apartment and put under surveillance. A few months later, Obata's colleagues at Berkeley helped him put his paintings into storage as his family prepared to move to the Tanforan holding center and then the Topaz internment camp. Miyatake locked up his Little Tokyo studio and was forced into Manzanar. Meanwhile, Shimizu continued island hopping with the Japanese Navy, sending drawings of Polynesians sitting under palm trees to Tokyo.

---

6. For more on U.S. Depression-era artists solidarity movements see Matthew Baigell and Julia Williams eds., *Artists Against War and Fascism: Papers of the First American Artists' Congress, Congress* (New Brunswick, N.J.: Rutgers University Press, 1986) and Andrew Hemingway, *Artists on the Left: American Artists and the Communist Movement, 1926-1956* (New Haven: Yale University Press, 2002), Nicolas Lampert, *A People's Art History of the United States* (New York: The New Press, 2013), Richard D. McKinzie, *The New Deal for Artists* (Princeton: Princeton University Press, 1973), Susan Platt, *Art & Politics in the 1930's: Modernism-Marxism-Americanism* (New York: Midmarch Arts Press, 1999).

World War II certainly ruptured the artists' lives, although not in the ways one might first imagine. Kuniyoshi aided the Allied effort by drawing anti-Japanese propaganda and sending radio broadcast messages targeting Tokyo artists and intellectuals. (He might have wondered if Shimizu was listening.) Ishigaki's troubles really began when the war was over, and communists replaced fascists as the declared enemy; eventually, he and Ayako were arrested and forced to return to Japan in 1951 because of their leftist activities prior to the war. He never painted again. Obata taught art to his fellow inmates at Topaz, instilling them with hope as they waited in the dust storms. After he reclaimed his teaching position at U.C. Berkeley after the war, in 1954, Obata became a naturalized U.S. citizen. He then supported the new U.S.-Japan alliance by becoming a cultural ambassador by guiding American tourists through a highly aestheticized version of Japan. Miyatake returned from Manzanar to reopen a Little Tokyo studio and photographed Japanese and Japanese-American life in Los Angeles, marking weddings, funerals, and visits from Japanese dignitaries and celebrities until his death in 1979. Shimizu died in 1945 soon after Japan's surrender from stress and exhaustion. His daughter claimed that he died of a broken heart after losing his son during the last weeks of battle at sea. Only Kuniyoshi remained standing in the art world after the war, though emotionally battered by his wartime experience in New York. He continued to teach at the Art Student's League, but his journals and paintings reveal his disillusionment with the war's aftermath. Fascism was trounced, but Kuniyoshi's paintings of headless carousel horses, melancholic clowns, and dystopian carnivals reflected a global anxiety in the grips of the Cold War.

Since they were significant and recognized artists during their lifetimes, it is puzzling that these artists have been so much forgotten. Occasionally, Kuniyoshi receives some recognition, but not in accordance with the fame he enjoyed during his lifetime.[7] Obata

---

7. In 2018 the Smithsonian American Art Museum held a Kuniyoshi retrospective that garnered background articles about his life and work. This was the first *solo* Kuniyoshi show in decades and did not travel to other museums.

Chiura is in San Francisco museum collections collections and has monographs dedicated to his life and work thanks to the tireless efforts taken by his granddaughter, Kimi Kodani Hill. Nevertheless, Obata's paintings rarely travel outside California to receive a wider audience. Shimizu is virtually unheard of in the United States, but scholar Shipu Wang has reintroduced works by Ishigaki Eitarô in his studies of Asian American artists. Miyatake's photographs taken inside Manzanar have produced iconic images of the internment experience, but there is less appreciation of his prewar innovations.

Given the artists' prominence in the interwar art world, understanding why American art lovers are hard-pressed to name them invites observations about art history and regional studies. There are several possible explanations. The most obvious answer is that none—from Japan or otherwise—of the social realist, Ashcan School, or American Scene painters receive much attention from today's art world. Outside the occasional exhibition, those artists are simply not in fashion. Another reason is that except for Obata Chiura, the artists featured in this book did not do work that is recognizably Japanese. They worked in a modern, expressionist idiom that rejected traditional allusions both to conventional Japanese and Western genres. Soon after trade with Japan restarted in the mid-nineteenth century, Americans were enthusiastic for traditional Japanese art, summed up by the fashion for *Japonisme*. Not only were the artists featured here determinedly modern and aside from Obata uninterested in such traditions, but they also arrived in the United States after the fervor for Japanese arts and crafts had largely passed. After World War II, American fascination with Japanese culture returned in the form of Zen gardens, rustic *wabi-sabi* aesthetics, and eventually Sanrio characters of mouthless cats. Both U.S. and Japanese cultural diplomacy redirected Americans to think of Japanese aesthetics as beautiful and gentle, or cute and harmless, so that the wartime enemy could be transformed into an ally in Cold War Asia. Pre-World War II Japanese artists active in the United States—except for Obata with his brush-paintings and guided tours of Kyoto gardens—had no place in this new cultural lexicon.

Another reason for their comparative obscurity is that they fell in between a categorical divide that often leads to lost or limiter stories. Academics, museum curators, and art book publishers assign individuals to Japan or a Japanese-America, but there is difficulty allowing actors to occupy both groups. Although Japanese curators include these artists in the modern Japanese art canon, their assignation in the United states as "Asian-American artists" means the American art world writ large does not consider their influence on Japanese art. Scholars in the United States tend to compartmentalize these artists as Asian American rather than as pioneers of American modernism. Worse, they miss them completely. Western scholars of Japan have missed how these artists figure in the history of Japanese modern art. Scholars of Asian-America who have claimed them tend to over-emphasize their Americanness with a reliance on English language sources, rather than allow them to straddle the fence between the United States and Japan. This book attempts to locate them as occupying a more complicated space than any one of these, a realm that both transcends national or ethnic identity and one that has multiple points of entry.

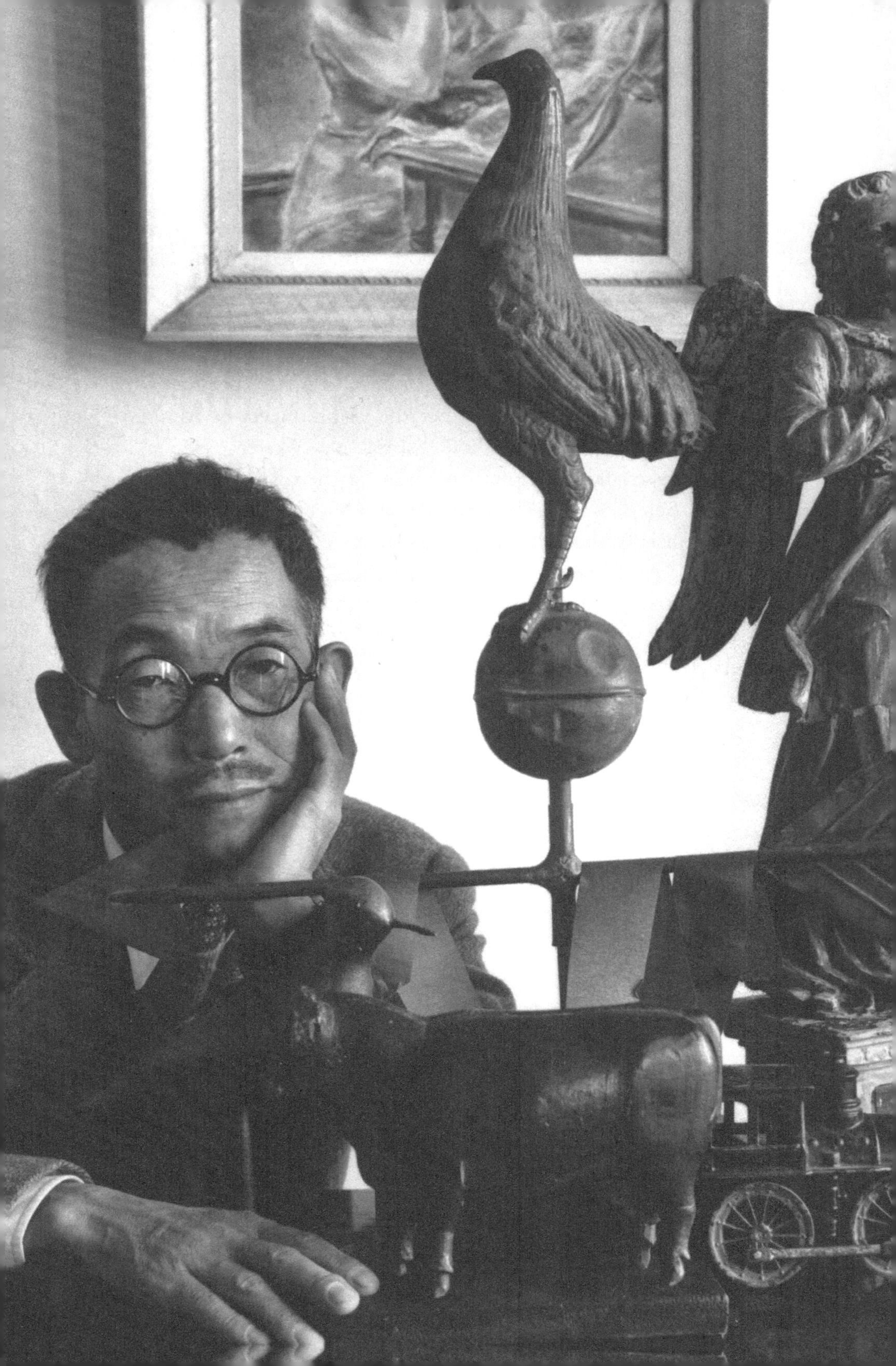

Chapter One
Kuniyoshi Yasuo
Kuniyoshi-ism: Transcending Citizenship and Race

As a pioneer of American modernism, Kuniyoshi Yasuo was a successful artist during his lifetime–an art star cavorting with other art stars. He was a respected and popular teacher at the Art Students League in New York. He had multiple exhibitions at galleries and museums, including the Whitney Museum of American Art, where he was the first living artist to have a solo show. He was the head of powerful and influential art associations. Art critics at the *New York Times*, *The New Yorker*, *Art News*, and other periodicals tracked his decades-long career.

But now he is largely forgotten.

Compared to other artists featured in this book, Kuniyoshi is the best-known Japanese artist who lived in the United States during the first half of the twentieth century. Nevertheless, apart from the noble efforts of a few scholars, little has been written about Kuniyoshi

(Opposite): Kuniyoshi Yasuo, 1948, Hirshhorn Museum and Sculpture Garden, Smithsonian Institution, Washington, DC, The Joseph H. Hirshhorn Bequest, 1981, Original photo by Arnold Newman, digitally reproduced by Cathy Carver.

in English since World War II.[1] Comprehensive art history books capture some of his basic biographical information, but the extent of his contribution to the modern American art scene has largely been overlooked. On the other hand, one can regularly view Kuniyoshi's work in Japan's modern art museums, and major art collections include his canvases. This is a shift: Prior to World War II, Kuniyoshi was unknown in the Japanese art world, but a darling of New York's. Today, books about Kuniyoshi's art and career line Tokyo's art bookstore shelves. Whereas the American art world celebrated Kuniyoshi while he was alive, Japan's art establishment has preserved his legacy.

Kuniyoshi Yasuo and Japan's modern age arrived at about the same time. He shared his birth year with the municipal establishment of his hometown, Okayama City, a centuries-old castle town with a large, famous garden. Kuniyoshi was born in 1889, the same year the Meiji Emperor promulgated the Japanese Constitution, establishing new political structures that lasted until the end of World War II. Japan was an old country, which had shuttered its gates to exchange with Westerners since the 1600s. When American gunboats thrust open Japan's doors once again in 1853, a few insurgents from southern Japan used the subsequent chaos to overthrow the Tokugawa military government and replace it with their own, under the auspices of direct imperial rule. Almost three hundred domains became seventy prefectures and castle towns like Okayama became municipalities. When the class system was upended—privileges for the samurai class were erased—young Japanese like Kuniyoshi could imagine more exciting futures. Suddenly, Japan's modern metamorphosis invited Kuniyoshi's generation to imagine their place in the world in a completely new way.

---

1. Tom Wolfe's efforts to bring recognition to Kuniyoshi's contributions to American modern art have been heroic. He has written scholarly articles and promoted exhibitions — including at the Smithsonian American Art Museum—that demonstrate the importance of Kuniyoshi's art. In addition, Shi-Pu Wang, *Becoming American? The Art and Identity Crisis of Yasuo Kuniyoshi* Honolulu: University of Hawaii Press, 2011.

After finishing primary school, Kuniyoshi entered the Okayama Industrial School, which had opened just a couple of years after his birth. He studied two subjects, textiles and dyeing, out of the three offered at the school. He was fifteen years old and dissatisfied with what the fledgling school could offer him. Two years later, he left before graduating. Okayama was progressing at a slower pace than Kuniyoshi's ambitions. Rather than join the hordes of young people then descending on Tokyo, Kuniyoshi resolved to leave Okayama for the United States. He planned to return as a success, a savior to his family, a star. Kuniyoshi daydreamed about the local journalists rushing to interview him about his adventures when he disembarked at Yokohama wearing waistcoat and trousers and speaking perfect English. He did not return to Japan for twenty-five years after leaving in 1906.

Magazines such as *Amerika* and *Seikô* (Success) encouraged ambitious young men like Kuniyoshi living in the countryside to travel to the United States for self-advancement. Articles assured readers that studying English while doing menial labor would precipitate triumphant returns to their hometowns carrying bags of gold and prospects for future employment. Don't go to Peking or Seoul, declared Fukuzawa Yukichi, writer, teacher, and the future face of the 10,000-yen note. Neither the Chinese nor the Koreans knew how to progress either personally or as a nation, he declared.[2] Traveling East across the Pacific was the more promising and practical option.

Kuniyoshi's father protested his decision to move to the United States. (His mother and father had divorced, and his father remarried.) He did not want his only child to board a ship, travel months across the ocean, and live in a place where he did not know the language. Kuniyoshi persisted. If he did not move to the United States, then he would join the Japanese military like the rest of his friends. Joining the Japanese imperial effort in East Asia was even less appealing to his father, who read newspaper accounts of the carnage at Port Arthur and

---

2. Fukuzawa Yukichi, "*Datsu-a Ron*" (On Saying Good-bye to Asia), *Japan: A Documentary History. The Late Tokugawa Period to the Present*, ed. David J. Lu (New Jersey: Routledge, 1996), 351-353.

Mukden, where Japan was battling Russia. In 1905, Japan won the two-year war, but 50,000 Japanese families suffered dearly owing to the bloodbath. Sojourning in the United States was a relatively safer compromise. His father gave his blessing and provided Kuniyoshi with some money to help him after he arrived.

Seventeen-year old Kuniyoshi regretted his choice to move to the United States within days of his arrival. He could not speak to anyone except for a few Japanese, who were equally baffled by Seattle. Advertisements shouted incomprehensible English words. Seattle police forced one of his co-patriots to pay a fine for ringing a fire station box, after he mistook it for a place to post letters. Unfortunately, in an impetuous moment no doubt fueled by adrenaline when his feet touched solid ground, Kuniyoshi immediately wired back the money that his father gave him. If he had held on to the money, Kuniyoshi later recalled, he would have boarded the next ship back to Japan.[3]

Art was not on his mind as Kuniyoshi sat on Seattle's docks, eating peanuts, and wondering how he could get back to Japan. (Kuniyoshi later insisted that he would never eat peanuts again after those lonely days.) Arriving as the doors closed to Japanese immigrants as a result of the 1907 Gentlemen's Agreement, Kuniyoshi had not traveled to the United States intending to become an artist. He did not aspire to one day join the *gadan* (Japanese art world), nor, did he know what was on display in Japanese national museums, galleries, or art journals flourishing during the Meiji era's appetite for "civilization and enlightenment." Before landing in the United States, Kuniyoshi claimed to remember having seen only one painting while in Okayama—a Western-style oil painting of a battle scene. It would be years before Kuniyoshi would find his place in American art society.

Survival in the United States required finding work, but Kuniyoshi soon discovered that sleeping on hay and carrying buckets of water for Spokane railroad laborers was not what he had in mind. He resolved to travel south, where the weather promised to be better, skipping San

---

3. Yasuo Kuniyoshi, *Yasuo Kuniyoshi* (New York: American Artists Group, Monograph Number 11, 1945), 1.

Francisco, which was recovering from a catastrophic earthquake that occurred only months before his arrival. In addition, San Francisco was hostile toward the Japanese immigrant population. Kuniyoshi landed in Los Angeles, where the population was booming. During the winter, he worked as a hotel bellboy and custodian. The sunshine calmed Kuniyoshi and he felt less in a hurry to race back to Okayama. He became a seasonal farmworker. Grapes, he later told his students, took on a special significance to him, so that paintings of grapes were steeped in these memories. In the Central Valley vineyards, he ate enough to make himself ill before loading his baskets.

Kuniyoshi struggled to learn English. His teacher, either exasperated by his incapacity to speak or believing all Japanese to be artists at heart, encouraged him to go to art school based on a drawing he did of a map of China. Kuniyoshi entered a downtown Los Angeles art school and learned to draw for the next few years. Other Japanese students attended the school, so he had opportunities to socialize. Adventure was still alive in him and he started air pilot's school, but this was far too frightening a venture only seven years after the Wright brothers took off at Kittyhawk. Seeing fellow students killed in airplane accidents, Kuniyoshi decided that to be an artist was far less risky than being an airplane pilot.[4]

At some point during Kuniyoshi's free time when not working in orchards under Central California's blazing sun or in hotels for Los Angeles' rough-and-ready clientele, he decided that "to become an artist was a wonderful thing."[5] The classroom, where he drew figures, still lifes, and a plein air study of the Los Angeles plaza, became a sanctuary from dirt and sweat. Art school, a space where Kuniyoshi would inhabit in the subsequent years of his life, became a place of respite. He did not have to speak to be understood. Nor did he have to grovel before landowners and hoteliers. Kuniyoshi Yasuo, perhaps frail on a farm, was dignified behind an easel. His Los Angeles art

---

4. Lloyd Goodrich, *Yasuo Kuniyoshi*, (New York: Whitney Museum of American Art, 1948), 7.
5. Kuniyoshi, *Yasuo Kuniyoshi*, 3.

class was the location for one of Kuniyoshi's dramatic milestones: he leaped from proletariat to aesthete, from *dekasegi* (immigrant worker) to artiste. John Berger wrote that the migrant worker has two ways to experience their life away from home: "Work time, and 'time-off,'" one that they are paid for and one they are not.[6] Free time can be a burden for a migrant worker, because it has no monetary value, since unproductive time when not in one's home country – Okayama, El Salvador, or Anatolia – is wasted time. However, Kuniyoshi transformed his "time off" in the art classroom into a potential space for "work time" as a professional artist. Kuniyoshi resolved to move to New York, the American artist's outpost, where officials and critics no longer debated whether to display nudes in public exhibitions as they did in the more conservative Los Angeles. To be an Artist became Kuniyoshi's objective, rather than saving money, learning English, and returning to Okayama with bags of gold.

In 1910, Kuniyoshi traveled across the country to live with a friend of his father's. New York was far bigger than Los Angeles, but it, too, was still expanding. Pennsylvania Station was completed shortly after Kuniyoshi arrived. The city was already dotted with skyscrapers. Cars were beginning to fill New York streets, but trolleys were still used to transport workers and shoppers. With 4.7 million people, New York had the largest population of any American city. His father's friend, also an artist, allowed Kuniyoshi to live with him for room and board in exchange for cleaning his studio. Kuniyoshi resolved to reenter art school full time despite having limited means. Following his host's suggestion that he join the one hundred-year old National Academy of Design, which was modeled after London's Royal Academy, Kuniyoshi walked from 66th Street to 109th and Amsterdam every day to study drawing from life models. Since he had spent the last few years on the same exercises, he was bored after two months.

Kuniyoshi's arrival in New York corresponded with its modern art revolution. New York's artists were frustrated with academic art that could not teach them how to capture the convulsive skyline or

6. John Berger, *A Seventh Man*, (New York: Verso Books, 2010), 190.

the city's modern pace. They started to rebel. Artists Robert Henri, John Sloan, and Walt Kuhn defected from the academy in 1910 to hold the "Exhibition of Independent Artists," a show that required participants only pay an entrance fee to show their works rather than be awarded entrance by jury. Henri explained, somewhat defensively, that members were not exiting the academy because it had rejected them, but by their choice.[7] Fearing audiences to the Independent Artists show would dismiss their experimental paintings, Henri beseeched them to accept the art on display even if they did not immediately understand it. The show exhibited almost 300 works and received a lot of media attention, but only five pieces sold for a total of $75.

Undeterred, Walt Kuhn and others formed the Association of American Sculptors and Painters, with the idea for an artist-curated exhibition featuring modern European and American artists. They wanted the show to represent a broad swath of modern art, including paintings even the organizers might not necessarily like. Kuhn had lived and studied in Europe for several years before conceiving the 1913 exhibition. He was also savvy about the benefits of a cause celebre: Publicity, he wrote to Vera Kuhn during the show's planning stages, was part of the exhibition's goal.[8] Organizers conspired to use their European contacts to wrangle paintings for the show. Some of the works on display were familiar to an American audience: impressionist landscapes, still lifes, and portraits of distinguished white men. Old World masters like Ingres and Delacroix were included. Other canvases, however, were new and sent shockwaves throughout the art world as Kuhn planned. When association members unpacked exhibition pieces shipped from Europe, the paint on Georges Braque's "Violin: Mozart Kubelick" was barely dry.

---

7. Robert Henri, "The New York Exhibition of Independent Artists," *The Craftsman 27*, no. 2 (May 1910): 160-172.
8. Letter to Walt Kuhn's wife, Vera, dated December 15, 1911. Milton W. Brown, "Walt Kuhn's Armory Show," *Archives of American Art Journal 27*, no. 2, 1987: 5.

European and American artists exhibited twelve hundred works at New York's 69th Armory Regiment in 1913, what became simply known as the "Armory Show." As the scene of battle for America's first "art war," the Armory was an appropriate setting. It was the Europeans that caused the most fuss among critics and viewers. Media warned of a European art invasion: Few American artists, headlines screeched, would avoid being hit by the European modern art bomb. The *New York Times* compared some of the pieces to children's art and cave paintings recently found in France. Critic Bolton Brown called the paintings "very ugly" and nothing but "a jumble of lines and patches" in which "brains and taste" were not deployed to create them.[9] Young New Yorkers, however, anticipated a revolution: Stuart Davis described it as "a masochistic reception whereat the naïve hosts are trampled and stomped by the European guests at the buffet."[10] (Not all artists were excited: When called upon to explain the new art, Kenyon Cox proclaimed that the Futurists and Cubists were "destroying the art of painting.")[11] The show was an enormous commercial success. Lines to enter the Armory continued from ten in the morning to ten at night for weeks. When the exhibition traveled to Boston and Chicago, an additional two hundred and fifty thousand viewers attended, many having traveled from the West Coast to view the works.

Most visitors flocked to what some described as the "Chamber of Horrors" (Gallery I), where Cubist works by Picasso, Braque, Robert Delaunay and others were on display. Marcel Duchamp's "Nude Descending a Staircase, No. 2" (1912) inspired the most guffaws. American *Art News* offered a $10 prize to anyone who could locate

---

9. Bolton Brown, "'Art' in the Armory; Resembles the Ancient Brushstrokes of Prehistoric Man," *New York Times*, March 1, 1913.
10. Ken Johnson, "Reliving the Show that 'Dropped Like a Bomb'" *New York Times,* October 10, 2013.
11. "Cubists and Futurists Are Making Insanity Pay: Kenyon Cox, Member of the National Academy, and Recognized Here and Abroad as One of America's Foremost Painters, Gives a Straight-from-the-Shoulder Opinion of the New Movements of Art," *New York Times*, March 16, 1923.

the nude in the work.[12] Not everyone laughed. President Theodore Roosevelt chimed in, appreciating the exhibition's efforts to keep the American public up-to-date on European trends, but withheld his approval.[13] While critics battled in their newspaper columns about whether the Fauvist and Futurist works were ludicrous or laudatory, New York's artists leaped into a new era. The Armory Show toppled the National Academy as the hegemonic power in the American art scene. Anything that reeked of the academy —crisp portraits of East Coast blue bloods and military heroes, landscapes featuring America's bountiful natural resources, blond-haired couples playing pianos in sitting rooms—was out. Art students abandoned academy schools for more progressive ones in droves.

Kuniyoshi did not see the Armory Show, because he was working at a hotel in Syracuse, but he heard about it when he returned to the city. He found his friends transformed and the swirl of Armory excitement caught up Kuniyoshi as well. He stopped caring about allegory, romance, and billowing—though sheer—taffeta on nubile maidens like his then favorite painting at the Metropolitan Museum of Art (Pierre Cot's "The Storm" 1880). In the following year, Kuniyoshi left the National Academy for the Robert Henri School of Art, renamed the Independent School. Henri was a leading member of The Eight, a group of New York artists who rebelled against the National Academy's restrictive exhibition practices. His school beckoned artists like Kuniyoshi and eighteen-year old Stuart Davis, who had been so impressed by the Armory.

Kuniyoshi stayed at Henri's school for two years. He next moved to the Art Students League in 1916. His friends told him that he was "going to the dogs," but soon Davis, and even Henri himself, followed him there. At the League, students could study for any number of years with an instructor of their choice; there was no curriculum from which to graduate. Popularity determined how much money

---

12. Lindsay Pollock, "Top Ten Artnews Stories: Naming the Dame," *ARTnews*, November 2007.
13. Tom McCormack, "The 1913 Armory Show: America's First Art War," *art21 magazine*, March 8, 2017.

instructors received, because pay was based on how many students signed up for class. Students also served as the school's management. The League became the mainstay of anti-academicism in New York, owing to its liberal governing structure. It was not necessarily a leader of the avant-garde, but a place that fostered individual talent as well as community among students.

The Armory Show caused tremblers, but it did not completely topple American realist art, despite the numerous attempts at Cubism that subsequently lined art school hallways. Walter Pach lamented that a new type of Impressionist academicism had arrived after the 1913 show. Kuniyoshi and his cohort steered away from impressionism and emulated Ashcan artists instead. Known at the time as the "Revolutionary Black Gang," because of their paintings' dark palette, Ashcan artists depicted urban, working class America. They showed Americans as messy and disheveled and living in a chaotic world. Instead of addressing subjects through shattered, multiple lenses as the Cubists did, New York's artists focused on the city street, where classes and cultures collided. Sometimes they used tenement rooftops, hanging laundry, and water towers as their landscape. New York's artists depicted modern life as they saw it, rather than through a modernist stylistic frame. In their point of view, city life was adequately fractured without having to apply a stylistic device to prove the point. They illustrated—rather than expressed—New York's contradictions, demanding pace, and chaotic skyline.

New York had an additional feature that captured the imaginations of the Ashcan school and their progeny: the city's immigrant culture and society. Immigration was defining New York's character in dramatic ways. Kuniyoshi was one of over nine million newly arrived immigrants to the city, making its streets a jumble of foreign languages. While the Armory Show did not make all New York artists Cubists, it dislodged any lingering aspirations that one could succeed in the modernist art world by painting only Euro-American gentry. Although they welcomed commissions to do portraits for uptown old money and new wealth, artists searched the city's streets to find new characters. They painted Hungarian girls with golden braids,

African-American jazz musicians, Italian opera singers, and Russian shopkeepers.

Living on the margins, Kuniyoshi was cold and hungry. His legs were tired as he commuted between home and the Art Students League. He did not have money to buy a winter overcoat. Despite the physical hardships, Kuniyoshi found at the school kindred spirits, who became his lifelong friends. Upon entering the League, Kuniyoshi joined Kenneth Hayes Miller's class. More than an art instructor, Miller mentored his students, which accounted for his popularity, despite his more conservative taste. Though these post-Armory Show artists craved antidotes to academicism, Miller made them look at the Old Masters at the Met. He emphasized the importance of artists like Honoré Daumier to imbue his students with an appreciation for history and social relevance. Although his depictions of nineteenth century Paris seemed out-of-date to twentieth century New Yorker's, Daumier's satirical approach taught Miller's students about how to approach illustrating everyday life. His students were loyal to him for teaching them art history and practical drawing skills, while he also encouraged their individual expression. In a 1969 interview, painter Katherine Schmidt proclaimed that Miller's success as a teacher was owing to his wanting to "bring out in you what was best for you to do," so that none of his student's works looked like another's.[14] As a result, Miller fostered some of the most influential American artists of the twentieth century.

Miller was known for making regular, intellectual pronouncements and speaking in aphorisms, difficult for a non-native English speaker like Kuniyoshi to understand. (Apart from Miller's proclamation that he "did not like flowers," which Kuniyoshi regularly recalled to others.) He instructed Kuniyoshi to absorb New York life by visiting museums, going to cafes, and attending music concerts. At first Kuniyoshi took Miller's advice to study Daumier literally: his first submission to the Society of Independent Artists annual exhibition

---

14. Oral history interview with Katherine Schmidt, December 8-15, 1969. Smithsonian Archives of American Art.

was entitled "Crucifixion," a dark and heavy-handed allegorical piece with Daumier echoes. New Yorkers, however, were not interested, and Kuniyoshi had to start again.

In Miller's class, Kuniyoshi gained the essential piece that had been missing since his arrival in 1906—a social life. As much as he learned from Miller, the class highlight was socializing with other students.[15] The daily trials of living in New York became far less acute because he had friends that lived in similar circumstances and shared his interests. Kuniyoshi claimed that it was at the League where his "life began to take on real meaning." He joined weekend field trips to museums to see masterworks in person with classmates like Alexander Brook, George Bellows, and Reginald Marsh. Kuniyoshi also discovered the opposite sex; women artists had found sanctuary at the League unlike in New York's academic art schools. Marsh recalled entering a teacher's studio to find a bevy of female students, who all "scared him to death."[16] Kuniyoshi's lonely days eating peanuts at the harbor were over.

Kuniyoshi began exhibiting his works with an international coterie of artists in addition to his League friends. After organizing the Armory Show, Walt Kuhn founded the Penguin Club in 1917.[17] Kuhn had started out in vaudeville with trick bicycles; he knew the importance of spectacle and humor. Kuhn had organized masquerade balls at the Kit-Kat Club at the turn of the century and understood how to attract a crowd. Located near Union Square, membership in Kuhn's "sketch club" was based solely on his approval. An introduction from Louis Bouché provided Kuniyoshi entre to the Penguin, and soon he was exhibiting alongside Max Weber and Jules Pascin. The Penguin Club was most famous for its all-inclusive annual ball, which raised funds to support the space's overhead costs. Fun, according to Kuhn, was the key word. In order to build elaborate sets for the parties, he deviously enlisted commercial artists, who aspired to be part of the

15. Robert Laurent, "Memories of Yas," *College Art Journal* 13, no. 1 (Autumn 1953): 9.
16. Oral history interview with Katherine Schmidt.
17. Oral history interview with Louise Bouche′, 1959, August 7, Archives of American Art, Smithsonian Institution.

avant-garde crowd, because they had good carpentry skills. Barred from the all-male studio, the parties also welcomed women—labeled "Penguinettes"—to join in the fun.

Each ball had a theme, often accented with self-mockery and irreverence. Flyers advertised lectures on male grooming by the denim-clad and hirsute George "Pop" Hart. More ironic touches included a lecture by Bouché on the immediate need to suppress immorality in art—particularly the nude. The invitation to a 1918 Strawberry Festival depicted a wedding photo of Robert Ament dressed in billowing white dress and veil, clutching a bible and nosegay. Seated next to him was the self-satisfied groom, Wood Gaylor. The wedding invitation instructed attendees to wear a straw hat or dress "like a rube." Everything was tongue in cheek except for the club's decree to wear costumes to the balls. Instructions to guests were severe: if you did not show up in costume, you would not be admitted. The Ball Committee decided whether you were trying to get away with fancy dress, or, if you had made every effort to wear a costume related to the ball's theme (for example, Fete Day for a Spanish-American Village). Flyers warned that there would be absolutely no onsite rentals, so come to the Penguin Club prepared. Plus, the Volstead Act was not yet in effect, so one could expect to drink. New York's artists were reveling in full view. "People knew how to play in those days," Kuniyoshi later wrote.[18] They were considered the rebels of their time, fighting conservatism with humor.

Hamilton Easter Field, another student of Kenneth Hayes Miller's, entered Kuniyoshi's life around this time. This friendship with the heir of a prosperous family eased Kuniyoshi's life in New York. Art collector and artist, Hamilton Easter Field's patronage enabled Kuniyoshi to pursue painting full-time. Until his death in 1922, Field supported Kuniyoshi by providing him with a rent-free apartment in Brooklyn, a residence at Field's summer art colony in Ogunquit, Maine, and a stipend. Having lived and traveled in France during the height of the *Japonisme* craze in the late nineteenth century, Field amassed an

18. Kuniyoshi, *Yasuo Kuniyoshi*, 5.

extensive and celebrated collection of Japanese woodblock prints by Hokusai and Hiroshige. He curated shows that juxtaposed *ukiyo-e* with living artists like Frederick Childe Hassam.[19] Soon after meeting him, Kuniyoshi's black ink drawings began to reflect something of the flatness of the Japanese woodblocks Field showed him. Seeing Field's collection was most likely Kuniyoshi's first exposure to Japanese prints.

In the summers, some Art Students League classmates traveled to Field's country home in Maine, where he ran the Ogunquit School of Painting and Sculpture. Many of Miller's students, including Kuniyoshi, joined the group. Gathering in shacks along Perkins Cove, there was nothing fancy or fussy about the art colony. They often went on picnics into the backcountry. Robert Laurent reminisced that one summer, a hike ended with sleeping in a hayloft as Kuniyoshi left the barn doors open and sang Japanese love songs while they watched the moon.[20] The colony hosted many leading artists and writers of the era: Edward Hopper, Harold Weston, Samuel Halpert (married to Edith Halpert, who later established the influential Downtown Gallery), and John Dos Passos all frequented the colony, which continued after Field's death in 1922. Many of its visitors were immigrants like Kuniyoshi. On one venture over the Canadian border to purchase alcohol following Prohibition, Kuniyoshi, Laurent (born in France), and Bernard Karfiol (born in Austria) returned empty-handed, because they were stopped at the border for not having brought identification.

Field decorated the artists' cabins sparsely with American folk art, largely with hook rugs and furniture. His friend and companion, Robert Laurent, collected sculpture and painting.[21] Whereas Kuniyoshi's

---

19. Doreen Bolger, "Hamilton Easter Field and His Contribution to American Modernism," *The American Art Journal* 20, no. 2, (1988): 84.
20. Robert Laurent, "Memories of Yas," *College Art Journal,* 13, no. 1, (Autumn 1953): 7.
21. Elizabeth Stillinger, "From Attics, Sheds, and Secondhand Shops: Collecting Folk Art in America, 1880-1940," *Drawing on America's Past: Folk Art, Modernism, and the Index of American Design*, edited by Ulrike Mills, (Washington D.C., National Gallery of Art, 2002), 53.

contemporaries in France were looking at objects from West Africa and Oceania for inspiration in the Cubist and Fauvist movements, many modern artists in the United States turned to so-called naïve American art for their own "primitive" references. Artists who stayed in Ogunquit observed that modernism's fundamental characteristics were on display in American folk-art pieces. They were simple, but strong in form, with abstract qualities that modern artists admired.[22]

Collectors had not yet discovered America's local antiques, so artists with limited funds like Kuniyoshi were able to form their own collections. Kuniyoshi bought prints by Currier and Ives, a nineteenth century print shop that produced idealized American life scenes. He purchased dolls with thick, round arms, porcelain complexions, and wide-set eyes. His figure paintings took on the dolls' characteristics —stiff, round, and white. Kuniyoshi's portraits of babies had bright eyes with penetrating gazes that resembled a doll's glassy stare. Critics at the time saw in the figure's "almond shaped eyes" references to the East, but Kuniyoshi's source of inspiration was from New England. Trained for years in Los Angeles and New York academic art schools, Kuniyoshi started to reject his draftsmanship studies and sought naive sources for his works.

Kuniyoshi had been in New York for almost a decade by the time he visited Maine's farms and fishermen hamlets. New Yorkers were listening to jazz and watching the buildings on its skyline grow taller, but after several years living in the city, Maine's cows and dairy farmers were more exotic to Kuniyoshi. While many of his peers continued to paint urban settings even during their Maine summers, the rural and rugged New England landscape and community drew Kuniyoshi's attention. He embraced country life: A local fisherman friend was in awe of how Kuniyoshi grew his summer vegetable crop, given the sandy coastline. (Kuniyoshi said his secret was learned from the fishermen in Japan, where they used dried seaweed and fish as fertilizer.) Laurent praised Kuniyoshi for painting his local chicken nemesis, responsible

---

22. Virginia Tuttle Clayton, "Picturing a 'Usable Past'," *Drawing on America's Past: Folk Art, Modernism, and the Index of American Design*, 21.

for destroying his tomato crop, rather than resorting to violence.[23] In 1920 Kuniyoshi began visiting Peggy Bacon and Alexander Brook, at their home in Woodstock, New York. It was much closer to the city than Ogunquit and soon Kuniyoshi became a member of that art community, later building a home there. Kuniyoshi maintained a country residence throughout his life as an escape from the city, a place for socializing and community.

Summers in Maine were productive. Kuniyoshi was painting every day while living among artists—one of whom, Katherine Schmidt, he would marry. Art critic and friend, Lloyd Goodrich, claimed that Schmidt, who had lived in New York City since she was eight years old, was instrumental in helping Kuniyoshi make friends. She was naturally social and gregarious; he was not. The couple had already known each other for two and a half years before deciding to marry. Their decision to marry was not a frivolous one. The costs would be great for Schmidt: Because of the Expatriation Act of 1907, Schmidt lost her U.S. citizenship for marrying a Japanese national.[24] Schmidt's family opposed her marriage to Kuniyoshi and cut her off financially. Marriage between Art Students League classmates was common, but according to Arnold Blanch, there was controversy among their friends about whether a Japanese man should marry an American woman."[25] Laurent remembered the couple spending long nights consulting with Field about what they should do. At times, the talks became heated and Kuniyoshi "stomped out" during the discussions.[26] When they finally married in Maine in 1919, Kuniyoshi made a wreath of field flowers to decorate Schmidt's hair.

---

23. "Cock Calling the Dawn." Ogunquit, Maine, 1923 Oil on canvas 30 x 25. Columbus Museum of Art, Ohio. Gift of Ferdinand Howard, 1931.
24. In 1922, the Cable Act reversed loss of citizenship for women when they married, but excluded marriage to Asians, because they were not eligible for naturalization. In 1931, the law was changed to include Asians.
25. Oral history interview with Arnold Blanch, June 13-August 3, 1963. Smithsonian Archives of American Art.
26. Laurent, "Memories of Yas," 6.

Field gave the couple a studio and room at one of his Brooklyn properties as a wedding present. When Field backtracked and decided the couple needed to pay rent, Schmidt chose to work rather than be beholden to his whims.[27] She ran the League's lunchroom and Kuniyoshi started photographing friends' artworks to earn extra income. Kuniyoshi eventually stopped taking classes at the League in 1920, so that he could earn more money. Despite off and on financial hardships, the couple's Brooklyn residence soon became a gathering place for New York's artists. Marsden Hartley and Stefan Hirsch as well as poet Hart Crane also lived at the property. A group of around ten artists regularly met to sketch models and then hold an auction to bid on each other's works. Eventually, they brought other artworks for the group to bid on. A vase decorated by Jules Pascin won the highest bid of twenty-five dollars to Wood Gaylor. Kuniyoshi introduced board games with toys, some of which he decorated.[28] The club then moved on to bowling, an activity Peggy Bacon drew in 1932 called "The Ardent Bowlers," featuring Kuniyoshi and other members of the group.

By 1917, Kuniyoshi had established an exhibition record at the Society of Independent Artists where he showed a few pieces. He regularly displayed works at the Penguin Club's East 15th Street brownstone headquarters. However, he lacked gallery representation. Schmidt was devoted to helping Kuniyoshi's career. Friend and fellow artist, Isabel Bishop, remembered Schmidt carrying Kuniyoshi's work from gallery to gallery, even though she did not have representation for her own work. The couple regularly visited Alfred Stieglitz's "291 Gallery." Stieglitz had wanted to represent him, but Kuniyoshi did not care for the notoriously difficult gallery owner.[29] Instead, he chose the Daniel Gallery in 1920 after it showed two of his paintings. The works received positive reviews, and Charles Daniel gave him a solo show the following year.

---

27. Oral History interview with Katherine Schmidt 1969, December 8-15, Archives of American Art, Smithsonian Institution.
28. Laurent, "Memories of Yas," 8.
29. Oral History interview with Katherine Schmidt 1969, December 8–15, Archives of American Art, Smithsonian Institution.

Charles Daniel had opened his gallery on West 47th Street the year after the Armory show. Like Stieglitz's 291 Gallery, the Daniel Gallery was unusual, because he represented a diverse group that included photographers, women, and immigrant artists. In 1915, Daniel held a solo exhibition of paintings by Man Ray, who was known primarily for his avant-garde photography in Paris. The gallery also represented Stuart Davis, William Glackens, Marsden Hartley, and Stanton Macdonald-Wright, the premier American artists of the time. The group represented various styles and forms: Glackens was associated with the Ashcan School, Hartley synthesized Cubism and Expressionism, and Macdonald-Wright developed Synchronism, an early American abstract art that attempted to synchronize color with sound. For a Japanese man doing oil paintings of Maine landscapes inspired by American folk art, Kuniyoshi had found an appropriate home.

Kuniyoshi's first solo show received good reviews, though Daniel Gallery shows were generally panned. Critics called Kuniyoshi a "humorist"—particularly his many paintings of cows. Kuniyoshi wrote later that he could not understand the comedian label assigned to him. He explained that he painted so many cows because they were "decorative as well as ugly."[30] He also expressed a connection to bovines because he was born in the Year of the Cow according to the lunar calendar. (Kuniyoshi became known for his cows, to the extent that they became a constant motif that decorated exhibition announcements and catalogs.) All the paintings sold well. After the horrors of World War I and the disparity between the rich and poor of New York's "Jazz Age," Kuniyoshi's paintings of rural America were nostalgic for another era, but were also fresh and almost exotic. By the 1930s, only reproductions were available to art viewers, because most of his early paintings were squired away into private collections and museums.

Having arrived earlier, Kuniyoshi became a leader among Japanese artists living and traveling through New York. Kuniyoshi was not the only Japanese artist at the Art Students League in the 1920s. Shimizu Toshi and Ishigaki Eitarô also rejected New York's academic institutions

30. Kuniyoshi, *Yasuo Kuniyoshi,* 7.

in favor of the more liberal school. Kuniyoshi established New York-based, Japanese-member art societies. The Gachôkai (Japanese Painters and Sculptors Society), became one of the more resilient groups, lasting from 1922 through 1930. In its first exhibition in 1922, the Gachôkai hosted an exhibition of fifteen artists held at the Civic Club on West 12th Street. Although New York-based Japanese artists came together as a group for exhibitions and their social lives often intersected, their different interests conspired to make for independent lives. Kuniyoshi, for example, had no interest in Ishigaki's leftist reading group that helped export communist literature to Japan. Shimizu was married with a young child and lived far uptown. He socialized more often with League teacher and painter John Sloan and the photographer Nakayama Iwata, who had a studio on 5th Avenue. Kuniyoshi favored Brooklyn and Maine country life.

Despite running in international art circles and doing paintings of Maine's barnyards, Kuniyoshi's Japanese-ness fascinated critics. If they could not understand Kuniyoshi's canvases, they explained that it was owing to Kuniyoshi's "Oriental" exoticism, a convenient, if somewhat lazy, analytical frame. They assumed that it was Kuniyoshi's "Eastern sense of humor" when they did not get the joke: A critic for *The New Yorker* wrote in 1942 that "One of the few really Oriental things about Kuniyoshi's work is its humor, which is a mingling of the impish, the grave, and the subtly sophisticated that is entirely un-Occidental in character."[31] Kuniyoshi's foreignness, in other words, made his paintings seemingly impenetrable and allowed the American viewer to quickly give up trying to unravel the puzzle. Unable to locate his references or grasp Kuniyoshi's meaning, the critics concluded that it "could not come from a Western mind," otherwise his intent would be clearer to a Western audience.[32] Kuniyoshi, too, often relied on

31. "The Art Galleries: A Kuniyoshi Retrospective," *The New Yorker*, May 16, 1942. Scrapbook of printed materials relating to Yasuo Kuniyoshi, 1934-1945. "Yasuo Kuniyoshi Papers, 1921-1993." Smithsonian Archives of American Art.
32. Jane Myers and Tom Wolf, The Shores of a Dream: Yasuo Kuniyoshi's Early Work in America, (Fort Worth, TX: Amon Carter Museum, 1996).

his Japanese origin to explain his ideas to critics: Why do you paint so many cows? Because I was born in the Year of the Cow according to the lunar year. Kuniyoshi's explanations were also practical, since it would not have been economically prudent for him to deny any Japanese artistic heritage. Most critics and collectors preferred a hybrid version of Japanese and Western art, which they claimed to observe in Kuniyoshi's ink drawings more than the oil paintings. Black ink, they said, was his birthright as a Japanese. For a Japanese artist establishing himself in the 1920s art world, there was no worse critical condemnation than to be accused of "swallowing Western art whole."

Some critics applauded Kuniyoshi's individualism rather than seeking out traces of the East in his work. One *New York Times* critic complimented him by writing "Kuniyoshi is himself in everything he does, being neither touched by the 'East' nor 'Cezanne.'" (The critic, Henry McBride, condemned most modern Japanese artists for all painting like Cezanne.) At one point, McBride declared that Kuniyoshi had a perspective as though he were from Mars, more alien than foreign.[33] During the 1930s, his friend and fellow artist Julian Levi wrote that Kuniyoshi's critics focused too much on identifying "Oriental" and "Occidental" elements in his work. Looking for "Oriental ingredients," Levi wrote, "neither explains nor evaluates his painting."[34] Levi asserted that most sophisticated art came from a "multiple fountainhead." Nevertheless, McBride and Levi's commendations of Kuniyoshi's humanist point of view were rare, compared to explanations of his Japanese-ness. As a member of an "artistically expressive race," most critics praised Kuniyoshi's innate Oriental attributes and sensitivity, which they declared to be a compliment to his American training.[35]

---

33. Henry McBride, *The New York Herald*, January 13, 1924.
34. "Scrapbook of printed materials relating to Yasuo Kuniyoshi, 1934-1945." Yasuo Kuniyoshi Papers, 1921-1993, Smithsonian Archives of American Art.
35. *Brooklyn Eagle*, May 10, 1942. Scrapbook of printed materials relating to Yasuo Kuniyoshi, 1934-1945. "Yasuo Kuniyoshi Papers, 1921-1993." Smithsonian Archives of American Art.

When in 1923 Kuniyoshi's friend Alexander Brook became associate director of the Whitney Studio Club, the precursor to the Whitney Museum of American Art, his career received another boost. Kuniyoshi had a long-standing relationship with the Whitney art institution in its various manifestations. Several years before the 1913 Armory Show, Gertrude Vanderbilt Whitney started an open studio next to her own in Greenwich Village for informal exhibitions of young artists' works. The function and influence expanded. The studio's eventual director, Juliana Force, established one of New York's central institutions for American artists as well as a site for revelry and food for those that were hungry.

Whitney Studio Club artists paired modern and folk elements for their exhibitions. Force had a personal collection of folk art, as did the Ogunquit art colony members. Henry Schakenberg's 1924 exhibition, "Early American Art," was most likely the first show of American folk-art. Kuniyoshi lent a painting of a locomotive and a carving of a cow from his personal collection. Brook also asked Kuniyoshi to curate a show. Called "Portraits and Religious Works," Kuniyoshi selected American and European contemporary art and again combined them with folk art from his collection.[36] His curation included Henri Matisse and Joseph Stella hanging on walls next to model trains. The combination reflected the juxtaposition between modern and traditional, urban and rural, secular and sacred, as well as industrial and agriculture landscapes, all references that Kuniyoshi and his peers esteemed.

Kuniyoshi and the painter Jules Pascin became close friends when they were neighbors at Field's Brooklyn home. Pascin, originally from Bulgaria, had been something of a Paris art world celebrity prior to his arrival in New York. Fearing that he would be forced to join the German army, he left Europe just before the start of World War I. New York's art world was already familiar with Pascin's work, notable for its erotic subject matter, having viewed it at the 1913 Armory Show.

---

36. *The Shores of a Dream: Yasuo Kuniyoshi's Early Work in America.* Jane Myers and Tom Wolf (Fort Worth, TX: Amon Carter Museum, 1996), 33.

Pascin, four years older than Kuniyoshi, introduced him to European artists passing through New York and later provided Kuniyoshi with entre to Parisian art circles. He influenced Kuniyoshi's painting subject matter and style, coaxing him away from Maine's rural motifs. Traces of Pascin's paintings started appearing in Kuniyoshi's portraits of sensual and somewhat melancholic women wearing lingerie. The solid, wide-eyed, chalky mannequins swimming off Maine's coastline disappeared.

By 1925, Pascin convinced Kuniyoshi that it was time to visit Paris. Members of the Whitney Studio Club hosted an enormous party to send Kuniyoshi and Schmidt off. A Japanese artist friend lent the couple housing when they first arrived, but they did not stay long in the bedbug-infested apartment. Schmidt knew some French, but Kuniyoshi did not bother to learn any. French was ultimately unnecessary, since their Parisian circle were emigres—Japanese, Russians, Bulgarian, Germans—with few French except for friends of Pascin's like Chaim Soutine. The couple financially struggled to keep up with their social group. Schmidt described Kuniyoshi and herself as "puritanical," in shock at the extravagance and libations they witnessed while in Paris.[37]

Pascin was the center of their social circle, though he and Kuniyoshi were something of an odd couple. Pascin was known for selling a painting on Friday and spending all the proceeds on Saturday. Pascin drank alcohol and Kuniyoshi drank tea. Pascin caroused all night and Kuniyoshi often stayed in. Pascin started fights in bars and Kuniyoshi was introverted. Pascin divided his time between his wife, Hermine (David), his lover, Lucy (Krohg), and hundreds of models, while Kuniyoshi stayed only with Schmidt. On one occasion, Pascin convinced the couple to visit a Marseilles neighborhood, which turned out to be a red-light district. A group of women pushed the couple up the stairs of one establishment and then danced off with Kuniyoshi's hat. Schmidt was not amused.

Schmidt remembered Paris as overwhelming for them. They thought Americans in Paris were "flying too high" and were poseurs,

---

37. Oral history with Katherine Schmidt 1969, December 8-15, Archives of American Art, Smithsonian Institute.

wearing berets and bike-clips on their pants. She enjoyed socializing with Aline Bernstein, a renowned costume designer and writer Thomas Wolfe's lover, but avoided most other Americans in Paris.[38] The couple left France and traveled to Italy, where they saw more art than created it. In Spain, they struggled to move around, because few people spoke English or even the limited French that Schmidt could understand, but they managed to visit as many museums as possible. They ended their trip in the south of France, where many of their friends lived, including Reginald Marsh. Schmidt recalled that they spent as much time with writers like Susan Glaspell and Elmer Rice, as they did with other artists. In 1926, the couple returned to the United States. Kuniyoshi had felt like a small fish in a big pond: "France (was) so rich in art and artists, and America so poor," he told friends when they returned.[39]

After a flurry of exhibitions at the Daniel Gallery, Whitney Studio Club, and the Art Center's Exhibition of Japanese Artists in New York, Kuniyoshi once again heeded Paris' siren's call—or maybe Pascin's. Kuniyoshi and Schmidt returned to France in 1927, but she did not like it anymore the second time. She struggled to paint and Kuniyoshi was falling more under Pascin's spell. He turned his attention to lithography, which proved a satisfying endeavor, because of the technical challenges. He had created his first lithograph in 1922, "Milking the Cow," at a Whitney Studio Club workshop. During the 1920s, many painters—Matisse, Picasso, José Clemente Orozco—were making lithographs. According to Ishigaki Eitarô, Kuniyoshi's choice was a business decision as much as it was creative, because they generated a regular revenue stream unlike more expensive canvases.

Schmidt returned to New York earlier than planned, telling Kuniyoshi that she never wanted to live outside the United States

38. Oral History Interview with Katherine Schmidt 1969, December 8–15, Archives of American Art, Smithsonian Institution.

39. Cynthia Jaffee McCabe, *The Golden Door: Artist-Immigrants of America, 1876-1976* (Washington DC: Hirshhorn Museum and Sculpture Garden, Smithsonian Institution, 1976), 144.

again. Following Pascin from cafe to cafe, where he would eventually pick fights was too much for her.[40] Kuniyoshi stayed on with Pascin. Convinced that Kuniyoshi's career would not advance in the United States, Pascin tried to persuade him not to return. Nevertheless, Kuniyoshi went back to New York. His letters to Schmidt had become bleaker over time. She credited his decision to leave Paris as a realization that he was more American than he believed—less a cosmopolitan and more rooted to his life in New York.

After he returned, Kuniyoshi's painting style dramatically shifted. He replaced the playful colonial, folk art references with a greater realism and a darker, more melancholic mood. Critics described his paintings as more "serious," and less "naive."[41] Pascin had encouraged him to paint live models, rather than from his imagination or memories. Painting from life brought out emotive qualities in his subjects. Leaving Brooklyn, Kuniyoshi took up residence on 14th Street in a studio with high ceilings and a view of the street action below. Downtown Gallery owner, Edith Halpert, recalled that you had to walk through a lingerie store to access the studio; wealthy collectors hesitated navigating various underwear racks before climbing the four flights of stairs to Kuniyoshi's space.[42] Fourteenth Street painters, including Reginald Marsh and Ishigaki, were neighbors, as were burlesque shows and Union Square political rallies.

Schmidt and Kuniyoshi built a summer home in Woodstock with money they saved and an inheritance from Schmidt's family, presumably a member who had recovered from her marriage to a Japanese. Artists had already started settling in the Woodstock area, and the couple had many friends there. Older residents welcomed the young couple and supported them. Kuniyoshi spent every summer in

---

40. Oral History Interview with Katherine Schmidt 1969, December 8–15, Archives of American Art, Smithsonian Institution.
41. "Kuniyoshi Glorifies the Humble Stove," *The New York Times*, March 6, 1930.
42. Speaking of Art: Sections from the Archives of American Art, Oral History Collection (1958-2008), Archives of American Art, Smithsonian Institution, Winterhouse Editions, 2008, 53-54.

their Woodstock home. It became a popular destination for New York City artists escaping for the weekend. (Schmidt recalled the endless cooking and cleaning for guests to be a "nightmare.")[43] Although soft-spoken and at times reclusive, Kuniyoshi craved the company of artists, always fearful of returning to his lonely days on the West Coast.

The Museum of Modern Art in New York first opened its doors only a couple of weeks after the October 29, 1929, stock market crash. The museum's first exhibition showcased Paul Cézanne, Paul Gauguin, and Vincent van Gogh, but its second show, "Paintings by 19 Living Americans," highlighted local talent. Identified as "American, born in Japan," Kuniyoshi was one of the nineteen. Kuniyoshi's inclusion in the exhibition made his status as an American artist explicit. The museum's press release stated that the painters were selected because they represented mature artists of both conservative and radical styles. The show included his former teacher, Kenneth Hayes Miller, as well as John Sloan, Edward Hopper, and Walter Kuhn. It included five of Kuniyoshi's paintings: early examples like "Boy Stealing Fruit" (1923), "Landscape, Maine," (1925), and "Self-Portrait as Golf Player," (1927) as well as more recent ones: "Nude" (1929) and "Still Life" (1929). Sara Mazo, Kuniyoshi's second wife, who later worked at the Museum of Modern Art, credited curator Alfred Barr's inclusion of Kuniyoshi as a milestone in her husband's career.[44]

The museum's curators choice to include so-called "non-Americans" became an instant cause for criticism and comment in art circles. Some questioned why painters like Kuniyoshi, Pascin—who became a U.S. citizen in 1920—and Max Weber (born in Russia) were included in the "19 Americans" exhibition, since they had not been born in the United States.[45] Some critics, however, did not mention

---

43 Oral History Interview with Katherine Schmidt 1969, December 8–15, Archives of American Art, Smithsonian Institution.

44. Interview with Sara Mazo, November 18, 1993. The Museum of Modern Art Oral History Program, 13.

45. Ibid.

where Kuniyoshi, Pascin, or Weber were born at all; their attention was given to the canvases themselves.[46] However, the choice to identify the artists as "living Americans" remained a talking point. Some celebrated the diversity of American art. Art critic for the *New York Times*, Edwin Alden Jewel, proclaimed that American art in 1930 had become a melting pot; it was a hybrid of different influences, people, and media.[47] Art dealer and writer, Samuel Kootz, stated that the American assignation for the "19 Living Artists" had "nothing to do with painting," but was merely "a descriptive word representing the nation in which the artist works."[48] According to Kootz, being an American painter was to occupy an American space, or, state of mind. The exhibition covered a broad range of painters: realists like Sloan and modernists like O'Keefe, Impressionists like Ernest Lawson and Precisionists like Charles Demuth. What united the painters (sixteen of the nineteen) was their association with the Art Students League as instructors or as students. The artists represented the New York art world more than it did an "American" one, which might explain the inclusion of three painters not born in the United States, but who were New York residents.

Despite his successes in 1930, Kuniyoshi was tense. The stock market crash affected sales as well as photography commissions. He was devastated to learn that Pascin, who Kuniyoshi considered the "father of the contemporary art scene in America," had killed himself in Paris. His marriage to Schmidt was strained. The Daniel Gallery gave Kuniyoshi a one-man show before closing its doors for the last time in 1931. The gallery had been his champion, home, and exhibition site throughout the 1920s, and its loss caused him anxiety. Kuniyoshi turned his attention back to Japan. Since leaving Japan in 1906, Kuniyoshi had regularly exchanged letters with his father, who always pleaded with

46. Maurice Stern, "The First and Second Exhibitions at the Museum of Modern Art," *Parnassus* no. 8 (Dec., 1929), 13-16.
47. Edward Alden Jewell, *Modern Art: Americans*, (New York: Alfred A. Knopf, 1930).
48. Samuel Kootz. *Modern American Painters*, 1930.

him to return.[49] Kuniyoshi did not feel that he was "ready," having not yet reached a point when his father would be "truly proud" of him. When his father became ill in 1931, Kuniyoshi returned to Japan and used the opportunity to exhibit his paintings. Friends like sculptor Dorothea and her husband, Edward Greenbaum, lent him money to transport twenty-nine oil paintings and sixty lithographs to show in Japan. Though he received a warm welcome from the *gadan* (art world), only three of his paintings sold, and Kuniyoshi boarded a ship back to the United States within four months.

His time in Japan made a strong impression on Kuniyoshi. He observed how Japanese art associations supported their members, which inspired his later efforts to organize and strengthen artist groups in New York. By the 1920s, the Japanese government had established a secure, though somewhat conservative in taste, salon system that hosted exhibitions. The U.S. government-sponsored Federal Arts Project did not intervene on behalf of artists suffering during the economic depression until 1935. Unlike the United States, in Japan gallery owners were not the captains of the art market; Japanese newspapers and department stores sponsored group exhibitions in major cities. Without bases of support, American artists were more vulnerable to economic cycles, and patrons became scarcer after the stock market crash. Recognizing the importance of structured art associations, Kuniyoshi adopted an even greater leadership role in organizations to advocate for artists after his return.

Absent from Japan since 1906, everyday life had become so transformed as to be virtually unrecognizable to Kuniyoshi. Journalists compared Kuniyoshi to the legend of Urashima Tarô — Japan's version of Rip Van Winkle. In an interview with a Japanese art journal, Kuniyoshi claimed that he felt as though he was visiting a "foreign land."[50] He noted with trepidation Japan's increased militarism. Despite feeling somewhat alienated from the transformed landscape, Kuniyoshi described for local journalists feeling a connection to

---

49. Kuniyoshi, *Yasuo Kuniyoshi*, 9.
50. Unno Hiroshi, "Kuniyoshi Yasuo: shoku modan stairu saihô," *Aato* 93 (Winter 1980), 24.

the scenery. Walking around Okayama's famous garden, Korakuen, he recalled his childhood interest in *sumô*, Japanese wrestling. The trip inspired a new, "fresh" impression of Japan.[51] He explained to journalists that although he was an "American painter," as a Japanese, he would never "become a local" in the United States. But, Kuniyoshi continued, he believed that the trip would instill "Japanese meaning" in his work from that point on.[52] What that signified to Kuniyoshi is unclear; while the influence of his Parisian sojourns is obvious in his canvases, "Japan" does not have an obvious presence.

Kuniyoshi's return to Japan became the occasion for his first interaction with the gadan. He had neither experience nor art world connections before his 1906 departure. Kuniyoshi had never created artwork with the Japanese market in mind; he would not have known how. Upon arriving, he immediately went to Okayama to see his father. The *Chugoku Minpo Press,* a regional newspaper, hosted an exhibition at the Meiji Confectionary Company, which was well-attended by residents and his family and childhood friends.[53] When he returned to Tokyo, Kuniyoshi relied on Japanese contacts that he had made while in New York and Paris for admission to Japanese art societies. Painter Fujita Tsuguharu, whom Kuniyoshi had met in Paris, wrote letters of introduction for him that facilitated solo exhibitions. Kuniyoshi ignored Fujita's recommendation to make a visit to the imperial family (Obata Chiura, however, chose to follow Fujita's advice when he visited in 1929, which might partially explain his relative commercial success.) Kuniyoshi did not reject all paths into the *gadan*, however. His friend from New York that relocated to Japan, Shimizu Toshi, was a leading figure in the Nika-kai, a relatively progressive art society. The group rallied to support Kuniyoshi's visit. In November 1931 members of the *gadan*, including forty painters, threw Kuniyoshi a

---

51. "Yasuo Kuniyoshi," *Atorie* (January 1932).
52. Ibid.
53. Hideo Tomiyama, "Yasuo Kuniyoshi and his Native Country, Japan," *Yasuo Kuniyoshi, 1889-1935: A Retrospective Exhibition.* (Austin, TX: University Art Museum, 1975), 61.

welcome party at the Frank Lloyd Wright-designed Imperial Hotel, which catered to Western visitors to Japan. In addition to the five-day exhibition held by the *Tokyo Nichi-Nichi* newspaper, Kuniyoshi had a five-day exhibition in Osaka. Nevertheless, according to biographer, Yamaguchi Taiji, the Japanese public was only interested in Kuniyoshi as a curiosity, a Japanese living in the United States.[54] Most Japanese critics paid less attention to the work itself, because they were more interested in Kuniyoshi's personal story. Kuniyoshi claimed that critics thought his work too "European," and he had a difficult time convincing them that there was "such a thing as American art."[55]

Many art journals featured stories about Kuniyoshi, his work, and his career abroad. Shimizu wrote articles that described Kuniyoshi's unusual history as an adventurer in California, who transformed himself into a successful New York artist, and whose work was represented in major American museums. For art critic Kaneko Yoshio, Kuniyoshi's paintings "transcended citizenship and race."[56] Kuniyoshi, Kaneko claimed, was his own "ism" (*kuniyoshi-izumu*). Critic and artist Yanagi Ryôsuke highlighted Kuniyoshi's relationship with Pascin, with whom Japanese art readers were familiar.[57] Comparing the Parisian neighborhood of Montparnasse to New York's Greenwich Village, Yanagi wrote about the activities of the Penguin Club, unjuried exhibitions, and the democratic management of the student-run Art Students League. Members of the Japanese *gadan*, many of whom had studied in Paris, would more easily understand the American art world when compared to France.

Despite the exhibitions, media attention, and gadan acceptance, Kuniyoshi believed that his painting style did not suit the 1930s Japanese art world, which he felt was more interested in *nihonga* (Japanese-

---

54. Yamaguchi Taiji, *Amerika bijutsu to Kuniyoshi Yasuo* (Tokyo: Nippon hôsoku shuppan kyôkai, 2003), 96.
55. Kuniyoshi, *Yasuo Kuniyoshi*, 11.
56. Kaneko Yoshio, "Yasuo Kuniyoshi no koto," *Bijutsu Shinron* 6-12, 1931.
57. Yanagi Ryôsuke "Kuniyoshi" *Atorie,* December 1931.

style) than Western-style works. When Kuniyoshi arrived, there had been a resurgence of interest in woodblock printing, which led to the *shin-hanga* (New Woodblock) movement.[58] As Japan became more nationalist, Kuniyoshi felt that many Japanese rejected anything that reeked of the West. He believed that the gadan's mission was to revive a state-codified version of Japanese traditions, aesthetics, and heritage. Kuniyoshi was cynical about his prospects in Japan and whether he could compete in an art world that seemed interested in retreating to nativism. Indeed, there was resurgent chauvinism in the 1930s, but *yôga* (Western-style painting) had not been eclipsed as Kuniyoshi perceived it to be. *Yôga* artists were still part of the establishment. For example, the *yôga* artist Yasui Sôtarô, who often did oil paintings of nudes, enjoyed positive reviews and was nominated to the government-sponsored Japan Art Academy in 1935. Kuniyoshi's impression of the Japanese art world as being in the throes of Japanese tradition was a reaction to his observations about its 1930s nationalist political context.

Although Kuniyoshi did not achieve instant success in terms of sales that he had expected, he remained a recurring subject for the *gadan* after he returned to New York. Renowned art critic and artist, Arishima Ikuma, writing about Kuniyoshi in 1934, found Kuniyoshi's works to be humorous. The article highlighted Kuniyoshi's personal affability, which Arishima credited to an American influence. (American art critics had credited Kuniyoshi's humor to being Japanese.) In fact, Arishima stated that by meeting Kuniyoshi, he felt that he "learned what was good about America for the first time."[59] Kuniyoshi's geniality was evidence that the United States was a "good" country where "good" people lived. Arishima qualified his statement, however, by saying that Kuniyoshi's open personality was also because of his upbringing in western Japan, where people were thought to be friendlier than in Tokyo.

---

58. As a *nihonga* artist, Obata Chiura, who visited Japan from California in 1929, had critical and commercial success.
59. Arishima Ikuma, "Hajimete Kuniyoshi-kun ni atte. Zaibei nihon sakka no shôkai: Kuniyoshi Yasuo," *Chûô Bijutsu* (June 1, 1934).

Kuniyoshi later said that he felt that the Japanese viewed him as a "foreigner," going so far as to say that he no longer considered Japan to be "home."[60] He told a writer for *Atorie* magazine in 1932 that he knew "very clearly" that he was Japanese, adding "However deeply a Japanese enters a Western country, ultimately he cannot become a Westerner."[61] He accepted that he was also an oddity to the Japanese media, agreeing with journalist's comparisons to Urashima Tarô. In less than a year, Kuniyoshi decided to leave Japan and return to New York. After he returned in February 1932, his marriage to Katherine Schmidt officially ended. She had chosen not to join him in Japan, believing that her "irrepressible" nature would not suit Japanese society. The four-month separation convinced the couple that their marriage could not last. A fellow artist, she had been a companion and partner in his ascension as a leader in the American art world. She remarried the following year, but Kuniyoshi and Schmidt remained close until his death in 1953, when she was present to support not only him, but also his second wife, Sara Mazo.

When he received word on his return across the Pacific Ocean that his father had died, Kuniyoshi decided at that moment never to return to Japan. (Prior to leaving, he applied for membership to the Nika-kai art association, perhaps hedging his bets. Records show that he maintained his membership until his death.) Kuniyoshi's return to Japan had caught the attention of *The New Yorker* "Talk of the Town" section. Although there was no mention made of the incident in the Japanese press, the writer claimed that Okayama's Buddhist priests had objected to Kuniyoshi's exhibiting paintings of nudes. (Kuniyoshi was the likely source of this anecdote.) By 1931, nudes in Japanese art were commonplace, but the article's inclusion of this story suggested that Japan was provincial and prudish. It congratulated the United States for its modernity.

---

60. Unno Hiroshi, "Kuniyoshi Yasuo: Modan sutairu saihô," *Aato* (Winter 1980): 24.
61. Alexandra Munroe "The War Years and Their Aftermath" *Yasuo Kuniyoshi: tanjô 100nen kinen—nyû yôku no yûshû* (Tokyo: Tokyo Teien Art Museum, 1989). 43.

Returning from Japan, Kuniyoshi was met with professional challenges. The winter of 1932 was the low point of the Depression in the United States: monthly wages were sixty percent of those in 1929 and industry operated at one half its 1929 volume. Kuniyoshi, however, was able to endure while many artists struggled in the wake of the stock market crash. The Daniel Gallery had closed its doors, but Kuniyoshi found a new home at Edith Halpert's Downtown Gallery. Halpert exhibited Georgia O'Keefe, Stuart Davis, Ben Shahn, and Charles Sheeler, all members of Kuniyoshi's circle. A Russian Jewish immigrant from Odessa, Halpert was one of the pioneers of the American modernist movement and helped to put it on the art world map. In 1933, the Downtown Gallery hosted their first solo show of Kuniyoshi's latest work, where reviewers noted Jules Pascin's influence in his portraits of women. When O'Keefe abandoned the project, he received a commission to paint murals of flowers for the women's powder rooms in the Radio City Music Hall. He also assumed a teaching post at the Art Students League in 1933. The position guaranteed steady income for himself and his second wife, Sara Mazo, until his death twenty years later.

Art associations gave Kuniyoshi countless accolades throughout the 1930s. He received a Carnegie Institute award for "Odd Objects on a Couch" in 1931, which was followed by a Temple Gold Medal from the Pennsylvania Academy of Fine Arts in 1934. He continued to have exhibitions in New York and beyond: In addition to regular shows at the Downtown Gallery, shows at the Art Institute of Chicago, the Musee du Jeu de Paume, Baltimore Museum of Art, the Santa Barbara Museum of Art, the Carnegie Institute, and Whitney Museum of American Art showed his work. In 1935 Kuniyoshi received a Guggenheim fellowship, previously awarded to many of his friends like Alexander Brook, Peggy Bacon, and Arnold Blanch. The fellowship saved Kuniyoshi financially and allowed him to travel west to New Mexico as well as to Mexico. Sara Mazo accompanied him on the expedition. Although Kuniyoshi painted barren western landscapes and steam engines following his trip, a critic commended him for being too much of an "individualist" to have suddenly changed his point of view because of a visit to Mexico. The critic was grateful that he did not find one "Mexican sombrero, nor a conventional sunny market place" in Kuniyoshi's canvases when he returned to New York.[62]

Kuniyoshi was neither a leftist nor a communist, but he was fervently anti-fascist, particularly after returning from Japan. While his friends and colleagues looked to the Spanish Civil War as an indication of impending doom, Kuniyoshi was keenly aware of the global threat that Japan's military posed. Between 1930 and 1932, young military officers were carrying out assassinations and assassination attempts on politicians. Only weeks before Kuniyoshi's arrival, in August 1931, Prime Minister Hamaguchi Osachi died from gunshot wounds inflicted by a right-wing youth the previous year. While Kuniyoshi was organizing exhibitions in Tokyo and Osaka, ultranationalists murdered a former finance minister and head of the Mitsui business conglomerate. Kuniyoshi's return to Japan also coincided with the Manchurian Incident on September 18, 1931.[63] In the same Japanese newspapers that featured interviews discussing his life in the United States, front-page headlines celebrated Japan's mission in Manchuria. By January 1932, the Japanese military occupied Jinzhou in Manchuria and left the League of Nations the following year. In addition to its aggressions on the continent, Kuniyoshi was disturbed by what he had seen as a more dictatorial regime in Japan. Kuniyoshi had observed in

---

62. Rosamund Frost, "Kuniyoshi, American of Two Decades," *The Art News*, May 15, 1942. Scrapbook of printed materials relating to Yasuo Kuniyoshi, 1934-1945. Yasuo Kuniyoshi Papers, 1921-1993. Smithsonian Archives of American Art.
63. China and Japan had competed for control over Manchuria in northeastern China since the Russo-Japanese war ended in 1905 and Japan won control of the Manchurian Railway (Mantetsu). Intent on fomenting war with China and frustrated by what they perceived as the government's cautious foreign policy, Japanese military officers took action on September 18, 1931. They blew up a portion of the southern Manchurian railway track and blamed the act on Chinese military forces. The military used this as pretext for an attack on Chinese regional armies. Japan then installed a puppet regime in the form of the last emperor of China's Qing dynasty, Puyi, as head of Manchuria, calling it 'Manchukuo'.

person Japan's authoritarian shift: He recounted how he had stopped to ask a policeman for directions, but the officer sternly reprimanded Kuniyoshi for not removing his hat when addressing him. Imagine, Kuniyoshi asked, a New York policeman behaving in such a way.

During the 1930s, Kuniyoshi's political activism took the form of art association leadership to protect artists' rights and ensure their financial support. Artists were banding together to take political action: From the fall of the stock market until World War II, American artists united to protest injustice, fascism, militarism, and war. Using art as a catalyst, they established galleries, associations, and journals to spur others to action and shape public consciousness about mounting global crises. Kuniyoshi was one of the 1930s art association movement's primary leaders. Kuniyoshi's experience as leader of Salons of America following Hamilton Easter Field's death in 1922 prepared him for a leadership role. Salons of America's board of directors had included "radicals, conservatives, and those on the fence," requiring Kuniyoshi to wrangle strong personalities and big egos with political and self-serving agendas.[64] He used this experience to establish the American Contemporary Art (ACA) Galleries in 1932, along with Herman Baron, Stuart Davis, and Adolf Dehn. The gallery did not censor artists and often exhibited socially conscious artworks. Like the Art Students League and the leftist John Reed Club, founded in the fall of 1929, the ACA Gallery was inclusive, showing work by women, African-Americans, Japanese, Chinese, Latin Americans, and Russian artists on a regular basis.

The ACA Galleries became the regular meeting place for the American Artists' Congress (AAC), which was a center for pre-World War II artist activism. International in scope, the AAC included artists with varying degrees of art world success, artistic styles, and media. The AAC's anti-war stance was its primary political position, so membership included everyone left of center. Some supported social realist art as a vehicle to fight fascism, while others were vehement anti-Stalinists. In addition to staunch anti-fascism, the Congress was

64. "Salons of America: A New Art Society." *New York Times*, July 3, 1922.

opposed to censorship, which had become a critical art world topic since the removal of Diego Rivera's Rockefeller Center mural. The Congress also voiced concern about the decline of art patronage and criticized the inadequacy of government programs supporting artists.[65]

Kuniyoshi was one of the AAC's first leaders, until Harry Glintenkamp replaced him in 1937. Almost all the Congress members were established figures in leftist movements, except for Kuniyoshi, whose political neutrality engendered his selection as the group's initial leader. Under Kuniyoshi's direction, the AAC sponsored a show, "Against War and Fascism: An International Exhibition of Cartoons, Drawings and Prints," at the New School for Social Research in spring of 1936. The scope of the New School show was vast: it included Francisco Goya, Daumier, Pieter Breugel, as well as Albrecht Dürer's 15th century "Four Horsemen of the Apocalypse." Kuniyoshi also contributed paintings to Congress shows such as "In Defense of World Democracy: Dedicated to the Peoples of Spain and China," which included works by Pablo Picasso. Funds raised at the exhibition were used to help refugee groups in Spain and China.

Although Kuniyoshi was involved in activist groups, his art from this period did not reflect an explicit political ideology. He did hundreds of paintings and drawings of dark-haired women during the 1930s and 1940s. (Japanese women never figured in Kuniyoshi's canvases.)[66] Kuniyoshi abandoned his 1920s paintings of robust female figures standing confidently on rocks in the ocean, their hair cascading down over large, white thighs, or swimming with rainbows. In the 1930s, Kuniyoshi's women were languid and thin with dark circles under their eyes. Most of them smoked cigarettes and read newspapers, which were perceived as masculine activities at the time. Reading newspapers made

---

65. For more information on the AAC, please see the chapter on Ishigaki Eitarô in this manuscript as well as Andrew Hemmingway, *Artists on the left: American Artists and the Communist Movement, 1926-1956*. (New Haven, CT: Yale University Press, 2002), 23. One AAC member, Noda Hideo, who was a protégé of Kuniyoshi and Ishigaki, had assisted Rivera with the mural.
66. Unno Hiroshi, "Kuniyoshi Yasuo: shoku modan stairu saihô," *Aato* 93 (Winter 1980), 28.

them seem interested in the outside world, but Kuniyoshi's women look bored, if not depressed by what they read. The paintings were not portraits of named individuals, nor were they identifiable as Sara Mazo or other friends. Instead, they were representations of a general emotional state embodied in a female figure. Art critic Unno Hiroshi described Kuniyoshi's women as "tired of being alone, thinking about what they can do in today's society."[67] Julian Levi, Kuniyoshi's friend as well as a painter, wrote that the women were certainly not "good girls" with their black hair, packs of cigarettes at the ready, and lace-trimmed nightgowns.[68] Ishigaki Eitarô described Kuniyoshi's women as what Americans would call "beautiful, but dumb."[69] Ishigaki explained that Kuniyoshi was trying to find a universal humanity in his subjects, which reflected the turbulent times. Kuniyoshi's own explanation of his many paintings was simpler: "I like to paint women," he said.[70]

Kuniyoshi's women reflected the Depression era's gloom, but an expectation that artists should lift people's spirits during dark days emerged in some art circles. Masculine images of breadwinners wielding iron tools to build skyscrapers were meant to instill audiences with a sense of hope. American Regionalists depicted women as the backbone—hoeing rows of vegetables, carrying babies or chickens—of this effort. Kuniyoshi's women, however, did not appear optimistic, nor were they hard at work. They were portraits of ennui, a psychic depression that matched an economic one. Biding time was a theme; his canvases were titled "Waiting" and "Still Waiting." His portraits of melancholy and dejected women, bored or dismayed by the headlines about war looming in Europe, were the antithesis to the male hero and their sturdy homemaker wives. Art critics praised Kuniyoshi's portraits

---

67. Unno Hiroshi, *Aato*, 1980.
68. Julian Levi, "Yasuo Kuniyoshi." Scrapbook of printed materials relating to Yasuo Kuniyoshi, 1934-1945. Yasuo Kuniyoshi Papers, 1921-1993, Smithsonian Archives of American Art.
69 Ishigaki Eitarô, "Kuniyoshi no gyôseki," *Geijutsu Shinchô*, July 1953, 61.
70. Lloyd Goodrich, *Yasuo Kuniyoshi*. 31.

for deeper thought and feeling than his previous works.[71] The women were "alone," but not lonely, they noted.[72] Just as the cow had become a motif in the 1920s, (what critic Henry McBride called Kuniyoshi's "Cow Period,") the languid woman with newspaper became symbolic of Kuniyoshi in the 1930s. At one event, when artists lampooned each other, Kuniyoshi included himself in the joke: Kuniyoshi posed with a model, who was smoking a cigarette, holding a newspaper, and barely able to keep her eyes open.

Though he did not paint Japanese women, questions about Kuniyoshi's "Japanese-ness" lingered for critics. One *New Yorker* critic claimed Kuniyoshi's women were "half-humorous."[73] As in his paintings of cows, the reviewer credited the "humor" with his Japanese heritage. Kuniyoshi intentionally incited such "East versus West" speculation by alluding to Eastern traditions and Western stylistic devices. His paintings of women included what he "knew" and what he "sensed" about all women. Condensing what he understood about women into his female figures was part of an Eastern tradition, Kuniyoshi explained, though his painting style was Western.[74] As tensions with Japan heightened, however, this explanation became more treacherous: Critics once again analyzed his paintings in racial terms, explaining that the texture of his canvases derived from his Japanese "race." Alluding to heightened tensions with Japan, one critic comforted his readership that they had nothing to fear from Kuniyoshi, because he was a Greenwich Village artist—not a Japanese.[75]

---

71. Scrapbook of printed materials relating to Yasuo Kuniyoshi, 1934-1945. Yasuo Kuniyoshi Papers, 1921-1993 Smithsonian Archives of American Art.
72. "The Art Galleries: A Kuniyoshi Retrospective," *The New Yorker*, May 16, 1942. Scrapbook of printed materials relating to Yasuo Kuniyoshi, 1934-1945. Yasuo Kuniyoshi Papers, 1921-1993 Smithsonian Archives of American Art.
73. Ibid.
74. Lloyd Goodrich, *Yasuo Kuniyoshi*, 31.
75. "The Art Galleries: A Kuniyoshi Retrospective," *The New Yorker*, May 16, 1942.

Although Kuniyoshi rejected Japan's militarism, nationalism, and increasing isolation from other global powers, he still had to confront his Japanese-ness upon his return to New York. The importance—or usefulness—of Kuniyoshi's Japanese identity in the art world had ebbed and flowed with changing trends and newly emerging "isms." Like a geopolitical weathervane, the more Japan was in the headlines, the more critics looked for Japanese references in his artwork. Japan was not at the center of the international community's attention during the mid-1920s, so a critic could write a favorable *New York Times* review of his solo show at the Daniel Gallery in 1924 without mentioning Japan or identifying Kuniyoshi as a Japanese.[76] However, this changed as an aggressive Japanese military expanded its territorial reach and it became a subject in the world's headlines. As the Japanese military invasion of China dominated 1938 headlines, one critic observed that Kuniyoshi was becoming "older and more Japanese." The critic's evidence was Kuniyoshi's painting, "Summer Storm," which depicted a horse tethered to a tree. (There are no visible Japanese techniques or stylistic references on the canvas.) The critic recalled how the writer Lafcadio Hearn, known for his writings about Japan, had predicted that his son, whose mother was Japanese, would become "more Japanese with age." This was not to detract from the quality of Kuniyoshi's art, the critic declared, because "blood was thicker than ink, at least, the ink used in naturalization papers."[77]

The Carnegie Institute awarded Kuniyoshi with its first prize in 1944 for "Room 110" as part of its "Paintings in the United States" exhibition. Most art critics were not surprised that Kuniyoshi would be awarded the prize, since he was a perennial Carnegie favorite,

---

76. "Kuniyoshi Glorifies the Humble Stove." *The New York Times*. March 6, 1930.
77. *The New York Sun*, October 15, 1938, from Scrapbook of printed materials relating to Yasuo Kuniyoshi, 1934-1945. Yasuo Kuniyoshi Papers, 1921-1993 Smithsonian Archives of American Art.

having received second prize in 1939.[78] Others were shocked that a Japanese national would receive the award. Local Pittsburgh media outlets lambasted the committee for awarding a "Jap" the prize. They challenged their readers to come up with an appropriate title for the still-life, which they called a "pile of junk" that seemed on the verge of collapse.[79] The *Pittsburgh Post Gazette* accused members of the Carnegie jury of smoking "reefers" or partaking of the director's private stock of vodka when selecting "Room 110" as a winner.[80] The *Pittsburgh Press* photographers created a caricature of the Kuniyoshi painting, calling it "Padded Cell 7-11," or, "Maid's Day Off" and saying that it was "Tokyo Fujiyamo O'Toole" who actually painted the piece. Other critics surmised that most artists would understand why Kuniyoshi was awarded first prize: "It's a painter's painting," Dr. Harvey Gaul wrote. He claimed that the common citizen would not understand the selection once they found out he was a Japanese national, however.[81]

"Room 110" was one of many still-lifes that Kuniyoshi painted in addition to female figures. They were deeply personal. For years, he stored things that he had picked up when they had caught his eye in Maine's antique stores or from trash piles on the street. (Accusations of "Room 110" being a pile of trash were not far off the mark.) Over time, he rediscovered objects among his collection and they took on meaning for him when assembled with other objects. The hard part for Kuniyoshi was putting the various items together for a composition.

78. "Kuniyoshi Captures Carnegie," *Newsweek*. December 1944. Scrapbook of printed materials relating to Yasuo Kuniyoshi, 1934-1945. Yasuo Kuniyoshi Papers, 1921-1993. Smithsonian Archives of American Art.
79. Douglas Naylor, "Winner Depicts Pile of Junk." Scrapbook of printed materials relating to Yasuo Kuniyoshi, 1934-1945. Yasuo Kuniyoshi Papers, 1921-1993 Smithsonian Archives of American Art.
80. Charles Danver, "Pittsburghesque," *Pittsburgh Post Gazette* "The Art Galleries: A Kuniyoshi Retrospective," *The New Yorker*, May 16, 1942. Scrapbook of printed materials relating to Yasuo Kuniyoshi, 1934-1945. Yasuo Kuniyoshi Papers, 1921-1993 Smithsonian Archives of American Art.
81. "Japan-Born Artist Tops Carnegie Exhibit," *Pittsburgh Post Gazette*, October 13, 1944. Scrapbook of printed materials relating to Yasuo Kuniyoshi, 1934-1945. Yasuo Kuniyoshi Papers, 1921-1993 Smithsonian Archives of American Art.

Even if they seemed like a haphazard and random selection, Kuniyoshi spent hours putting the objects together in a specific way that would eventually inspire a painting. Claiming that he did not know what a weathervane or a mask or a toy tiger symbolized, he said the objects merely drew his attention in that moment. Kuniyoshi held on to objects for years before they became subjects of his canvases. They were mementoes of certain times and places. Kuniyoshi tried to explain to his Art Students League students that to paint something was to paint the totality of the emotion contained in that object. He often used grapes as an example in his classes: when I paint grapes, he told his students, I am painting my youth in California. He described for his students that he gobbled as many grapes as he could upon arrival to the vineyards, remembering that he got sick of the taste and his hands were covered in juice. Now, he said, drawing grapes was a way of accessing those memories. Fruit was tricky, Kuniyoshi said, because he let it decay as he finished the painting. If he painted a slice of watermelon, he did not replace the fruit with a fresher version as the days went on. He left it there until it was covered in flies.

The 1941 attack on Pearl Harbor "woke him from a dream," Kuniyoshi said, and forced him to face global crises. He remained in New York during World War II and, thus, avoided interment on the West Coast as decreed by Executive Order 9066. Nevertheless, he was classified as an "enemy alien" because of his Japanese nationality. Authorities froze his bank account, took possession of his camera, and restricted travel to his Woodstock home. Kuniyoshi wrote that in only a few days, his status in the United States had changed, "although (he himself had) not changed at all."[82] Living under house arrest during the first few days after the bombing of Pearl Harbor, Kuniyoshi frantically campaigned his friends to serve as character witnesses. His longtime friend, Debbie Greenbaum, who was a Kenneth Hayes Miller alum, testified to authorities about Kuniyoshi's loyalty to the United States, while her husband acted as his legal counsel. He also wrote a series

82. Yasuo Kuniyoshi letter to George Biddle, December 11, 1941. Yasuo Kuniyoshi Papers, 1921-1993 Smithsonian Archives of American Art.

of letters to various government officials professing his loyalty to the United States and his opposition to Japanese aggression.

Kuniyoshi claimed that he was afraid to leave his home unescorted and did not ride subways alone, fearing anti-Japanese violence. Nevertheless, Kuniyoshi continued to teach classes at the Art Students League throughout the war, which guaranteed him some income. Ishigaki claimed that Kuniyoshi's sensitivity to his treatment as an enemy alien by Americans made the war experience even more agonizing than if he were in the battlefield.[83] Ishigaki recalled that some of his League students were unsure of Kuniyoshi, observing that their "facial expressions betrayed their suspicions and narrow-mindedness."[84] In another account, a friend noticed that pedestrians eyed Kuniyoshi with hostility, "as if an enemy were in their midst" as they walked together to a church to attend a funeral.[85] Art critics, who did not like Kuniyoshi's work, started referring to him as a "Jap." A critic for a Pittsburgh newspaper claimed never to have liked Kuniyoshi, "even before Pearl Harbor." The process of re-categorizing Kuniyoshi's identity started in the latter days of World War II: for some he was a "Jap," and for allies, he became a "Japanese-American," a new category that emerged during the war. Kuniyoshi was rarely called "Japanese" again by the American press.

In public, Kuniyoshi did not waiver between supporting United States or Japan; he was firmly on the side of the Allies. As a member of the Committee of Japanese Artists Living in New York City, Kuniyoshi signed his name to a "declaration of loyalty" letter, stating that he supported the national defense of the United States as an "artist and as a man," whether that meant utilizing his artistic skills

---

83. Ishigaki Eitarô "Kuniyoshi no gyôseki," *Geijutsu Shinchô* (July 1953), 60-62.
84. Ibid, 60-63.
85. Robert Laurent quoted in ShiPu Wang's *Becoming American: The Art and Identity Crisis of Yasuo Kuniyoshi.* (Honolulu, HI: University of Hawai'i Press, 2011), 5.

for the war effort or "taking up arms."[86] He asserted from first-hand observation that Japan had been taken over by fanatical militarists that restricted freedoms and marched the country into war. Kuniyoshi had romantic associations of Japan as a "beautiful country with flowers and pines," and as a place of "custom, tradition and culture." The military threatened those memories and Kuniyoshi believed that the United States had a responsibility to free the Japanese from the military's grip.

During the war, Kuniyoshi demanded that the Allies accept only "unconditional surrender" from the Japanese army, often making public statements in the guise of his leadership of art groups. He believed that any compromise with Japan would preserve seeds of fascism. Since he no longer had familial ties in Japan, Kuniyoshi could support bombing campaigns without thinking about personal consequences. Other Japanese members of his circle were not as vehement as Kuniyoshi in his call for eradicating the militarists at any cost to civilians. The Ishigakis, for example, were terrified that family members would be victims of the air raids. Kuniyoshi's understanding of the war campaign was limited to American media. Unlike Japanese living on the Pacific coast listening to Japanese radio, Kuniyoshi had little access to Japanese media and depended on American news outlets for his information. When friends asked him for insights about Japan, he countered that he knew no more than they did, because he read the same newspapers.

Although Kuniyoshi insisted that his knowledge about Japan was reduced to distant memories, he accepted an Office of War Information (OWI) assignment to illustrate Japan in propaganda posters. One of his proposed drawings showed a warrior wearing samurai armor from Japan's middle ages, suggesting that Japanese culture had a long military history and culture, which led to the conflict. The OWI wanted a more "journalistic" feel that would document the current situation, however, and they rejected this early submission. The OWI selected

86. "Declaration of Loyalty: Committee of Japanese Artists Resident in New York City, 1941," Yasuo Kuniyoshi Papers, 1921-1993 Smithsonian Archives of American Art.

two of Kuniyoshi's other posters: one featured a man seen from the back with his wrists bound with rope and another of a woman who had been stabbed with a bayonet while a child sat by her side. Whereas his early pieces were obvious references to Japanese culture, the new figures did not show any specific ethnicity or nationality.

In addition to the OWI posters, Kuniyoshi contributed to the war effort by broadcasting to the Japanese public. He wrote his statement in English and translated it into Japanese. Addressing the Japanese art and intelligentsia community, he described an idealized egalitarian society in the United States. He called upon listeners to not "blindly" follow their leaders, but to reject them. He declared that it was not "money madness" that had drawn people from around the world to the United States.[87] Rather, it was the global community's desire for freedom that the United States offered. He referred to artists like Max Ernst and Marc Chagall who fled Europe to the United States, because they could create art more freely. Kuniyoshi stated that the Committee of Japanese Artists residing in New York had pledged loyalty to the United States in a letter to President Roosevelt and that they believed the Japanese militarist clique represented a "dire threat to all mankind." He tried to convince listeners that they were members of an international community of artists, rather than to a Japanese national one.

The New York intelligentsia lauded his wartime efforts. A photograph, called "Three Good Hates," in *Time* magazine in 1942 showed artists George Grosz, Jon Corbino, and Kuniyoshi posing in front of a large mural of Hitler, Mussolini, and Hirohito, which they had prepared for the Art Students League United Nations Ball. The extreme caricatures reflected standard propaganda images of the time. In 1942, *The New Yorker* magazine identified Kuniyoshi as a Japanese who was doing his "damnedest" to help the United States in its war against Japan.[88] Claiming that he was a long time "anti-Japanese

87. Yasuo Kuniyoshi, "Radio Broadcast, Japan Against Japan, 1942," Yasuo Kuniyoshi Papers 1921-1993 Smithsonian Archives of American Art.
88. "Talk of the Town: Telling Tokio," *The New Yorker* (March 28, 1942).

man" since Japan first invaded China, the article lauded the painter for helping the war effort. The writer also commented on Kuniyoshi's short stature, a common way to belittle Japanese, but declared that he was "purely American" despite his "shortcomings."

Kuniyoshi continued to do portraits of women throughout the war. His subjects displayed heightened melancholy, tension, and anxiety. Before Pearl Harbor, Kuniyoshi and Sara Mazo had separated, increasing his emotional turmoil. They reunited in 1944, but the separation during the war years must have exacerbated his feelings of vulnerability.[89] Kuniyoshi's allegiance to the Allied war effort was definite, but he was experiencing inner turmoil. Although he blurred the text in earlier canvases, newspaper headlines about Nazi expansion in Europe became legible in his canvases. Kuniyoshi claimed that people accused him of being a "cynic." He had not agreed at the time, but in 1944 he was beginning to accept that he might be forlorn about the state of the world. He wrote in the summer of 1944, "Morbidness has helped to shape and lead to (a) feeling of depression." Kuniyoshi claimed that these feelings stemmed from feelings of frustration and seeing only the "darker side of life."[90]

On June 29, 1945, the U.S. Army Air Force dropped incendiary bombs on Okayama City, Kuniyoshi's hometown. Fires burned most of the city and 1,700 people lost their lives. Tokyo had been incinerated a couple of months earlier and nearly 100,000 people were killed. On August 15, 1945, Japan accepted unconditional surrender—as Kuniyoshi had insisted was the only way to end the war.

89. *Yasuo Kuniyoshi: tanjô 100nen kinen—nyû yôku no yûshû* (Tokyo: Tokyo Teien Art Museum, December 1989). Pgs. 204-205.

90. Archives of American Art. Letter. General Correspondence 1941-1962, 1971-189, undated; Box 1, Folder 2.

(Opposite): Kuniyoshi Yasuo and Katherine Schmidt, 1925. Stowall Studios. (Rosalie Berkowitz collection of photographs), (1927-1950). Archives of American Art, Smithsonian Institution.

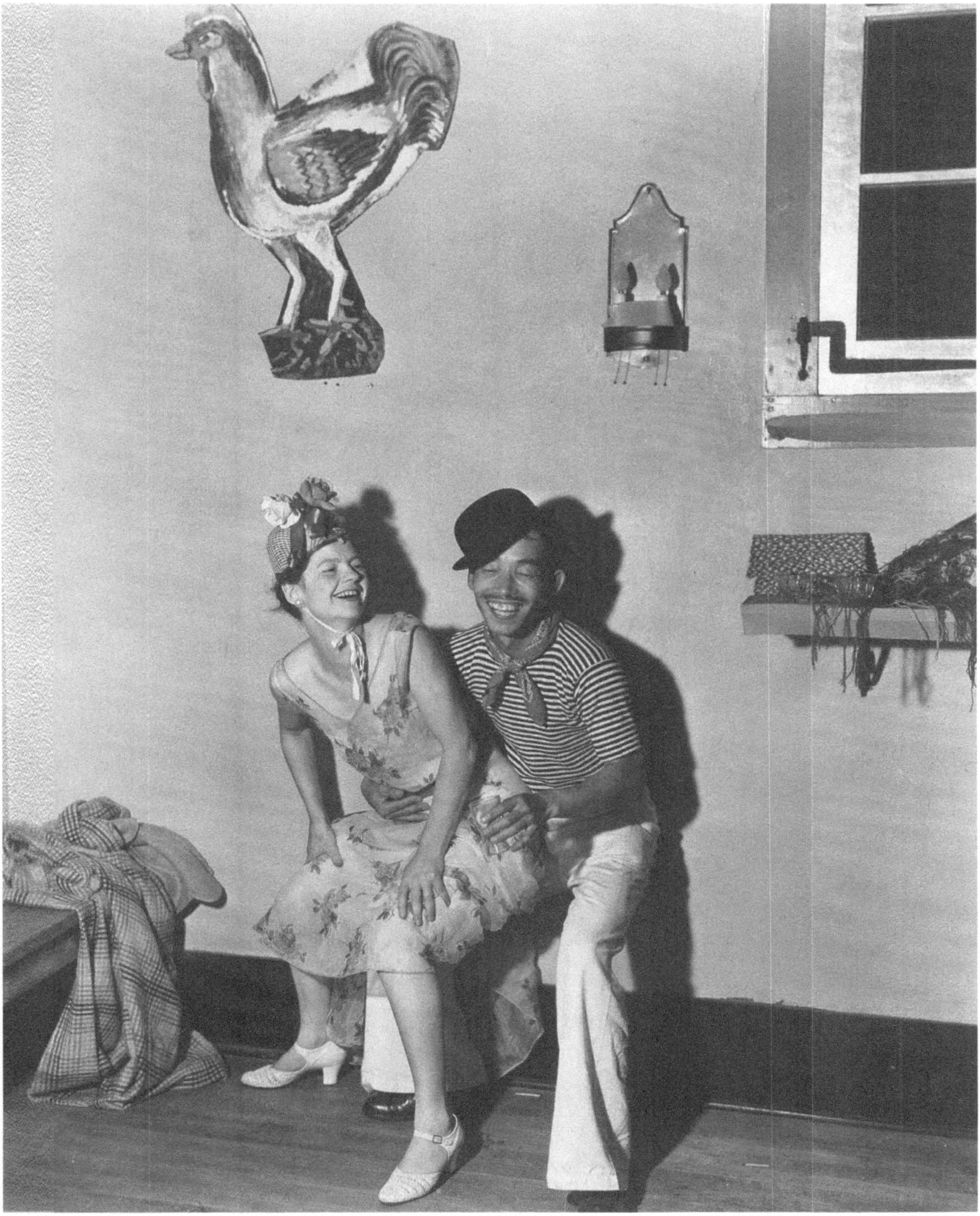

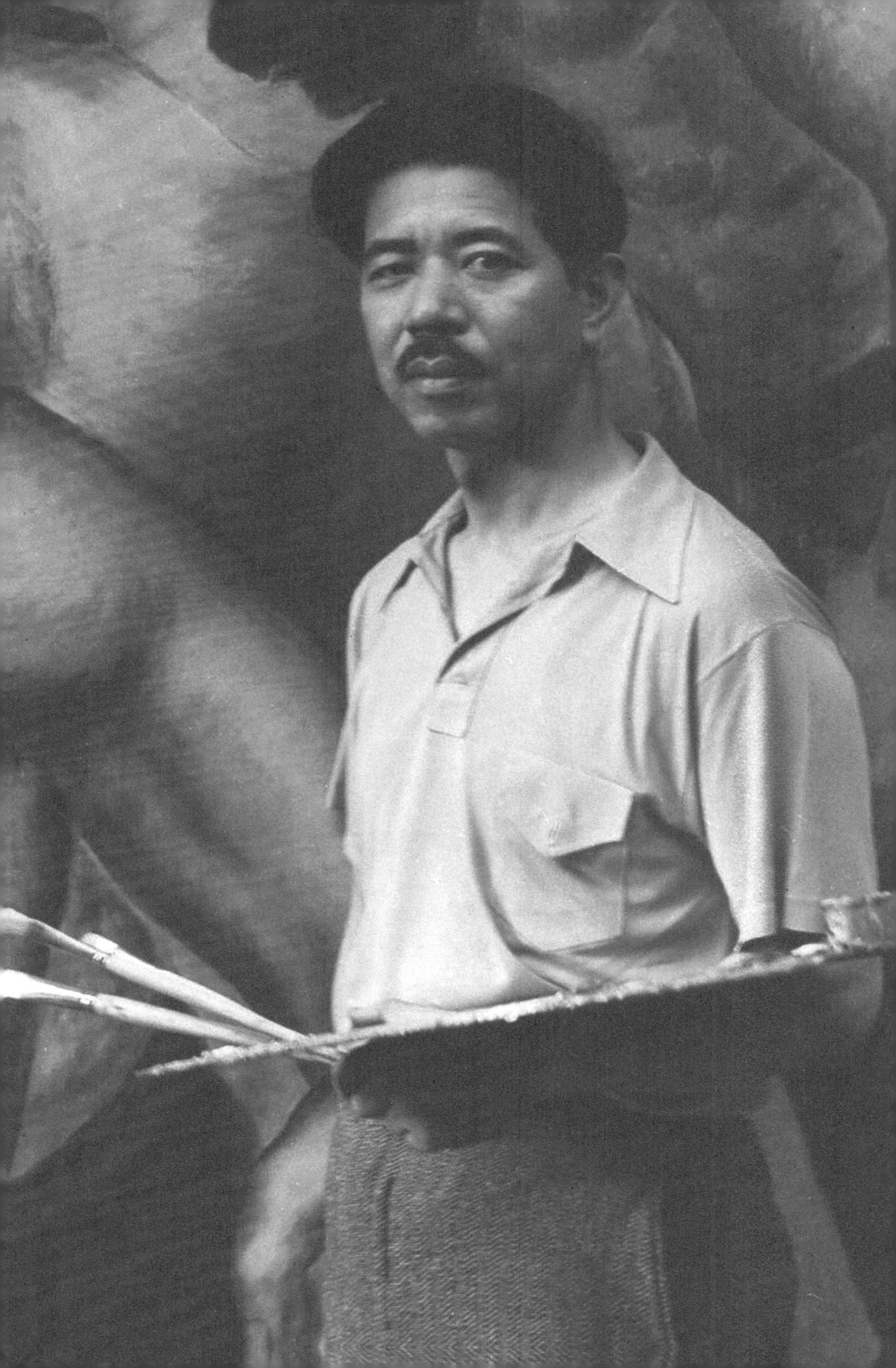

Chapter Two
Ishigaki Eitarô
Artist on the Left

As a young boy, Ishigaki Eitarô spent each morning sketching the Taiji shoreline, where workers built whaling boats. The smell of carved cedar was a strong childhood memory.[1] Ishigaki understood that in addition to seagulls and the ocean, he was also illustrating local hardship as fewer men worked to build boats. Taiji had fallen into economic decline during the late nineteenth century, because its whaling industry was unable to compete with Norwegian ships that had started sailing along Japan's coastline. His father's shipbuilding business had also been damaged. Ishigaki's early sketches that fused art and social consciousness anticipated themes that characterized his life and career.[2] Eventually, Ishigaki's father moved to Seattle for work in 1901 when his son was seven years old. He asked Eitarô to follow him nine years later.

1. Yasugi Masahiro, "Ishigaki Eitarô no Amerika—aru tobei gaka no shôgai," *Amerika no naka no Nihon—Ishigaki Eitarô to senzen no tobei gakatachi.* (Wakayama: The Museum of Modern Art, Wakayama, 1997), 8.
2. Ibid.

(Opposite): Eitaro Ishigaki, ca. 1940. Federal Art Project, Photographic Division collection, circa 1920-1965. Archives of American Art, Smithsonian Institution.

Hearing that there were better work opportunities to the south, father and son left the Pacific Northwest to move to Bakersfield in California's Central Valley. Bakersfield had become a boomtown in the 1880s when gold was discovered in the nearby Kern River. When they arrived in 1910, it still had a frontier mystique. Years later, Ishigaki recounted his time there for the Japanese periodical, *Chûô kôron*, by describing Bakersfield as a "hot jungle," not only in terms of its climate, but its culture of lawlessness. "Violence," he recalled, "occurred there with a degree of calm."[3] Laborers like the Ishigakis had flocked to Bakersfield, "like bees to honey" in pursuit of higher wages, but the town also attracted gamblers and speculators. Despite the fighting, rampant gambling, and even shootings, the police never showed up.

When Ishigaki arrived in Bakersfield, Japanese and Chinese immigrants were at the bottom of California's social hierarchy.[4] Japanese were often targeted for assault. Ishigaki felt safer staying close to the local Japanese community. A voracious reader since his childhood, Ishigaki spent his free time at Bakersfield's Methodist Mission reading Japanese scholars, though he commented later that he should have been studying English. Japanese churches provided solace as well as reading materials like the Christian socialist, Uchimura Kanzô, who had studied theology in Boston.[5] He also became motivated to read another Christian socialist writer, Kinoshita Naoe, a co-founder of Japan's Social Democratic Party in 1901, along with Katayama Sen and Kôtoku Shûsui. Kinoshita's writing led Ishigaki to understand Bakersfield society as divided by class and race. He concluded that the town's lawlessness was a symptom of social inequality. The wealthy, white upper classes served as the town's (inattentive) law enforcement,

3. Ishigaki Eitarô, *Ai ni tsuite no kokuhaku: otoko to shite, onna to shite* (Osaka: Heiwa Shobo, 1971), 23.
4. Ishigaki explained to Japanese readers in the 1950s, however, that second and third generation Japanese in the United States were solidifying their positions and occupying more professions. He also stated that the state of Hawaii had a Japanese as a member of the Senate. Ishigaki Eitarô, *Ai ni tsuite no kokuhaku*, 26-30.
5. Ishigaki Eitarô. *Chûo Kôron* (June 1952).

while the non-white and immigrant classes were confined to the filthiest menial labor. Influenced by Kinoshita's opposition to legalized prostitution, Ishigaki observed Bakersfield's prostitute community, which reflected the town's racial hierarchy and division. Prostitutes only served members of their own racial group.[6]

Bakersfield was home to a Buddhist Hall, established by the Japanese government by way of the Japan America Association (JAA). Ishigaki felt that it was far too lavish for the three hundred Japanese living in Bakersfield. He resented the hall as being an extension of the Japanese state, believing that it was a way for the government to maintain control over Japanese nationals living abroad.[7] The JAA used the hall to host ceremonies and festivals, show Japanese movies, and present *naniwabushi* performers and music recitals. Children studied Japanese textbooks at the hall, which Ishigaki feared would prevent them from assimilating into American culture.[8] Ishigaki blamed anti-Japanese racial prejudice in California for forcing the isolation of the Japanese community, but he also argued that the Japanese state's influence over emigrants contributed to its insularity.

The Buddhist Hall in Bakersfield demonstrates how Japanese immigrant communities in California were not as distant from their country of origin as the vastness of the Pacific Ocean might suggest. The Japanese government tightened its control over the Japanese diaspora following the Great Treason Incident of 1911, when several Japanese socialists and anarchists were accused of leading an unsuccessful plot to assassinate the Emperor Meiji. One of the incident's protagonists, Kôtoku Shûsui, had been active in California prior to becoming embroiled in the affair. Kôtoku was a founding member of socialist political parties, which the government sought to suppress during the

---

6. Ishigaki Eitarô, *Ai ni tsuite no kokuhaku*, 24.
7. Eiichiro Azuma, *Between Two Empires: Race, History, and Transnationalism in Japanese America* (Oxford and New York: Oxford University Press, 2005) and Yuji Ichioka's *The Issei: the First Generation of Japanese Immigrants 1885–1924*, (New York: Free Press London, 1988).
8. Ishigaki Eitarô, *Ai ni tsuite no kokuhaku*, 36-40.

Meiji era. Following his 1905 release from Tokyo's infamous Sugamo prison, Kôtoku left for California to more freely organize within immigrant communities against the Japanese government. Other Japanese socialists along with his young nephew, Kôtoku Shiei, who became a painter in California, joined him. Because of Kôtoku and his larger network, Japanese state authorities monitored California's immigrant population fearing a ricochet effect on the home country.

Two years after the Ishigaki's arrival, a landmark incident shook Bakersfield's Japanese community and propelled the younger Ishigaki out of the town. The Japanese held a ceremony at the Bakersfield Buddhist Hall to commemorate the late Emperor Meiji's birthday, an occasion that Ishigaki described as probably "no different from what occurred throughout the Japanese countryside."[9] Bakersfield's 1912 commemoration for Emperor Meiji occurred the year after the accused Great Treason Incident members—including Kôtoku—were executed in Japan. California's Japanese community became uneasy, fearing guilt by association. Ishigaki was present when a member of the Bakersfield Japanese Methodist Mission, Takeda Shojiro, refused to bow in front of a portrait of Emperor Meiji during the commemoration ceremony. In 1891, a similar incident had occurred when Uchimura Kanzô, an English teacher at a Tokyo school, refused to bow to an imperial signature, because it amounted to "idol worship" and violated his Christian beliefs. Takeda was most likely inspired by the event. At a church meeting two days later, Takeda accused those Japanese Mission members who did bow of "idolatry." The Japanese America Association and then local newspapers cast Takeda as a traitor. Because he had frequented the Methodist Mission and had associated with Takeda and others involved in this so-called

---

9. Ishigaki noted in his memoirs that the year was 1912, but according to Yuji Ichioka's scholarship the ceremony took place in November of 1911, almost a year before the emperor's death.

lèse majesté incident, his father recommended that Ishigaki move to San Francisco to distance himself from scrutiny.[10]

Rather than saving money to open a small business back in Taiji and marry a "good person" as his father advised, Ishigaki was a self-described romantic with "big dreams" that did not include immediately returning to Taiji in Wakayama.[11] When he moved to San Francisco in 1912, Ishigaki entered art school and worked at his aunt's store in Japantown. San Francisco's Japanese community had moved away from its Chinatown neighbor following the 1906 earthquake and begun to expand. In Japantown, Ishigaki had access to imported publications like the feminist magazine *Seitô* (Blue Stocking), and the literary journal *Shirakaba-ha* (The White Birch Society). *Seitô* led him to reading translations of the playwrights Henrik Ibsen and Anton Chekov as well as American feminist and anarchist, Emma Goldman, who Ishigaki later met in New York. A *Shirakaba-ha* essay by Yanagi Sôetsu, philosopher and leader of the Japanese folk craft movement, introduced Ishigaki to William Blake's writing.[12] *Shirakaba-ha* artists and writers espoused individualism and personal cultivation unlike Japanese naturalists, who had previously dominated the early

---

10. Although Ishigaki made no mention of it in his memoirs, he was further connected to the Great Treason Incident beyond the shadow it cast on his life as a Japanese in California. He and Ôishi Seinosuke (1867-1911), came from the same hometown in Wakayama Prefecture. Ôishi studied medicine during the 1890s in the United States and then returned to Wakayama to set up his practice. His home became the gathering place for socialist study groups. During the Great Treason Incident, he became implicated along with Kôtoku. As he was a valued member of the community, the people of Wakayama protested Ôishi's inclusion in the plot against the emperor and his subsequent execution. It is likely that news of Ôishi's involvement reached Ishigaki and his father while they were in California, given their connections to Wakayama immigrants. Yasugi Masahiro, "Ishigaki Eitarô no Amerika —aru tobei gaka no shôgai," *Amerika no naka no Nihon – Ishigaki Eitarô to senzen no tobei gakatachi* (Wakayama: The Museum of Modern Art, 1997), 8.
11. Ishigaki, Eitarô, "Amerika hôrô yonjûnen," *Chûô kôron* (1954) Ishigaki Ayako, *Umi o watatta ai no gaka*. (Tokyo: Ochanomizu-shobo, 1988), 24.
12. Ishigaki Ayako, "Ishigaki Eitarô, 40 Years' Wandering in America," *Ai ni tsuite no kokuhaku: otoko to shite onna to shite*. (Tokyo: Heiwa shobo, 1971), 37.

twentieth century's literary world. Naturalists were known for the "I Novel," which expressed interiority and emotional states, which the *Shirakaba-ha* members viewed as being a solipsistic preoccupation with the dark side of human experience. Instead, they advocated a positive approach to improving one's lot.[13] They also rejected what they saw as the naturalists' retreat from social issues. The *Shirakaba-ha* position eventually characterized Ishigaki's art: he depicted social inequities and injustice, while professing a belief that wrongs could be righted if light was cast upon them.

In 1913, Ishigaki met the poet Kanno (Takeshi) Isen at a lecture on Henry Wadsworth Longfellow.[14] Kanno remembered that at the time of their meeting, Ishigaki was more concerned with politics than with poetry. He introduced him to his wife, the sculptress Gertrude Boyle, and their circle of painters, sculptors, and writers, who helped expose Ishigaki to non-Japanese friends outside the church. Unlike his aunt, who called him a "fool" (*baka*) for wanting to be an artist destined to a life of poverty, Kanno and Boyle fed Ishigaki's creativity with exposure to other artists, musicians, and poets.[15] The couple invited him to join a Bohemian group at poet Joaquin Miller's Oakland hills home, where Japanese writers like Noguchi Yonejirô had also visited.[16] He met Noguchi later in New York along with his son, Isamu, who Ishigaki mentored. Miller's circle was dedicated to artistic expression and to living outside societal norms. Ishigaki's participation in Miller's Oakland hills society of international writers and musicians provided a respite from racial conflict then consuming California politics. The 1907 Gentlemen's Agreement between the United States and Japan, which barred Japanese migrant laborers, had not quelled San

---

13. Gennifer Weisenfeld, *Mavo: Japanese Artists and the Avant-Garde 1905-1931*, (Berkeley: University of California Press, 2002), 20.
14. Ishigaki Eitarô, *Chûô kôron*, 47.
15. Ishigaki became acquainted with the composer, Henry Cowell (1897-1965), whom he continued to see when the two lived in New York City in later years. Ishigaki also met the poet Edwin Markham (1852-1940) there.
16. Ishigaki did not meet Noguchi Yonejirô until the poet visited him in his New York studio following World War I.

Francisco's anti-Japanese sentiment. While Ishigaki sketched in an Oakland cabin and took walks with Boyle, the California state senate passed the Alien Land Law of 1913, which prohibited Japanese from owning land.

Ishigaki's job at a Japantown church introduced him to socialists operating in California like the writer and activist, Katayama Sen, whose work he became familiar with in Bakersfield. Katayama was born in 1858 in Okayama to small farmers. After moving to Tokyo, he pursued education in the United States at Maryville College in Tennessee, Grinnell College in Iowa, and then Andover College, where he started to study theology. Studying Christianity and social problems became intertwined. By the time he returned to Japan in 1897, Katayama was ready to enter the labor movement, while remaining committed to Christian humanism. He returned to the United States again to become a Texas-based rice farmer, but also managed to attend a convention for the Socialist Party of America in Chicago and then the Congress of the Second International in Amsterdam in 1904. The rice venture failed, and Katayama continued to move between Japan and the United States. His commitment to fomenting socialism never faltered, culminating in his imprisonment for being a union organizer in Tokyo in 1911. Katayama moved to California again in 1914 after he was released from prison, never to return to Japan.

Reading in a newspaper that Katayama was visiting northern California, Ishigaki went to Sacramento hoping to invite the activist to give a lecture in Japantown. Finding him in the Japanese laborer's rest area, Ishigaki described Katayama as using an orange crate as a desk, which was surrounded by books, including the three volumes of Karl Marx's Capital.[17] Hearing that Ishigaki was a burgeoning artist, Katayama showed him a woodblock by Tobari Kogan that he carried with him. Although twenty years separated them in age, the pair formed an immediate bond. Katayama agreed to accompany Ishigaki to San Francisco, where he lectured about the Japanese Constitution and socialism. Katayama remained one of the most influential figures

---

17. Ishigaki Eitarô, *Chûô kôron*, 69.

in Ishigaki's political life and later followed him to New York in 1917. Their friendship and collaboration continued until Katayama's death in 1933.

While Katayama nurtured his political studies, Gertrude Boyle influenced Ishigaki's creative exploration. When Ishigaki met her, Boyle was a known in the San Francisco area as a portrait sculptor of California luminaries like John Muir and Luther Burbank. Sixteen years his senior, Boyle trained Ishigaki's artistic eye, encouraging him to meet other artists and see as many exhibitions as he could. Boyle arranged for Ishigaki to study privately with landscape painter Arthur William Best and later to attend classes at the California School of Arts, where other Japanese students had attended. According to Ishigaki, he lacked an "eye that could see art," until Boyle taught him how. Boyle's example also led him to see that the divide between artists and intellectuals was not as stark as Ishigaki had imagined.

Their relationship soon developed from a mentorship into a romantic affair. Ishigaki claimed later that their deception of Kanno was "wrong," but believed that Boyle would be his lifelong partner in activism, intellectual pursuits, and the arts.[18] Boyle was a well-known enough San Francisco figure that California newspapers widely reported the scandal when the affair came to light. Kanno threatened violence. Her family's opposition forced the couple to leave San Francisco. A friend recommended that they move to New York, where he assured them that they could live among likeminded artists and writers, who were less likely to interfere with their affairs.[19] After a month working in Los Angeles fruit orchards to earn money and a brief stop to bid farewell to his father in Bakersfield, Ishigaki and Boyle headed to New York in 1915. Boyle was thirty-seven years old and Ishigaki was twenty-one.[20]

---

18. Ishigaki Eitarô, "*Hôrô yonjûnen*," in *Amerika no naka no Nihon: Ishigaki Eitarô to senzen no tôbei gakatachi*, (Wakayama: The Museum of Modern Art, Wakayama, 1997), 121.
19. Ibid, 94.
20. Ishigaki Ayako, *Umi o watatta ai no gaka: Ishigaki Eitarô no shôgai* (Tokyo: Ochanomizu-shobo. 1988), 51-53.

The couple settled in Harlem, where Ishigaki tried to find work. He contacted the local Japanese community, which gave him leads. He tried to work in an umbrella factory, but the paint fumes and working conditions proved unbearable. Another friend introduced him to a Japanese curio shop, where he repaired broken toilette sets and carved monograms into ivory. Friends suggested that the couple go to Rye Beach and work at a concession stand for the summer, a popular job for local Japanese. Ishigaki was too shy to generate many sales, while Boyle shunned the summer crowd wearing all black and a shawl over her head. Walking home with her young, Japanese lover attracted unwanted attention in the community. Expecting to return to New York City with $500, they arrived with a mere $50.

Throughout his life, Ishigaki maintained close friendships with strong and influential women. Five years after Emma Goldman sent a letter to American newspapers protesting the execution of Kôtoku Shûsui in the Great Treason Incident, she helped Ishigaki and Boyle to settle in New York. Newspaper articles with headlines like "Again in Love with Japanese: Gertrude's Family Call Her Insane," attracted Goldman's attention. As an advocate of "free love," Goldman wrote to Boyle to lend her support to the sculptress and her lover.[21] Upon their arrival in New York, Goldman introduced them to local leftist circles connecting the couple to social leaders like female reproductive rights advocate, Margaret Sanger. Boyle became the arts editor for Sanger's *Birth Control Review*. Later, Ishigaki facilitated Sanger's extending her message to Japan, helping her publish an article for a leading progressive journal, *Kaizô*, to which he also sometimes contributed

---

21. "Again in Love with Japanese: Gertrude Boyle's Family Call Her Insane. Married Eight Years Ago to Kanno, She Now Prefers Ishigaki," *Boston Daily Globe,* March 28, 1915.

articles. *Kaizô's* editors invited Sanger to visit Japan in 1922.[22] Sanger, in turn, introduced Ishigaki to Agnes Smedley, a journalist and activist in support of the Indian independence movement and later China's liberation from Japan. During the second Sino-Japanese war, Ishigaki collaborated with Smedley to inform Americans about Japan's aggression in China and to raise funds for civilians.

Whereas Ishigaki's political collaboration with women remained central to his New York life, his romances with American women were more difficult to manage. After their move to New York, Ishigaki tried to take care of Boyle as she became increasingly socially disengaged and physically weakened. Boyle continued to sculpt, but despite her exhibitions at art shops near Washington Square, she was not able to sell her work as she had in San Francisco. To support them, Ishigaki took on illustration jobs under a pen name for Japanese newspapers in New York, like the *Nyû Yôku shinpo* and *Nichibei shûhô*. The couple moved to Greenwich Village, where they found an affordable space that had an appropriate studio for Boyle. At her urging, Ishigaki started to attend the Art Students League, where he became friends with John Sloan, Kuniyoshi, and others. Her career continued to flounder, however, compounding her depression as Ishigaki started to blossom with his new circle of friends. Oil paintings he made in 1917 of himself and Boyle—dark circles under Ishigaki's eyes and Boyle's sharp cheekbones—reveal the strain the couple was under.[23]

Ishigaki's life in New York continued along two intersecting paths—art and politics—as it had in California. Ishigaki and Boyle lived on 14th Street near Union Square, which was a hub for political activity. A

---

22. In the early 1920s, the Ishigakis befriended Ishimoto Shizue (later Kato Shizue) when she visited New York with her husband. Her husband, Baron Ishimoto Keikichi, was also interested in socialism. When Sanger visited Japan, Ishigaki asked Ishimoto Shizue to act as Sanger's guide. Later, Ishimoto Shizue became one of the leading figures advocating for female reproductive rights in Japan and became a politician during the postwar period. Sakamoto Hiroko, "The Cult of 'Love and Eugenics' in May Fourth Movement Discourse," *positions* (Fall 2004).
23. Robert Boyle, Gertrude's great nephew, questions whether the portrait is of Boyle, since the painting does not resemble her photographs.

leftist political party occupied the first floor of their building, Margaret Sanger's sister's human rights activities on the second, a single mother with two children were on the third, and Ishigaki and Boyle's studio was on the top floor. The room had tall ceilings and direct light, which both artists appreciated. Because Ishigaki was often in his studio, the working mother's children often came over to play. The studio became a gathering place for Japanese residents, activists, and artists.

The Art Students League nurtured Ishigaki's painting skills, while introducing him to like-minded artist-activists. Ishigaki found in his primary teacher, John Sloan, a synthesis between art and leftist politics that he could emulate. Known for his paintings of the working and immigrant classes, Sloan was a pioneer proletarian artist in the New York scene at the turn of the 20th century. Associated as a leader of the Ashcan School of art, Sloan integrated American realism with social concerns, illustrating the lives of the urban poor with dignity. (Sloan did not like the "Ashcan School" moniker, because he felt it lumped together a diverse group of artists.) In 1912, Sloan joined the leftist publication, *The Masses*, as an art editor and invited Ishigaki to contribute illustrations. Sloan continued to play an advisor role in its successor, *New Masses*, until he was replaced by Stuart Davis.[24] For Ishigaki, Sloan remained a life-long mentor, who embodied his goal of integrating art and socialism.

After arriving in New York, Ishigaki wrote poetry in addition to studying painting at the Art Students League. Inspired by the Russian Revolution in 1917, he participated in the publication of a small magazine, called *Kyôson* ("Coexistence") that featured Japanese writers,

---

24. Although his work is known for its ideology, Sloan's early work tended to the more decorative. John Sloan had been acquainted with Japanese artists from the late nineteenth century: he befriended Kubota Beisen (1852-1906), a newspaper illustrator for the *Kokumin Shinbun*, at the Chicago World's Columbian Exhibition in 1893. Scholars have observed that Sloan, too, had been caught up in the Japonisme fervor at the time. Gabriel P. Weisberg, "Japonisme: The Commercialization of an Opportunity." *Japonisme Comes to America: The Japanese Impact on Graphic Arts: 1876-1925* (New York: Harry N. Abrams, 1990), 91-92.

poets, and journalists. Ishigaki provided the illustrations and some poems. *Kyôson* included proletarian writer, Maedakô Hiroichirô, who helped to introduce the proletarian novel to Japan. Maedakô arrived in the United States in 1907, moving from Chicago to New York in 1915. Like Ishigaki, Maedakô was friends with Katayama Sen as well as Kôtoku Shûsui, whose execution deeply affected him. After he returned to Japan in 1920, Maedakô worked as a journalist covering United States-Japan relations, often writing in English. Unlike Maedakô and others who translated Russian reports and essays on communism for *Kyôson*, Ishigaki wrote existential poetry that was often dark in tone. In "Night Before Release" (*Shutsugoku no zenya*), Ishigaki compared death to liberation from a prison cell where "his tears freeze under the stars' shadows."[25] The poem was overwrought, but Ishigaki's anxiety and strain were keen, since he was responsible for supporting himself and Boyle.

Ishigaki's involvement in *Kyôson* had stemmed from his reunion with Katayama Sen, who in 1916 followed Ishigaki to New York, where he hoped to continue agitating for Japan's revolution by working within its immigrant communities. New York had become a hotbed of leftist activity: both Nikolai Bukharin and Leon Trotsky were in the city in early 1917 prior to returning to Russia to launch the October Revolution. At an infamous Brooklyn meeting, Katayama participated in a group that included other Russian exiles to discuss divisions within the left (radicals versus moderates) as well as the future of American socialism.[26] Katayama's activities were rooted in an international movement, but he remained focused on Japan's socialist future. Although he did not plan to return to Japan, he hoped to make the United States a "school of communism" for Japan. Graduates would return to Japan one day to "preach its gospel." Katayama formed a study group of New York-based Japanese intellectuals to translate and debate literature emerging from Russia. They translated treatises imported from London—Lenin's

25. Ishigaki Eitarô, "Shutsugoku no zenya," *Kyôson* (1917).
26. Jacob Zumoff, *The Communist International and US Communism, 1919-1929*, (Chicago, IL: Haymarket Books, 2015), 33.

writing was not yet published in the United States—and sent them to Japan, where there was limited access to Marxist writings emerging from the Russian Revolution. Ishigaki's 14th Street studio became the gathering place for the group, where they ended their evenings drinking, dancing, and eating Katayama's home-baked cakes.[27]

As a member of the Comintern, Katayama left New York for Mexico in 1921 after escaping arrest at a labor strike in New York. (The dancer, Itô Michio, who also lived on 14th Street, provided a safe haven, before Katayama fled to Atlantic City.) Soon after arriving in Mexico, Katayama moved to Moscow, maintaining the hope that a significant leftist party would form in Japan. Katayama continued to write letters and postcards from the Hermitage museum, and sent issues of the magazine *Pravda* to Ishigaki until his death in 1933. In addition to canned foods and medicine, Ishigaki sent Katayama Japanese magazines, newspapers, and periodicals.

Ishigaki maintained relations with the remaining New York study group members despite the dissolution of the Katayama reading group. Former sailor, cowboy, and socialist writer, Maniwa Suekichi, was a regular correspondent with Ishigaki. Maniwa had left the socialist study group for Vladivostok, Russia. He then returned to Japan and was arrested in the April 16 Incident of 1929, when the police rounded up and imprisoned hundreds of suspected communists. In a letter to Ishigaki from prison in Ichigaya, Maniwa sardonically wrote that he had arrived at his "villa." Letters from Maniwa continued to arrive from prison, though written on tiny scraps of paper.

All the members of the Japanese socialist study group eventually left New York, but Ishigaki remained—not to return to Japan until after the Second World War. Ishigaki was sympathetic to communism, but he did not feel compelled to become a member of the Comintern nor to return to Japan to participate in socialist movements. He never converted to Christianity as Katayama had, despite his years working in California's churches and reading Christian writers.

Ishigaki claimed that politics—whether it was conservative

27. Ishigaki Ayako, *Umi o watatta ai no gaka*, 70.

or progressive—was neither "pure nor clean" and he found this incompatible with his "single-minded" personality. Instead, he would commit his life to painting.[28] Furthermore, regular communications with friends in Japan reminded him how difficult state oppression of leftists was. His involvement in the New York art scene and romantic relationships tied Ishigaki to the United States. New York was Ishigaki's city—not Tokyo—which he had never visited much less had art world connections.

After Katayama's departure, Ishigaki refocused his attention on his artwork and career. Together with Kuniyoshi and Shimizu Toshi, Ishigaki established the Gachôkai, the Japanese Painting and Sculpture Society, of New York in 1922. According to his future wife, Ayako, one of the instigations to form the group was the rescindment of Shimizu's first place prize at a 1921 Chicago art exhibition, after the judges discovered that he was Japanese.[29] The episode, which received wide publicity and letters of protest from supporters like John Sloan, convinced Japanese artists in New York that they needed to join together as a united front. Alienation from American forums compelled the self-conscious formation of a nationally identified, insular group like the Gachôkai. For the first show, the group's pamphlet, bound with thread in a "Japanese style," declared that member artists should aim to "introduce Japanese art to the world."[30] There were no pretenses that they were Japanese exhibiting their "American art." Nor did they promote themselves as "Japanese-American" artists, an anachronistic category in 1922. Their identification as Japanese was resolute. Japanese artists in the United States had to be flexible: performing as American artists when allowed and asserting their Japaneseness when barred at the door.

To publicize the Gachôkai's first exhibition, the *Evening Telegram* published an extensive interview with Ishigaki as one of the participating artists. Ishigaki posed in kimono for the photograph,

---

28. Ishigaki Ayako, *Umi o watatta ai no gaka*, 84.
29. Ibid, 86.
30. Ibid.

an indication of how the group was branding the art exhibition as Japanese. When asked to compare Japan and the United States, a familiar interview topic for foreigners, Ishigaki deliberated on differences in its art worlds despite having little information outside of New York. Ishigaki had no direct experience with the Japanese *gadan* outside reading imported art journals or meeting members passing through the city, but this did not stop him from theorizing about its art world. Japan's art appreciation, according to Ishigaki, was more developed than in the United States, because American critics paid attention to only a small number of artists, whereas Japanese critics commented on a larger group that included international artists. He went on to say that American art critics had become "too biased by commercialism."[31] To gain recognition, artists and writers had to go abroad before they received attention in the United States (Of course, this was also true of Japanese western-style artists, who traveled to Paris for legitimacy.) Ishigaki had never been to Europe, which he believed would serve an artist's commercial success more than his creative gifts. Despite opining on both East and West, Ishigaki's stance in the interview firmly aligns himself with being Japanese. He never speaks from a American artist's vantage point despite years spent living and studying in the United States.

Ishigaki's paintings illustrated his political fervor, now that his socialist circle had withdrawn from New York. Nearly a decade before the Great Depression, the advent of social realism, and the arrival of the Mexican muralists to New York, Ishigaki's art reflected his political viewpoint and social concerns. In 1925, he submitted two paintings to the Ninth Annual Society of Independent Artists exhibition. Their positive reception established his place in New York's modern art scene and ensured him subsequent success. "Boxing Match" and "Whipping," are highly stylized, almost abstract in their approach.

---

31. "Young Japanese Artist Finds Strange Contrasts in American Men and Women: Eitaro Ishigaki Marvels That Women Are So Much More Cultured and Better Educated Than Opposite Sex Members." (Interview with Ishigaki Eitarô.) *Evening Telegram* New York. November 4, 1922.

Ishigaki's painting of two boxers, one black and the other white, is reminiscent of George Bellows' 1909 painting called "Both Members of This Club," which also depicted black and white figures in the ring. Bellows' painting, created when the legality of boxing was still in question, highlighted the brutality and masculinity of the fighters. A frequent audience member at boxing matches, Ishigaki's more stylized painting, in contrast, showed two figures abstracted to the point of being machine-like. Ishigaki depicted audience members looking like skeletons with red-rimmed eye sockets, chomping on cigars as they cheered the violence in the ring. The skulls suggest German Expressionists like Otto Dix more than Sloan and the Ashcan School. The conflict between black and white boxers reflected the racial tension in the United States at the time and a theme that Ishigaki regularly returned to. By 1925, Ku Klux Klan from Birmingham to Detroit, and Dallas to Denver, membership had reached its peak across the United States. As the Jazz Era blew its horns, a white supremacist, nativist reactionary movement blew back.

Although Ishigaki often depicted racial tension in his paintings, the conflict occurred between whites and blacks – not white versus Asian. Perhaps because he lived in New York, where there was a smaller Japanese population and less contention with whites than in California, Ishigaki never painted the anti-Japanese racism characteristic of the time. Following the outbreak of the Sino-Japanese War in 1937, he painted violence inflicted on Chinese civilians, but not domestic injustices targeting Asian immigrants. At times, he inserted his second wife, Ayako, as a subject of his paintings, but she is never portrayed as a victim or a revolutionary, mingling with other characters as an equal and without duress. Although he did not depict anti-immigrant violence in his paintings, Ishigaki regularly returned to the theme of violence being inflicted on African-Americans. In the 1930s, Ishigaki painted a dark and haunting image of a night lynching in the south. In another painting, "Bonus March," (1932), a protest by World War I veterans that ended in brutal suppression by federal troops, Ishigaki depicted a muscular African-American male figure holding up the body of an unconscious white man. The image is striking in terms of the United States racial landscape; both men are shirtless, touching skin to skin, with homoerotic overtones. An image of a black man rescuing and carrying a wounded white man, contradicted notions of African-Americans as both threatening and powerless. Two years later, Ishigaki painted "Rescue," which showed both white and black dockworkers carrying a wounded African-American to safety. Ishigaki depicted blacks and whites in solidarity, both victim and savior, protesting as a unified front against uniformed police.

The second painting Ishigaki submitted to the 1925 Society of Independent Artists exhibition was "Whipping," an allegorical illustration of conflict between workers and capitalist overlords. His sympathies with the left and the labor movement were made explicit. By 1925, paintings such as "Whipping" led some United States newspapers to label Ishigaki as a "Japanese communist artist."[32] Using a penname, Ishigaki described "Whipping" for a local Japanese-language newspaper as an illustration of Marx's class struggle.[33] The canvas' central figure is faceless and dark, riding a horse and brandishing a curling, snake-like whip to threaten and control the crowds below him. "Whipping" made a strong impression on art critics at the time and garnered Ishigaki significant media coverage with articles singling it out for praise.[34] Ishigaki's canvas told a story, but expressed it in a stylized, geometric form and in a dramatic palette that was modern. The *New York Times* art critic said that Ishigaki's submissions made the "most striking impression" in the exhibition and that Ishigaki had added "grace and strength" to his modernist rendering. Like Kuniyoshi's paintings, critics located Ishigaki's work in the American modern art scene. The painting, the critic said, "caught an 'American rhythm.'" The critic qualified his statement by saying it was too early to declare what the "American rhythm" might become, but he did not

32. "Makes Ethiopians of Adam and Eve." *New York Times*, March 5, 1925.
33. "Iro-toridori na bijutsu-ten: hôjin shuppinsha jûroku nin hatsuratsu na seiki tsuyoi shikisai no shigeki to kosei o daitan ni jiyû ni hôsha shite." Review of the 9th Independent Artists' Association Exhibition, *Japanese Times,* March 11, 1925.
34. "American Rhythm," *New York Times*, March 15, 1925.

shirk from suggesting a Japanese immigrant could represent American modern art.

In addition to his more allegorical and stylized works, Ishigaki's paintings captured New York's downtown city life, the favorite site of inspiration for local artists like Sloan, Reginald Marsh, Peggy Bacon, and others following the Ashcan School. Ishigaki explored 14th Street, where he often took walks near his studio, for ideas. Writing years later for a Japanese audience about his New York experiences, he described the neighborhood with a nostalgic fondness. Ishigaki guided his readers on a walking tour, describing each block from memory. Running from the Hudson to the East River, Ishigaki recounted seeing cargo ships with black smoke rising from their stacks. There was a Catholic Church, attended by Italian and Latin American immigrants. The street was lined with department stores, ten-cent shops, and movie theaters, which Ishigaki wrote was similar in feeling to Tokyo's Asakusa neighborhood – an area that Ishigaki had never visited, but he understood in the popular Japanese imagination. Young men lined up to enter strip tease joints, penny arcades, bars, and restaurants. At Union Square, laborers gathered daily to listen to and debate speeches by anarchists and International Workers of the World members. Ishigaki also observed what he called "country hicks" (*onoborisan*) and foreigners hanging about, while pickpocket artists and loan sharks trolled the street. He was at home in 14th Street's working-class atmosphere, saying that he liked the "feeling of comfort it gave (him)."[35] He made no mention of feelings of alienation or loneliness as a Japanese.

Ishigaki's 1925 painting "City" is the visual representation of his daily stroll. The painting's characters occupy the canvas as though they were actors on a stage. It is an egalitarian slice of the city's inhabitants:

---

35. Ishigaki Eitarô. *Ai nit suite kokuhaku – otoko to shite, onna to shite*. (Osaka: Heiwa Shobo, 1971), 25-130.

a beggar with hat in hand leaning on a crutch, a young girl selling newspapers, a mother with child in tow, a policeman talking to a young woman, a political activist yelling into a bullhorn, and two nuns casting stern glances at a short-haired flapper in a fur coat. The large scale of the painting (three by eight feet), renders the characters lifelike, as though the viewer was walking among them.[36] When the painting was exhibited at the Tenth Annual Society of Independent Artists exhibition in 1926, a critic for the New York Times commented on Ishigaki's keen ability to portray the variety of city life with his depictions of young women in torn stockings, nuns, and beggars.[37] Ishigaki's cast of characters was not random. They were loaded with social comment. Similar to German Expressionist themes that depicted the brutal effects of war, Ishigaki depicted a "beggar" on crutches, who was most likely a wounded World War I veteran. The Salvation Army volunteer ringing a bell appealing for donations, evokes the social upheaval of an era that left many in need while others celebrated the Roaring '20s with bootleg liquor.

Women on the move in New York City was a favorite subject of Ishigaki's 1920s canvases. In "City," nuns shoot chastising looks and a mother darts an envious glance at the young flapper at the center of the canvas. Not only men, but also women, were confounded by society's "new woman." In "City," the flapper's luxurious coat, green hat, and red lips demands the crowd's attention as she walks unaccompanied through the street. Conservative reactions to social change were a regular Ishigaki subject. He painted another canvas in 1925 that again showed two disapproving nuns glancing at two

---

36. Severed by Ishigaki in a fit of rage, the left panel featuring the nuns and the flapper is at the Wakayama Museum of Modern Art and the right panel that depicts the policeman and activist with bullhorn is in Kamakura's Museum of Modern Art.

37. "Shows Vitality of Modernism." *New York Times*. March 21, 1926. *Time Magazine* discussed another painting of Ishigaki's from the show, no longer extant, which seems to have been more critical of the city experience. The critic described the picture as a "phantom on the point of being crushed by a thousand elevated trains and run over by a horde of cockroach taxicabs." "Art: Independent Artists," *Time Magazine,* March 15, 1926.

young women, who sultrily look over their shoulder at the viewer. A large woman boards a train in one 1926 canvas and a group of flappers share a newspaper onboard another. (Interestingly, it is a male passenger who holds the hand of a child, while women wait to board the train.) Society might not yet understand how to conceive the new role of the working American woman, who had only had the right to vote since 1920, but Ishigaki celebrated her.

In 1927 Ishigaki was balancing a relationship between a new partner, named Heather, and Gertrude Boyle, who had moved to an adjoining apartment on the same floor of his building. Neither Ishigaki nor Ayako wrote about Heather in detail, so little is known about her—much less her last name—other than that she might have worked as a church secretary or nurse. Not long after, Ishigaki met Ayako Tanaka, who became his lifelong partner, collaborator, and ally. She had attended college in Tokyo, where she became interested in debates about social issues. Arriving in the United States in 1926 when she was twenty-three-years old, Ayako lived with relatives who were working as diplomats in Washington, D.C. She was employed at the Japanese embassy and attended classes at George Washington University, but she found the environment stifling and resolved to move to New York City on her own. Marxist economist Inomata Tsunao, whom Ayako had met when he was a professor at Waseda University, recommended that she introduce herself to Ishigaki and his New York circle of socialist friends. When she arrived in New York in 1927, Ayako contacted Ishigaki, who became a friend and mentor, and then romantic partner.

For Ayako, Ishigaki was unlike any Japanese man she had ever met. He did not care about social norms. Ten years his junior, Ayako had been raised in a middle-class home in Tokyo and found Ishigaki "bold" and "unpolished," but kind and attentive.[38] They joined protests against the execution of Nicolo Sacco and Bortolomeo Vanzetti, which erupted on New York's streets throughout 1927, and Ishigaki took her to art galleries and introduced her to his friends. She started to

38. Interview with Ishigaki Ayako. "Watashi to Ishigaki Eitarô." *NHK Nichiyô bijutsukan*. December 6, 1977.

appear in his canvases. His painting of out of work musicians ("Jobless Musician Band," 1928) riding the Staten Island ferry, included Ayako in a red dress, peeking out from the right side of the canvas. Walking her home (she lived uptown) and drying her feet following protest marches in the snow, led to romance.

Reactions to Ayako's appearance in Ishigaki's life were mixed. Katayama wrote from Moscow to say that he was concerned about their ten-year age difference, based on a photograph he received of the couple.[39] Heather was furious, and the couple was forced to temporarily move uptown to avoid her. In a fit of rage over Heather's resistance to the ending of their relationship, Ishigaki severed "City" in to two pieces, each now stored in separate Japanese museums.

Boyle gave her blessing, but she took Ishigaki's relationship with Ayako hard. She had continued to battle depression, which included time in a hospital. Ayako noted that she felt Boyle's presence in Ishigaki's studio, although they lived separately. Boyle and Ishigaki had continued to regularly share meals and he called Boyle to say "good night" before going to bed.[40] Once Ayako moved into Ishigaki's studio, Boyle continued to live next door until she returned to Kanno, who had moved from San Francisco to Brooklyn.[41] After divorcing Heather (some reports say they had married; others do not) and Boyle safely with Kanno, Ishigaki was free to marry Ayako, who supported his art as well as Ishigaki's activism until he died in 1958.

The 1929 stock market crash had immediate effects on artists' lives. Ishigaki had just sold one of his paintings prior to the crash, but the gallery canceled the sale days after because the buyer was bankrupt. Ishigaki lost his job working at the curio shop, which had supported him, Boyle, Heather, and Ayako. He could no longer sell illustrations to periodicals. Ayako started to work as a housecleaner, cashier, and

39. Ishigaki Ayako, *Umi o watatta ai no gaka: Ishigaki Eitarô no shôgai*. (Tokyo: Ochanomizu-shobo, 1988), 110.
40. Ibid, 100.
41. Kanno and Boyle moved to Japan to live until the outbreak of the Sino-Japanese War when they returned to San Francisco in 1937. Boyle died upon arrival and Kanno in 1938.

even posed for sketching classes held at the Metropolitan Museum of Art. The idea of working at the museum had occurred to her while she pounded the pavement attempting to sell Ishigaki's drawings. She returned home to fetch her red kimono and offered to pose in it. She was hired right away. (Though out of fashion in modernist circles, Metropolitan patrons still admired Japonesque.) Ayako and Ishigaki left the city for summer beach resorts, where she made waffles and he oversaw carnival games, an occupation of last resort that he had tried with Boyle.[42] The Proletarian Art Museum in Moscow purchased two of Ishigaki's paintings in 1932, providing the couple with some relief to purchase food. Jack Shirai, a member of New York's Japanese Laborers Club, brought them leftover food from the restaurant where he worked.[43]

As global crises began to unfold following the crash, many artists felt compelled to create works that a mass audience could both easily understand as well as inspire action. The 1929 stock market crash and the subsequent Depression, the rise of Hitler and the Nazi Party, Japan's aggression in East Asia, and the Spanish Civil War seemed to render modernist abstractions and subjective expression irrelevant in the face of international crisis. Marxist philosopher and literary critic György Lukács asserted that "art for art's sake" was over. He announced that the time and place for an artist's subjective solipsism had passed. Ordinary people could not understand the avant-garde, much less relate what they saw to their own experience.[44] Artists had a more important mission: to incite revolution. Although Ishigaki had long addressed social and political issues in his art, his representations became more straightforward representations of class conflict. He created allegorical depictions of the masses' struggle—free of abstraction.

Like Ishigaki, many of the artists who engaged in socially relevant

---

42. Interview with Ishigaki Ayako. "Watashi to Ishigaki Eitarô." *NHK Nichiyô bijutsukan*, December 6, 1977.
43. Shirai was active in the anti-war movement and other socialist activities, eventually joined the Lincoln Brigade, and died in Spain in 1937.
44. György Lukács, "Realism in the Balance," *Aesthetics and Politics* (London and New York: Verso, 1977), 28-59.

art in the United States were immigrants. The migration of newcomers in the early twentieth century challenged earlier notions of what the United States looked like. Japanese, Russians, Ukrainians, Italians, Chinese, Brazilians, Mexicans and others created artworks with an overtly political purpose. For many of them, experience on the lower rungs of the social ladder disposed them to empathize with the plight of the urban poor. Their collective goal was not only to document, but also to improve the human condition by depicting it in its starkest terms. Questioning whether they had been merely satisfying bourgeois desires for culture, politicized artists redefined their purpose in the 1930s. Some celebrated an indelible "American spirit," while others revealed the hypocrisies at the heart of capitalism that rendered such mythologies empty. As these artists responded to the Depression by mobilizing into art associations to tackle problems of inequity, they supported each other during the lean times, and created a unified voice of protest.

When "Los Tres Grandes"—the Mexican muralists, Diego Rivera, José Clemente Orozco, and David Alfaro Siqueiros—visited New York, they had a profound effect on the art world and Ishigaki in particular. Art, politics, and social causes invited common ground between Ishigaki and the muralists. They had a dramatic effect on his stylistic choices. In 1933 Ishigaki again adopted the theme of the overlord whipping the oppressed when he painted a Cuban plantation owner riding a horse and striking a slave with his whip. The 1933 painting was more representational, had a warmer color palette, and was realistically rendered. Unlike the dark and anonymous monster in the 1925 "Whipping," the plantation foreman wears a white uniform representative of a colonial power, while the brown-skinned slave wears only pants and a straw sun hat. The scene Ishigaki presented in 1925 was a universal nightmare; his subsequent works depicted specific scenes like a slave revolt in Cuba, lynchings in the southern United States, and protest marches in Washington.

International tension inspired Ishigaki and others to organize and lead leftist art groups. Responding to calls from Lukács and others, artists formed a "cultural front," using their art to exert political influence.[45] In the shadow of the Depression, proletarian writers and artists formed dozens of literary societies, theater troupes, and painters' associations in order to serve a socialist cause, advocate for artists' freedom of expression, and provide practical support for each other. Ishigaki was on the frontlines of this call to action and he was accompanied by the energetic and eager Ayako. Ishigaki had never the leftist activist scene, participating in the 1926 launch of the *New Masses*, the successor to *The Masses* that had merged the arts and socialism, but the Depression instilled him with new energy. The Ishigakis became friends with *The Masses* writer and editor, Michael Gold, who they regularly shared meals with to discuss how to integrate social revolution and art. Ishigaki became a contributing artist to the revived journal, which heralded a new era of socialist-minded artists in New York.

In 1929 Ishigaki became one of the founding members of the John Reed Club, an influential group that supported leftist artists and writers. They wrote letters of protest, organized art exhibitions, and advocated for the working poor.[46] Named after an American journalist, who wrote a firsthand account of the 1917 Bolshevik Revolution, the club served as a gathering place for artists and writers, who feared encroaching global fascism. In addition to explicit promises to defend the Soviet Union and to fight fascism, the group protested racial injustice in the United States. Noda Hideo also joined the club along with Ishigaki. Noda had been born in California, but had returned to Japan for his education, common for Japanese immigrants. Like Ishigaki, Noda also worked on social realist subject matter, including assisting Diego Rivera on his mural at Rockefeller Center. The club expanded Ishigaki's circle, introducing him to Rivera and Orozco. Feeling a kinship with their Mexican heritage, Ishigaki claimed his early experiences in Bakersfield working as a dishwasher in a Mexican

---

45. Refer to Michael Denning, The Cultural Front: The Laboring of American Culture in the Twentieth Century (London and New York: Verso, 1998).
46. The first of their exhibitions was held at the United Workers' Co-Operative Apartments in December of 1929.

restaurant led to instant feelings of camaraderie with the muralists.[47]

Although colleagues for more than a decade, Ishigaki's relationship with Kuniyoshi had become closer after they weathered failed marriages and the ups and downs of New York's art market. Since returning to New York from Japan in 1932, Kuniyoshi became more inclined to participate in political movements. In 1932, Kuniyoshi Yasuo, Herman Baron, Stuart Davis, and Adolf Dehn founded the ACA Gallery in New York. In 1936, the ACA Gallery hosted Ishigaki's first solo exhibition. Compared to the days of the Gachôkai, post-1929 crash artists in New York were more concerned about politics than ethnic or national identity. Painter and John Reed Club member, William Gropper, wrote the introduction to Ishigaki's ACA exhibition catalog and made no reference to his friend's Japanese heritage. Gropper highlighted Ishigaki's background as a student and laborer during his early years in California and claimed him as a member of the "American Scene." Gropper's omission of addressing Ishigaki's Japanese heritage signifies how the politically charged era inspired artists, curators, and critics to emphasize political viewpoints more than nationalist identities.

Nevertheless, artists descended from Japan continued to use their national identity depending on the art circles if it gained them an advantage. Despite a common political ideology that united artists in the 1930s, national identity continued to be a means for mutual support among Japanese artists. They participated in Japan-centered exhibitions, despite the internationalist efforts of other New York art groups. The local Japanese-language newspaper, *Nyû Yôku shinpô*, hosted thee exhibitions (1935, 1936, and 1938) for "Japanese Artists Living in New York" at the ACA Gallery and elsewhere that featured works by Ishigaki, Kuniyoshi, Shimizu Kiyoshi (Shimizu Toshi's brother), and Usui Bunpei, all veterans of the city's art scene. Inclusion in the exhibition was determined by one's nationality rather than political ideology. Sawada Miki, granddaughter of the founder of the

47. Ishigaki Eitarô. "40 Years' Wandering in America," *Chuo Koron* 67. June-September 1952, 7-10,12-14.

Mitsubishi zaibatsu and wife of General Counsel Sawada Renzo, was living in New York after studying art in Paris and submitted a painting for the exhibition. Visiting from San Francisco at Kuniyoshi's invitation, the show included Noda Hideo, Yamasaki "Jack" Chikamichi, and Suzuki Sakari—all students at the Art Students League. Although they banded together for "Japanese" artist exhibitions, traces of Japan as a subject or as stylistic device were largely absent from their work. For their 1938 exhibition at the Municipal Art Galleries, the *New York Times* art critic noted that the nine Japanese-born artists showed little to no Japanese aesthetic references in their paintings. Painter Nakamizo Fuji explained that he "painted New York scenes in the American manner, because Japanese pictures did not sell."[48] Although noting the absence of Japan in the paintings, critics did not condemn the artists for being "mimetic" of Western art traditions or abandoning their artistic heritage as they might have in previous years.

The 1935 "Japanese Artists Living in New York" exhibition also included sculptor Isamu Noguchi, born to Noguchi Yonejirô and American Leonie Gilmore in 1904. Boyle and Kanno Isen had been friends with Yonejirô when they lived in San Francisco, and Ishigaki later became friends with him as well, when he passed through New York. Noguchi Isamu had been traveling between New York, Japan, and Paris, where he had studied with Constantin Brâncuşi. As a half Japanese, half American, he occupied a rare, liminal space between the two nations. Upon Noguchi's return from Paris, Ishigaki and Ayako were his only expatriate Japanese artist friends in New York. Ayako believed the sculptor to be "lonely," despite his many romantic affairs, and he was a regular on Ishigaki's couch.[49] Ishigaki acted as an older brother and mentor, providing a sanctuary for Noguchi to vent his frustrations about the art world and share stories about his latest love conquests.

One of the ACA Gallery's important functions during the 1930s was to host meetings for the American Artists' Congress (AAC),

48. "Japanese Artists Have City Exhibit," *New York Times*, June 23, 1938.
49. Masayo Duus, *The Life of Isamu Noguchi: Journey without Borders.* (Princeton University Press, 2004), 152-153.

another effort at forming a popular front to protest fascism. In 1935 Ishigaki was instrumental in the founding of the AAC (his studio was used for its first organizational meeting), whose membership included Kuniyoshi, Alexander Calder, Stuart Davis, Ben Shahn, Isamu Noguchi, and 360 other participants.[50] Stating that they wanted to form new relationships, receive new audiences, seek out new exhibition sites, and oppose censorship, the Congress held twenty-two exhibitions in a range of cause-oriented shows, such as "War and Fascism" (1936), as well as mounting annual shows for its members. It was also responsible for bringing Picasso's painting, "Guernica," to New York exhibition in 1939. One exhibition at Rockefeller Center featured works that depicted labor strife, industrial accidents, the threat and horror of war, and Ishigaki's painting of racial violence.

Leftist ideology generated international solidarity among artists. Despite a few exhibitions featuring Japanese artists, ethnic differences mostly dissolved in favor of political allegiances during the Depression. Ishigaki's paintings were emblematic of an internationalist and humanist spirit. Social realism, which reached its peak during the Depression-era, had long been Ishigaki's oeuvre. As social realism began to dominate more canvases, some critics feared its homogeneity, owing to common stylistic devices and subject matter. They insisted on a distinction between art and propaganda, which they said social realism tended to veer toward. During the 1930s, the most damning art critique was that an artist created works of "propaganda" rather than art. Critics declared that Ishigaki, however, was successful at walking this tightrope. *New York Times* art critic Howard Devree wrote that to classify Ishigaki as a "socialist artist" was to do him a disservice, because he was no "mere cartoon propagandist."[51] His 1936 solo exhibition had twenty-six paintings on display including depictions of the unemployed, images

---

50. Communist party member, Henry Glintenkamp (1887-1946), who was known for his anti-war illustrations, followed Kuniyoshi as head of the Congress.
51. Howard Devree, "A Score of Art Shows: Sculpture, Oils, Watercolors, and Work in Black-and-White in Current Openings," *New York Times*, March 15, 1936.

of war, street scenes, and muscular arms pounding metal. Many of them were common tropes emblematic of the time. Yet Devree praised Ishigaki for conveying his political message while maintaining a "full sense of aesthetic design." In 1938, Edward Alden Jewell also singled out Ishigaki's submission, "Victims of War," as a "good example" of the marriage of art and propaganda.[52] Despite its omnipresence before World War II, with the advent of the Cold War, a-political abstract expressionism dominated the art world. Cultural front works from this era were largely dismissed and purposefully forgotten, with few exceptions. Ishigaki Eitarô was one of many 1930s leftist artists, whose work has been discounted as a phase in American art history, because its moment had passed.

In 1935, the Works Progress Administration (WPA)[53] hired Ishigaki to create a mural as part of its Federal Art Project. For a weekly salary of thirty-seven dollars, he was enlisted to paint the walls of the Harlem courthouse on 121st Street. Ishigaki separated his piece into two parts, each focusing on aspects of United States history: "The Independence of America" and "The Emancipation of the Slaves." Much like his painting "Bonus March," the mural's preparatory sketches reveal that it was an ode to masculinity: portraits of Presidents Washington and Lincoln hovered over muscular, shirtless workers, building and restoring the country. Praising the mural as "patriotic," the *New York Times* publicized the mural, reproducing the "Human Rights in the United States" section of his work.[54] Ishigaki was photographed for

---

52. Edward Alden Jewell, "Art Under a Democracy," *New York Times*, May 8, 1938.
53. In 2020 the Whitney Museum of American Art's exhibition "Vida Americana: Mexican Muralists Remake American Art, 1925-1945," featured paintings by Ishigaki. Shipu Wang also wrote about the influence of Mexican muralists on Ishigaki as well as other Japanese artists in the United States for the exhibition catalog. Shipu Wang, "Picturing Transracial Alliances: Mexican Muralists and Asian American Art*ists," Vida Americana: Mexican Muralists Remake American Art, 1925-1945*," (New Haven: Yale University Press, 2020), 214-219.
54. Patriotic Mural Painted by WPA Artist for Harlem Court, *New York Times*, February 17, 1937.

the article while he painted. There was no protest when the public witnessed that a Japanese artist painted a historical allegory of the United States in Harlem.

After working on the piece for almost three years, WPA administrators removed Ishigaki from the project only days before its conclusion. The stated reason for his removal was his Japanese citizenship. The WPA had been fielding complaints that its federal funding was not serving "Americans" and consequently removed many non-citizens from similar projects. Ishigaki's murals had also become controversial, because some viewers objected to how he depicted Presidents Washington and Lincoln. They believed his portrait of George Washington had a "cruel" expression. Ishigaki countered that the president was "serious-looking, not like politicians who wear sugar-coated smiles for babies and old ladies." Others claimed that Abraham Lincoln "look(ed) too dark," and described it as appearing, "Negroid."[55] Within twenty-four hours of the unveiling, visitors' protests forced committee members to remove the murals.

Since newspapers like the *New York Times* had already reproduced mural sections as he worked without a negative public reaction, Ishigaki was unprepared for such censure. Responding to the controversy in a 1938 interview with the *Daily Worker's* Louise Mitchell, Ishigaki interpreted the criticism as "slander against the WPA" by Roosevelt administration opponents.[56] When Harry Webber reported on the murals for the newspaper, *Afro-American*, the murals had already been removed. Members of the crowd that Webber interviewed claimed that "Lincoln seemed to have the heavy lips, dark skin and features

---

55. "Dark-Skinned Lincoln in WPA Mural Stirs Harlem," *Daily News*, April 1, 1938.
56. Louise Mitchell, "Eitaro Ishigaki, Well Known Anti-Fascist Japanese Artist, Answers Slurs Against Murals in Harlem Court." *Daily Worker*, April 5, 1938. Reproduced in Amerika no naka no nihon Ishigaki Eitarô senzen no tobei gakatachi. *Japan in America: Eitaro Ishigaki and Other Japanese Artists in the Pre-World War II United States* (Wakayama: The Museum of Modern Art, Wakayama, 1997), 117.

generally ascribed to colored persons."[57] Ishigaki defended his portrait of Lincoln to the *Daily Worker* saying that the darker palette used in the painting was meant to convey a "somber tone." Ishigaki went on to accuse those who criticized the mural by saying that Lincoln was painted to look like an African-American were "also attacking the Negro People."

Although he had focused his artist's lens on United States social and political issues, mounting war in East Asia forced Ishigaki to address crises affecting his homeland. Japan's aggression in China started in 1931, but formal war between China and Japan broke out following the Marco Polo Bridge Incident on July 7, 1937. Ishigaki and Ayako became outspoken anti-war activists. Together with Kuniyoshi, they attended a 1937 ball in New York with proceeds going to relief efforts in China.[58] To protest the war and to plea for solidarity between the two nations, New York-based Chinese and Japanese artists hosted joint art exhibitions, which were co-sponsored by the American Artists Congress and the Artists Union.[59] The war's effect on Chinese civilians became Ishigaki's recurring art theme during the late 1930s. For the American Artists Congress annual exhibition, "An Exhibition

---

57. Harry Webber, "Protests Oust Lincoln Mural." *Afro-America*, April 9, 1938.
58. Leonard Lyons, "The Post's New Yorker," *Washington Post* (October 18, 1937).
59. Cooperation among Japanese and Chinese artists was not limited to New York. Japanese and Chinese art associations in California had been joining group exhibitions since the mid-1930s. The Foundation of Western Art in Los Angeles held exhibitions between 1934 and 1937 called "Contemporary Oriental Artists" that included Terada Takeo, Ueyama Tokio, and Chinese painters Tyrus Wong and Wing Kwong Tse. Unlike the New York shows, the California shows were not explicitly political in their message: they were not dedicated to Chinese suffering in the face of Japanese military aggression. Not all Japanese artists in New York supported the exhibition. Critic Emily Genauer wrote that many Japanese artists had refused to include their paintings in the 1937 joint show with Chinese out of loyalty to Japan, but she did not name them. Tom Wolf, "The Tip of the Iceberg: Early Asian American Artists in New York," *Asian American Art: A History, 1850-1970*, Editors Gordon H. Chang, Mark Dean Johnson, Paul J. Karlstrom (Stanford: Stanford University Press, 2008), p. 94.

in Defense of World Democracy, dedicated to the Peoples of Spain and China," Ishigaki submitted a painting featuring a Chinese family running away from burning buildings.

Where critics had once commented on his international leftism, they started to write about Ishigaki as a Japanese, who openly expressed sympathy with the Chinese.[60] One *Daily Worker* critic, Ray King, praised Ishigaki for bringing an "Oriental sense of rhythm and color with a Western feeling for realism . . . that showed the shattered streets of Shanghai and the hills of Bilbao."[61] Gone were references to Ishigaki's "American rhythm," which they used to describe his work during the 1920s. In addition to praise, King also criticized Ishigaki's paintings, writing that though earnest, his figures would benefit from less "heroic posturing." By 1940, Ishigaki's painting style had become firmly identified with social realist symbols and figures. Stylistic techniques seen in "Whipping" and diversity represented in "City" were no longer as important as his desire to present humanity as capable of resistance.

Following the German invasion of Poland in 1939, some Japanese artists who were living in Europe started to arrive in New York on their way back to Japan. Both Ishigaki and Kuniyoshi regularly went to the docks to greet and help them while they were in New York. Influential painters like Miyamoto Saburô, Kawabata Minoru, Oka Shikanosuke, and thirty other Japanese artists stopped in New York on their way back.[62] Although Ishigaki had never visited Paris and Kuniyoshi had not traveled there for many years, their willingness to help indicates the strong bonds between Japanese artists living abroad. The community relied on one another in the twenties and thirties when there were financial difficulties, and they continued to do so during the war.

Ayako's career as a writer blossomed during the 1930s. At the recommendation of Pearl Buck, Ayako conducted a series of anti-war

---

60. "Japanese Artists Have City Exhibit," *New York Times*, June 23, 1938.
61. Ray King, "Japanese Painter Ishigaki Portrays Chinese Struggle," *The Daily Worker*, May 16, 1940.
62. Ishigaki Ayako, *Umi o wattata ai no gakka: Ishigaki Eitarô no shôgai* (Tokyo: Ochanomizu shobo, 1988), 173-174.

lectures throughout the United States. She gave talks on Japanese art and religion to promote a more positive image of Japan, while condemning the war in China.[63] She also wrote a commercially successful memoir under the penname, Haru Matsui, called *Restless Wave*, published in 1940, about her life as a young Japanese woman. She concluded the book before Japan's attack on Pearl Harbor, but the threat of conflict with Japan loomed in its final pages. Ayako ended her memoir with a description of her activities and experiences as a journalist in the Little Tokyo area of Los Angeles, where she was temporarily posted. Compared to the relative freedom that she and Ishigaki enjoyed in New York, Ayako remarked on the treatment of Japanese in California as an "inferior race," who were kept on a "lone island cut off from American society."

Ishigaki provided decorative illustrations of Japanese lanterns, waves, and kimonos for *Restless Wave's* title pages. Ayako claimed that he used woodblock artist Hokusai's Tokugawa-era print, The Great Wave Off Kanagawa, as a model for the cover of the book. Although the illustrations were dramatically different from his canvases, they were like many of the illustrations Ishigaki had created for Japanese-language newspapers and journals over the years. Ayako said that they provided the right "simple Japanese style" appropriate to the book, reinforcing Japan's image as decorative and unthreatening rather than as the military aggressor in China. The first book published in English by a Japanese woman, the book's strong sales helped the Ishigakis financially during the war.[64]

Ayako was traveling with a Chinese woman to Massachusetts to conduct a joint lecture when she heard about the Pearl Harbor attack on the radio.[65] The lecture continued as scheduled, but Ayako was not permitted to participate. Like Kuniyoshi and other Japanese in New York, the Ishigakis came under FBI surveillance. When agents appeared at their apartment to interrogate them, Ishigaki readily renounced

---

63. Ishigaki Ayako, *Umi o wattata ai no gakka*, 76-179.
64. Haru Matsui (Ishigaki Ayako), *Restless Wave: An Autobiography*, (New York: Modern Age Books, 1940), 230-231.
65. Ishigaki Ayako, *Ishigaki Ayako nikki* (Tokyo: Iwanami Shoten, 1996), 10.

the Japanese emperor as a god as required.[66] Over the years, Ishigaki had gathered many letters, postcards, and clippings from Katayama Sen and other friends active in socialist groups. Unwilling to turn the letters over to the FBI, who were collecting correspondence between Japanese, and not knowing where to hide the materials, Ishigaki burned them all in their fireplace.[67] Government agents offered to return the Ishigakis on one of the "exchange ships" between the two countries (their friend Itô Michio had returned on one of these ships), but neither wanted to return to "fascist" Japan.[68]

During the war, Ishigaki continued to paint and submit canvases for exhibitions. The war's toll on civilians became a recurrent theme. Although several of these works focused on Chinese civilians suffering at the hands of the Japanese, Ishigaki also painted scenes that portrayed a wide swath of humanity—featuring multiple races, ethnicities, genders, and ages— suffering from war's effects. In "Fear" (1941), fire consumes blond women and African American men, all tangled together trying to escape the inferno. War, for Ishigaki, was not a contest between nations, but a disaster inflicted upon humanity.

Kuniyoshi, who was making anti-war broadcasts to be played in Japan, invited Ayako to contribute as well. In 1942, she began doing broadcasts as well as translation work for the Office of War Information. In 1943, the studio where Ishigaki had worked until the Depression, rehired him to repair antiques. For artists living in New York, World War II brought very little change to their lives compared to their compatriots on the West Coast. The war had an emotional impact that was reflected in their work, but their productivity did not halt. Despite living under surveillance, they were able to go to jobs, attend exhibitions, and mostly live as they had before the war. Although relieved that they were allowed to move about the city freely, unlike incarcerated ethnic Japanese on the West Coast, the Ishigakis experienced the same emotional strain that Kuniyoshi did. According

66. Ishigaki Ayako, *Umi o watatta ai no gaka*, 180.
67. Ibid, 179-180.
68. Ishigaki Ayako, *Ishikai Ayako nikki ue*, 12.

to Ayako, she had never once seen Ishigaki sick, but during the war, the stress left him physically frail, and he was often bedridden. He began to speak more frequently of his hometown, Taiji in Wakayama, and his family. His sympathies had been with the Chinese for years, but he was concerned about the bombings of the Japanese countryside as the war continued.[69] In July of 1945, Ishigaki began to write a series of essays for a memoir:

> Since the beginning of World War II, I must have permission from the American Department of Justice to take walks around New York, because I am an alien from an enemy nation. Every Sunday, Ayako and I walk to Washington Square Park. New York's parks always have a playground for children. Mothers carry babies in carriages, while some small children waddle about, and others run. There are some children who play baseball, while little girls jump rope. All of the children are innocent and cute. Since Ayako and I do not have a child, we enjoy watching children play in the park.[70] America's children and Taiji's children all play in the same way. Whenever I watch children play, I always think of my younger days when I also played."[71]

Ishigaki devoted much of his memoir to his childhood, Taiji's boat builders, and his early years in Bakersfield with his father. He recounted so much detail, Ayako said, that the process exhausted him and he stopped after writing about his early adulthood, never completing nor publishing the work.[72]

According to Ayako, the Ishigakis' reaction to Japan's surrender on August 15 was mixed. Relieved that the war was over, they were also overcome by the momentousness of the defeat of their "homeland" (*sokoku*). In one painting that depicted the aftermath of the atomic

69. Ishigaki Ayako. *Umi o watatta ai no gaka,* 186-188.
70. Ayako suffered two miscarriages during the 1930s. Their first baby lived ten days before he died. She discusses the emotional heartbreak of the experience in some detail in *Restless Wave*, 217-224.
71. Ishigaki Ayako, *Umi o watatta ai no gaka,* 186-188.
72. It later became serialized in the journal *Chûô Kôron* in 1952.

bomb dropped on Hiroshima, Ishigaki rendered the loose skin dangling from victims' hands in much the same way as survivors would in their own illustrations of the bomb's aftermath. Once communication reopened, they immediately began inquiring into the fate of their family members. Ishigaki's younger brother had died of illness in February 1945. His sister-in-law and their three children lived with his parents in Nagano Prefecture, where they fled to escape the bombing. However, Ishigaki's sister-in-law was delivering X-ray equipment to Tokyo when the March air raids occurred, and her body was never found. The three orphaned children returned with their grandparents to Taiji, but Ishigaki's father died of a heart attack five days after the surrender, leaving his mother to raise the three grandchildren on her own. Ayako's family, who lived in the Waseda area of Tokyo, all survived. But they had read in a Japanese newspaper during the war that Ishigaki and his wife had been killed in California as enemy aliens and did not learn that they were alive until after the war.[73] Ishigaki and Ayako spent the first months after the surrender organizing care packages with clothes, bedding, and food to send to Japan.

By 1947, the American political landscape had changed. Having survived the war as "enemy aliens," the Ishigakis faced political persecution at the war's end. Friends working in the government warned Ishigaki and Ayako that conservative bureaucrats and politicians were targeting suspected leftists. Artists who had been members of the John Reed Club and who had participated in exhibitions like the Chinese Emergency Relief exhibition were labeled "Red." Formerly social realist artists stopped making works that might be considered leftist. Ishigaki felt constrained by the new political climate, because he knew he could no longer comfortably paint works critical of social injustice.[74] Ayako recalled that Ishigaki was overjoyed when the first African-American player, Jackie Robinson, joined his favorite baseball team, the Brooklyn Dodgers, but his spirits fell when concerts by Paul Robeson, a singer

73. Ishigaki Ayako, *Ishigaki Ayako nikki ue*, 189-191.
74. Interview with Ishigaki Ayako. "Watashi to Ishigaki Eitarô." *NHK Nichiyô bijutsukan*. December 6, 1977.

whose politics Ishigaki admired, were canceled. In addition to Isamu Noguchi and twenty-one others, Ishigaki participated in an exhibition held at the Riverside Museum in New York for "Japanese American Artists," the first time the group used this designation instead of "Japanese." Although he had distanced himself from the leftist artist groups he had associated with in the 1930s, Ishigaki participated with his old coterie of Japanese artists. Ishigaki had been painting at the Yaddo artists' colony in Sarasota Springs and contributed some of his new works to the show.[75] He included a painting critical of the KKK, which had begun to target leftists after the war.

As their friends had warned, in 1949 the FBI summoned Ishigaki and Ayako to question them about their involvement in socialist movements. For the next two years, agents tracked their activities, appeared at their home unannounced, and regularly brought them in for questioning. They were asked to identify names of suspect *nisei* (second-generation Japanese), but neither Ishigaki nor Ayako were acquaintances with any of the people in the FBI inquiries. They were asked about Agnes Smedley, whom they had not heard from since she left New York for England. The FBI also inquired about their involvement in the Friends of China Association[76], Smedley's East and West Association, and the John Reed Club. When agents asked how the couple felt about the Prime Minister of Japan, Yoshida Shigeru, they claimed not to have any opinion about him. Ishigaki continued to commute to work, although he was often intercepted on the way

---

75. The Yaddo colony had become a regular meeting place for many artists including the Ishigakis regularly spent time there in 1947 and 1948. FBI agents entered the Yaddo colony seeking out communist members.
76. Ishigaki's friend, Agnes Smedley, who had been sympathetic toward the Chinese Communist Party, was the first to be arrested and accused of espionage. Smedley had spent the years 1938 through 1941 as a war correspondent in China, visiting both the Chinese Communist Party and Guomindang forces in the war zone. Smedley also had romantic affairs with convicted Soviet spy Richard Sorge, who had operated in Japan. Ozaki Hotsumi, who was accused of being a member of the Sorge Spy Ring, translated her book, *Daughter of the Earth*, into Japanese. At the Yaddo colony, Smedley introduced the Ishigakis to journalist Edgar Snow, whose earlier sympathies for Mao Zedong made him an FBI target.

for more questioning. When they learned that agents had tracked articles Ishigaki had written during the 1920s appealing for Soviet Union famine relief, the couple became anxious about their future.

Ishigaki later discovered that they had become implicated with the Richard Sorge spy circle operating in Tokyo during the war, which explained the intensity of the government's surveillance. Agnes Smedley's association with the communist group, and love affair with Richard Sorge, might have aroused suspicions that the Ishigakis were also involved. The Japanese authorities, which had rooted out the communist spy circle during the war, now informed Occupation authorities about potential spies living in the United States. In 1951, Major General Charles A. Willoughby and one of the Japanese prosecutors and investigators of the Sorge group testified before the U.S. House of Representatives Committee on Un-American Activities on the spy ring's origins and connections to the United States. Los Angeles-based artist Miyagi Yôtoku's interviews conducted while in Sugamo prison were used as evidence. In one of the statements read aloud before the group, Miyagi identified a member of his Los Angeles-based Social Problems Study Group (*Shakai Mondai Kenkyûkai*) as being a "close friend and associate of Katayama Sen's." Because Miyagi was a painter, the investigators might have made a link with Ishigaki, who they knew to be connected with Katayama.[77]

With the rise of Senator Joseph McCarthy in 1950, Ishigaki concluded that he no longer had a place in New York or its art world. Old friends were distancing themselves from the couple, fearing that they, too, would be implicated and targeted by the FBI. Ishigaki also recognized how the art world was changing as abstraction, which Ishigaki never engaged in, replaced the 1930s social realism in critical favor. Unlike Kuniyoshi, who adapted his style to the postwar art world, Ishigaki felt alienated and detached from the New York art

---

77. "Hearings on American Aspects of the Richard Sorge Spy Case, Based on Testimony of Mitsuda Yoshikawa and Major General Charles A. Willoughby," Hearings Before the Committee of Un-American Activities, House of Representatives, 82nd Congress (August 9, 22, 23, of 1951) Harvard College Library, Gift of the Government of the United States.

community. He continued to do figurative works in the postwar era, but he depicted scenes of his daily life with Ayako rather than political protest.

Ishigaki and Ayako resolved to return to Japan. The FBI investigation blocked the couple's proposed departure, but after they hired a lawyer to represent them, they were permitted to leave based on their status as "illegal aliens." Forced to depart within three weeks, Ishigaki worked day and night packing his canvases and saying farewell to friends, leaving all other possessions behind. On the day of their departure, agents appeared once again for more questions about Katayama Sen, Taguchi Unzô, and other members of the New York-based Japan Socialist Club. Their experiences in New York left Ishigaki bitter. Yamaguchi "Shirley" Yoshiko, who was their longtime friend and Isamu Noguchi's wife, warned the couple: "When you get back to Japan it would be better if you didn't talk about what you really think for a while. Otherwise you'll get tripped up right away."[78] When he arrived in Yokohama in July of 1951, Ishigaki Eitarô had been away from Japan for forty-two years.[79]

---

78. Masayo Duus, *The Life of Isamu Noguchi: Journey without Borders*, (Princeton, NJ: Princeton University Press, 2004), 261.
79. The Ishigakis stayed with his aunt in San Francisco for a couple of days. Onboard ship, they befriended Tsunoda Ryûsaku (1877-1964), who was responsible for assembling the Japanese literature collection at Columbia University.

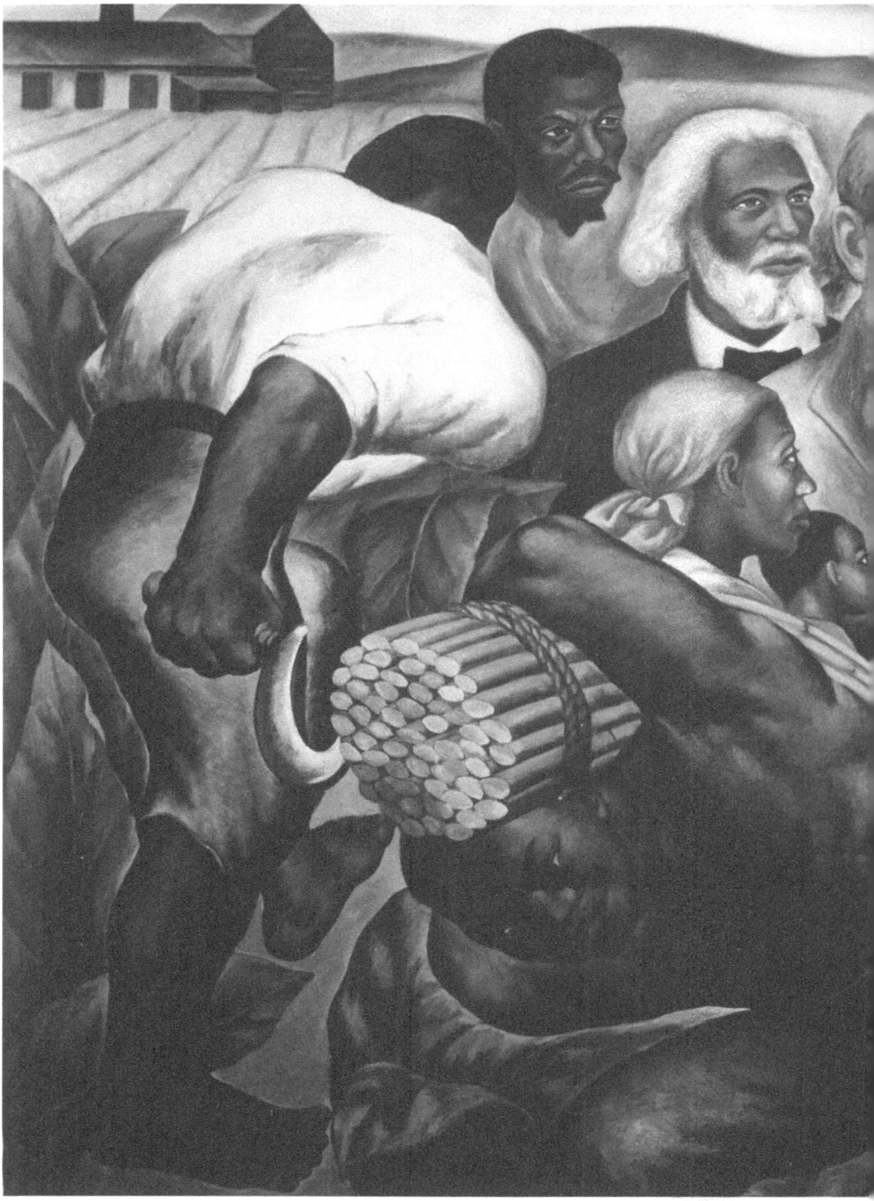

The completed *Emancipation of the Negro Slaves* panel of Ishigaki Eitaro's *The Civil War* mural at the Harlem Courthouse in New York, circa 1937. Federal Art Project, Photographic Division collection, circa 1920-1965. Archives of American Art, Smithsonian Institution.

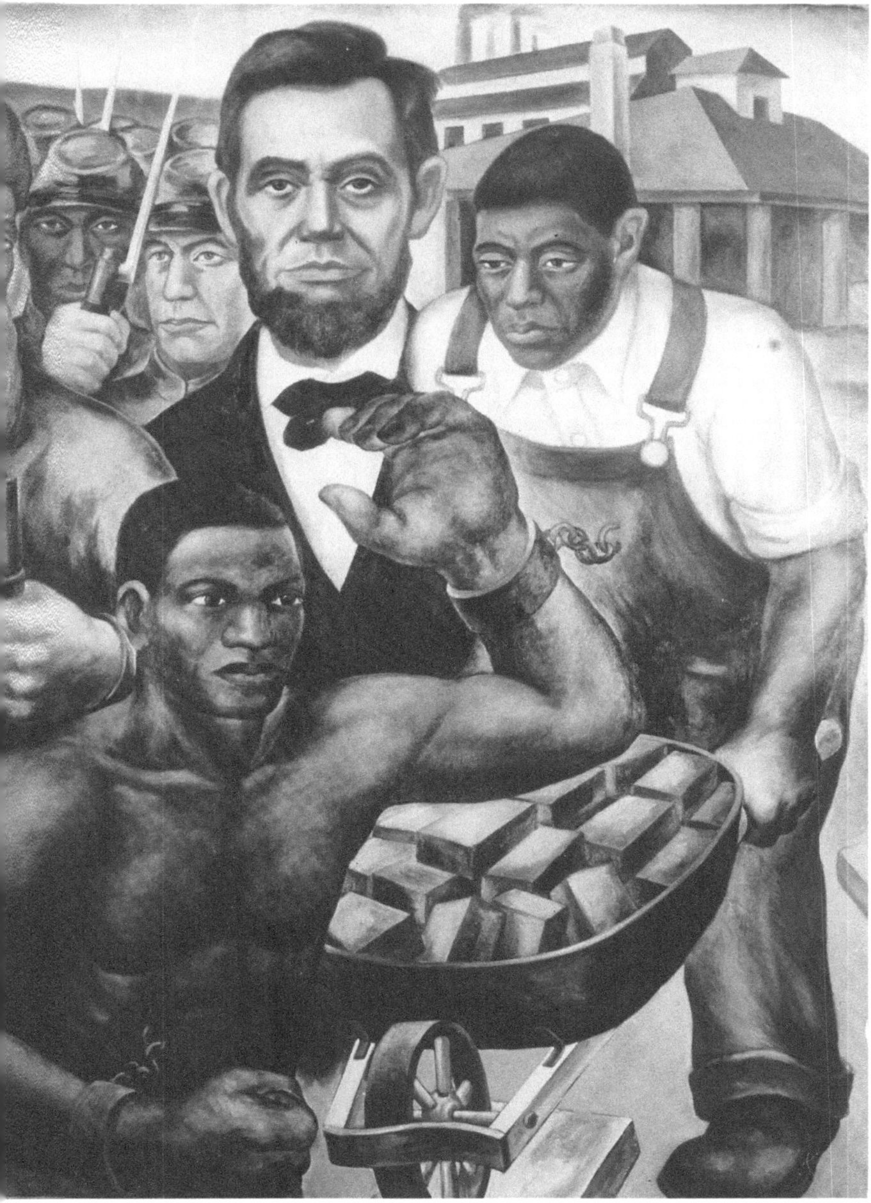

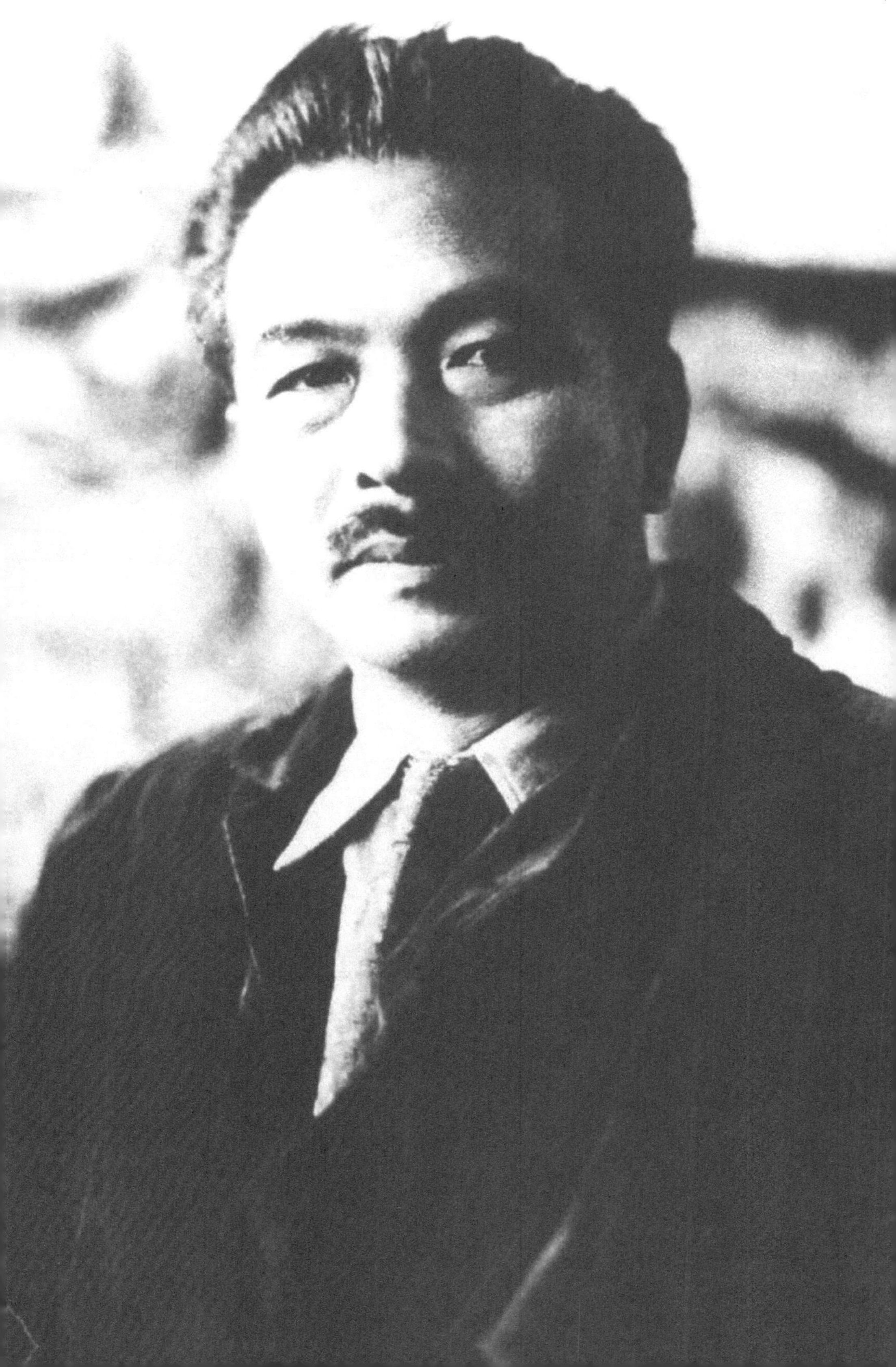

Chapter Three

Shimizu Toshi

Limits of Cosmopolitanism

Shimizu Toshi was born on New Year's Day in 1887, six years before Kuniyoshi Yasuo and Ishigaki Eitarô. Shimizu was their *senpai*—their elder—and New York's man about town in the teens and 1920s. Like Kuniyoshi and Ishigaki, Shimizu entered exhibitions, joined art societies, and studied at the Art Students League. But he also differed from Kuniyoshi and Ishigaki; Shimizu never intended to stay in New York and remained focused on courting the Parisian art world before returning to Japan. The United States was a mere stepping stone in Shimizu's art career. He made choices in his personal life that supported access to the Japanese art world (*gadan*) upon his return. He avoided relationships with American women, temporarily returning to Japan to marry. Despite enjoying success in the New York art world and establishing an international coterie of friends and colleagues, Shimizu never lost sight of his ultimate goal: to return to Japan and join its *gadan*.

The Shimizu family's social class might explain his desire to return to Japan, whereas other members of his New York-based Japanese

---

(Opposite): Shimizu Toshi in the 1930s. Photographer unknown.

cohort felt no immediate longing. Neither Kuniyoshi nor Ishigaki had families occupying a high social status. Shimizu was the eldest son of five siblings to a landed family with a long lineage located in Tochigi Prefecture. Educating five children taxed the family, but their home and farmland covered the fees. His father was known to enjoy art, and he regularly bought new musical instruments—an accordion and violin—as well as a camera, a gadget only a few could afford at the time. Shimizu often absconded with the heavy camera into their village—to his father's chagrin—but his main interest was painting and drawing. Family members recalled that Shimizu insisted on having reams of white paper and a brush at all times and asked visitors to pose for him. Friends and family said that he maintained a similar posture in his later art studios. He worked furiously, head down, and determined. Shimizu's obstinacy was revealed in other ways: he insisted upon dressing like a *samurai*, and if his mother did not create appropriate outfits for him, he refused to go to school.[1] As the eldest son, Shimizu took his position and his family's lauded history seriously. His father described him as someone who, "always wanted to walk first down any road." Scolding made young Shimizu erupt into a temper tantrum.[2] He was proud, headstrong, and creative.

Shimizu's early ambition was to follow in his uncle's footsteps and become an officer in the military, but he failed the exam in 1906. Shimizu was devastated. Depressed and fearing that he would become a financial burden to his family, Shimizu's next plan was to move to the United States to earn money. Although he left Tochigi hoping to return with riches, Shimizu arrived on American shores in 1907 with the seed of artistic possibility already planted. He later credited his artistic ambition to a visit from the Emperor Meiji to his Tochigi elementary school.[3] The school principal presented the emperor with

---

1. Quoted from "Aruite kita michi" in Sugimura Hiroya. "Toshi Shimizu Shôgai to gagyô." *Shimizu Toshi ten. Shimizu Toshi Retrospective Exhibition. November 1996-January 1997.* (Tochigi Prefectural Museum of Fine Arts 1997), 8-9.
2. Sugimura Hiroya, *Shimizu Toshi ten*, 8-9.
3. Ibid, 9.

Shimizu's portrait of an American general (sometimes reported as the German statesman, Otto von Bismarck, but Shimizu's diary states otherwise), that reportedly earned him praise. The incident instilled confidence in Shimizu, but he remained committed to his plan to join the military.[4] When he failed, he spent the year before his departure to the United States drawing portraits of Japanese casualties of the Russo-Japanese War. Shimizu's desire to be a part of the military was never completely forgotten, given his multiple canvases of uniformed soldiers in military formation throughout his career. Whereas hardship among the poor was a constant theme in Ishigaki's paintings, Shimizu returned to the military in his.

After two weeks at sea, Shimizu arrived in 1907 in Seattle's Japantown, where he saw some of his countrymen in laborer's clothes and others wearing white gloves and bowler hats.[5] Arriving only months before the Gentlemen's Agreement shut the door to Japanese immigrants, Shimizu worked at any job available after disembarking in Seattle. He washed dishes at a restaurant, worked as a house cleaner, and then toiled on a farm in Bellingham. Railroad and mining work in Butte, Montana paid well enough for Shimizu to put money aside. Along with another Japanese friend, Shimizu started a business venture installing irrigation systems on the Wapato reservation in 1908. In his memoirs, he observed that while Americans abused Native Americans, he enjoyed cordial relations with them, because Japanese immigrants shared the same "skin and hair color."[6] The project did not prove lucrative, however, because he underestimated how long it would take. Shimizu returned to Seattle after four years to start again with nothing.

Shimizu started art school five years after arriving in Washington. Despite years working at hard labor, he never lost sight of his interest in becoming an artist. A friend who had worked with Shimizu on the reservation had also traveled to the United States to study art, and each

---

4. Yaguchi Kunio, "Shimizu Toshi nenpu," *Shimizu Toshi gashû*. (Nichido shuppan, 1975), 126.
5. Sugimura Hiroya, *Shimizu Toshi ten*, 10.
6. Unno Hiroshi, "Shimizu Toshi: shoku modan sutairu saihô," *Aato* 92 (Autumn 1980).

supported the other to achieve this goal. Although he had intended to travel south to study art in San Francisco, Shimizu started formal art lessons in 1912 with the Dutch-Indonesian painter Fokko Tadama, who had migrated to Seattle in 1910. According to Shimizu, Tadama was born in Borneo, the son of a colonial administrator. He had studied art in Amsterdam and Paris and became a successful landscape painter, but sales had been slow, prompting his move to the United States.[7] Tadama's class attracted other Japanese students such as Tanaka Yasushi and Nomura Kenjirô, who both became well-known artists in the 1920s and 1930s. Shimizu committed to studying with Tadama for several years and spent the summer working at an Alaskan fish cannery to save money for tuition. Tadama's instruction was academic: he taught practical technical skills, valued portraiture above all else, and praised nineteenth-century romanticism. (Tadama considered Van Gogh "insane.")[8] Prior to the 1915 Panama Pacific Exposition in San Francisco, the West Coast had little exposure to modernism, so his more conservative teaching was popular in Seattle. Tadama's instruction earned Shimizu local success and a series of solo exhibitions. Whereas local critics panned Tanaka Yasushi's exhibition of nude paintings, which were eventually covered up, they singled Shimizu out as being the most skilled of Tadama's students. They praised his "Portrait of Mrs. C" (1915), a demure woman in formal dress.[9] Shimizu's portrait shows his instructor's Dutch influence, a style associated with careful attention to the play of shadows and light coming from a single source.

Developments in the rapidly changing modern art world seemed to pass Seattle by, prompting Shimizu to move to New York in 1917 after ten years of toil and some artistic success. Tanaka also left soon after

7. Asano Toru, "Shimizu Toshi." *Amerika ni mananda Nihon no gakatachi: Kuniyoshi, Shimizu, Ishigaki, Noda to Amerikan shiin kaiga Japanese Artists Who Studied in U.S.A. and the American Scene.* (Tokyo: National Museum of Modern Art, 1982), 181.
8. Yui Shôichi, "Shimizu to ano koro no nyû yôku jazu shiin." *Shimizu Toshi ten*, (Tokyo: Musashino Cultural Center, 1991), 19.
9. Iwasaki Yoshikazu, "Amerika ni okeru Shimizu Toshi." *Shimizu Toshi ten,* (Tokyo: Musashino Cultural Center, 1991), 16.

with his American wife to Paris, where his nudes could be displayed without causing a scandal. By the time of Shimizu's arrival, the Armory Show had already come and gone and New York's artists scrambled to paint their modern lives rather than idealized portraits like those he had made in Seattle.

On the day he arrived in New York, April 19, 1917, Shimizu headed for a Society of Independents show as well as to the Metropolitan Museum.[10] He did not care for the "imitations" of post-impressionism and Cubism that he saw at the Independents exhibition. Tadama's prejudices about modern art would take more than one day to fade. Like Kuniyoshi, his escape from Seattle's conservative art schools meant that Shimizu was soon impatient with New York's academic institutions. Unwittingly following Kuniyoshi's footsteps, he tried the National Academy of Design, but abandoned the school after one month for the Art Students League. In addition to two friends that he knew from his time in Seattle, Kuniyoshi and Ishigaki also became Shimizu's close friends and colleagues. After a decade in the United States, Shimizu effortlessly navigated New York's art circles.

Shimizu joined classes taught by George Bellows and Kenneth Hayes Miller's class, where he met Kuniyoshi, but changed his schedule to take John Sloan's night class so he could work at a store doing basket design during the day. Sloan became a friend and mentor throughout Shimizu's stay in New York. As a teacher, Sloan was known among League students to be too harsh for "thin-skinned weaklings."[11] They appreciated his critique, however, as much as they dreaded it. Shimizu was talented, welcomed instruction, and was impervious to critique, making him an ideal student for Sloan. In his diary, Shimizu highlighted Sloan's practical help, appreciating how hard Sloan worked

---

10. Sugimura, Hiroya. "Toshi Shimizu Shôgai to gagyô." *Shimizu Toshi ten. Shimizu Toshi Retrospective Exhibition. November 1996-January 1997.* (Tochigi: Tochigi Prefectural Museum of Fine Arts, 1997), 12.
11. From an anonymous poem written by one of Sloan's students at the Art Students League. *The Touchstone: And the American Art Student Magazine*, 5, (1919), 180.

to find buyers for his students' paintings.[12] Sloan encouraged Shimizu to go out on to New York's streets to find subjects to paint rather than be limited to the studio. Shimizu began painting what he saw outside and rarely entered a studio to do a portrait or a still-life ever again. He didn't join Ishigaki's socialist study groups nor did he join Kuniyoshi to visit Old Master exhibitions or summers in Maine. Shimizu took to New York's streets with his easel and brushes.

Sloan's political influence was also evident in Shimizu's 1919 canvas called "People Passing a Church," which had a parenthetical sub-title, "Poor People Ignored by the Rich." An older couple wearing coats lined with fur pass a beggar on the street in front of the church, hat in hand asking the couple for help. Although Shimizu's canvases continued to represent a diverse cast - black, white, young, old, workers, the leisure class, flappers, soldiers, and many others - "People Passing a Church" was the last canvas with such an explicit message.

Shimizu and Sloan's close relationship garnered attention: In 1919 a writer for an art student's magazine, *The Touchstone,* described Shimizu as his instructor's "experiment." The instruction was mutual. Shimizu for Sloan—in the writer's telling—was a unique opportunity to see the United States through the "Oriental mind." Shimizu represented a test case: his art showed the "quality of the Japanese point of view and technique," while providing insight about what a Japanese found important in Western art. The writer claimed that as a Japanese, Shimizu would be too "surprised by American civilization," to be able to render it as it was, and could only illustrate it through his "shocked sensibilities." Shimizu had not received formal art training in Japan except for elementary school, so his canvases could not translate an American setting through Japanese stylistic techniques—as Obata Chiura was able to do. Nevertheless, Sloan expected that Shimizu's canvases held a clue to the Japanese mind and its interpretation of the West. If only one could solve the puzzle.

Shimizu's painting style and subject matter shifted immediately and dramatically from his Tadama studio days. In his diary, Shimizu wrote

---

12. Sugimura Hiroya, *Shimizu Toshi ten*, 13.

that he wanted to "hold up a mirror" to people in their daily lives, rather than show their interior and emotional ones.[13] His canvases were like short stories: No longer posed behind neutral backdrops, Shimizu's subjects were shown in action on an urban stage. E.B. White wrote that New York gave the "gift of loneliness" in exchange for the anonymity it provided. Its "visual and linguistic strangeness," was shadowed by solitude. Shimizu used this anonymity to paint snapshots of New York. He painted people in Central Park, fish markets, ice cream parlors, movie theater box offices, pastry shops, and tennis courts – the settings as important as the actors. His portrait of New York is often sunny and optimistic, diverse and welcoming. Unlike Ishigaki's urban scenes, Shimizu does not include obvious victims of society's class system; there are no beggars or political activists in his paintings. Everyone—including Shimizu—seemed to be enjoying New York life.

Although his New York figures are simply outlined and somewhat naïve compared to the "Portrait of Mrs. C," his canvases still reflect Shimizu's diligence and careful rendering of detail. He recorded in his diary the multiple visits to locations to capture specific details. For "Child's Bakery," painted in 1924, he braved winter storms to record a bakery's window display. He paid careful attention to clothing—a flapper's coat, a soldier's uniform, or child's school outfit—to identify his character's social role. Shimizu never created caricatures, however. Rather, he pulled away the curtain for glimpses into urban and rural New York. Shimizu's paintings were like postcards of American life, as though he anticipated bringing images back to Tokyo's galleries to instruct Japanese how other people lived and to provide proof that he had lived among them.

Shimizu submitted paintings to the 1919 Society of Independent Artists, an un-juried art show with no prizes, which tried to provide greater access for a wider variety of artists than other exhibitions offered. Participating artists paid an entrance fee in order to show their work at the society's annual exhibitions, which had been founded

---

13. Iwasaki Yoshikazu, "Amerika ni okeru Shimizu Toshi." *Shimizu Toshi ten.* (Musashino Cultural Center, 1991), 16.

in 1916 by Marcel Duchamp, Joseph Stella, Man Ray, and others. For its first exhibition in 1917, Duchamp tested the limits of the Independent's professed creative freedom by submitting his ready-made piece, "Fountain." The committee rejected the urinal-as-art and Duchamp resigned. John Sloan assumed the group's leadership position and remained its head until his death in 1951. While Kuniyoshi left the Independents when Field established a competing salon, Salons of America, Shimizu continued to contribute paintings to both groups.

In autumn 1919, Shimizu returned to Japan for the first time in twelve years. His sojourn abroad was not complete, however, and he returned to New York the following year with his bride, Kozawa Sumiko. Prior to marrying, Shimizu had lived on the Upper West Side and had a studio downtown. Hoping to start a family, the couple moved to Manhattan's far northern corner on Sherman Avenue near Inwood Park, a somewhat more suburban part of the island at the time. One year after his wife's arrival, their son Ikuo was born. His journals indicate that Shimizu was an active, hands-on father and that he spent much of his time with his wife and son. They accompanied Shimizu as he explored New York's streets as well as to gallery exhibitions and parties and Chinatown restaurants. They also had cameos in many of his paintings. His brother, Kiyoshi, followed him to New York to become a painter and was a fixture at their Inwood apartment. His wife's cooking and warm welcome became a sought-out refuge for Japanese living in or passing through New York.

Upon his return from Japan with Sumiko, Shimizu submitted "Yokohama Nights" to the fifth annual Society of Independent Artists exhibition as well as the Art Institute of Chicago's 34th Annual Exhibition of American Paintings and Sculpture. "Yokohama Nights" won a top award in Chicago, but the exhibition directors reversed the group of artist judges' decision when they received complaints that Shimizu was not an American. A Japanese subject was acceptable, but not a Japanese artist. The loss of the $200 monetary award was significant for Shimizu, since he was perpetually saving funds to travel to Europe. Sloan, who was one of the judges, tried to argue in an article called "Chicago Overrules Jury and Bars Japan," that Shimizu deserved the award, because his entire art education had been in the United States, which made him an "American artist."[14] The case became well-publicized and hotly debated within art circles. Inadvertently, Shimizu's name became the talk of the town. His journal reveals that he did not particularly care about losing the award, since he was his own harshest critic, but he minded losing the prize money.[15] The incident confirmed to Japanese in the United States that despite their acceptance in some American art circles, they were forever foreign. In addition to establishing the Gachôkai, formed by Shimizu, Kuniyoshi, Ishigaki, and others, in New York, California-based artists like Watanabe Torajirô, Miyagi Yotoku, and Ueyama Tokio formed spin-off groups in Los Angeles. Feeling alienated from American art circles, Japanese artists embraced their minority status and used it as a marketing strategy.

Despite the loss of his Chicago award, Shimizu exhibited widely in 1922 and 1923. He worked at the Woodstock art colony, exhibited with the Gachôkai, the Society of Independent Artists, and Hamilton Easter Field's breakoff group, Salons of America. Art dealer and collector, Joseph Brummer, gave Shimizu a solo show at his gallery in 1923. At the start of World War I, Brummer had closed his Parisian gallery, which showed African and Pre-Columbian art as well as Japanese woodblocks. He continued to show these works at his new E. 57th Street gallery as well as American artists like Peggy Bacon and Alexander Brook. Shimizu's paintings, wrote Brummer in the show's catalog, possessed the same strong qualities of Parisian painters, casting a penetrating gaze on New York streets and its inhabitants. When he first saw Shimizu's vivid portrayals of New York life, Brummer claimed that he had imagined that the painter must be a native New Yorker to have such a keen understanding of its scene. When Brummer learned that the painter he admired was neither a New Yorker nor Parisian, but a Japanese, he related Shimizu's skill to his Japanese heritage. According to Brummer, since Shimizu was from the same world that

---

14. "Chicago Overrules Jury and Bars Japan," *American Art News*, November 12, 1921.
15. Sugimura Hiroya, *Shimizu Toshi ten*, 14.

had recorded the Floating World (*ukiyo-e*), he could handle New York with insight and dexterity. Shimizu was never a part of the "floating world," nor was he trained as an *ukiyo-e* artist, but Brummer assumed that he must have inherited his skills by simply being born a Japanese.

Shimizu's days were full. His canvases became snapshots of their daily lives: tennis playing, ice skating, going to the beach (Shimizu recorded his first swim in the ocean at Brighton Beach in his diary.)[16] Shimizu enjoyed dining out— cheap Chinese was a favorite—with other artists and attending balls and events. Although working full time and painting every day in his studio, Shimizu managed to regularly travel from his Inwood apartment to midtown art galleries or the Whitney Studio Club in Greenwich Village, often with his family in tow. At one opening, he introduced his young son, Ikuo, to Sloan and Walter Pach. He commented in his diary that the party (probably a Penguin Club gathering) was so packed with costume-clad viewers that the paintings themselves could not be seen. Kiyoshi was omnipresent at home, and if Sumiko and Ikuo were unavailable, a partner to visit galleries and artist studios. Kuniyoshi, Shimizu, and Kiyoshi often visited their painter friend Usui Bunpei's studio to drink and talk until late. Shimizu Toshi relished New York's Jazz Age.

One of Shimizu's close friends in both New York and later in Paris was Nakayama Iwata. After living in New York and Paris for a decade, Nakayama returned to Japan to become one of its most influential modernist photographers. Nakayama was the first Tokyo School of Fine Arts student to receive a photography degree, which earned him a government scholarship to study in the United States in 1919. With funds earned from summers at Rye Beach and work as a photography assistant, Nakayama bought a portrait studio on 5th Avenue. Nakayama managed the studio, which became a hub for Japanese artists living and visiting New York, until he left for Paris in 1927. Like Miyatake Tōyō in Los Angeles, Nakayama created fine art prints in addition to commercial studio portraits. He regularly contributed to international photography salons as well as to Alfred Stieglitz's

16. Sugimura Hiroya, *Shimizu Toshi ten*, 143.

Camera Work. Like Miyatake, dancers were one of Nakayama's favorite subjects. He photographed Itô Michio years before Miyatake met him, as well as a Balinese dancer, named Nyota Inokai, and the Futurist performer, Enrico Prampolini. Nakayama and his wife, Masako, also had a son the same age as Ikuo, forming a strong bond between the two families. While in Europe, the Shimizus and Nakayamas traveled together in Spain. Once they returned to Japan, however, their paths diverged: Nakayama moved to Kobe and became a pioneer avant-garde photographer, avoiding Japan's growing militarism, and engaging in an international coterie of artists and dancers. Shimizu, on the other hand, joined the art world establishment, and followed the Japanese imperial army into the field. Nakayama retained his cosmopolitan leanings, while Shimizu retreated into nationalism.

One of Shimizu's favorite New York haunts was Chinatown. Since the Chinese Exclusion Act of 1882, Chinese had congregated in ethnic enclaves, where they endured economic and political discrimination, occupying the bottom rung of American social and racial hierarchy. Faced with exclusion and violence, they formed insulated communities to avoid harm. Artists, however, seized upon Chinatown for inspiration, creating images that revealed their desires and fantasies more than the reality of the place.[17] These metropolitan Chinatowns became scenes of exoticism and degeneracy, cheap food and vice for Americans. Columnist Winifred Ward advised in a 1919 newspaper article that when seeing the "real" New York one should not go to Chinatown with a group of sightseers and police escorts; instead, in order to see Chinese as "normal human beings," one should go alone on Sundays when the shops were closed.

Chinatowns also became extensions of China's political chaos following the 1911 Revolution. Many Chinese immigrants blamed the Japanese for the upheaval, since Japan had joined other imperial powers seeking access to the Chinese market. In response to the

---

17. Please see Anthony W. Lee's *Picturing Chinatown: Art and Orientalism in San Francisco,* for an in-depth look at how artists represented these communities. (Ahmanson Murphy, Fine Arts Imprint, University of California Press, 2001).

Treaty of Versailles, which transferred German territories to the Japanese, thousands of New York Chinese signed a cable in protest and gathered to demonstrate on Mott Street. While Japan, which had sided with the Allies, eventually conceded its claim to the peninsula, it retained economic rights formerly held by the Germans. It was in this geopolitical context that Shimizu, whose uncle had been a soldier in the first Sino-Japanese War, painted New York's Chinatown in 1922.

Shimizu's painting of Chinatown showed one corner of a red-light district, where only a few years earlier, writer Nagai Kafû, had also headed when he was in the mood for "frightful vice or degradation," when he was in New York.[18] Nagai's short story, "Chronicle of Chinatown," is almost the literary version of Shimizu's painting. The canvas shows shadowy, dirty buildings with red details, a hue that Nagai likened to the color of a "woman's eyes swollen from crying." Shimizu's nighttime Chinatown was a shadowy place, like the one "without stars and without moon" as described by Nagai. (Perhaps because of the nighttime version's positive reception, Shimizu painted a daytime Chinatown after he returned to Japan.) Nagai and Shimizu's Chinatowns were home to poverty and immorality: beggars lay in the street or against narrow staircases flanked by naked gaslights and red doors, while partially dressed prostitutes hung out of windows with their lovers.

Shimizu later reminisced about his Chinatown memories when he spoke of the painting, His description echoes Nagai's short story. Shimizu reported that American streets smell of butter and Japanese streets smell of soy sauce, but Chinatown smells like pork. Even the "feet, breath, and hair" of Chinese women had the same smell, he said.[19] Nagai, too, wrote about the smell of pork combined with incense and opium.[20] Although he avoided Nagai's vicious descriptions of the Chinese "screeching like monkeys," Shimizu described what he called a "typical" Chinatown scene as a place of alcohol, women,

18. Nagai Kafû, "Chronicles of Chinatown," *American Stories*. Translated by Mitsuko Iriye (New York: Columbia University Press, 2000), 195.
19. "Modan sutairu saihô: Shimizu Toshi," *Aato* (Autumn 1980), 25.
20. Unno Hiroshi, *Aato* (Autumn 1980).

gamblers, immorality, corruption, and sickness, which made it "death's showroom" (*shi no tenrankaijô*). Ironically Shimizu's canvas shows more Western tourists and revelers than Chinese residents; a few men dressed in Chinese clothes look down from a balcony on the scene before them, but few other Chinese populate the scene.

Shimizu had visited Seattle's Chinatown as well, making him something of a connoisseur. When he was particularly exhausted from work, he stated that he was at risk of being tempted to enter Chinatown's "dark abyss of corruption and degradation." Even poetry and flowers, Shimizu said, were not as beautiful as the "mysteries, ugliness, and depravity" that he found behind Chinatown doors marked with "Open Day and Night" signs.[21] His 1922 painting of New York's Chinatown was a portrait of a world he knew, feared, and had once seduced him. By 1922 he had a wife and a son, and his baser needs became a nostalgic memory projected on a place and people. Shimizu concluded his comments on the painting, saying "I dream of Chinatown."

Shimizu spent his final year in New York preparing for his move to Paris, buying Sumiko and Ikuo new coats and himself new brushes. Like many Japanese artists in the United States, Shimizu wrote that he had "intended to study in France seventeen years earlier, but instead settled for New York."[22] Finally, he was reaching his lifelong goal. Ishigaki and a friend from his Seattle days accompanied the Shimizus to the harbor, where they joined Miyake Kokki, an established artist who had trained in the United States and Europe, onboard the ship. Miyake helped the Shimizu family get settled in Paris. Shimizu also reconnected with Tanaka Yasushi, who had been in Paris since they parted in Seattle. Shimizu was grateful for Tanaka's assistance getting settled, but he was disappointed to see that his friend was still creating "academic" work.[23] Tanaka was not the only target of Shimizu's criticism. He often complained in his diary that he was disappointed

21. Unno Hiroshi, *Aato*, (Autumn 1980).
22. Iwasaki Yoshikazu. "Amerika ni okeru Shimizu Toshi," *Shimizu Toshi ten* (Tokyo: Musashino Cultural Center, 1991), 15.
23. Sugimura Hiroya, *Shimizu Toshi ten*, 16.

with the Japanese artists he met. There were many of them, he wrote, but none were very serious. At the beginning of the month, when funds from Japan generally arrived, Shimizu observed them wandering Parisian streets and drinking in cafes. By the end of the month, Shimizu griped, they were knocking at his studio door, looking for a meal, and never leaving. Although he was sorely disappointed in them, Shimizu impressed his cohorts.[24] Miyake Kokki believed that Shimizu would become one of the most revered Japanese painters living in Paris, like Fujita Tsuguharu.[25]

For the next two years, Shimizu lived in Paris and traveled to the Netherlands, Italy, and Spain with friends like Miyake and Nakayama, who arrived from New York in 1926. He visited museums wherever he could, seeking out the old masters that he had only seen in reproductions. Having saved for years in New York for his European sojourn, Shimizu spent all he had going to museums and travel. Shimizu was prolific while in Europe and exhibited widely, but he did not stay long enough to become enveloped in the art world there. He painted as many scenes as he could, avoiding abstraction, cubism, or anything too expressionistic. Shimizu was wary of "modern art" and the "isms" in general. (Paradoxically, he wanted to be understood as a modern artist, so his diary reveals an ongoing conflict.) He painted many canvases of café and street scenes in Paris and Madrid, still paying close attention to fashion details, café signs, and newspaper headlines that underscored the European setting. In "Cafe with a Sailor" (1926), a sailor smokes a cigarette, while a young woman's languid gaze is engaged elsewhere. Shimizu painted himself sitting at a table with his family while he sketches. Only Ikuo looks out of the canvas at the viewer. Newspapers, signs, and cigarettes indicate that this scene was a typical day in Paris, where the Shimizu family felt perfectly at home.

After working, living and painting abroad for nearly two decades, Shimizu returned to Japan in late 1926. He had created a body of

---

24. Sugimura Hiroya, *Shimizu Toshi ten*, 16.
25. Yaguchi Kunio, "Tokushû Shimizu Toshi—Shimizu Toshi, sono hyôdenteki shiron," *Sansai*, 315 (March 1974), 36.

work while in Paris and Madrid to exhibit upon his return and had developed sufficient connections among *gadan* members sojourning in Europe that would ease his entrance. On his way back, as though to test the waters, he stopped in Shanghai, where one of his brothers had arranged a solo exhibition at the Japan Club. Japanese empire had expanded the *gadan* territory, so its international settlement in Shanghai eventually became a regular outpost for Shimizu's exhibitions, where he visited and showed his work.

Shimizu embraced his homeland with a renewed fervor. Shimizu Toshi's return in 1927 can be understood as an example of *nihon-gaeri*: a spiritual, cultural, and ideological return to Japan. He praised Japanese culture, his countryside roots, and nationalist ideology that permeated the early Showa era. He wrote that he identified with a "Japanese spirit" and regularly evoked his family's samurai lineage. Shimizu Toshi left New York's Greenwich Village and Paris' Le Chat Noir to rediscover the "earth from which he was born" in the Tochigi countryside. Soon, rural Tochigi prefecture's peasant families, rather than Parisian flappers and Spanish priests, became his painting subjects. He referred to his time abroad in New York and Paris as a "phase," that, now complete, could be remembered in nostalgic terms. Part of the Japanese mythos about living abroad was the fantasy of the "glorious homecoming" (*kokyô ni shiki o kazaru*) upon their return. After years spent in foreign lands, the idea was to return to one's family and hometown successful and refined. In this spirit, Shimizu held his first solo exhibition in his hometown in Tochigi prefecture.[26] Shimizu's return to Japan was as much a state of mind as it was a physical relocation and entrance into its art world.

Shimizu recognized that to succeed in the gadan was to participate in Tokyo's group shows like those organized by the Bunten and Nika-kai. For Nika-kai's 14th Annual exhibition, Shimizu contributed five of his Parisian paintings, which won awards. His medals garnered

26. Oka Yoshiaki, "Niki ni miru. Shimizu Toshi. Taiô soshite kikoku ato no kiseki," Okawa Museum. http://www.kiryu.co.jp/ohkawamuseum/kikakuten/44-shimizutoshi/nikki_oka.html

him attention in art journals and newspapers. In the following year, Shimizu exhibited works at the group exhibitions sponsored by the *Chûô* art journal and another at Fukuhara Shinzô's Shiseido Gallery in Ginza. Inspired by the Society of Independent Artists in New York, Shimizu became a founder in 1930 of a similar organization in Tokyo called the Independent Arts Association (*Dokuritsu-ten*). In 1931, the Dokuritsu-ten had its first exhibition, for which he also submitted works. Shimizu's diary entries reveal, however, that he was depressed and frustrated.[27] He became more fixated on death, particularly since his children were sick after their return to Tochigi. He was also dissatisfied with his critical success. Writing in his diary in 1930, he dismissed the Nika-kai's *Chogyû* prize as "pathetic."[28] He was also discouraged by the quality of art he saw represented in the *gadan*. Looking at the art magazine, *Atorie*, he complained that he would "welcome just one stroke of genius among all the mediocrity."[29] Though better received than Kuniyoshi proved to be, Shimizu expected greater financial and even greater critical acclaim in Japan.

At the time of Shimizu's return to Japan, artists recently back from France were influenced by the painterly quality and strong colors of the Fauves and Henri Matisse. Shimizu's canvases were colorful but not expressionistic. Art critics commended Shimizu's individual style, writing that his paintings were refreshing by employing vivid colors, making his canvases bright and lively.[30] They approved of how he painted his figures in a simple, "primitive" manner.[31] Others, like Suzuki Yasunori, observed that Shimizu was able to capture "Americanism." They commended Shimizu's ability to tell stories about people set in

---

27. Oka Yoshiaki.
28. Ibid.
29. Sugimura Hiroya, *Shimizu Toshi ten,* 20.
30. That same reviewer criticized Kuniyoshi's palette as being too brown and dull. Inoue Chôzaburô, "Minshû no ga—Shimizu Toshi," *Bijutsu Gurafu* 2 (August, 1983, Originally printed in 1970).
31. Yaguchi Kunio, "Tokushû Shimizu Toshi—Shimizu Toshi, sono hyôdenteki shiron," *Sansai* 315 (March 1974), 33.

a certain time and place.[32] They called him a "people's artist," because he presented characters that were spirited and strong, not merely worn down by circumstances or an emotional interiority.[33] Indeed, Shimizu showed people living; the people that inhabited his canvases were not passive, but were engaged in activity and their environments.

Shimizu continued to mark the location of his paintings after his return to Japan as he had in New York, Paris, and Madrid. When he painted a Japanese woman in kimono having her teeth attended to by a dentist, he included a Japanese *hinomaru* flag seen from the window in the opposite building. The idea for the 1928 dentist painting germinated during his time in the United States, Shimizu said, although it was completed after his return to Japan. Commenting on the image, Shimizu explained that a close friend who was a dentist in New York inspired the painting.[34] Shimizu found the dentist's probing a beautiful woman's mouth with his tools to be amusing, emblematic of the new "machine age." The author Tanizaki Junichirô also wrote of modern dentistry in his 1933 work, *In Praise of Shadows*. The Japanese, Tanizaki explained, "hate(d) to go to the dentist" because of the "scream of (the) drill" as well as the "excessive glitter of glass and metal (that was) equally intimidating."[35] Thinking of the many *geisha* then living in the Shinbashi area of Tokyo, Shimizu captured the scene of a dentist using his cold tools to beautify a woman in traditional Japanese garb as a visual interpretation of modern paradoxes.

Despite his efforts and positive reviews, Shimizu struggled to find buyers for his paintings. Friends recommended that he locate a patron for financial support in exchange for small portraits and landscapes.

---

32. Suzuki Yasunori writing in Dokuritsu Bijutsu, 1933. Reprinted in *Shimizu Toshi ten* (Musashino City: Musashino shimin bunka kaikan. 1991), 90-91.
33. Many related this quality to Kitagawa Tamiji's paintings as well. Inoue Chôzaburô, *Bijutsu Gurafu*.
34. Shimizu Toshi, "Watashi no sakuhin: kansô," *Shimizu Toshi ten* (Musashino City: Musashino Cultural Center, 1991), 93.
35. Tanizaki Junichirô, *In Praise of Shadows* (Leete's Island Books. 1977), 12.

Shimizu conceded and did the small pieces "only for food."[36] He traveled throughout Japan, meeting with various provincial leaders, doctors, and wealthy individuals who might have an interest in the arts. He expanded his solo exhibitions to include western Japan in Kobe and Osaka as well as to the Japanese empire in East Asia. Writing about his experiences in the United States and Europe for art journals became a way to promote the originality of his works. In an attempt to legitimate his influences, which were largely unknown in Japan, Shimizu wrote essays on American Scene painters like John Sloan.[37] The 1929 stock market crash had not spared Japan, however, and Shimizu had difficulty making ends meet with his paintings and he was forced to work as an illustrator as he had in New York.

When Shimizu returned from New York and Europe, he entered an intellectual landscape that was grappling with modernity. Between the two world wars, industrial and technological change in the form of electric power and machine production had swept Japan. Since the Meiji era, critics thought that the adoption of a new culture – clothes, food, media, aesthetics – was an extension of this modernization, thereby conflating industrialization and Western culture. Authentic Japan, they contended, was somewhere buried underneath. Japanese critics (and foreign fans of Japan like Fenollosa) denounced Japan's adoption of Western "masks and costumes"; only a few understood that removing masks would simply reveal an additional mask.[38] Shimizu's paintings from New York and Paris celebrated foreign space and time and maintained an objective space as observer. Sensitive to those voices calling for a restoration of an authentic Japan, from the 1930s, Shimizu pivoted away from foreign scenes to Japan's rural areas and extended empire.

On the other hand, Shimizu's friend, Nakayama celebrated the modern scene. He was at home in a chaotic urban landscape, where

---

36. Oka Yoshiaki. Okawa Museum.
37. Shimizu Toshi "Beikoku etching kai keni. John Sloan," *Chûô Bijutsu* Vol. 153 (August 1928).
38. See Harry Harootunian's *Overcome by Modernity: History, Culture, and Community in Interwar Japan*. (Princeton: Princeton University Press, 2000).

change seemed to occur overnight. The city was home to the machine, factory, cabaret, department store. Nakayama made dream-like (or nightmarish depending on the viewer's point of view) scenes, using montages of mannequins, neon signs, matchbooks, and cocktail glasses. His cinematic images captured the pace, seediness, and shadows of the Japanese metropolis, while showing modern life as dystopian as well as seductive. Nakayama's cityscapes were dens of corruption, where one's Japanese identity could be subsumed under modern life.

Shimizu renounced urban life as his primary artistic theme, choosing instead the countryside. While Nakayama reveled in the metropolis, Shimizu answered the call for the Japanese to "overcome" modernity's siren call by featuring farmers harvesting hemp (1929) instead of Parisians waiting for the subway (1925).[39] Writers, intellectuals, and artists, who feared that past traditions were being lost in the tidal wave of the present, were nostalgic for a place and time that they imagined still existed unchanged in the countryside. This nostalgia led to interest in folk art.

Japan was not alone in its attempt to overthrow modernity in a cultural war. Japan's interest in folk art and folk ways was part of a global reaction to modern life. Mourning an idealized past, when culture seemed rooted to a particular place, unscathed by the passage of time, became an integral fixture in discourses about modernity.[40] Hitler-approved German painters celebrated the *volk*, while American Regionalist painters sought out mid-western haystacks and ruddy, Euro-American farmers as subjects for their chauvinist and nativist points of view. Particularly in fascist regimes, art held the potential for perpetrating and constructing state-sanctioned identity. By the 1930s, the fascist ideology of an agrarian mystique had become entrenched in Japanese thought. Japanese painters like Shimizu found the oasis of purity, where time stood still, in *inaka*—Japan's countryside. Many

39. Harry Harootunian *Overcome by Modernity: History, Culture, and Community in Interwar Japan.*
40. Andreas Huyssen, "Present Pasts: Media, Politics, Amnesia," in *Present Pasts: Urban Palimpsests and the Politics of Memory* (Stanford: Stanford University Press, 2003), 24.

intellectuals equated modern society with the West: Nakayama's mannequins, cabaret signs, and bar accessories were Western imports and not the "real" Japan. In the countryside, however, farmers maintained age-old customs to ensure the nation's harvest. Their simple clothes, hearty lifestyle, and superstitious rituals and folklore remained uncorrupted by the West. Authentic Japan could still be found in rural Japan, among the folk.

By painting glorified scenes of rural life and commenting on those works in terms of a nostalgic past, Shimizu Toshi became complicit with this ideology. After commuting between Tokyo and Tochigi after his return in 1926, Shimizu began to spend more time in his hometown in the early 1930s. "I am a country person again," he announced in the 1933 Independent Arts Association journal. Given his family's holdings and status in the Utsunomiya area of Tochigi, Shimizu might have felt less alienated and more entitled to his place than in Tokyo. Critic Suzuki Yasunori commented in 1933 that perhaps after seeing the great cities of New York and Paris, Tokyo tired Shimizu out, and he sought rest in the countryside.[41] Shimizu's daughter, Tomiko, speculated that since her father's adult life was spent in foreign countries and cities, he embraced his rural origins more than most.[42] No longer an outsider, a dishwasher, or an artist whose

41. Suzuki Yasunori, "Shimizu kun no geijutsu," *Shimizu Toshi ten* (Musashino City: Musashino shimin bunka kaikan. 1991), 91.
42. Nakano Tomiko, "Chichi no omoide," *Shimizu Toshi ten* (Musashino City: Musashino Cultural Center, 1991), 89.

prize was rescinded, Shimizu regained his social status in Tochigi.[43]

Writing about his painting, "At Rest on the Land," (*Chi ni ikou*, 1930), Shimizu professed that his "appreciation for the earth" was hereditary as a farmer's son. When he thought of the land's "blessings," Shimizu wrote, he became inspired to paint farmers and the terrain where they lived. Although Shimizu wanted the work to depict something "quiet at its center," he also wanted the image to express strength.[44] In the painting, a father and mother relax after toiling in the fields, while their son stands with a teakettle ready to serve. The father prepares a pipe as his wife extends a helping hand. In Shimizu's rendering, patriarchal hierarchy maintained the family unit and, thus, preserving social harmony. In the distance, the hills are cleared and ready to be planted, while a large farmhouse can also be seen. The painting was more inspired by his grandparents than the parents who raised him. Shimizu described his mother as *haikara*, or stylish in a Western manner, but his grandmother was a large-built farmwoman and the inspiration

---

43. Another painter who had been active in New York also rejected Tokyo upon his return to Japan. In 1924, Kodato Gadô (1880-1954) returned after living in New York City for many years. Kodato had also exhibited with Shimizu, Ishigaki Eitarô and Kuniyoshi Yasuo in the *Gachôkai's* exhibitions. As art historian Tom Wolf has indicated, Gadô created some of the more memorable modernist paintings of New York in the 1920s. Wolf compared his painting "Subway" (1923) to urban landscape works by Max Weber done in the previous decade. In "Subway," people swarm like bees as they board and disembark the subway. When Gadô returned to his hometown, Utsunomiya in Tochigi Prefecture, in the year after the Great Kantô Earthquake, he imported materials from the United States to build a fabricated home. Kodato's reason for importing the home to the area remains unclear, but there is speculation that he feared a scarcity of building materials following the Kantô earthquake the previous year. There are only a few of Gadô paintings still extant. Retreating from crowds, subways, concrete and steel, Gadô returned to the rice fields and wooded hills of Tochigi— to live in an American house.
44. Shimizu Toshi, *Shimizu Toshi ten* (Musashino City: Musashino shimin bunka kaikan, 1991), 93.

for the canvas.[45] Shimizu reminisced about how his grandmother took him to the fields with her, cradling Shimizu during rest periods. He said that the smell of earth, mowed bean sprouts, and milk invoked this past for Shimizu, when his personal mythology of being born and raised from the soil became mixed with primal memories.

The land in Shimizu's rural landscapes promised bounty and serenity rather than the uncertainty of annual crop yields. He left no evidence of Depression-era rural hardship–or the region's history of famine–in this oasis of tradition. Others acknowledged that Japan's *inaka* had not escaped modernity's grasp: writers like Tanizaki Junichirô wrote that "all hope was lost" in the countryside's battle against modern life. Writing in 1933, Tanizaki claimed that the countryside was becoming more and more like the city with bright lights lining the streets. For most city inhabitants, however, Shimizu's paintings depicted a *furusato* (hometown) that they left behind and were nostalgic for. Some urbanites might have believed his paintings to be as distant and foreign as his renderings of American suburbs or Parisian cafés.

Money became scarcer and life more difficult for the Shimizu family during the Depression. Writing in May of 1930, Shimizu expressed fatigue for constant talk about economic hardship. "Today is the fourth day of continuing discomfort," he wrote in August of 1930. "I cannot continue to produce works easily in a day . . . I well know that all the money coming in is to ward off our hunger. I must muddle through and endure the unpleasantness until the end of this month." Commissioned work sustained his family, but Shimizu did it begrudgingly.

Shimizu found financial relief from the Japanese Imperial Army, which became his most reliable client until his death in 1945. The Japanese military had sent artists to sketch battlefields during the first Sino-Japanese and Russo-Japanese Wars, but the scale of its second war with China included more than 400 artists creating "war paintings" (*sensôga*).[46] The outbreak of total war in 1937 led to an even greater

45. Shimizu, Toshi, "Watashi no sakuhin—kansô," *Shimizu Toshi ten* (Musashino City: Musashino Cultural Center, 1991), p. 93-94.
46. Bert Winther-Tamaki, "Embodiment/Disembodiment: Japanese Painting During the Fifteen-Year War," *Monumenta Nipponica,* 52, no. 2 (Summer 1997), 146.

expansion of artist recruits. Dispatched to China in 1931 following the Manchurian Incident, by 1937, Shimizu was a veteran artist in the war effort. When Kuniyoshi visited Japan, Shimizu was again in China, which might might explain why they did not meet when Kuniyoshi was in Tokyo.

Artists participating in Japan's war effort had full schedules.[47] The military repeatedly dispatched Shimizu to China throughout the 1930s. Assigned to Shanghai in January 1932, Shimizu witnessed one of the first direct military engagements between China and Japan following the Manchukuo Incident. He then spent four months touring nearby battle sites. He returned to Japan to attend "Holy War" art exhibitions held at Tokyo's Nihonbashi Takashimaya Department Store followed by one at Osaka's Sumitomo Club. While his brother, Kiyoshi, submitted paintings to a New York exhibition protesting the Sino-Japanese war, Shimizu returned to China to cover the battle in Wuhan and the invasion of Hankou. Accompanied by twenty other artists, one of Shimizu's commissions was to visit a military hospital in the outskirts of Nanking to do portraits of decorated soldiers there. Commuting between battlefields and art gallery openings, Shimizu enjoyed as much artistic exposure as at any point in his career. Furthermore, his financial security was assured. By the time of Pearl Harbor in 1941, Shimizu Toshi had been working as an illustrator for the war effort in China for ten years.

Shimizu's military scenes show no evidence of violence or bloodshed. Soldiers prepare for some future skirmish, as in "Military Encampment (1932)," looking at maps and planning strategy, but do not engage in them. Among his early works, Shimizu's only painting illustrating the costs of war was of an ambulance with nurses and doctors attending to wounded Chinese civilians. In Shimizu's version of the 1937 battle of Nanjing, what is now known as one of World War II's most horrific civilian massacres, Japanese soldiers are depicted on a bridge rebuilding the conquered city's infrastructure. Painters could use greater "artistic license" than photographers, who would be

---

47. Bert Winther-Tamaki, Embodiment/Disembodiment," 145.

challenged to avoid showing civilian casualties lining Nanjing's streets. Two years after the invasion of Nanjing, one of Shimizu's paintings, "Roses and Lushan" 1939, featured a bouquet of roses in the foreground, while a fighter plane takes off from verdant mountains. It is a strange matching of the beautiful and mundane with a war scene, but the canvas is free of irony.

Most of Shimizu's illustrations seemed to be a travel log rather than a military assignment. In his versions of wartime Asia, civilian life continued as normal. While in Shanghai in 1932, Shimizu painted a group of Japanese nursery school children accompanied by their teachers wearing kimono. The group waits at a street corner, while members of the Japanese military protect them as they cross. The scene is placid and mundane in its everydayness. As a promoter of Japan's so-called Greater East Asian Co-Prosperity Sphere, Shimizu painted the continent's countryside as though he were on a grand tour of the military's recent acquisitions. While traveling with the military, Shimizu substituted the Japanese farmer for Chinese, Mongolian, and South Pacific islander inhabitants in native garb—making baskets, sitting in pavilions, preparing meals. He depicted the Japanese empire's newest members as exotic, but they were also extensions of his idealized versions of rural life in the Tochigi countryside. Men chopping trees, while women tended to children were themes in his *inaka* paintings as well. These sketches of half-naked islanders confirmed to viewers that the Co-Prosperity Sphere was not a war of conquest, but a "civilizing mission" that united Asians.

Some of his canvases became more expressive. During 1935 and 1936 while in north China, Shimizu did a series of paintings of a nomadic Mongolian family. He painted ochre faces, outlined in thick black. Over time, his brushstrokes became broader and coarser; the cheerful blues, reds and pinks of his New York and Parisian paintings were absent. Where the Tochigi landscape was green, the northern Chinese plains were harsh, dry, and brown. The barren landscape seemed to inspire Shimizu to paint in a more expressive manner, concentrating on texture and color. Shimizu's works became more abstract as the war went on. His backgrounds at times suggested Indonesian *batik* or bark cloth, which he might have seen during his trips to Southeast Asia. For over twenty years in the United States and Europe, Shimizu had made figurative paintings with simple lines and bright colors, paying attention to architectural details and fashion. During the late 1930s, Shimizu became more interested in abstract, geometric forms and the mere suggestion of figures.

Beginning in 1942, however, Shimizu radically transformed his approach to his military artist assignments. He began to paint in an almost photorealist style never seen before in his work, though early training with Tadama in Seattle must have prepared him for it. Roses, school children, and native basket weavers were gone: He created precise paintings of robust and muscular Japanese soldiers building a bridge in Malaysia, protecting an oil field, as well as advancing over a hill. Most likely, military officers insisted upon this "documentary" quality that showed soldiers on the battlefield. Paintings were more easily designed to show a victorious war instead of starving and overwhelmed forces isolated on islands.[48] Paintings of Japanese soldiers as well-supplied, robust, and capable figures boosted morale for Tokyo audiences.

Although he wrote in his diary about seeing a plane explode in one campaign in the south of China, Shimizu said little about the event and made almost no mention of battle scenes he may have witnessed. Scholar Oka Yoshiaki explained Shimizu's detachment from the violence of the battlefield as a result of his physical separation from the troops and action. While on these military tours, he stayed in hotels, traveled to scenic areas, and sampled local cuisine along with other artists.[49] Tours became social events for artists like Fujita Tsuguharu, who had returned from Paris to join the war effort as an artist.[50]

---

48. Bert Winther-Tamaki, Embodiment/Disembodiment, 154.
49. Oka Yoshiaki, Okawa Museum.
50. *Nanpô gakushin. Daitôa sensô* (Rikugun bijutsu kyôkai: September, 1942) Fujita was one of the more active members of this effort, participating in multiple trips overseas, exhibiting works, and holding conferences to discuss ways artists could contribute to the war effort.

Despite failing the 1906 officer's exam, Shimizu could finally participate in the action, merging his fascination with the military and his artistic skill. When journalists interviewed illustrators about their battlefield experiences, painter Kobayakawa Atsushirô singled out Shimizu for praise for his bravery. Shimizu responded to Kobayakawa, saying, "Everyone—soldiers too—is the same. When you hear a loud blast go off, somehow you become brave." He also insisted that the scale of the war and its effects were impossible for an artist to capture, indicating that despite the idealized character of his canvases, Shimizu was well aware of its horror and magnitude. By 1944, however, the government began rationing art supplies even for military illustrators.

Shimizu was an eager and early champion of the Japanese war effort and maintained his support until its final days by encouraging his eldest son, Ikuo, to sign up for the navy. Indicating his deep love for his son, Shimizu wrote in near obsessive detail about his son's life. (His daughter, born after his return from Paris is rarely mentioned.) Soon after joining, Ikuo died in a sea battle in 1944, but Shimizu was not informed of his death until 1945. Shimizu wrote:

> Ikuo, who never dreamed of being a soldier, died for Greater East Asia and for the emperor, as a splendid navy soldier. However, I am still alive—the one who had wanted to be in the military since I was a young boy, failed the exam, and stumbled about as an artist. It is ironic. The prestige of the house of Shimizu that has ancestors who were retainers of Toyotomi during the Tenshô era, will shine brighter with Ikuo."[51]

Soon after writing this, Shimizu composed a short biography of his son's life and also drew portraits of Ikuo with what scraps of paper he could find after the surrender. Shimizu's daughter remembered that her father tried to remain bright and lively in front of his family, but he regularly visited his son's grave, staying for hours before returning

51. Ueno Kenji, "Shimizu Toshi ten," *Bijutsu Techô* No. 467, (July 1980).

home at night.[52] Six months after Japan surrendered to the Allies, Shimizu Toshi died on December 7 at his family home in Tochigi. Family members attributed his weakened state to the loss of Ikuo. Japanese biographers of Shimizu have also speculated that Shimizu committed suicide.[53]

---

52. Although his remains had not been recovered, his grave held a fingernail and a strand of hair that he left prior to going to war. Nakano Tomiko, "Chichi no omoide," *Shimizu Toshi ten* (Musashino Cultural Center, 1991), 89.
53. Matsume, Shôkô. "Kaette kita Urashima Tarô gaka – Shimizu Toshi shoron." *Kôzô.* (Reprint.) March 8 1989, 30.

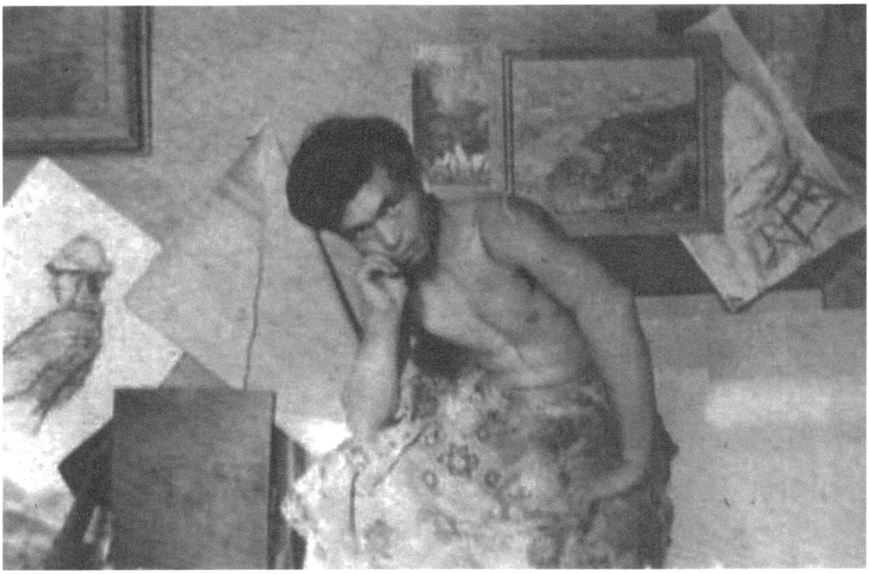

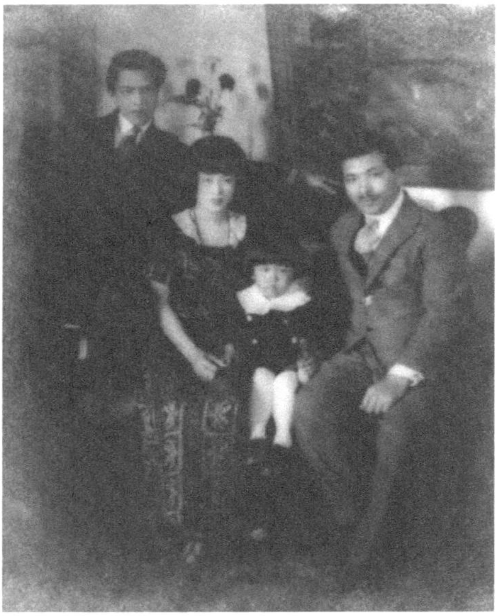

(Above): Shimizu Toshi in his Seattle studio, circa 1914.

(Left): From left to right: Shimizu Kiyoshi, Shimizu Sumiko, Shimizu Ikuo, and Shimizu Toshi, 1924. Photograph most likely taken by Nakayama Iwata.

(Opposite Above): From right to left: Shimizu Toshi, Nakano (Shimizu) Tomiko, and Shimizu Sumiko, 1943 in front of his painting, "Charge!"

(Opposite Below): Shimizu Toshi and his son, Ikuo, 1944.

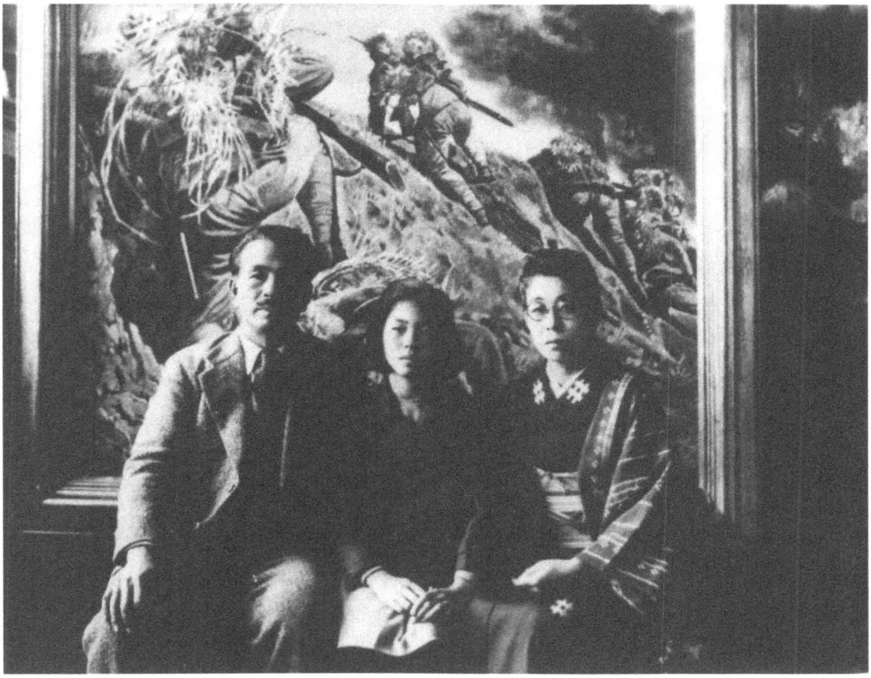

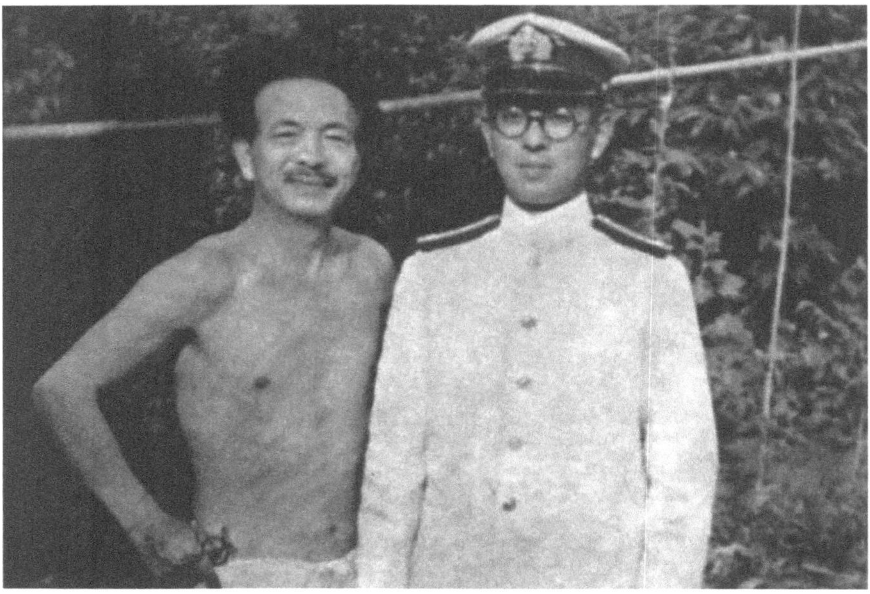

Art Across Borders

Illustrations

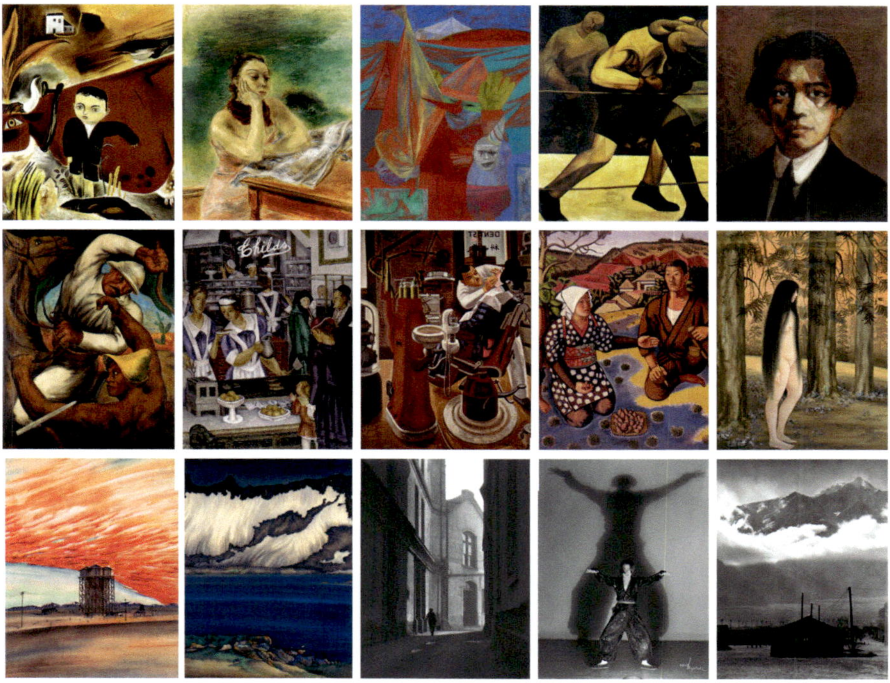

(Opposite): Eitarô Ishigaki, ca. 1940. Painting a Federal Art Project, Photographic Division collection, circa 1920-1965. Archives of American Art, Smithsonian Institution.

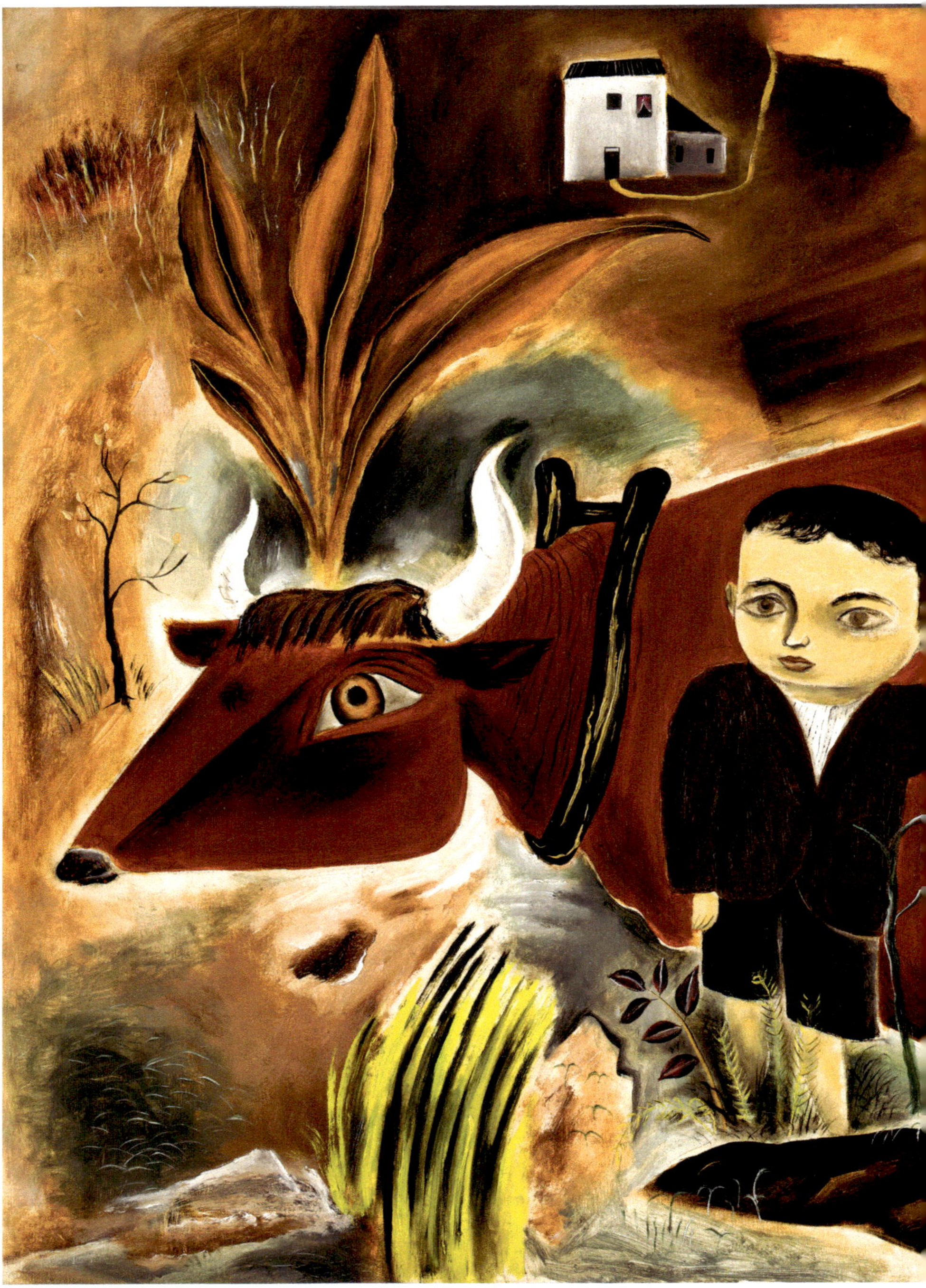

Fig. 1: Kuniyoshi Yasuo, "Little Joe with Cow," 1923. Oil on canvas. Crystal Bridges Museum of American Art, Bentonville.

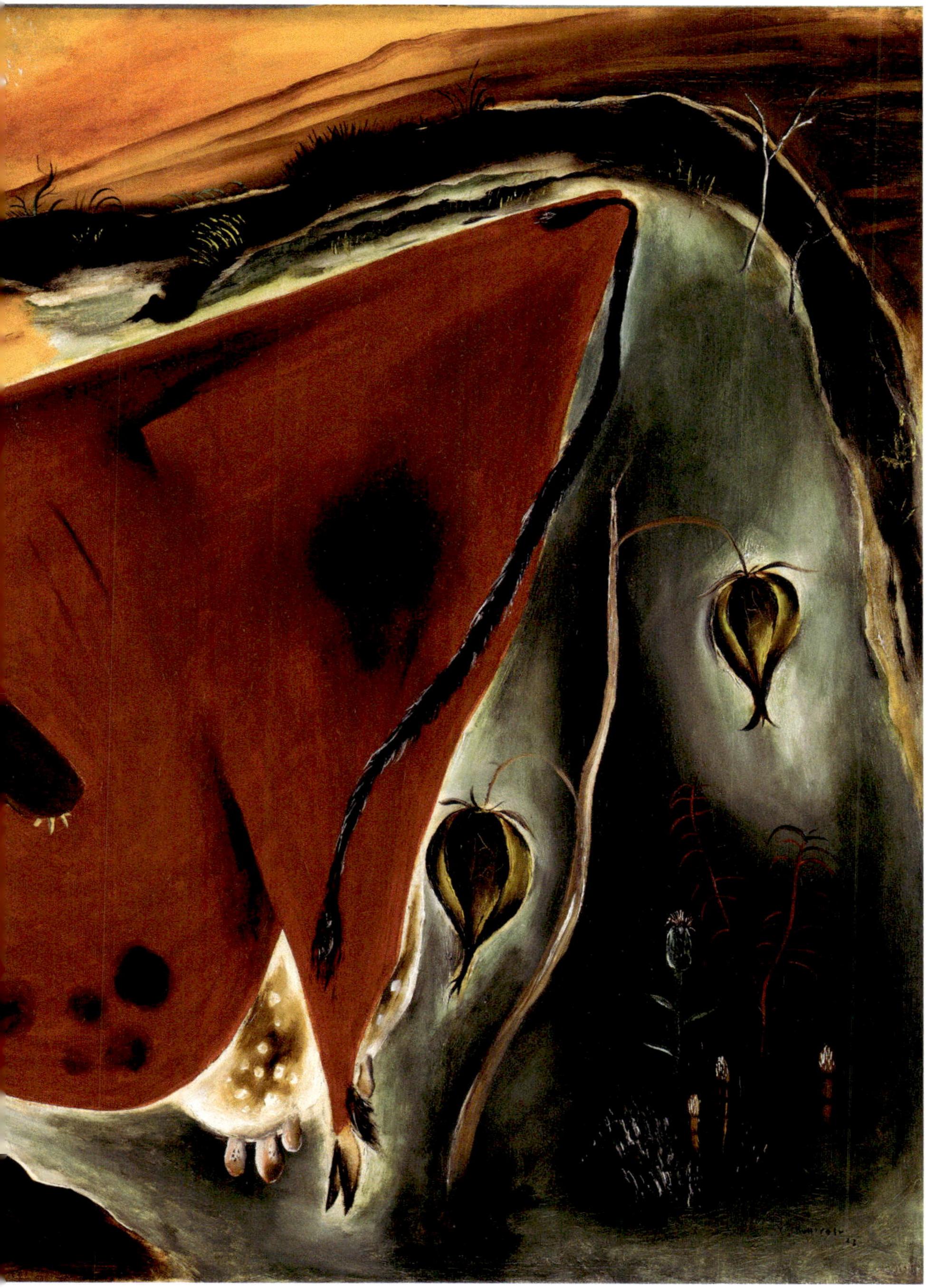

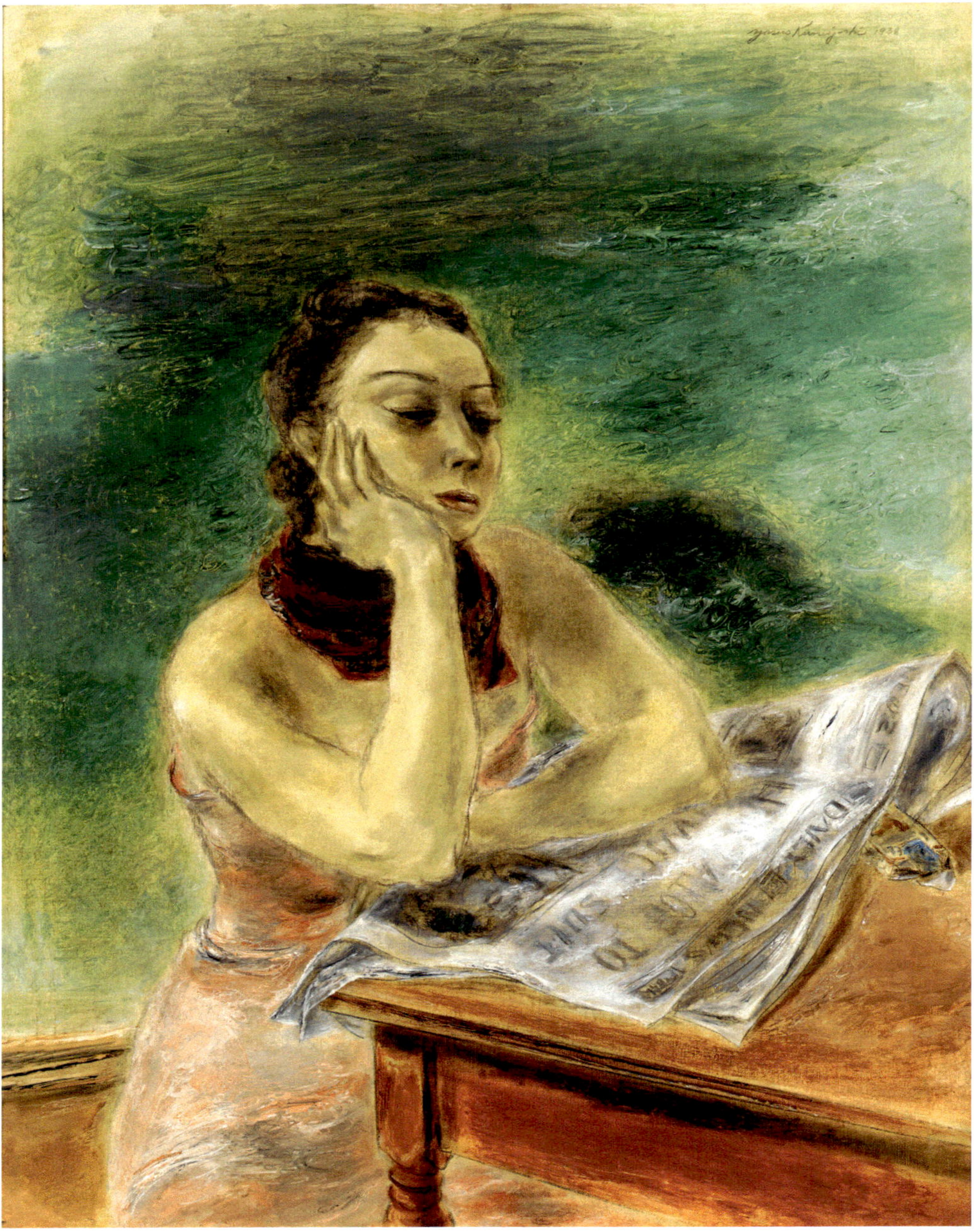

Fig. 2: Kuniyoshi Yasuo, "I'm Tired," 1938. Oil and charcoal on linen. Whitney Museum of American Art, New York.

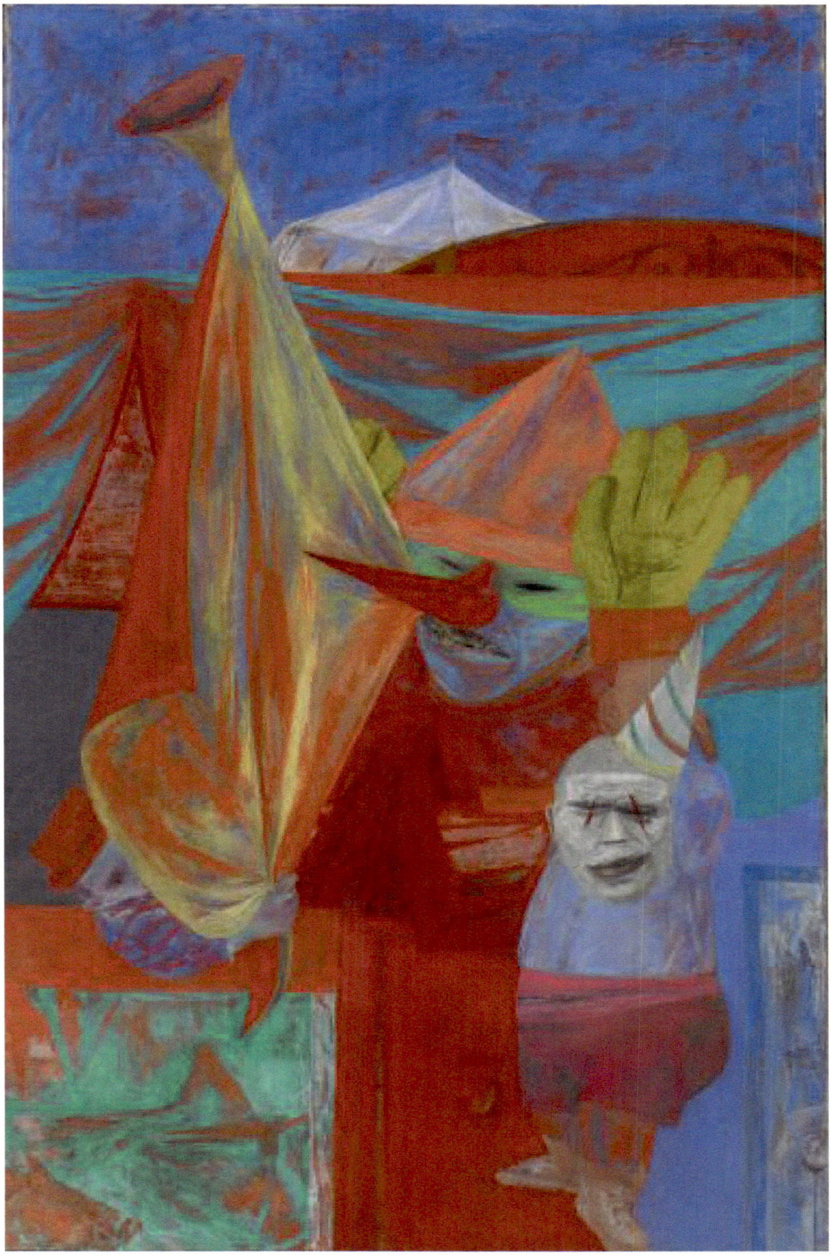

Fig. 3: Kuniyoshi Yasuo, “Fakirs,” 1951. Oil on Canvas. Smithsonian American Art Museum, Washington, DC.

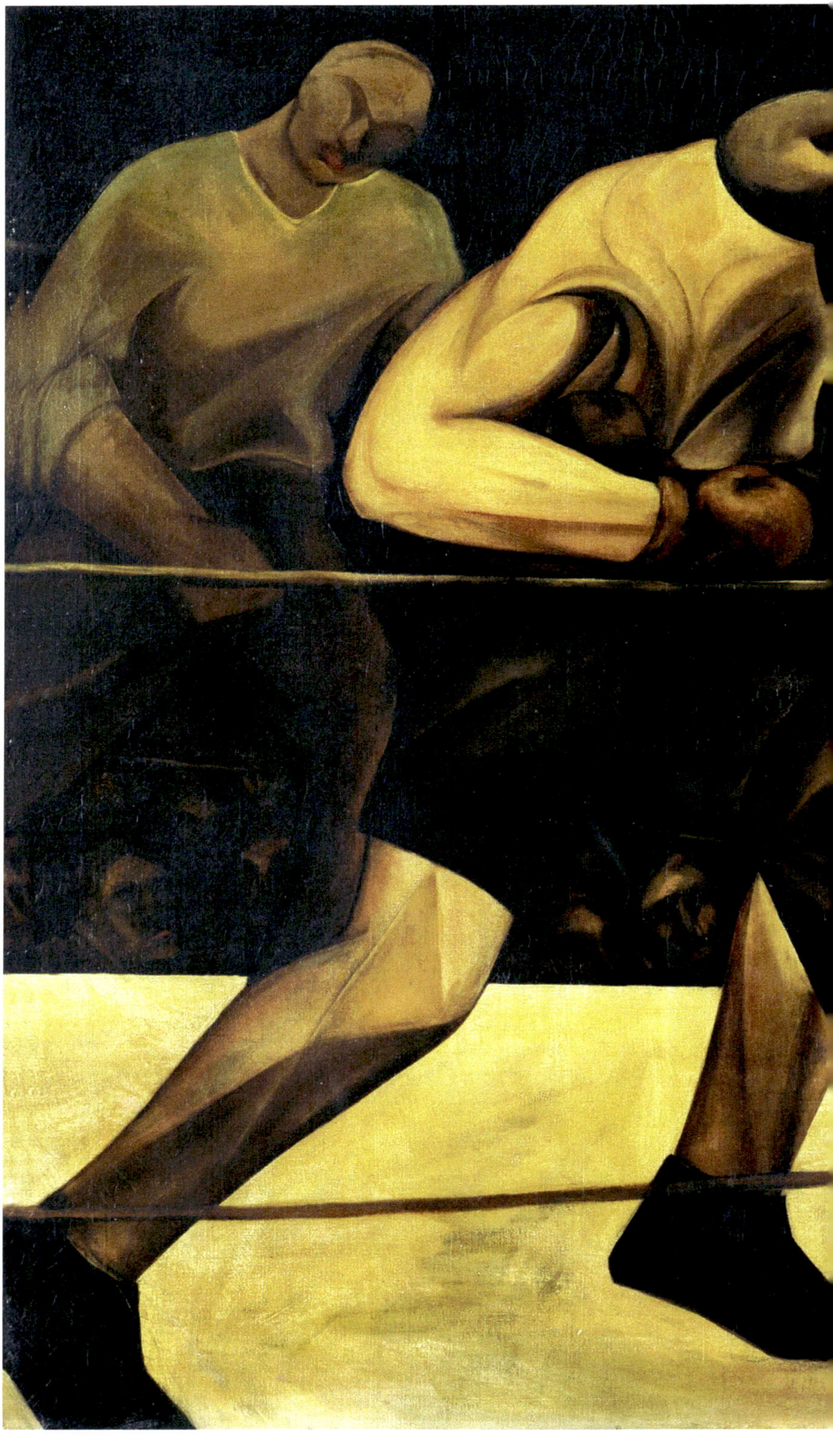

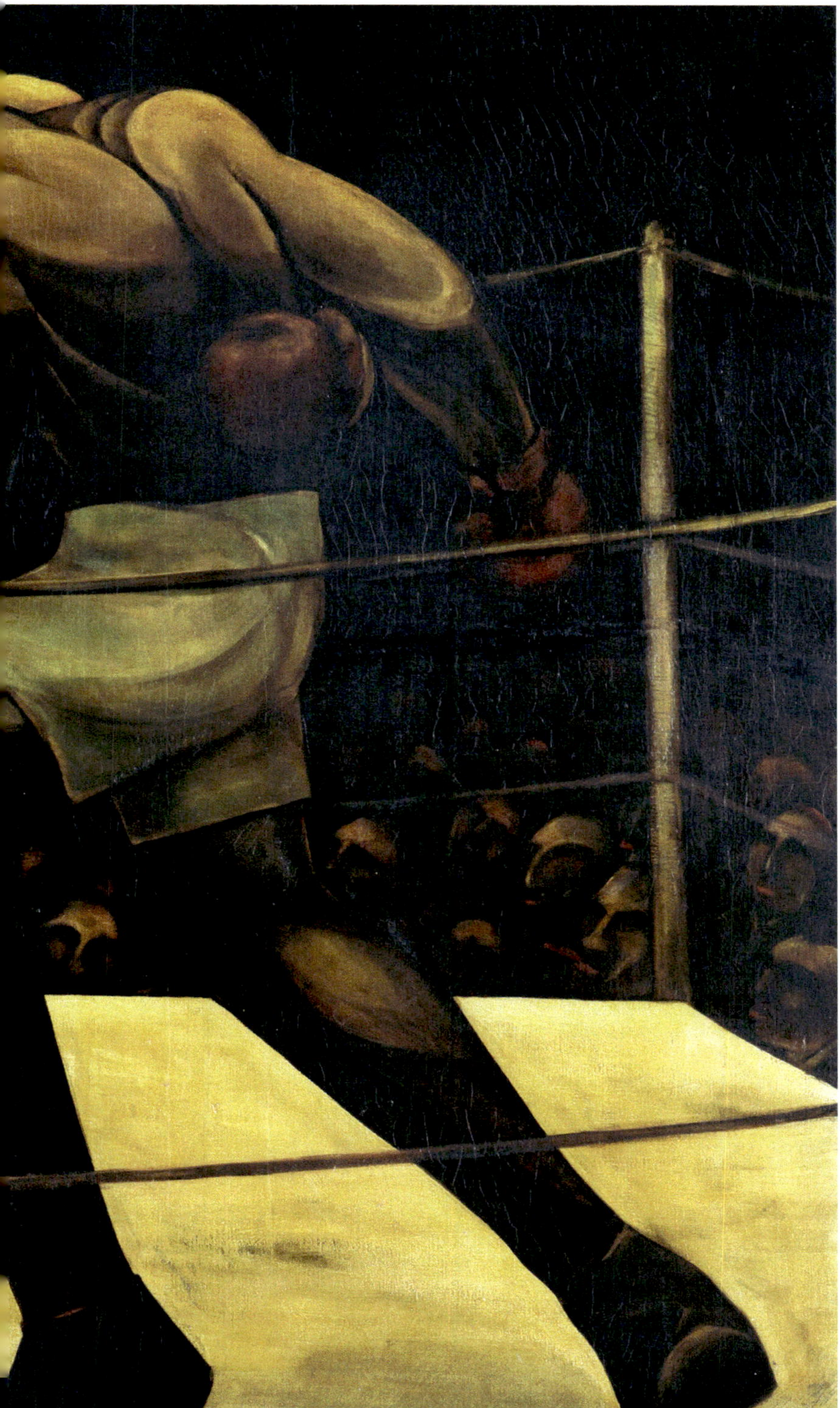

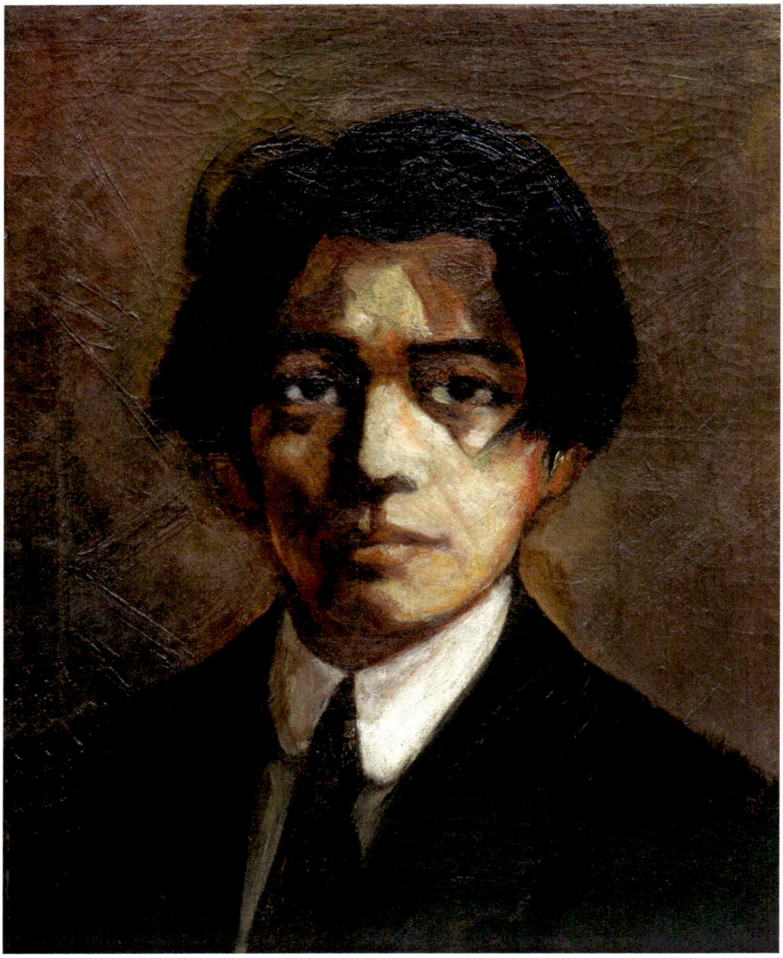

Fig. 4 (Previous Pages): Ishigaki Eitarô, "Boxers," 1925. Oil on canvas. The Museum of Modern Art, Wakayama.

Fig. 5 (Above): Ishigaki Eitarô, "Self Portrait," 1917. Oil on canvas. The Museum of Modern Art, Wakayama.

Fig. 6 (Opposite): Ishigaki Eitarô, "Cuban Revolution," 1933. Oil on canvas. The Museum of Modern Art, Wakayama.

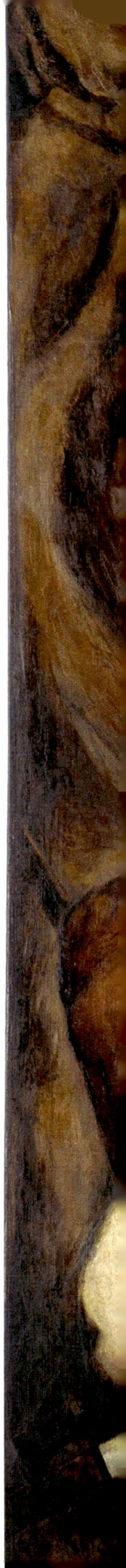

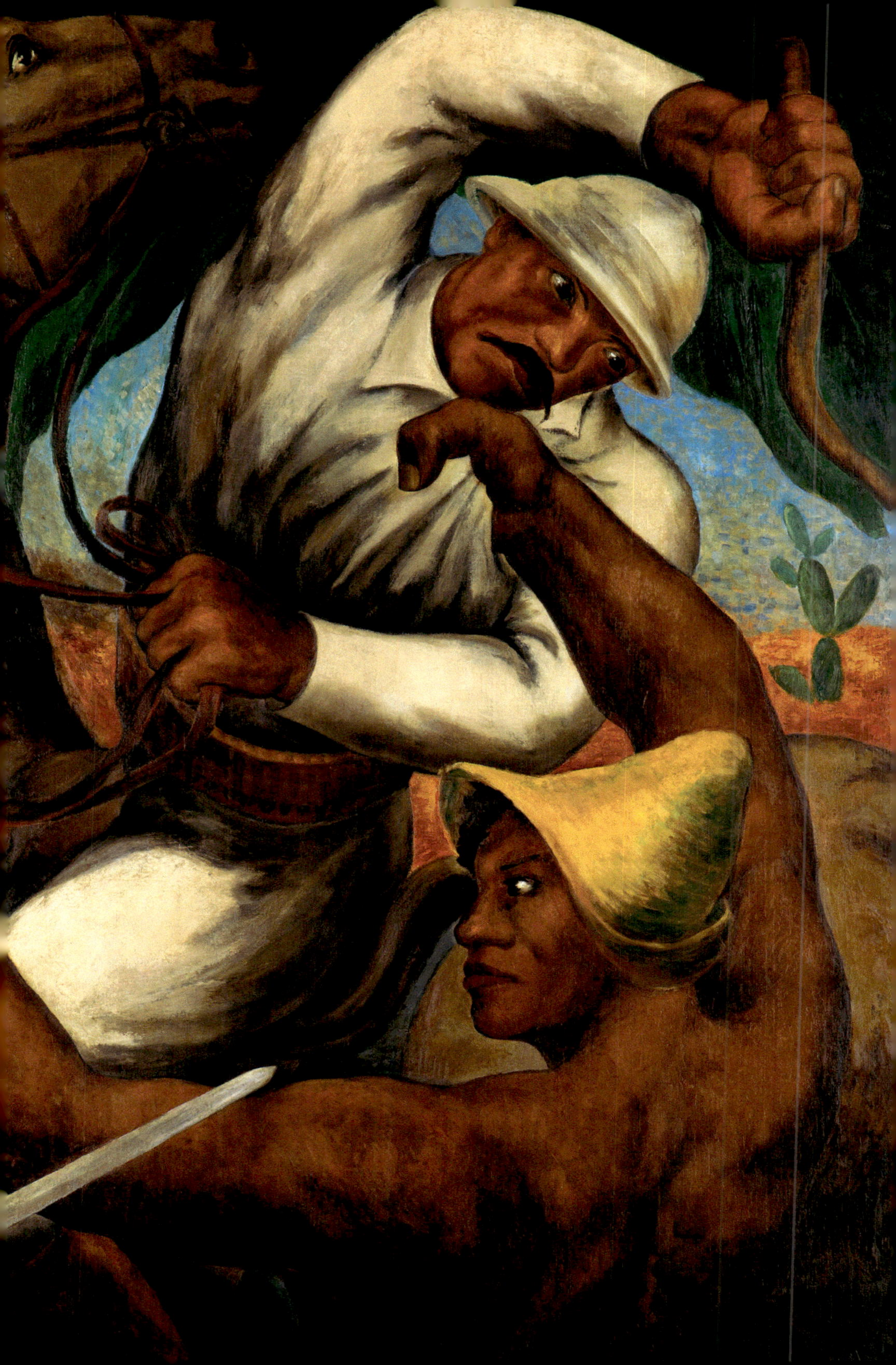

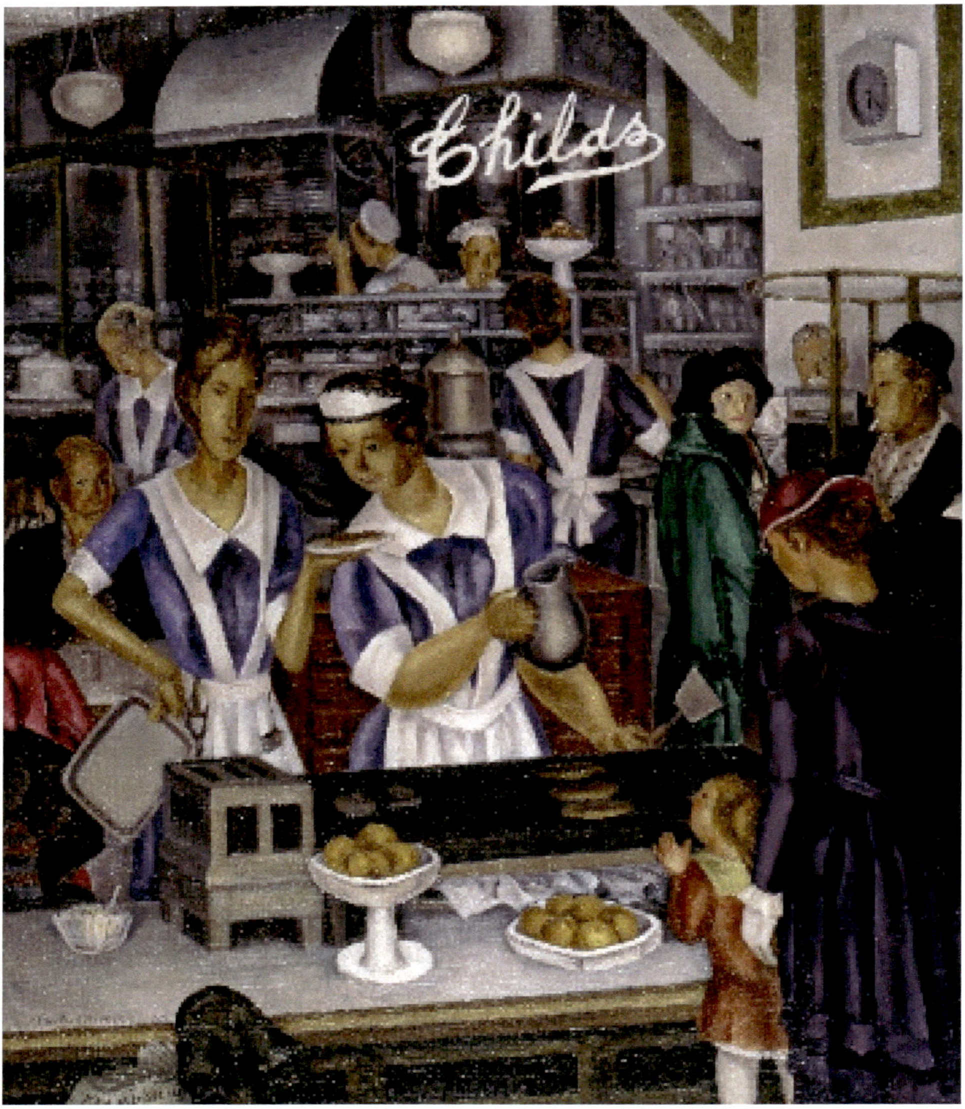

Fig. 7 (Above): Shimizu Toshi, "Child's Bakery," 1924. Oil on canvas. Fuchu Art Museum.

Fig. 8 (Opposite): Shimizu Toshi, "Dentist," 1928. Oil on canvas. Tochigi Prefectural Museum of Fine Art.

Fig. 9 (Following Pages): Shimizu Toshi, "At Rest on the Land," 1930. Oil on canvas. Tochigi Prefectural Museum of Fine Art.

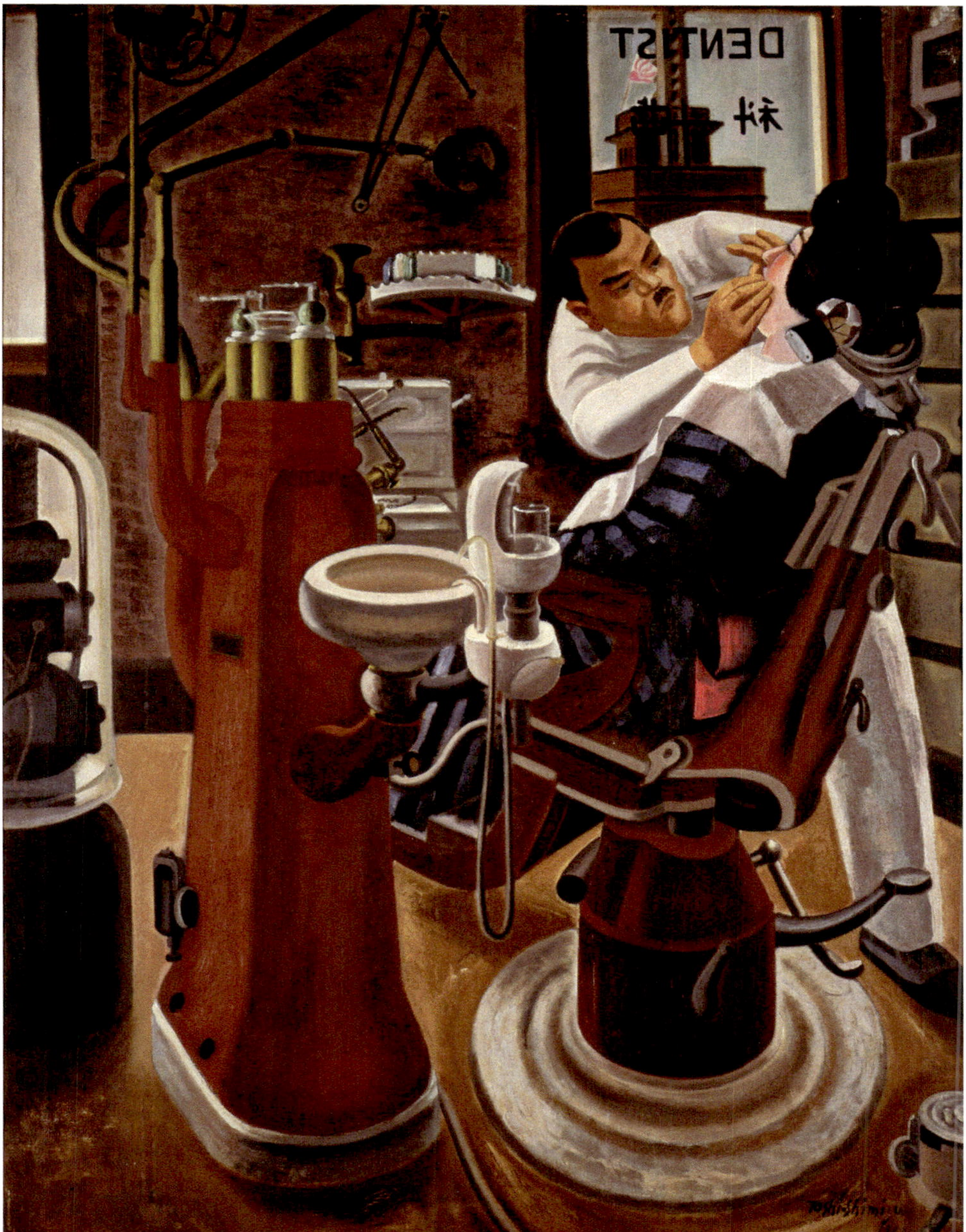
DENTIST

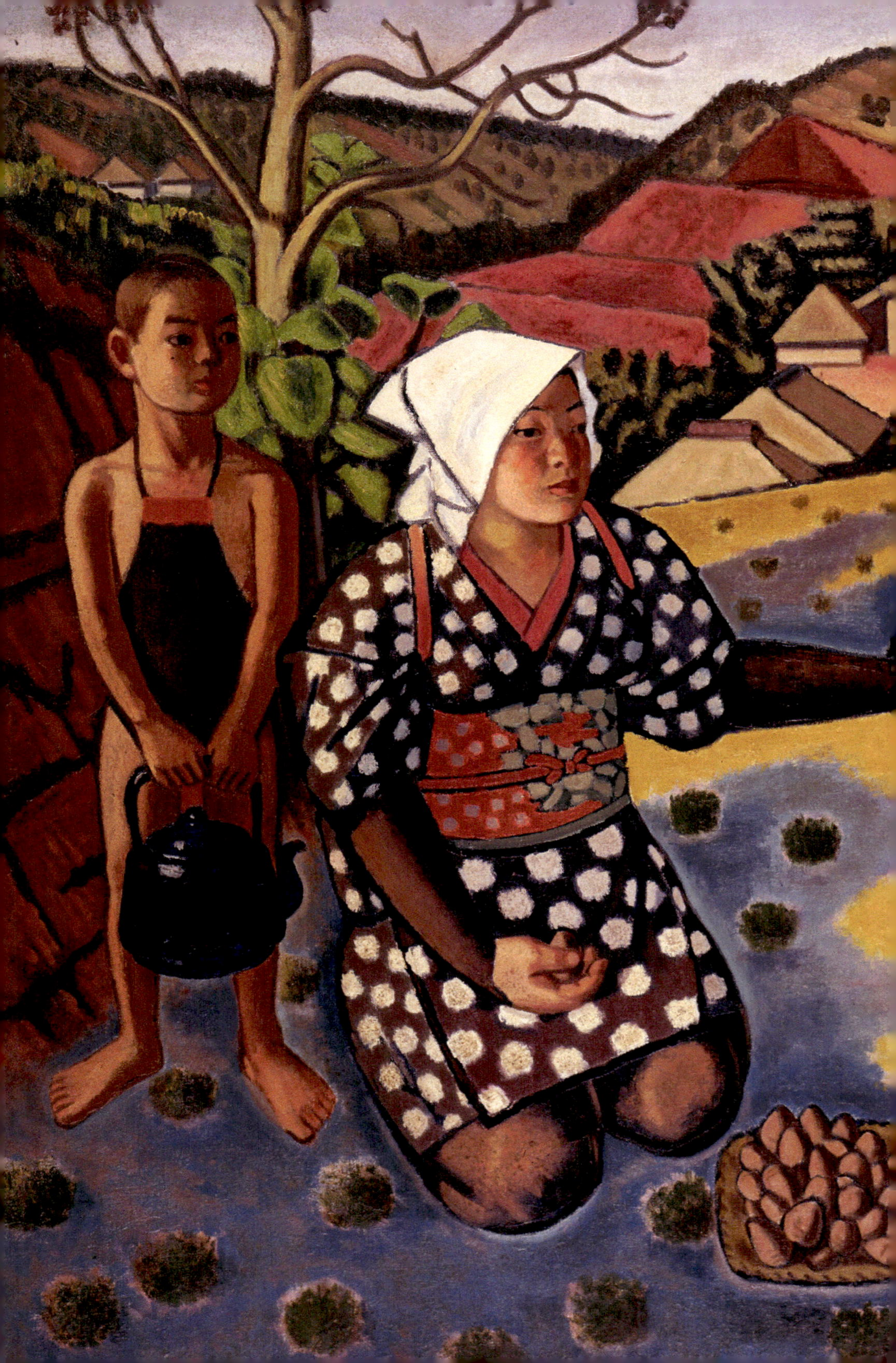

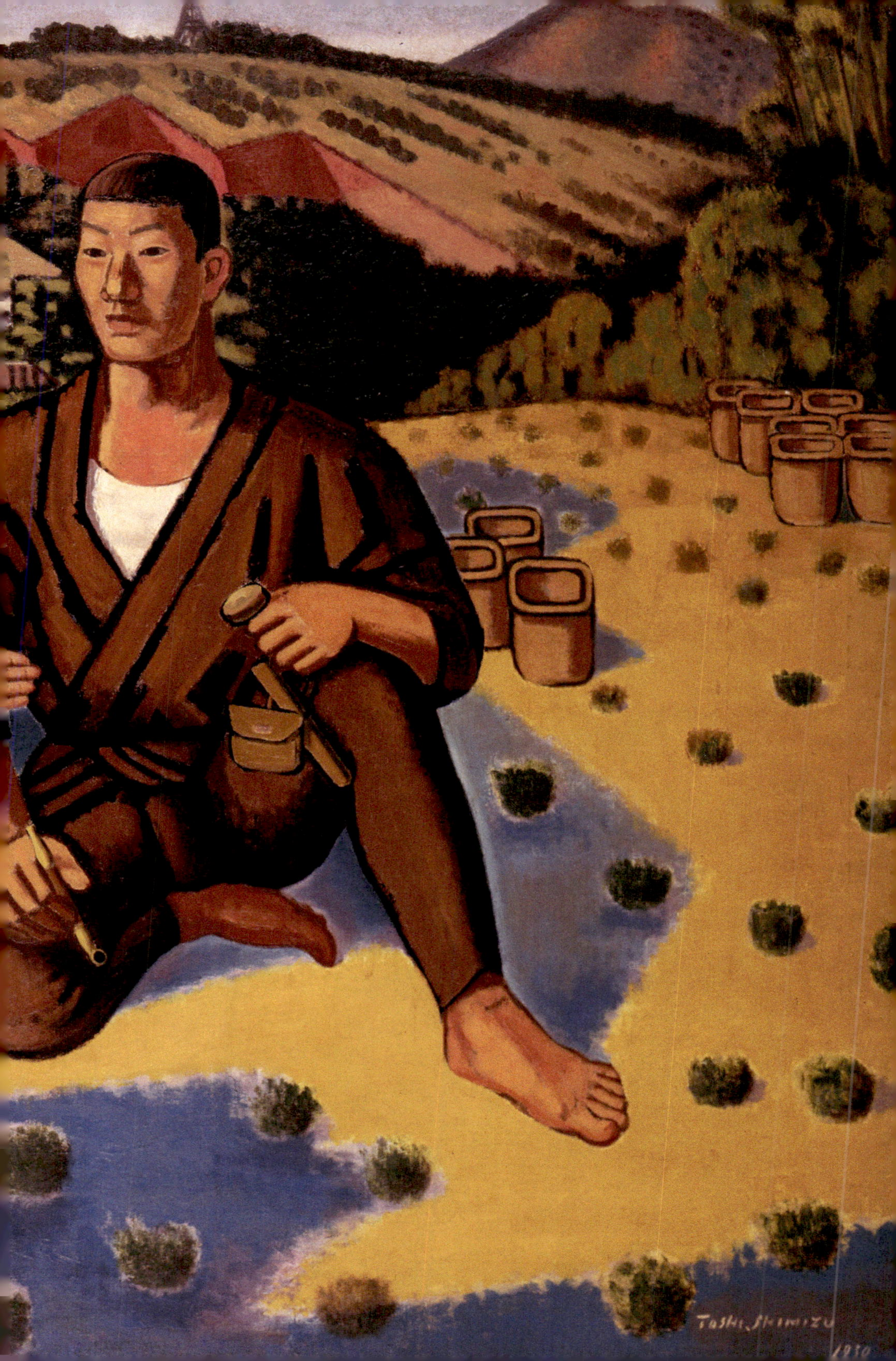
TOSHI SHIMIZU
1930

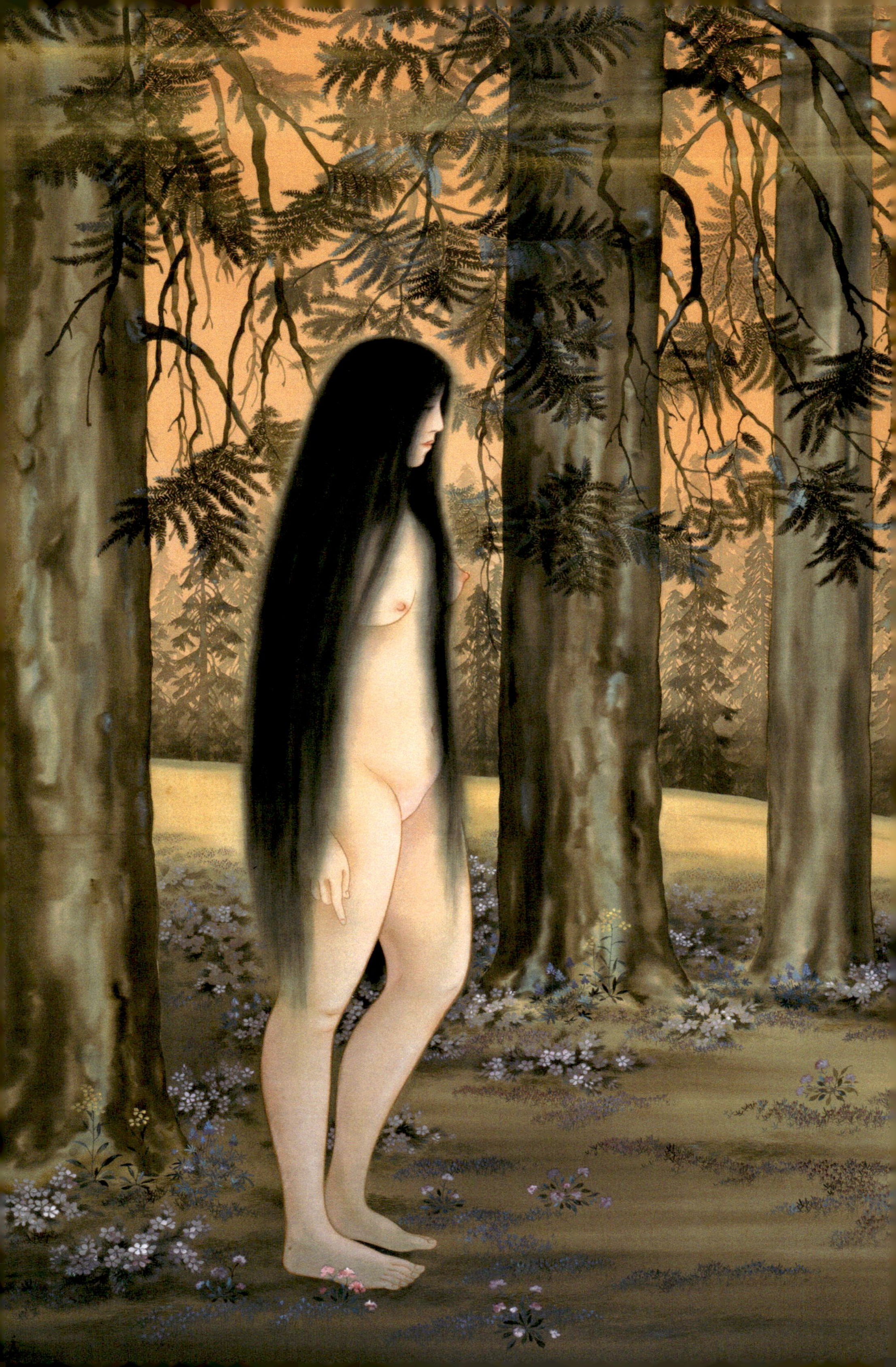

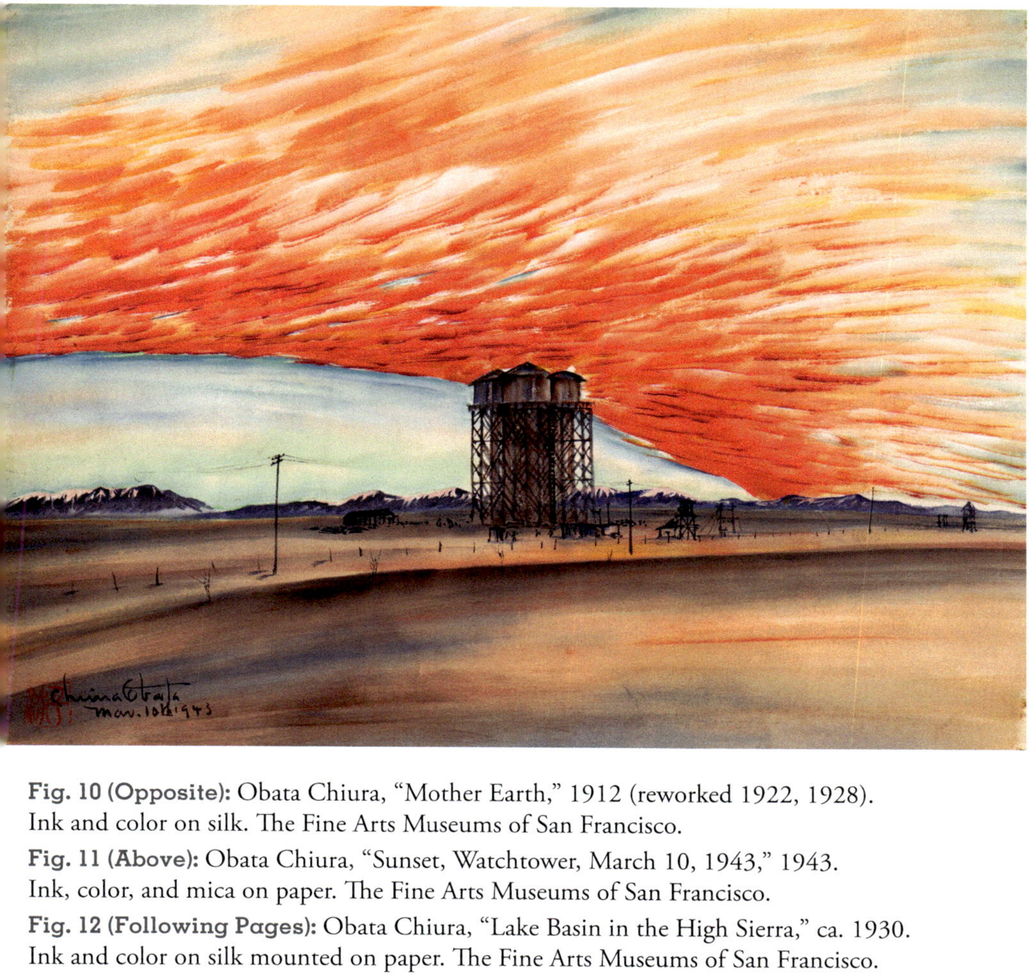

Fig. 10 (Opposite): Obata Chiura, “Mother Earth,” 1912 (reworked 1922, 1928). Ink and color on silk. The Fine Arts Museums of San Francisco.

Fig. 11 (Above): Obata Chiura, “Sunset, Watchtower, March 10, 1943,” 1943. Ink, color, and mica on paper. The Fine Arts Museums of San Francisco.

Fig. 12 (Following Pages): Obata Chiura, “Lake Basin in the High Sierra,” ca. 1930. Ink and color on silk mounted on paper. The Fine Arts Museums of San Francisco.

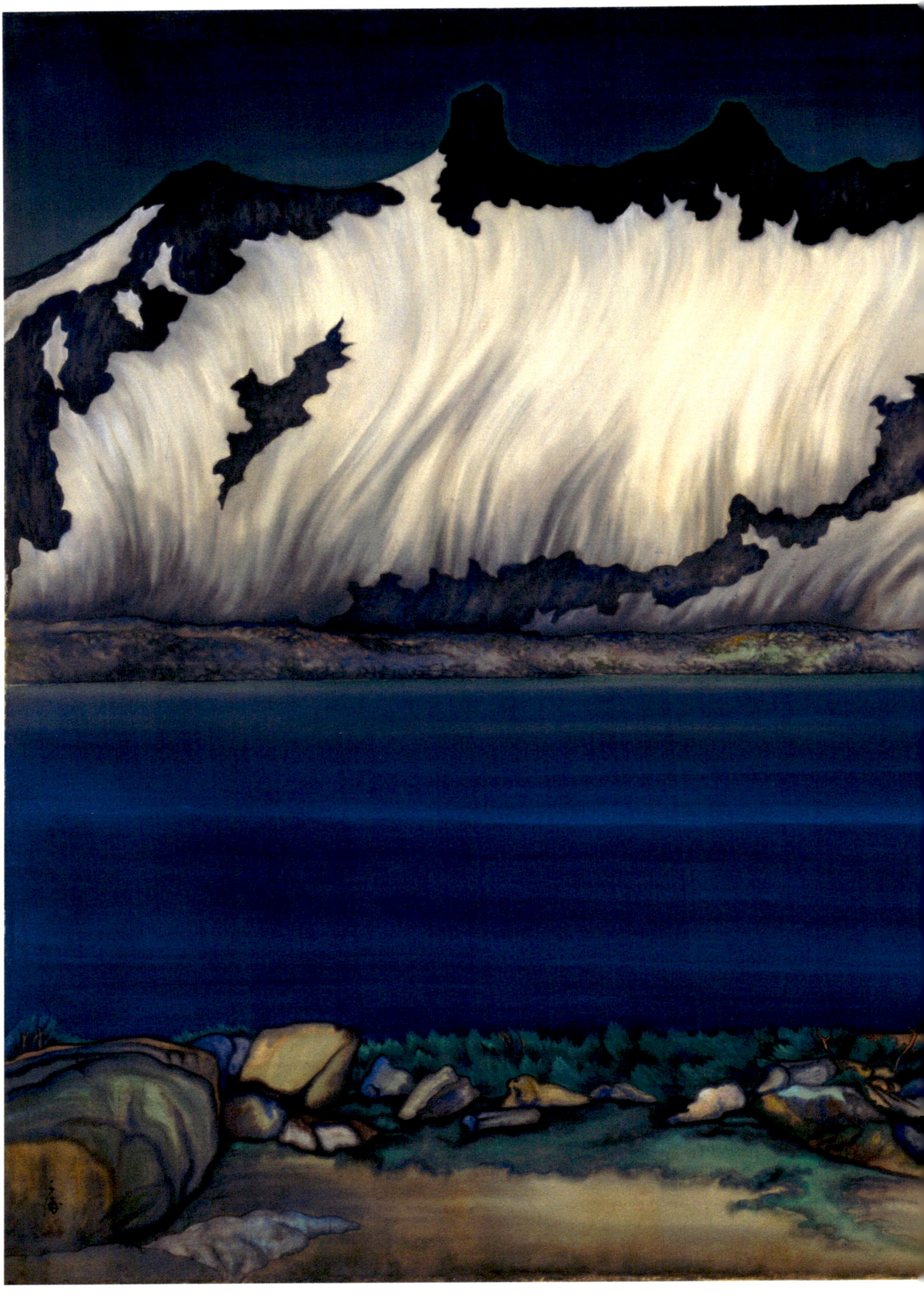

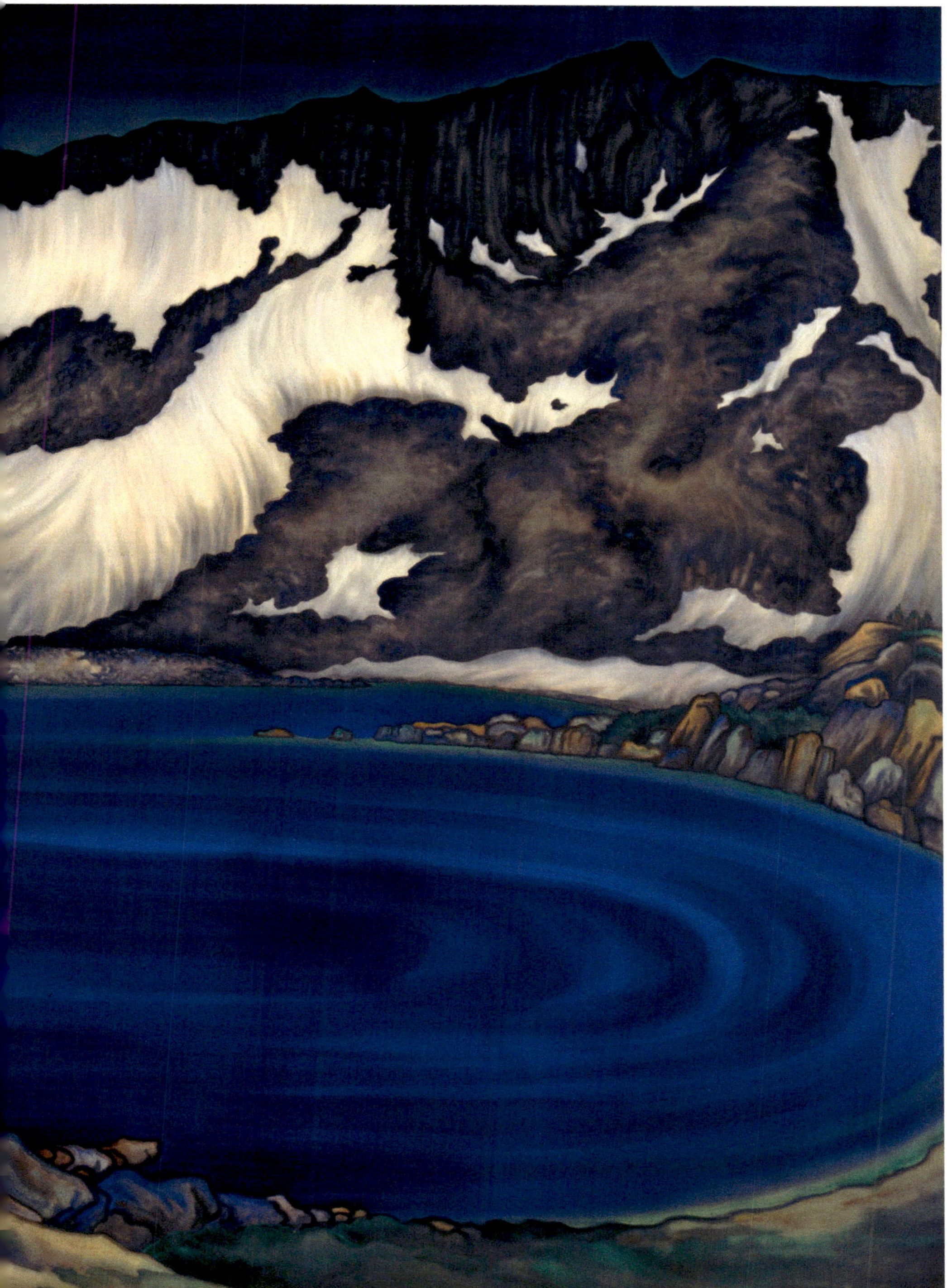

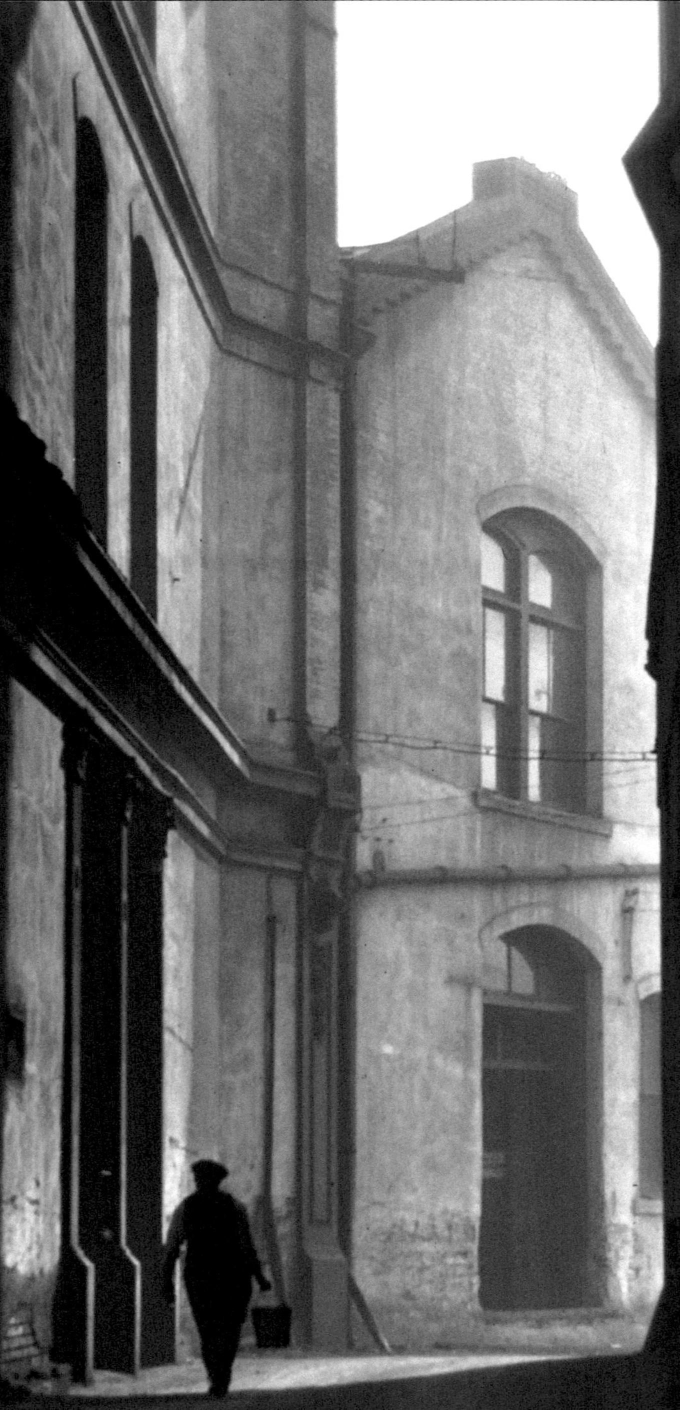

Fig. 13: Miyatake Tôyô, "Early Morning on Jackson Street, Little Tokyo, Los Angeles," 1925. Gelatin silver print. Collection of the Tôyô Miyatake Estate. © Toyo Miyatake Studio.

Fig. 14: Miyatake Tôyô, "Ito Michio in the Pizzicati," 1929. Gelatin silver print. Collection of the Tôyô Miyatake Estate. © Toyo Miyatake Studio.

Fig. 15 (Following Pages): Miyatake Tôyô, "Manzanar Barracks," 1943. Collection of the Tôyô Miyatake Estate. © Tôyô Miyatake Studio.

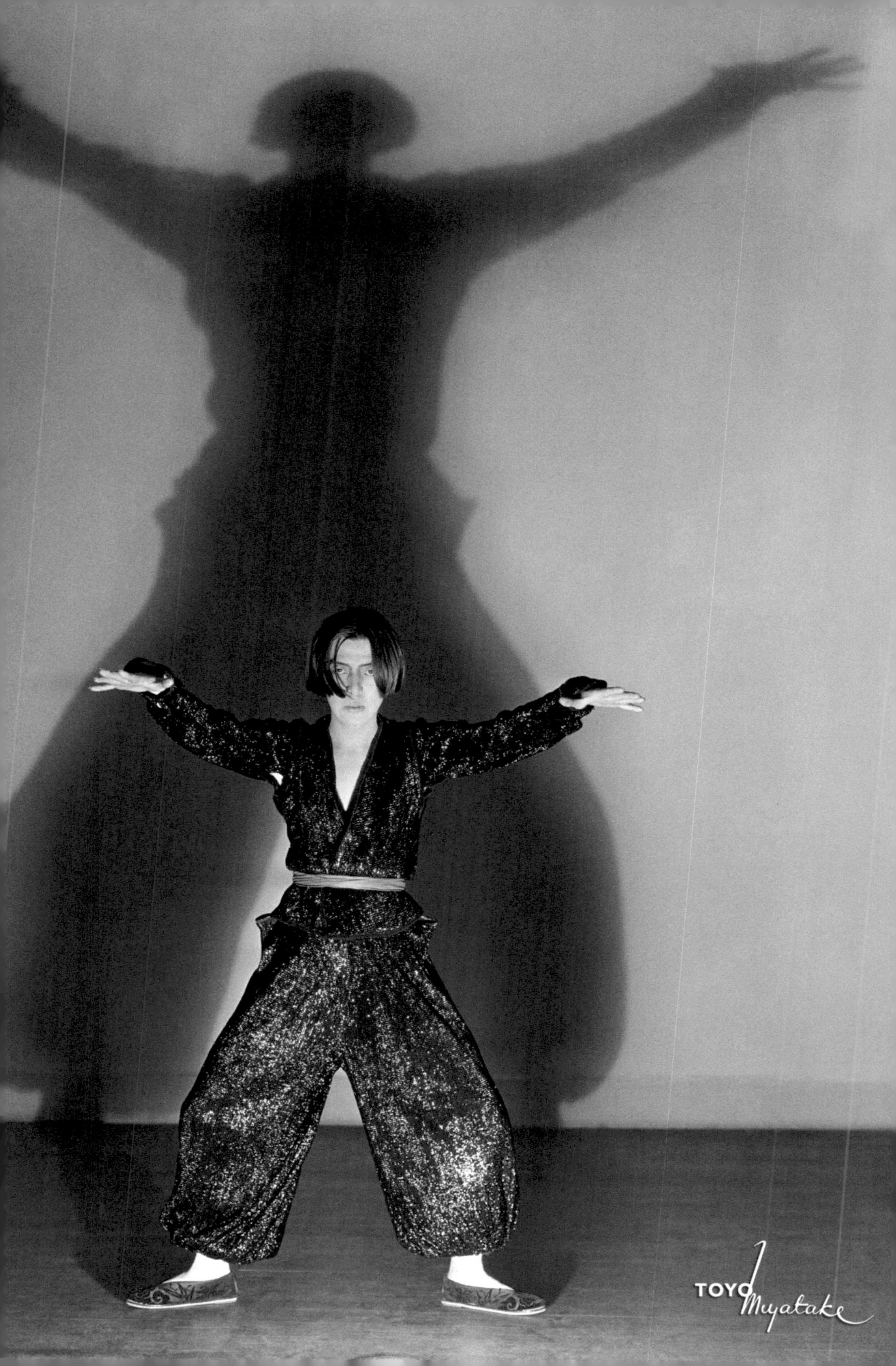
TOYO Miyatake

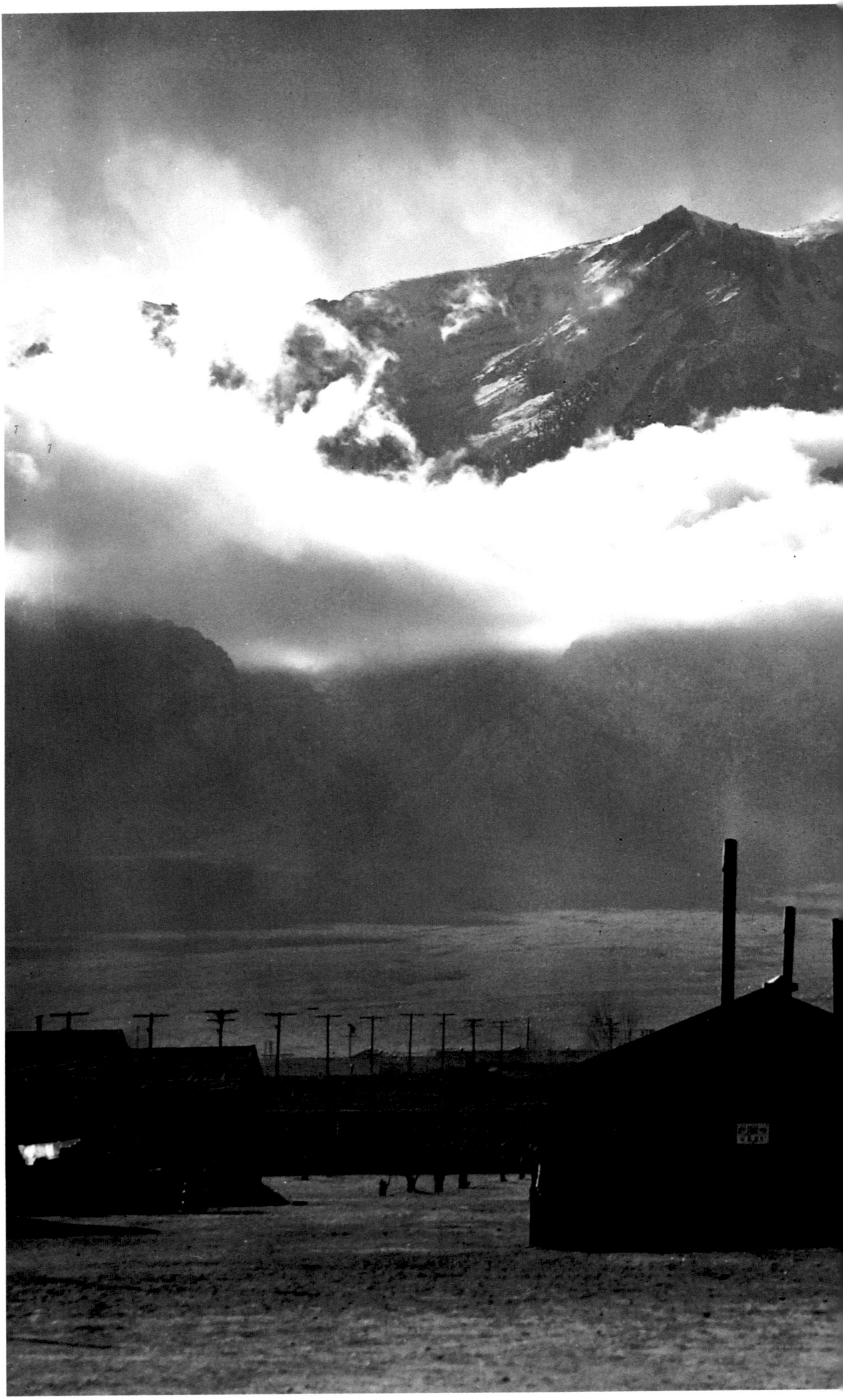

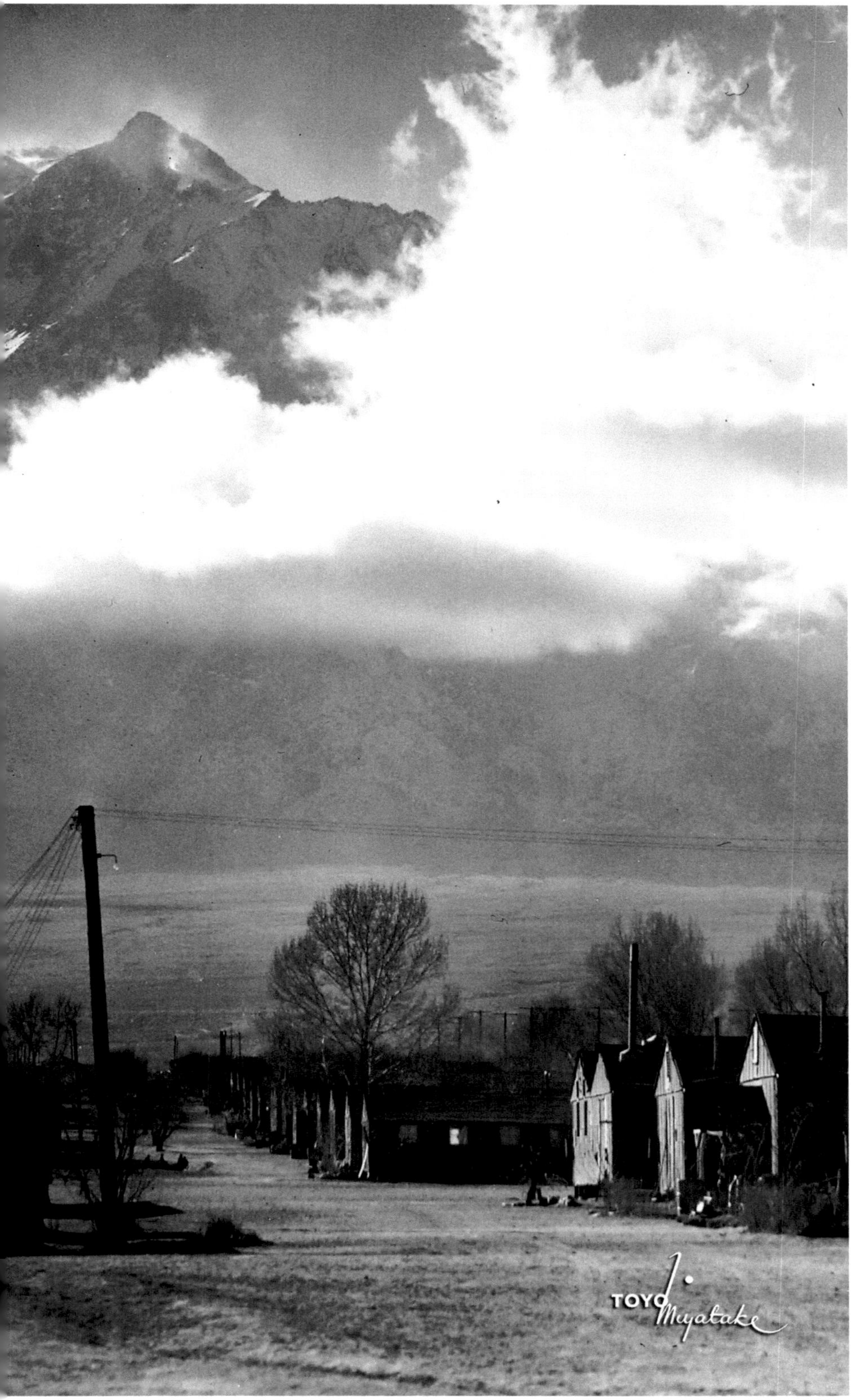
TOYO Miyatake

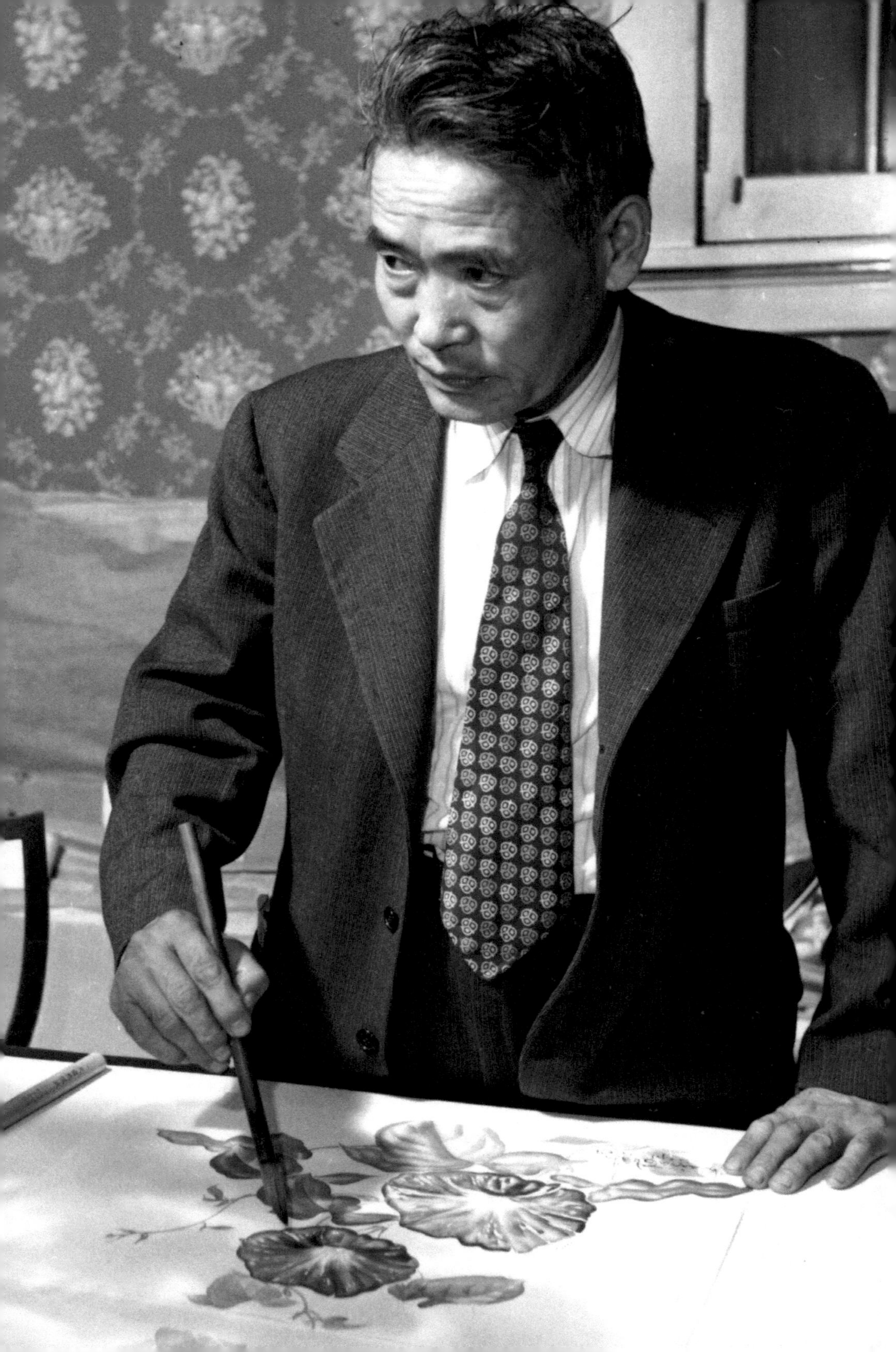

Chapter Four
Obata Chiura
Nature Knows No Depression

Obata Chiura was one of the most renowned Japanese artists living in California during the 20th century. He arrived in San Francisco in 1903 having trained since early childhood with masters in Japanese brush techniques and media. Before arriving on American shores, Obata had already received awards and worked on major commissions as a student in Tokyo. Although he had entertained the idea of traveling to Europe to study art, he stayed in California, where his skills provided him with steady commissions. Obata's fusion of Japanese stylistic devices applied to the Pacific Coast landscape made him one of the most popular California artists of his time. His paintings and woodblock series suited the West Coast: California's Arts and Crafts movement, the region's natural beauty, and the presence of Asian and Mexican immigrant communities contributed to an aesthetic distinct from the East Coast. Whereas regional folk art, social realism, and Ashcan school street scenes inspired Kuniyoshi, Ishigaki, and Shimizu, Obata found success applying his Japanese training to the California landscape.

Obata's training coincided with a period of tension between two schools of art: *yôga* (Western-style painting) and *nihonga* (Japanese-style

---

(Opposite): War Relocation Authority. Photograph of Chiura Obata painting, circa 1944. Chiura Obata papers, 1891-2000. Archives of American Art, Smithsonian Institution.

painting). The contentious relationship between *yôga* and *nihonga* was indigenous to Japan, where artists were forced to pick a side—though in reality lines between each category were often blurred. During the early Meiji era, artists were encouraged to adopt new styles, materials, and techniques entering Japan from Europe and the United States. Artists who painted in oils, used perspective and shading, and applied their works to canvas or paper to be hung on walls became known as *yôga* artists. *Nihonga*, on the other hand, employed *sumi* (black ink) and colors painted on hanging silk, handscrolls, folding screens, or fans. When the museum was adopted as a Meiji institution, folding screens, fans, and lacquerware became problematic for exhibition, because they could not be as easily displayed as canvases and sculpture. Japanese artists adapted their art to fit the museum setting by creating canvases that could easily be hung on walls and sculptures that sat on pedestals. As the Meiji era progressed, however, state enthusiasm and support for *yôga* artists waned, partially because there was little regard for it at international expositions. Late nineteenth century Western audiences viewed *yôga* canvases as too mimetic, an overthrow of Japanese tradition, which was simultaneously experiencing a boom in popularity.

Nihonga developed as a foil to *yôga* as scholars and collectors vowed to protect native culture and legitimize Japanese art, which they believed was under threat due to Western influence. Prominent art instructors, including Tokyo Imperial University professor, Ernest Fenollosa, and his pupil, Okakura Kakuzô (Tenshin), encouraged Japanese artists to return to native themes, techniques, and stylistic devices. Though there were many variations, *nihonga* became a fusion of Japanese-style (sometimes including oil) painting with Western techniques using Japanese themes. Each borrowed from the other, making it difficult to think of each school in binary terms.[1] By framing

1. Excellent scholarship on *yôga* and *nihonga* abound: See Alicia Volk's *In Pursuit of Universalism: Yorozu Tetsugorô and Japanese Modern Art.* (Berkeley, CA: University of California Press, 2010). Ellen P. Conant *Nihonga, Transcending the Past: Japanese-Style Painting, 1868-1968.* (St. Louis, MO: The St. Louis Art Museum and the Japan Foundation, 1995).

the genre as "Japanese-style," the *nihonga* compromise attempted to bring Japanese tradition into the realm of modern art. *Yôga* and *nihonga* categories often overlapped: Artists who used traditional brushwork elements in their work were considered to be in the *nihonga* camp, while those artists who painted oil on canvas, still-lifes of foreign fruit, were labeled *yôga* artists. If the woman in the painting was dressed in kimono, however, it might be considered *nihonga*. And, if the still life included cherry blossoms and a fan, it might be categorized as *nihonga*. Some *nihonga* pieces seemed to have emerged from *Japonisme* that had ricocheted back onto the homeland further confusing the categories. Although *nihonga* was a modern creation, its associations with a national aesthetic and the champions of tradition defined (and limited) the genre.

When Japanese artists arrived on foreign shores, Westerners were oblivious to the competition—much less the discourse on their distinctions—between the two schools. Obata's training was entirely rooted in both traditional Japanese and *nihonga* techniques, although his brother (who became his adopted father) was a trained *yôga* artist. He continued to paint in the *nihonga* style, while in California, but it was harder to find a market for those works at the turn of the century. Consumers on the Pacific Coast craved folding screens by Japanese artists more than the *nihonga* compromise of oil on canvas with Japanese themes. While he continued to independently create fine art painting, Obata earned income from commissions for his stylized and "traditional" decoration. His subject matter stayed rooted in nature, what he called "*Dai-shizen*," depicting California's beauty using Japanese brushes and *sumi* ink.

Obata's course was set early in life. Born Satô Zôroku in Okayama prefecture in 1885, Obata was one of eight children in a farming family. His mother was forty-four-years old and his father died soon after Zôroku was born. At the age of five, Obata went to Mizusawa in Iwate prefecture to live with his older brother, Rokuichi, and his wife. Rokuichi was a *nihonga* and *yôga* trained artist, who had studied in Tokyo's art schools, and Obata's mother believed that her "constantly drawing" youngest son would be better off with him.

Hundreds of kilometers north of his mother and sisters, the transition was difficult for Zôroku, who became known for his rambunctious behavior and disappearing into the forest, what he described as an "excellent playground for naughty children."[2] Located in the heart of northeastern Japan (Tôhoku), Mizusawa was conservative. Zôroku studied poems by Mito scholars favored by nationalists as well as epics of samurai valor at his primary school. In the nearby Kitakami River, he also developed his lifelong hobby of fishing. Nature was of preeminent importance to Zôroku: Inspired by the multiple inlets along Sendai's coastline, where natural beauty had also attracted poets like Matsuo Bashô, Obata eventually changed his name from Zôroku to Chiura, meaning "one thousand bays."

Though largely forgotten today, Rokuichi was well connected and regarded in the art world in his time. Rokuichi longed to return to Tokyo, sixteen hours away by train from Iwate, to continue with his art career.[3] As a compromise with his samurai-class in-laws, who objected to the couple moving to Tokyo, Rokuichi moved his wife and Zôroku from Mizusawa to Sendai, which was the largest city in the region. Life in Sendai seemed to calm Zôroku, who Rokuichi enrolled in art classes. Zôroku started a seven-year apprenticeship in *sumi* (black ink) painting with a notoriously strict teacher, Moniwa Chikusen. Moniwa was a member of the Nanga School, artists who admired classical Chinese culture and art. According to Obata, he spent two years, after school for two hours, drawing a circle and two straight lines, one line drawn with a downward stroke and the other with a left-to-right stroke.[4] His elbows were never allowed to touch the table. Eventually, Moniwa allowed Obata to paint flowers using only gradations of black ink. The disciplined apprenticeship did not dissuade him from life as an artist. Rather, Obata's interest deepened.

---

2. "Obata Chiura: An Oral History." Interview by Mauji Fujii, 1965. Japanese American History Project. The University of California at Los Angeles Special Collections Library. Shimojima Tetsurô, *Samurai to Kariforunia: Ikyô no Nihon gaka Obata Chiura* (Tokyo: Shogakukan, 2000), 18-22.
3. Ibid.
4. Obata Chiura, "How Painting Is Taught in Japan," *The Argus* (April 1928).

When members of the Japan Fine Arts Academy (Nihon Bijutsuin), including the renowned artist Yokoyama Taikan, visited Sendai, Rokuichi arranged to meet his former colleagues and friends and attend their traveling exhibition. Zôroku insisted that he also wanted to participate, but Rokuichi at first refused. Despite nurturing Obata's artistic talents, he felt that a family should have only one artist. Under relentless pressure, Rokuichi gave in and Obata viewed the Academy's exhibition. Founded by Okakura Kakuzô, the Academy exhibited some of Japan's finest *nihonga* artists. Obata was inspired to move to Tokyo to study, but Rokuichi objected and enrolled Obata in a military academy. Rokuichi's wife, who Obata had a much closer relationship, supported her stepson's choice and helped him board a train bound for Tokyo's Ueno Station. He was fourteen years old.

After viewing Murata Tanryô's paintings at an exhibition in Ueno, Obata resolved to study under him.[5] Murata, whose teacher had been a member of the Tosa School, had studied with Rokuichi in Tokyo. Because both Rokuichi and Obata had changed their names multiple times, Murata did not recognize the young man sitting on his doorstep as his friend's relative. Murata, who had been Rokuichi's junior in school, relented after receiving correspondence from Sendai and observing Obata's commitment. Obata became twenty-seven year-old Murata's "shadow," following him around the country to see masterworks in temples, castles, and shrines. Rokuichi reminded Obata that his task in Tokyo was to wake up early, study, and not to play. Obata caroused in Asakusa, drank sake, and ate far too many sweets. However, Murata informed Rokuichi that when he woke up at seven in the morning, Obata was already awake and working.[6]

Obata assisted Murata on several major commissions, including sixty screens for the famed Konpira Shrine in Shikoku.[7] Although still young, Obata's professional experience and exhibition record in

5. Obata Chiura, "How Painting Is Taught in Japan," 1928.
6. Shimojima Tetsurô , *Samurai to Kariforunia*, 42.
7. Susan Landauer, "Obata of the Thousand Bays," *Obata's Yosemite: The Arts and Letters of Chiura Obata from His Trip to the High Sierra in 1927* (Yosemite National Park, California: Yosemite Association, 1993), 20.

Tokyo were broadened. More than ten of his paintings were exhibited at annual shows hosted by *nihonga* art societies. Newspapers like the *Tokyo Asahi Shimbun* singled out Obata's paintings for praise in its reviews. He was awarded prizes for paintings like "Early Spring" (1902), an example of the *bijin-ga* ("beautiful woman") genre. *Bijin-ga* images were common among *nihonga* artists at the time, and critics praised Obata's careful use of color in the work. Although competing with older and more experienced artists, Obata's painting was awarded a bronze medal.[8] Some Japanese critics criticized the female figure's open-mouthed gaze, considered modern for the time and inappropriate for the genre. The work appealed to foreign tastes, however. Francis Larkin of Buffalo, New York, purchased the piece and donated it to the local museum.[9] After receiving the award for "Early Spring," he visited his family in Sendai and traveled throughout northeastern Japan on sketching trips. At seventeen years old, Obata was already receiving commissions, including illustrating a Japanese history book distributed in junior high schools.

Essays in exhibition catalogs in the United States describe Obata's style as "pure Japanese," but art from Japan cannot be understood in monolithic and homogenizing terms. Obata learned from a variety of masters, who had distinct influences, techniques, styles, and media. He was particularly influenced by masters from the Tosa and Kanô schools and employed techniques from both at different points in his career. Discourse at the time presented members of the Tosa School as "true" Japanese artists, whereas the Kanô School artists looked to Chinese subjects and ink brush techniques. In addition to training from the Tosa School-trained Murata, Obata studied with members of the Kanô School such as Hashimoto Gahô. Hashimoto, who had learned Song and Yuan dynasty traditions of Chinese monochrome ink painting, was a close associate of Ernest Fenollosa and a co-founder of the Japan Fine Arts Academy. Hashimoto was also a *nihonga* artist, who fused Edo-period Kanô School ink paintings with Western oil painting, a technique he had learned from European instructors. Obata started

---

8. *Tokyo Asahi Shimbun* (October 27, 1901).
9. Obata Chiura, "How Painting Is Taught in Japan," 1928.

absorbing various *nihonga* techniques from Yokoyama Taikan, Murata, and Hashimoto, who were formulating a "neo-traditional" genre in the 1890s and early 1900s.[10]

Obata learned Western techniques as well further qualifying his assignation as "pure Japanese." Rokuichi, who insisted on embracing Western plein air techniques, encouraged Obata to paint outdoors. Rokuichi directed his students to go outside and "paint what they saw," which differed from the instruction Obata received in Tokyo. Obata made visual diaries, sketching and painting the landscapes and people he saw. Teachers like Murata painted historical scenes, mostly images recreated from what were available in reproductions. Once he arrived in California, Obata's painting was most expressive when he painted while in nature. Obata's portfolio reveals that Japanese art is an amalgam of varying schools and techniques. Further, Obata's drawing upon this variety of wells to form his point of view reveals that his "traditional style" was distinctly modern.

Despite his growing success in Japan, Obata decided to leave for the United States in 1903. Unlike his peers, he later claimed that his reason for leaving was not for financial gain, but to broaden his horizons. Rokuichi could not understand his decision since Obata was already receiving critical success and awards. Confident after his move to Tokyo from Sendai, Obata wanted an adventure in the West while he was still young.[11] Though a committed *nihonga* artist, he intended to use the United States as a stepping-stone to study in Europe. Obata recalled that he convinced his brother to give him the money to travel to California by arguing that "the greater the view, the greater the art; the wider the travel, the broader the knowledge."[12] Another possible reason for going to the United States may have been to avoid military conscription. In 1903, relations between Japan and

---

10. John Clark, *Modern Asian Art*, (Honolulu, HI: University of Hawai'i Press, 1998), 73-87.
11. Shimojima Tetsurô, *Samurai to Kariforunia*, 45.
12. Kimi Kodani Hill, "Chiura Obata," *California Art Research*, First Series 120-160 (San Francisco: WPA Federal Art Project, 1937). *Topaz Moon: Chiura Obata's Art of the Internment* (Berkeley: Heyday Books, 2000), 3.

Russia were worsening over territorial rights in north China, and the outbreak of war seemed imminent.[13] Obata, who had left Sendai to avoid joining the military, may well have wanted to avoid conscription in the upcoming war.

Like many others boarding ships to cross the Pacific, Obata had every intention of one day returning to Japan rather than settling in the United States. Obata had no relatives or sponsors in the United States when he arrived in 1903. He only had a Tokyo church minister's letter of recommendation to a bishop at a San Francisco church.[14] Despite his lack of connections, Obata integrated himself into San Francisco's Japanese community. Obata's money from his family soon ran out and he worked at menial jobs to support himself. Every summer between 1909 and 1912, Obata traveled to southern California to work as a grape picker with other Japanese immigrants. Since he had come from an elite family and trained at top-level art schools, adjusting to his low social standing in California was a challenge. When he worked as a "school boy" (a Japanese term used for young servants), Obata recalled that on his first day of work he joined his employers at the dinner table and waited to be served.[15] He became quickly dissatisfied with the low pay and long hours, but he lacked connections to galleries and dealers that other Japanese artists coming to the United States had established. Obata entered the Mark Hopkins Art School (later the San Francisco Art Institute) to study Western painting, but soon left, complaining that the students were not serious enough and spent class time chatting.[16]

Trained professional artists, like Obata Chiura, who traveled abroad contended with ideas of Japanese art from the past. By the early 1900s, most Americans thought they knew what Japanese art

---

13. Shimojima Tetsurô, *Samurai to Kariforunia*, 46.
14. Obata Chiura: An Oral History. Interview by Masuji Fujii at the Obata home in Berkeley, 1965. Japanese American History Project, The University of California at Los Angeles Special Collections Library and the Department of Special Collections, Stanford University Libraries.
15. Ibid.
16. Shimojima Tetsurô, *Samurai to Kariforunia*, 67.

and style looked like. For some artists, shouldering Japanese cultural heritage abroad was a burden and limited their artistic expression. Not so for Obata, who was trained as a protector of those traditions. He had long studied, toiled, and lived to be a Japanese artist, trained in its techniques, media, and stylistic devices, and he was willing to make use of his skills to earn a living.

In addition to Obata, many Japanese artists left for the United States in the early years of the 20th century to sell their art. However, most were interested in *yôga*. Yoshida Hiroshi arrived in the United States around the same time as Obata. His goal was to sell art to earn money to travel to Europe, but Yoshida quickly discovered that he needed to create Japanese-style works for American customers. He was interested in studying European impressionists, but the American market did not want his versions of the French countryside. Americans were not interested in oil paintings by Japanese unless they featured dragons, chrysanthemums, and other Japanese motifs. After several selling trips to the United States, Yoshida abandoned oil painting and devoted his career to making woodblocks of Japanese scenery and famous sites from his world travels. During the 1930s, Yoshida became one of the leaders of the *shin-hanga* (new woodblock) movement, which was having its own revival in nationalist Japan.

Though he dabbled in *yôga* techniques in Japan, Obata abandoned Western style oil painting while in California." Instead, Obata followed in the footsteps of Japanese artists like Takahashi Katsuzô and Aoki Toshio, who had traveled to California during the late 1800s to sell Japanese-style works. Prior to moving to California, Takahashi Katsuzô had worked as an artist in Yokohama, a port town that had traded with the West since Japan's re-opening. In Yokohama, Takahashi painted handkerchiefs, shawls, and umbrellas with Japanese motifs to sell abroad, in what became known as the "art for export" market. Some American businessmen discovered that importing artists like Takahashi rather than their products was more cost effective.

Aoki Toshio also arrived in San Francisco during the 1880s to work as a commercial artist for the Deakin Brothers department store. After he moved to Pasadena in southern California, local elites hired Aoki to create traditional Japanese decorations during the "Japan craze" of the 1890s and early 1900s. Newspapers praised his "dragons and butterflies, ancient Mikado tragedies, and modern chrysanthemums."[17] Many of his works adorned the interiors of Arts and Crafts-style homes, an architectural design that fused Japanese and Western styles. Insisting on using only materials imported from Japan for his paintings (Obata imported his materials as well), Aoki nurtured his image as southern California's resident Japanese artist, which earned him fame and financial success. Californians remained interested in Japanese aesthetics for decades, providing artists like Aoki and Obata with ongoing commissions that gave him some financial security.

Obata's arrival in San Francisco coincided with racial violence targeting the Japanese community. Once the 1882 federal law passed that barred Chinese immigrants, the so-called Chinese Exclusion Act, San Francisco's labor groups turned their hostility to the Japanese newcomers. Because of their larger numbers, Japanese living on the West Coast confronted greater racial hostility than those living on the East Coast. During the first years of the twentieth century, the Hearst media empire, labor unions, and other agitators applied their anti-Chinese rhetoric and violence to the Japanese.[18] While Hearst's newspapers fanned the flames of racial hostility, American labor groups and legislators responded to Japanese immigrants with violence, racism, and a series of exclusion laws that made the Japanese into perpetual foreigners. When the Chinese Exclusion Act was renewed in 1902 and made permanent, anti-immigration groups in San Francisco called for a ban on Japanese immigrants as well. Nagai Kafû, who arrived in the United States the same year as Obata, wrote to a literary society in Japan, "The way Japanese people are ostracized in this place is almost unbelievable. It will be enough to tell you that no decent house or apartment will be rented to Japanese or Chinese." Another Japanese painter, Makino Yoshio, said that he fled San Francisco for

17. "Seen by Oriental Eyes: Our Civilization Viewed by a Representative of Another," *The Washington Post* (May 6, 1894).

18. Mae Ngai, Impossible Subjects: Illegal Aliens and the Making of Modern America (Princeton: Princeton University Press, 2004), 40.

London in 1897, because it was a "well known fact" that Californians hated Japanese.[19]

Owing to the hostility directed at their community during the 1900s, Japanese congregated in ethnic enclaves such as Japantown in San Francisco and Little Tokyo in Los Angeles, where they felt protected and had access to familiar foods and Japanese-language newspapers. But this isolation also aroused accusations that they were unable to assimilate to American culture. Writer Okina Kyûin, who lived in the United States from 1907 to 1924, wrote: "If there were no other Japanese beside me, nobody would call me Japanese. I am a 'Jap' because I am with them. If I left the Japanese, I would lose my identity as a 'Jap,' and I could find someone who does not see me as a 'Jap.'"[20] Kafû wrote that he preferred to be in Michigan, where there were not as many Japanese, instead of in the Washington State immigrant community, where he was treated like a "Jap."[21] Obata did not understand English and was only beginning to study at the Japantown Church, so he chose to remain safely within the Japanese community.

On April 18, 1906, a magnitude 7.9 earthquake in San Francisco created massive fires that nearly burned down the entire city. Escaping a falling chimney, Obata went out to document the disaster with a sketchbook. He went to Union Square, where he saw the St. Francis Hotel's guests screaming and sobbing with fear. As fires began to spread through the city, Obata returned to Japantown to help people evacuate. An army detail requisitioned Obata and eight other young men to help build sanitation holes; the others left, but Obata stayed on to finish the assignment.[22] For the next six months, Obata and other Japantown community members lived in tents in Lafayette Square. Prior to the earthquake, the Japanese community had lived next to Chinatown. Many of these residents lost their homes in the fire and moved south

19. Markino Yoshio, *A Japanese Artist in London* (Philadelphia: G.W. Jacobs, 1910).
20. Mitsuko Iriye, "Introduction," *American Stories* (New York: Columbia University Press, 2000), xix.
21. Mitsuko Iriye, *American Stories*, xvii.
22. Obata Chiura: An Oral History.

to Los Angeles. Gradually, the remaining Japanese moved their community west of the downtown area, though finding apartments willing to rent to them was difficult. Chinatown remained where it had always been.

The 1906 earthquake did little to temper the violence and discrimination targeting Japanese. Months after the earthquake, the San Francisco school board ordered the segregation of Asian students in public schools. Japan was asserting itself on a global stage, demanding to be treated on par with European powers. This discrimination did not coalesce with the Japanese understanding of its position in the hierarchy of nations. The Japanese military was expanding into East Asia and the idea of being lumped together with the Chinese made them indignant. Furthermore, Japan had just been victorious over Russia, a European power. The community was incensed that it should be targeted for abuse given its global position. President Theodore Roosevelt, who had negotiated the peace between Russia and Japan in 1905, was mortified by the San Francisco School Board's actions and rebuked the city's authorities. The debacle led to the so-called Gentlemen's Agreement of 1907, whereby Japan agreed not to issue passports to unskilled laborers wishing to enter the United States, and the latter agreed to end discriminatory practices. Japanese spouses and children were still allowed to join their husbands already working in the United States. Despite such diplomatic compromises, all Asian immigrants were ultimately excluded in the Johnson-Reed Immigration Act of 1924.

During his early years in San Francisco, Obata experienced racial hostility, including an episode that turned violent and landed him in jail.[23] He was a self-described "roughneck," who refused to submit to verbal and physical violence directed at him. Obata fought back. On one occasion returning from work, Obata became a target of violence by a group of construction workers. As he walked down the street, a group of eight men hurled racial epithets and one slapped him in the face. Obata did not back down and defended himself by hitting the man who spit on him and picking up a piece of iron railing to fend

23. Obata Chiura: An Oral History.

off the others. Police arrested Obata and charged him with attempted murder. He was eventually released from custody, but the men brought a lawsuit against him. Judge Timothy Fitzpatrick found it difficult to render a guilty verdict in a fight that was eight against one, when Obata was 135 pounds and five-feet, four inches tall and whose stated occupation was artist.[24] The Japanese Consulate used Obata's case as an example of anti-Japanese sentiment in San Francisco.

Despite facing racial violence, Obata's San Francisco life started to settle down, but he rarely left the safety of Japantown. If one stayed within its borders, a resident did not have to learn English. Many intended to return to Japan one day, so they did not see an immediate need to learn the language. As a result, many of the first-generation Japanese in the United States (*issei*) never learned English. Food markets, clothing stores, bookstores, inns, and bathhouses all catered to Japanese immigrants. Obata's social role in Japantown became more established, leading to more art-related work opportunities as people learned about his skills. He worked at a photography studio, hand coloring photographs for advertisements. Obata also made connections with the local Japanese-language newspapers and journalists. He produced thousands of illustrations between 1915 and 1927 as an illustrator for *Nichibei shimbun* (Japanese American News), *Shin Sekai* (New World), and *Japan* magazine. For the 1913 Portola Festival, a celebration of San Francisco's recovery from the 1906 earthquake, Obata was commissioned to decorate Union Square. (Labor groups objected to Japanese being allowed to participate in the project and attempted to sabotage Obata's projects.)[25] Soon his reputation as San Francisco's resident Japanese artist spread. Plans to travel and study in France were repeatedly postponed and then faded into the background.

Observing that Japantown's male population needed a pastime (men grossly outnumbered women), which provided a physical outlet as well as a way to engage with the white population, Obata

24. Obata Chiura: An Oral History.
25. Ibid.

established the Fuji Baseball Club in 1905 and served as its pitcher. Obata had had no interest in baseball while in Japan, a American import that was immediately embraced in 1872, but was impressed by a game he saw between Stanford and Waseda University (Waseda lost, 0-15). Baseball teams throughout Japan spread like wildfire as they did within California's Japanese immigrant communities. The games were also opportunities for fights, an activity that Obata happily joined in since childhood. The main event at Fuji games became the inevitable rumble that broke out. One Fuji game against a Chinese team quickly devolved into a rumble after Obata yelled a racial slur at the opposition. Police on horseback had to break up the fight, which the *San Francisco Chronicle* featured in a comic strip the next day. Perhaps craving more violent matches, he then established the Fuji Football team and played as its quarterback.

Obata's social life took a turn when he met Kohashi Haruko. Traveling alone, she had come to San Francisco from Fukuoka to study how to make Western-style clothing, intending to return to start a clothing school. Haruko was highly sought after by Japantown's single male population, because most arrivals were already destined for pre-arranged marriages. Haruko later recalled that when he promised to marry her, Obata insisted that they would soon go to Europe for him to study art and then back to Japan. She, too, wanted to travel to Europe. Haruko agreed to marry, but the pair never left the United States except for a temporary return to Japan in 1928. When they married in 1912 and she became pregnant the following year, they resolved to stay in California. Although he found work doing illustrations for newspapers and hand coloring photographs, Obata did not have enough money to make the trip and support a family. He was no longer interested in *yôga*, so a move to Europe lacked obvious benefits. Obata now had a family and a community that rooted him on the West Coast. Obata's "American adventure" would prove to be an enduring one.

One of Obata's most significant works during this period was "Mother Earth" painted in 1912. Although Obata had exhibited works in Tokyo and was an active member of *nihonga* societies, the necessity of earning a living in San Francisco left little time for fine art. The time spent on "Mother Earth" was a rare luxury. The painting's large scale (over six feet by five feet,) was a departure for him.[26] Obata used a new stylistic device—*môrô-tai*—in "Mother Earth," indicating his awareness of changes within the *nihonga* world. Influenced by Impressionism, the *môrô-tai* technique emphasized color gradations and shading more than line. *Môrô*—meaning "vague" or "hazy"—was initially a derogatory term invented by Japanese art critics to describe the new style.[27] One of Okakura Kakuzô's students, Hishida Shunsô, was a *nihonga* innovator credited with developing the *môrô-tai* technique. Obata was most likely exposed to Hishida's work when he was a student at the Japan Fine Arts Academy. It is also likely that Obata followed changes and experimentation in the *nihonga* world while living in San Francisco. Like Ishigaki, access to Japantown's imported art journals and newspapers ensured that Obata could stay abreast of Japan's artistic movements.

"Mother Earth," was a portrait of Haruko done soon after they married. In the painting, she was pregnant with their first child, Kimio, who was born five months after its completion. Despite her protests, Obata convinced Haruko to allow him to paint her in the nude; only the length of her hair, which reaches her knees in the image, provides any cover for her figure. Obata had long praised Haruko's hair and had forbidden her to cut it. A nude portrait was a bold choice for Obata, who had just been criticized for a paiting of a woman with a slightly open mouth. Painting a nude was not only new for him, but it had not yet become commonplace in Meiji Japan.[28] Obata's painting of his pregnant wife in a reflective, calm mood surrounded by nature presented her as being at peace unencumbered by their daily life. She walks through cypress trees along a forest floor strewn with flowers. Far from San Francisco's streets, the scene reveals Obata's longing for the serenity of nature. Although he reworked the painting in the

---

26. Seki Akio, *Amerika ni ikita nikkei gakatachi*, 24.
27. John Clark, *Modern Asian Art*, 78.
28. Shimojima Tetsurô, *Samurai to Kariforunia*, 111-113.

1920s, "Mother Earth" was a departure in Obata's career that he never replicated.

"Mother Earth" did not sell, and Obata did not paint nude figures again, but Haruko remained a central figure in Obata's creative and professional process. Throughout his career, Haruko was Obata's assistant, ordering supplies from Japan, cleaning his paints and brushes, and mixing his pigments. Interpreting his simple commands for "blue" or "light green" as he painted, Haruko could decipher exactly what shade and tone he needed. According to their granddaughter, Kimi Kodani Hill, Obata would wake Haruko at night if he decided he wanted to work on his painting and needed her assistance.[29] Later, Obata and Haruko exhibited together; she created *ikebana* (flower arrangements) to accompany his paintings.

By the early 1920s, Obata had begun to receive more art and illustration commissions. He had achieved a balance between Japanese aesthetics and Western sensibilities that appealed to an American audience. A 1928 article on Obata in *The Washington Post* claimed that he "interpreted America in the colors and lines of Japan," thereby creating a fusion between East and West that was popular among consumers and critics.[30] George Turner Marsh, who had lived in Yokohama and amassed a collection of Japanese arts and crafts, sought out Japanese artists based in San Francisco. Obata replaced Aoki Toshio as Marsh's source for Japanese-style illustrations. Marsh also hired Obata to illustrate his novel, *Lords of Dawn* (1916), a book featuring stories about Japanese samurai. Gump's department store, the City of Paris, the Emporium, and the Iwata Company all hired Obata to provide interior paintings for their Japanese arts and crafts showrooms. Obata became San Francisco's Japanese-themed interior decorator.

When an employer took Obata to see the San Francisco Opera's production of Puccini's "Madame Butterfly" set in Nagasaki, Obata insisted that the set was riddled with mistakes about Japanese culture.

29. Kimi Kodani Hill, *Topaz Moon*, 4.
30. "Won't Sell His Art." *The Washington Post*. February 12, 1928.

(Backdrops meant for spring showed chrysanthemums, an autumn flower. The soprano wore her kimono open. Obata told a friend that the set looked like a "mental hospital.")[31] In 1924, the opera company then asked Obata to do his own version, painting backgrounds for the production. He enlisted Haruko to help style the soprano's kimono and assist with costume changes throughout the performance.[32] Obata also fought off interfering stage directors who wanted to add lights around the Nagasaki bridge to indicate fireflies. ("There are no fireflies in the spring in Nagasaki.")[33] Critics lauded the production for being "authentic."[34] Obata remembered receiving a standing ovation for his designs, (he appeared onstage in his overalls), and that the opera received a patent for his backdrops.

Concerned that San Francisco's art world did not foster communication between Japanese and American artists, Obata established the East West art club in 1921— one year before Kuniyoshi, Ishigaki, and Shimizu opened the Gachôkai in New York.[35] Co-founded with artists Hibi Matsusaburô, Kôtoku Shiei, and Perham Nahl, the club aspired to facilitate an exchange between Asian and Western artists. In the years 1921 and 1922, the group of artists, which included Japanese, European, American, and Chinese members, hosted exhibitions and sponsored musical events. Its jury-free exhibitions were open to all who wished to participate. The San Francisco Museum of Art sponsored one of their events that featured nearly fifty different painters and musicians. Still-lifes and landscapes dominated the subject matter, evidence that California's art world was more conservative than New York's. Musicians and dancers performed a recital of "Sanbansô," while koto players performed *kagura*, dance and music associated with Shintô rituals. Japanese musicians also performed Beethoven and Schubert as well as scenes from Puccini's "Madame Butterfly," a Western fantasy of an exotic Japan that satisfied

31. Obata Chiura: An Oral History.
32. Shimojima Tetsurô, *Samurai to Kariforunia*, 133.
33. Obata Chiura: An Oral History.
34. Ibid.
35. Ibid.

the group's goal to fuse East and West. Although there were some non-Japanese members and the group aspired to be international, Japanese participants and content outnumbered the rest.

The East West Society's most lasting impact was to widen Obata's circle beyond Japantown's borders. Following its establishment, Obata went on nature excursions with friends outside of the Japanese community. Ever since he was a young boy living in Mizusawa along the Kitakami River, Obata's passion was fishing. He used it as a sort of meditation, watching how fish responded to the changing sun, clouds, rocks, and wind in their environment. Groups of artists and nature enthusiasts regularly traveled along the northern California coast. Its craggy rocks and cypress reminded Obata of Iwate's Sanriku coastline and a famed scenic location, Matsushima, near Sendai. Although he occasionally did sketches and watercolors of San Francisco city streets, most of Obata's paintings were of natural landscapes, what he called "Great Nature."

One friend, Worth Ryder, convinced Obata to join him on a two-month long hiking trip to Yosemite National Park and the Sierra Nevada in 1927. The trip became a turning point in Obata's life and career. A newly appointed art teacher at University of California, Berkeley, Ryder was a lifelong hiker, who often traveled with Obata to scenic areas in California. Ryder also invited Robert Boardman Howard, who had studied at the Art Students League with Kuniyoshi's instructor, Kenneth Hayes Miller, and was working at the time on a mural for the Ahwahnee Hotel in Yosemite. While in Yosemite, Obata made over one hundred pencil sketches, *sumi-e* brush paintings, and watercolors of the dramatic landscape. Howard described Obata in a 1931 letter to *Art and Artists* magazine as departing camp before the sun rose each morning to hike to a new location to paint and sketch in the sun, then hike back to camp before sundown, and repeat the process the following day. Obata also wrote journal entries about the trip coupled with poetry to capture the experience. Sitting around the campfire at night, Obata shared with Ryder and Howard his life philosophy: Artists, Obata declared, had the best life of all. As a result, they had a responsibility to be "cheerful and productive," and that it was "wrong to shed tears."[36] This, Howard insisted, was not mere idle talk. Obata seemed to practice his life philosophy, appreciating each moment. For his friends, Obata's company and approach to life was contagious. They became dedicated to supporting his art and career.

Obata returned from the Yosemite trip brimming with ideas, inspiration, and sketches from which to base large-scale paintings. The series he created led to his first solo San Francisco exhibition held at the Women's Gallery. Haruko provided *ikebana* to be displayed with the paintings. By 1928, her reputation as an *ikebana* artist had prompted a career as a flower arrangement teacher with loyal students scattered around the Bay Area.

One of the crucial elements of Obata's exhibition was his painting demonstrations. Watching Obata dressed in *kuro-montsuki* (formal black kimono) and using unfamiliar painting techniques captivated his audience. Haruko, as always, served as his assistant, handing him brushes, preparing paper, and mixing colors. Based on the popularity of his exhibitions and demonstrations in San Francisco, requests for similar shows came from around the country. When Ryder invited Obata to teach a painting class at UC Berkeley, students clamored for more sessions with him.

While Obata's career began to surge, Rokuichi fell ill and died in Sendai. Obata had intended to stay in the United States for only one year, but twenty-six years had passed. At the time of Rokuichi's death, Obata's friend and colleague, Perham Nahl, was in Japan. Obata introduced Nahl to his father by letter, so that he could meet and study with Rokuichi, but he had arrived in Yokohama just as Rokuichi died. Nahl returned to San Francisco, pressing Obata to return to Sendai to see Rokuchi's widow. On an annual basis, Obata consulted with Haruko to see when they should return to Japan, only to postpone the trip again. With four children ranging between one and sixteen years, and his eldest daughter having been born with intellectual disabilities, Obata struggled to save money for six tickets. Obata also might have

36. Obata Chiura, quoted in "Chiura Obata," California Art Research, 1st series (San Francisco: WPA Federal Art Project, 1937), 134.

postponed returning until he held a solo exhibition, so that he could return to Rokuichi feeling he had accomplished a milestone that his artist brother would appreciate.

The Obatas managed to return to Sendai in January 1929. Obata had left Japan when he was seventeen years old, during the Meiji era and before Japan's war with Russia. He arrived during Showa when he was forty-three years old and with a family in tow. Life in Sendai was difficult for the Obata family. Haruko hastened to find work teaching Western-style cooking and sewing to locals. Their eldest son, Kimio, was miserable in his high school and was allowed to return to the United States to prepare for college. Their youngest son, Gyo, was also unhappy. Unaccustomed to Tôhoku's harsh winter, Haruko and their children were freezing and all of them soon became ill. Obata understood how nature in the Tôhoku region was difficult: Not only did strong winds from neighboring Mt. Zao make Sendai's winters frigid, but famine, earthquakes, fires, and tsunamis also plagued the region. In 1896, when Obata was ten years old, a tsunami killed over 20,000 people along the Sanriku coast, only a few kilometers away from Sendai, and destroyed many thousands of homes. Obata's lifelong fascination with nature—his deep respect for its power as much as its beauty—was formed in Tôhoku, where nature was as cruel as it was beautiful.

As his family struggled to acclimate to their new lives in Sendai, Obata traveled to the coastline to sketch and to Tokyo to confer with members of Japan's art world. He also returned to his birthplace in Okayama, where he exhibited a few works while visiting his mother's grave. Sendai's prefectural library held a solo exhibition of his work that was well received and he sold a few pieces. Obata returned in 1929, the contest between *yôga* and *nihonga* for dominance within the art establishment had subsided and both groups were represented at government-sponsored exhibitions. Unlike many Japanese artists with established connections who went abroad, Obata did not maintain his relationship with the Japan Fine Arts Academy, where he had been associated before leaving for California. Nevertheless, they welcomed his return. Japanese newspaper articles praised Obata's paintings of California landscapes. While some voiced astonishment at his painting of his wife nude in "Mother Earth," as Obata feared that they might, his Yosemite watercolors were in high demand.[37]

Returning to Japan a few years after Obata, Kuniyoshi Yasuo did not enjoy the same commercial success as the former. Although he received substantial media coverage, Kuniyoshi was considered more of an oddity, and his personal history was given more attention than his artwork. Obata, however, created pieces that were familiar and accessible to the general Japanese public. Upon his arrival, he presented the emperor of Japan with one of his works, "Lake Basin in the High Sierra," which was exhibited in Ueno Park in 1930 after hanging in the imperial household. Ignoring Fujita Tsuguharu's recommendation to make an appearance at the imperial family, Kuniyoshi refused to go. He believed that *nihonga* was more popular in Japan at the time, when nationalism was on the rise as the army's military extended its reach in northern China. The success of Obata's Yosemite series might confirm Kuniyoshi's theory. But Obata was also savvier about navigating the *gadan* waters than Kuniyoshi; he entered juried group shows, where he was awarded prizes and sought out contacts within the academy. Kuniyoshi, on the other hand, focused on solo exhibitions, New York's primary means of exposure, though group shows that awarded prizes received more attention in Japan. Obata's previous experience working and showing in Japan had perhaps taught him how to operate in its art world, experiences that Kuniyoshi did not have.

Based on the positive response to his paintings, Obata approached the Takamizawa woodblock company to inquire about producing a series of Yosemite woodblocks based on watercolors that he brought with him from California.[38] In 1927 Takamizawa Tadao had visited

---

37. Shimojima Tetsurô, *Samurai to Kariforunia*, 185.
38. Obata pursued the Takamizawa family to produce his woodblocks; the publishing house's reputation, however, was mixed. Accused of refurbishing older prints, the Takamizawa seal became associated with forgery. The discovery was made when a forged print was discovered in Frank Lloyd Wright's collection. Janice T. Driesbach "Obata's Vision of Yosemite," *Obata's Yosemite: The Art and Letters of Chiura Obata from His Trip to the High Sierra in 1927* (Yosemite National Park: Yosemite Association, 1993), 51.

San Francisco, where he became acquainted with Obata's work and invited him to do the series. Particular about the touch, tone, and colors in the original paintings, Obata insisted that the printer make multiple, expensive changes to the colors and carvings. He rejected the first round of carvings for the series because he felt that the colors "looked like some place in Japan, not the High Sierras." He wanted a High Sierra pine tree, not a Japanese pine, he said. Even though a renowned carver, Kataoka, who had carved blocks for Hokusai, participated in the series, Obata still felt that the "High Sierra had gone on a trip to Japan," and did not reflect his vision of the California landscape. Obata often took the group of carvers and printers out to dinner to explain what the Sierras were like.[39] His ideas were specific, and it took the printer many attempts to capture his vision. In 1929 the stock market had crashed, and the world was plunging into economic depression, but Obata's exacting instructions were to be followed regardless of expense.

Obata's demands that the woodblocks have the look of his original watercolors were rewarded. The Yosemite woodblocks received critical praise and awards, including first prize in the 81st Japan Art Exhibition. Obata was an ascending *nihonga* artist when he left Japan and had established himself as a painter in California, but it was this series of thirty-five woodblocks made from his watercolors that solidified his reputation in both countries. Obata's use of *sumi* ink to outline the forms in his painting created a dramatic effect. It is unclear whether Obata had any prior experience working with woodblock printing while he was studying at the Tokyo School of Fine Arts. But when Obata returned, Japan was in the midst of a revival of interest in woodblocks led by artists like Yoshida Hiroshi, who had long since abandoned his *yôga* aspirations. He, too, found a lucrative market making woodblocks of scenes from his United States and European travels.

Despite his success, Obata and Haruko decided to return to California after living in Japan for two years. Ryder and Nahl had notified him that he could receive a position as an art instructor at UC

39. Janice T. Driesbach, *Obata's Yosemite*, 53-54.

Berkeley. With the global economic depression deepening, a steady salary was attractive to the Obatas. Another factor in Obata's decision to return was due to his children, who continued to be unhappy in Sendai. His eldest daughter, Fujiko, who had been born with disabilities, stayed with Haruko's family in Fukuoka. (Biographers note that neither Obata nor Haruko wrote or spoke about Fujiko, who died during the war.)[40]

When Obata returned with his family to California, his Yosemite woodblock series was exhibited widely, garnering as much success as it had in Japan. The *Los Angeles Times* praised the painstaking process required to make the prints.[41] Having brought Rokuichi's works back to California with him, Obata also held a "father and son" exhibition at the California Legion of Honor in 1931. Obata chose to show Rokuichi's *kakemono* and traditional Japanese pieces rather than his *yôga* works. Unaware of Rokuichi's study of Western techniques and of Obata's years of training, some critics claimed to identify "Occidental" tendencies in the son's work, whereas they asserted that his father was more "classically" trained in Japanese techniques.[42] Another critic claimed that Obata was "pure Nippon . . . with a suspicion here or there of Western influence."[43] Critics rewarded the pieces that they asserted were "Japanese," but remained skeptical of his adoption of other techniques that they interpreted as Western.[44] The works were well done, the critic noted, but "lacked some of the native charm" of his other works.

Whereas many artists struggled during the Great Depression, Obata's teaching position provided his family with financial stability. By 1932, he had a permanent position at the university. They moved from San Francisco to Berkeley to be closer to the campus. Obata, his wife, and two of his children helped to open the Obata Studio in Berkeley on Telegraph Avenue, where Haruko taught *ikebana* and

---

40. Shimojima Tetsurô, *Samurai to Kariforunia*, 194.
41. "Three Exhibits Reviewed." *Los Angeles Times*. (May 4, 1931).
42. *California Art Research*, 143.
43. Ibid, 149.
44. Ibid, 150.

he held private painting lessons. Obata's class on Japanese painting techniques was the only one of its kind in the United States, and people traveled to California to attend his sessions. Remarking on his teaching style, Obata claimed that he always taught his students "beauty." No one, he said, should pass through four years of college without being given the knowledge of beauty and "the eyes with which to see it."[45] Having embraced Rokuichi's methods as a painting instructor in Sendai, Obata often took his students on outdoors excursions, encouraging them to paint what they saw.[46]

Even after he moved to Berkeley with his family, Obata continued to socialize and carouse in San Francisco's Japantown when he had spare time. Although he had many beloved friends that were not Japanese, it was in Japantown that Obata felt most comfortable. Like many first-generation Japanese, Obata never became completely fluent in English. (Haruko recalled that his pronunciation was difficult for his students to follow at times. When he was elderly, he stopped speaking in English altogether.) Whether he wanted to or not, and he never indicated that he did, Obata did not eschew his Japanese identity in the decades that he lived in California. Critics did not grapple with how to identify Obata as a Japanese or an American artist. Obata was always Japanese, and he was always a Japanese artist. Haruko and Obata were unlike their children, who identified as *nisei* (second generation) and held U.S. citizenship, but it would not be until after the war that they legally received theirs. Furthermore, Obata was a *nihonga* "Japanese style" artist, identifying himself more with Japan in his artwork than second wave artists like Kuniyoshi and Ishigaki who worked on the East Coast. He taught his students Japanese traditions and techniques, presenting himself as a product of Japanese training. He wore kimono when he conducted his painting demonstrations. At a 1934 exhibition of his paintings at the UC Berkeley International House, Haruko gave demonstrations of Japanese-style flower arrangement, while Japanese

45. Obata Chiura, *Topaz Moon: Art of the Internm*ent (Berkeley: Heyday Books, 2000), 7.
46. Shimojima Tetsurô, *Samurai to Kariforunia,* 27.

women in kimono served tea.[47] Although he had lived in California for all his adult life, Obata presented himself as a Japanese national and cultural ambassador.

With the four artists thus far described in this book, it is possible to see the agency each had in determining their identities, indicating how arbitrary and fluid the assignation of categories can be. Though context and the art market's ebbs and flows contributed to defining them, Obata, Kuniyoshi, Ishigaki, and Shimizu had considerable control over how they were interpreted and received. Shimizu's many years in the United States had no bearing on his self-indentification as Japanese. He would never identify as an American artist, much less as a Japanese-American. Less definite were Obata, Kuniyoshi, and Ishigaki, who also lived decades in the United States, but their national identification varied. For Kuniyoshi, he was an American artist and a Japanese national, who aspired to U.S. citizenship and its attendant rights. Ishigaki was a leftist artist first; his identification as American or Japanese was immaterial to his art or person. Obata presented himself as a Japanese artist and national, but eventually applied for citizenship for his children's benefit. Identity is not innate, nor is it simply assigned by external structures. Not only can it shift over time depending on multiple factors, but the person can also steer its direction. For Japanese west of the Mississippi like Obata and – as we will see –Miyatake, war made blurry lines much sharper.

Obata watched Japan's aggressive expansion on to the East Asian continent with trepidation. After years of conflict, he was aware that the status of Japanese in California was tenuous. Hostility toward the community steadily reemerged when Japan left the League of Nations in 1933. Obata confided in his friends and colleagues that his existence, along with the larger community of *issei* and Japanese-Americans, became more vulnerable as Japan's militarism accelerated. Obata's fears were prescient. Wilder Bentley, a poet, calligrapher, and colleague at UC Berkeley translated a poem with Obata by the eighteenth-century writer and philosopher, Tanso Hirose:

---

47. *California Art Research*, 138.

Open the rustic bamboo gate at dawn.
All around us lies the frost, white as snow,
Until 'tis thawed by ten thousand summer suns.
'Tis bitter cold this morning.
Thus you and I had better learn to love one another.
You'd better fetch some water at the stream.
Whilst I gather kindling wood.

Bentley interpreted the poem as Obata's need to express the importance of reconciling former friends who had become political enemies. He believed that Obata shared the poem with him to communicate his sense of foreboding, and the poem became a kind of aesthetic and ethical pact between the two men as tensions between the United States and Japan grew.[48] Despite decades living in California, (Obata was fifty-seven-years old when WWII broke out), he knew that Americans would place him firmly on Japan's side of the conflict.

Obata first heard of the proposal to remove ethnic Japanese during a university faculty meeting before the bombing of Pearl Harbor. He was instructed to keep the conversation confidential. Disturbed by the term "evacuate," Obata voiced his disagreement and an argument ensued with a representative sent from Washington DC.[49] You evacuate people in the event of a natural disaster, he argued, but what was being proposed was an "artificial" evacuation. The government officials argued that removal of Japanese would prevent "lynchings." After the December 7 attack on Pearl Harbor, General John L. DeWitt, who was charged with West Coast security, stated that even those Japanese who were second and third generation and "Americanized," had "racial strains (that) were undiluted." DeWitt charged that they, too, would be ready to "fight and die" for Japan.[50]

48. Kimi Kodani Hill, *Topaz Moon*, 10-11.
49. Chiura Obata: An Oral History.
50. From Lt. Gen. J.L. DeWitt's letter of transmittal to the Chief of Staff, U.S. Army, June 5, 1943, of his Final Report; Japanese Evacuation from the West Coast 1942.

Obata understood that his family was at risk. He approached UC Berkeley officials to ask for help and counsel. Friends had sought to make a home for the Obata family east of the Mississippi River and outside the western exclusion zone, but they were unsuccessful. UC Berkeley's administrators explored housing the Obata's at Ansel Adam's camp in Yosemite.[51] Instead, Obata decided to "stay with the Japanese community."[52]

When President Franklin Delano Roosevelt signed Executive Order 9066 a few months later, the Obatas were forced to relocate to the Tanforan Assembly Center, a repurposed horseracing track and stadium in South San Francisco, used as a temporary holding station for ethnic Japanese. Haruko later complained that Obata insisted on painting constantly up to the moment they left for Tanforan, and she was left to handle the moving preparations on her own.[53] Obata's painting that night was his emotional crutch in the face of catastrophe. A colleague stored Obata's paintings on the Berkeley campus for the duration of the war, but most of their belongings including objects from their store were "dumped" or sold at low prices.[54] Many other Japanese artists who were forced into the camps did not have access to such storage facilities or sufficient notice to plan for safeguarding their works, which were lost together with their other possessions. Obata painted the rain falling on the Bay Bridge as his wife, two sons, and daughter traveled by bus to the relocation camp. The painting became the first of a visual diary that Obata made to document his and other prisoners' experiences.

For many Americans, the nature of the attack on Pearl Harbor seemed to confirm their prejudices that the Japanese were uncivilized and inscrutable, because they defied conventional warfare rules. The U.S. war against Japan became racially charged. Executive Order 9066 was purported to protect the western United States from domestic aid for Japanese attacks, but the majority of the prisoners were U.S. citizens

51. Chiura Obata: An Oral History.
52. Kimi Kodani Hill, *Topaz Moon*, 15.
53. Ibid.
54. Chiura Obata: An Oral History.

and could not speak a word of Japanese. All ethnic Japanese—70,000 American-born Japanese and 40,000 Japanese nationals—living on the West Coast were interned in ten camps scattered throughout California, Utah, Wyoming, and Arizona deserts. Unlike Kuniyoshi and Ishigaki, who lived in New York, Obata and other Japanese artists were confined in these camps for the duration of the war.

Before his transfer to the Topaz camp in Utah, Obata sketched people waiting in the cramped enclosure at the Tanforan Assembly Center. They arrived dressed in their best clothes, hoping to make a positive impression on the authorities. At its peak, Tanforan held 8,000 internees waiting for several months to be moved to their assigned camps. Heavy rains made the area knee deep in mud. Assured that they would be provided with bedding, the internees arrived to find piles of hay to stuff into cases. Obata recalled watching schoolchildren play hide-and-go-seek with armed guards.

Obata felt that it was crucial to provide a place for young people to learn to make up for the "intolerable sin" of forcing people to move from their homes into horse stables.[55] Recognizing that interminable waiting would cause psychological damage on all internees, Obata approached the camp administrators to start an art school only three days after his arrival. He wanted the school to be a "place of normalcy" for the prisoners as well as to provide a "sense of calmness."[56] In essence, Obata wanted to use art as a form of therapy for internees undergoing extreme psychological stress. A severe rainstorm broke out on the school's first day, May 25, 1942, and Obata was convinced that no one would come, but went to the designated mess hall in case someone did. He found two small girls waiting, drenched with rain; their parents had prepared them and sent them off to study.

Friends, former UC Berkeley students, and sympathizers donated money and supplies to help start the school. Visitors passed art supplies through holes in a chain link fence that surrounded the center. He organized sixteen other instructors, many with graduate

---

55. Obata Chiura: An Oral History.
56. Kimi Kodani Hill, *Topaz Moon*, 38.

degrees, to teach over twenty art classes, which included fashion and interior design, mechanical and architectural drafting, as well as oil, *sumi*, and watercolor painting.[57] The camp's administrative funds were not used to support the school, because students paid a fee (50 cents per child and one dollar per adult). Eventually, over 600 students ranging in ages from six to seventy years old attended classes, which were conducted from morning to night, five days a week. Many of the students had never taken art instruction before joining the school. Local newspapers wrote articles about the "Tanforan Art School," which also had an art exhibition at Mills College in 1942.

The Obatas stayed at Tanforan for five months, before they were transferred to the Topaz War Relocation Center in central Utah. As the family rode the train from California, Obata sketched the scenic beauty. As he learned to escape San Francisco's violence and prejudice by going on nature excursions and fishing, Obata found serenity and calm in the rivers, mountains, and fields of sage seen from the train window. While Haruko lamented how old and slow the train was as it traveled, Obata continued to sketch fellow passengers, even their exercise breaks when they were allowed to leave the train. After weeks on the train, the group arrived at Topaz.

As he documented the aftermath of San Francisco's 1906 earthquake, Obata kept a visual record of the internment experience, from sketches of Tanforan's muddy stables to the Topaz camp's dust storms. He captured the internee's daily life: medical examinations, administrator's speeches, funerals, mess hall meals, bus arrivals with newcomers, and makeshift classrooms. Cameras were forbidden to the Japanese during the war years, so Obata's drawings provide documentation from a camp inhabitant's point of view. He was also able to capture a wider variety of daily life scenes than a heavy camera requiring a flash. (Dorothea Lange took most of her photographs outside, because she feared invading the internees' privacy and didn't like to use a flash).[58] Guards accompanied

57. Kimi Kodani Hill, *Topaz Moon*, 40.
58. Linda Gordon and Gary Okihiro. *Impounded: Dorthea Lange and the Censored Images of Japanese American Internment.* (W.W. Norton & Company. 2006), 24.

photographers, including Lange, dictating what shots they could or could not take, and their prints were censored. The diary sketchbook became a way for Obata to process what he saw and experienced while at Tanforan and Topaz, but it was also documentation. In some instances, he recorded what residents relayed to him and not only what he witnessed. One of these drawings depicted the shooting of internee Wakasa Hatsuki, who had been walking his dog near the fenced perimeter. The man did not hear the sentry's verbal warning and was shot. Obata's image shows Wakasa buckling over with the impact of the bullet while his dog jumps in front of him. (Obata was recovering in the hospital at the time of the incident.)[59]

Obata had the remarkable ability to find solace in nature despite being confined in the harshest conditions. He tried to console others, who were distressed by the constant sand storms, that they should "just wait . . . that's the way to deal with Great Nature." He encouraged his children not to give into their emotions, but to appreciate the experience regardless of "how deep [their] hell."[60] Like many internees, both he and Haruko endeavored to improve their cabin surroundings by building a garden, gathering rocks, trees, and shrubs. They carved pieces of wood to make *ikebana* vases. Internees often searched for materials found around the camp to create crafts and lend some character to their bleak barrack existences. Obata credited a shared "spirit" that inspired the Japanese to plant gardens and clean their houses.

Writing to a friend about his ordeal, he described the Topaz scenery as beautiful.[61] He was unfamiliar with the visual allure of the desert and found a new beauty in its "enormous bleakness." Years later, Obata ironically remarked that without the camp, it would have "cost him a lot of money" to visit such a place with its grand views.[62] But Obata's appreciation of his surroundings in the face of misery was consistent with his life philosophy. Despite the humiliation of being a prisoner in both freezing and scorching conditions while being choked

59. Kimi Kodani Hill, *Topaz Moon*, 95.
60. Obata Chiura: An Oral History.
61. Kimi Kodani Hill, *Topaz Moon*, 71.
62. Obata Chiura: An Oral History.

by constant dust storms, he saw the desert location as a magical place of natural beauty. Unfamiliar desert colors, which he called "beyond description," inspired new works reminiscent of his series of Yosemite watercolors.[63] His paintings revealing the beauty of the desert landscape represent an alternative to the more common images of camp surroundings as exclusively barren, bleak, and dusty.[64] Obata was not creating idealized versions of a hellish experience, but he insisted on capturing Topaz in its totality. He even found himself feeling "profound gratitude" for his setting: the Rocky Mountains with snow on its peaks, the Sevier Desert, and Topaz Mountain. On occasion, he included the barracks with mountains and moonscape in the distance. His reverence for 'Great Nature' in his painting and writing supported Obata while living behind barbed wire in the Topaz desert.

Immediately upon arriving at Topaz, Obata set out to continue the Tanforan art school by establishing one at Topaz. By the end of 1942, the school had 3,250 students studying music, flower arrangement, sewing and knitting, English, as well as arts and crafts.[65] Finding supplies and a budget for all the students was a "stomachache" for Obata, not to mention his watercolor paints freezing during winter months.[66] His busy schedule as director and instructor for the school and his ongoing documentation of the camps and landscape paintings kept Obata preoccupied. Using crepe paper for flowers, gathered sticks and rocks, and sagebrush, Haruko, too, tried to allow for some prewar continuity by teaching *ikebana*.

A group in Cambridge, Massachusetts sponsored a "Relocation Center Art Exhibit," which welcomed art from ten evacuation camps. Representatives of the Japanese-American Citizens League went to Washington, DC and presented First Lady Eleanor Roosevelt, who

---

63. Obata Chiura: An Oral History.
64. Artist Kobashigawa Hideo claimed that Manzanar was a "paradise" compared to his life during the Depression. At Manzanar he did not have to work – he had nothing to do, but paint. Shimojima Tetsurô "Hideo Kobashigawa's World: A Biographical History," Hideo Kobashigawa Retrospective (Naha: 2000).
65. Kimi Kodani Hill, *Topaz Moon*, 70.
66. Obata Chiura: An Oral History.

had publicly called for fair treatment of American-born Japanese, with one of Obata's paintings. His desert landscape included a watchtower and fencing, not allowing the First Lady to be ignorant of the artwork's setting. (Photographers were not allowed to show watchtowers or barbed wire in their images.) She hung the painting in her office until her death.

Friends continued to appeal to the government for the Obata's early release from Topaz. In 1943 the couple were allowed to visit Brigham Young University to hold lectures. When asked to sign a loyalty oath to the United States, the Obatas signed the document. Haruko recalled that they made their decision to align themselves with their American home, because their children could never move back to Japan even if their parents could. Tension among internees grew between those who signed the loyalty oath and those who rejected it. To some internees, Obata's leadership position and choice to sign the loyalty oath made him appear complicit with the U.S. government. Rumors spread that he was a U.S. government spy. One night, Obata was ambushed at Topaz and put in the hospital for severe head wounds. He was unable (or unwilling) to identify his attackers. The incident convinced camp directors that he needed to be relocated out of the camp to ensure his safety.

When Obata and his family were allowed to leave Topaz, Obata's longtime friend and fellow art teacher Hibi (George) Matsusaburô continued to teach classes at the art school in Obata's stead. Hibi was a well-known member of San Francisco's Japanese community as a language teacher for *nisei* children and a leader in cultural events within the community. As an instructor at the California School of Fine Arts in San Francisco during the 1930s, Hibi also had extensive training in art instruction.[67] Hibi's works were more expressionistic

67. Hibi had entered the California School of Fine Arts, first as a student in 1919, and then later worked as an instructor. He modeled his art school at Topaz after the curriculum at the California School of Fine Arts. Hibi's work and life revolved around art school: in addition to working as a teaching assistant, he also worked at the school as a gardener, custodian, and store clerk. He met his wife, Hisako, who attended the School of Fine Arts between 1926 and 1929. Continuing his teaching position at the camp was crucial for Hibi's ability to survive the experience.

than Obata's and he used oil on canvas rather than *nihonga* techniques. Hibi's Topaz paintings emphasized less the area's natural beauty, and more the harsh conditions and the vulnerability of its residents. He depicted coyotes stalking the barracks in the moonlight and lonely figures trudging through the deep Utah snow.

After being released from Topaz in 1943, Obata, Haruko, and their daughter moved to St. Louis, where Gyo had been allowed to continue to study architecture at Washington University. At first Kimio had to stay behind, but he was eventually released as well. Their stay in St. Louis was a lonely period. They lived in a small town where there were no other Japanese. Obata was able to find some work at a commercial art firm. As soon as the war ended, Obata and Haruko moved back to Berkeley, where he was able to continue teaching art at the university. Kimio stayed in St. Louis to open an art studio and then later opened a second branch in Tokyo. Gyo received his architecture degree in 1945 with high honors and eventually co-founded an architecture firm, Hellmuth, Obata, and Kassabaum (HOK), in St. Louis. HOK became an internationally renowned firm and Haruko lived to visit her son's design at the National Air and Space Museum in Washington D.C. After the war, the Obatas committed their lives to building a cultural bridge between the United States and Japan that they hoped would forever preserve peace.

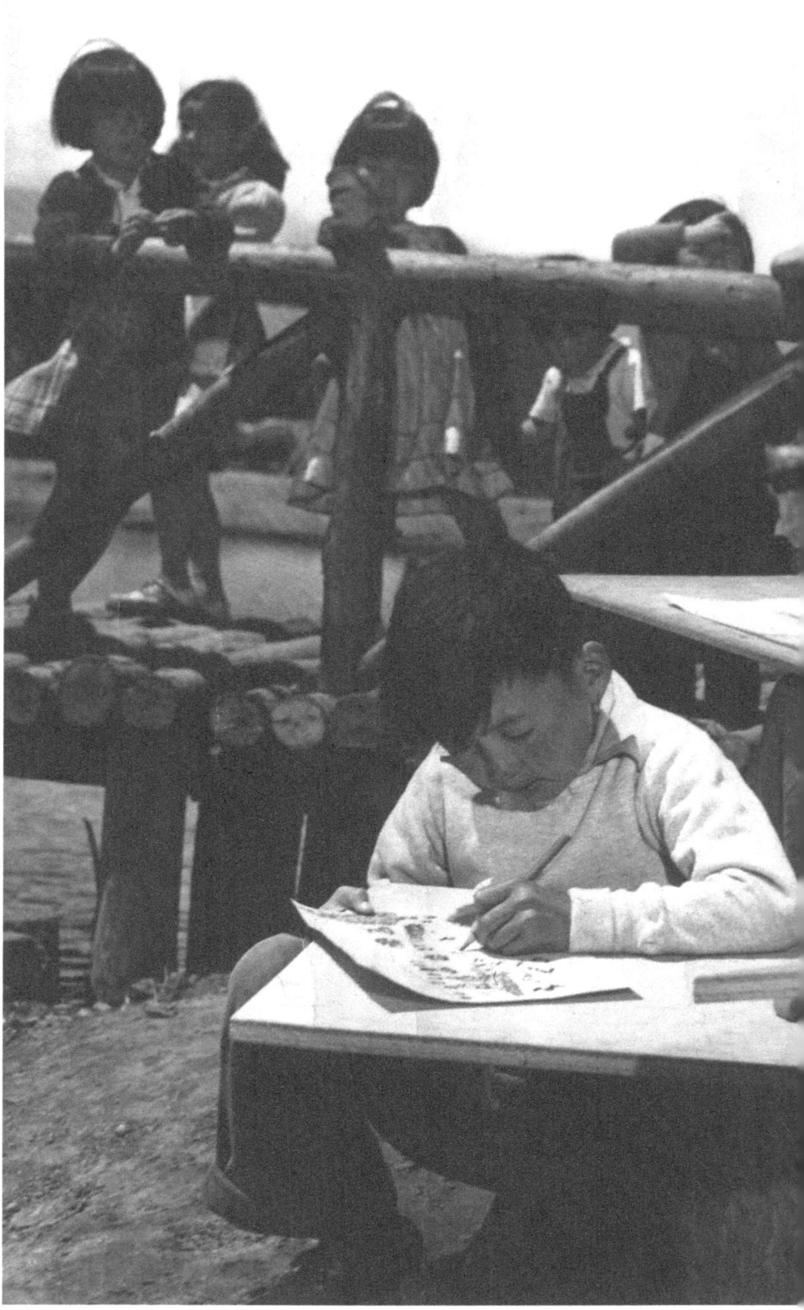

Obata Chiura teaching a children's art class at Tanforan Art School, 1942. Chiura Obata papers, 1891-2000. Archives of American Art, Smithsonian Institution.

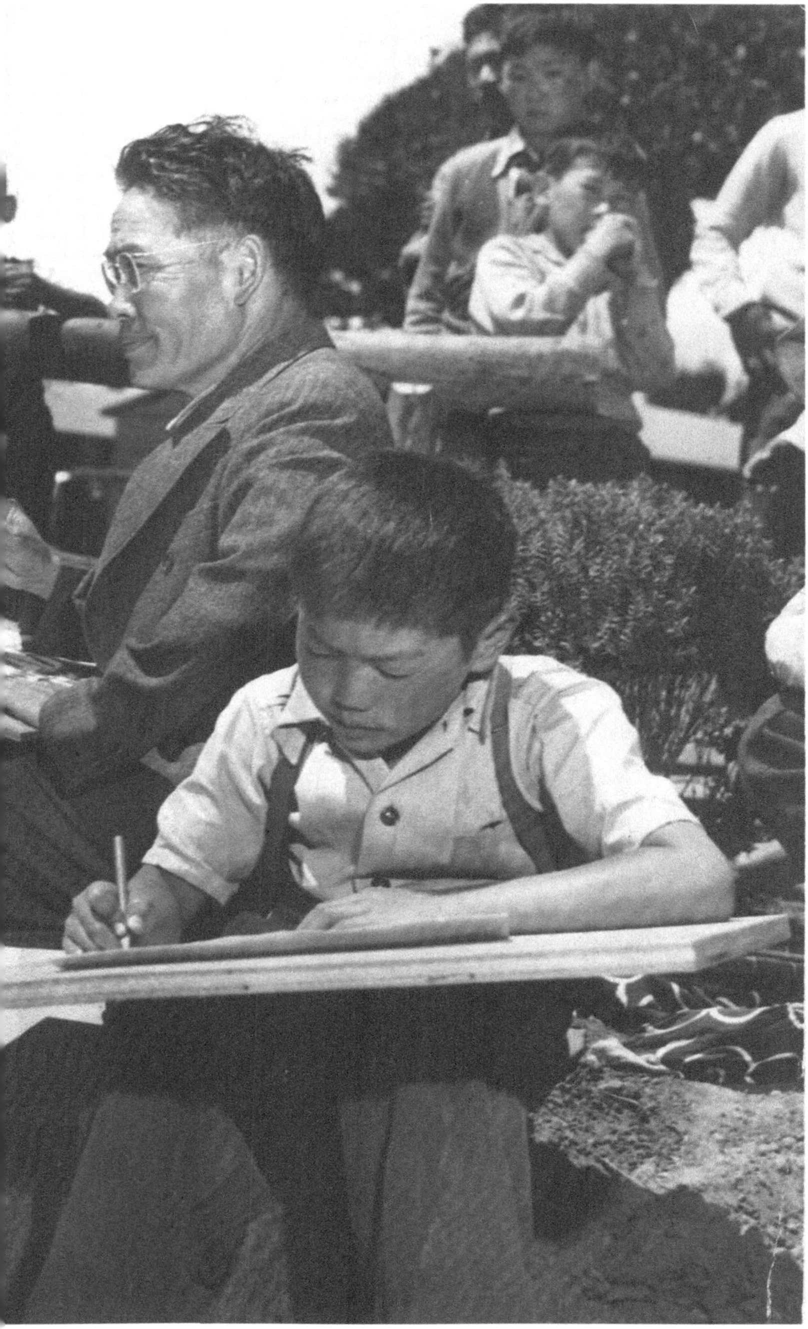

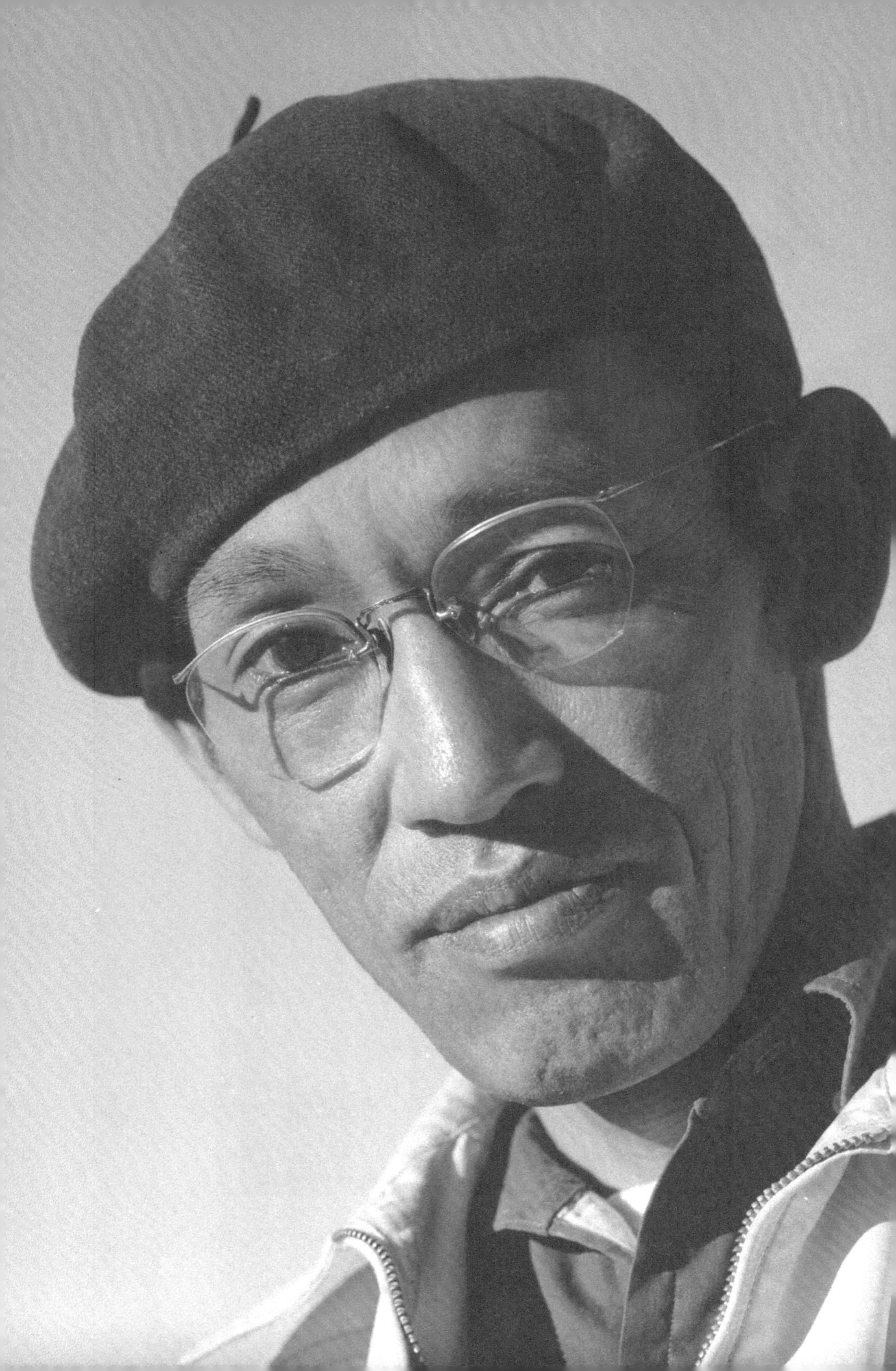

Chapter Five
Miyatake Tôyô
In Praise of Shadows

Carey McWilliams described Los Angeles as an "island on the land," America's remote corner bordered by mountains and ocean, and thriving on its own fantasies. During the first half of the twentieth century, real estate boosters and railroad magnates enticed Midwesterners to venture even farther west to southern California, where oranges dropped from trees in wintertime. Everything in Los Angeles, McWilliams wrote, was manufactured, a "gigantic improvisation." Like many of its plants and trees, water and energy, people, too, had to be imported. And people came. By 1920, Los Angeles had surpassed San Francisco as the largest city in California. Unlike New York City, where the majority immigrant population was a mix of northern and southern Europeans, Los Angeles hosted people from the Pacific Rim: Mexicans, Chinese, Filipino, and Japanese. As Los Angeles expanded, so did its Japanese community: In 1890, there were 58 Japanese living in southern California, but by 1940, there were nearly 50,000.

(Opposite): Miyatake Tôyô by Ansel Adams, 1943. Adams, Ansel, 1902–1984. Manzanar War Relocation Center photographs. Library of Congress.

Little Tokyo, McWilliams wrote, was an island within that island.[1] Los Angeles' Japanese immigrant population was marginalized from political and economic power and was forced to be self-sufficient. Japanese immigrants, many of whom traveled south after San Francisco's 1906 earthquake, settled in an area located between the downtown shopping district and Chinatown, making Little Tokyo another thriving ethnic enclave like San Francisco's Japantown. In 1928, builders completed the Los Angeles city hall and its 32 floors towered over its Little Tokyo neighbor. The center of Los Angeles political power was close in proximity, but Little Tokyo was contained within its own colony.

Most Japanese in southern California lived in Los Angeles, and almost all of these lived in Little Tokyo. Photographs taken in Little Tokyo often show the building towering in the background as a *hinomaru*, the Japanese national flag, flies outside shop windows. It became a bustling residential and commercial district with racial covenant laws and hostile whites guarding its borders. Living outside of Little Tokyo was not an option for Japanese. Los Angeles realtors often advertised that they did not sell to Japanese (or Mexicans), so they assured prospective white customers that racial segregation was maintained.[2] Scenes of 1920s Little Tokyo show streets teeming with Japanese; no white faces can be seen in the crowds. When artist Takehisa Yumeji visited California, traveling from San Francisco to Los Angeles to sell his works, he noted in his diary that he was relieved to arrive in Little Tokyo, where he felt more comfortable and safer.[3] Little Tokyo's resident artists, however, endeavored to traverse these borders and engage with a larger art network.

Japanese artists, writers, musicians, and dancers added to Little Tokyo's vitality. While it had its share of accomplished painters,

---

1. Carey McWilliams, *Southern California: An Island on the Land* (Salt Lake City: Peregrine Smith Books, 1946, 1973), 321.
2. Sheri Bernstein, "Selling California, 1900-1920." "Contested Eden, 1920-1940." *Made in California: Art, Image, and Identity, 1900-2000*. (Los Angeles County Museum of Art University of California Press, 2001), 105.
3. Tsurutani Hisashi, *Yumeji no mita Amerika*, (Tokyo: Shin Jinbutsu orai-sha, 1997), 122.

photography was one of the community's most active art forms. As Edward Weston and Margrethe Mather founded the Camera Pictorialists of Los Angeles followed by San Francisco's f/64 group, Japanese also established camera clubs to support their work. They went on photography expeditions, held exhibitions, published catalogs, and submitted images to international expositions. Most of the club members were amateur art photographers, but some owned photography supply stores and operated portrait studios. The local Japanese-language newspaper, the *Rafu Shimpo: Los Angeles Japanese Daily News,* supported their efforts by hosting juried exhibitions and publishing catalogs. In addition to local media attention, many of Los Angeles' Japanese photographers were celebrated in the most respected international photography journals of the time.

Little Tokyo's camera clubs—along with those that emerged in Hawaii, San Francisco, and Seattle—were an extension of amateur photographers in Japan, where middle class interest triggered a boom in camera consumption.[4] Predominantly male, they bought equipment, studied "how-to" manuals, took pictures, developed film, followed photo-journals, and attended traveling exhibitions. It was an expensive hobby, but one that captivated many middle class consumers. Their images were not mere snapshots of families on vacation, but conscious explorations of photography as a fine arts medium. Photography supplies, cameras, and photo-journals from Japan were available in Little Tokyo, where photographers explored diverse genres including pictorialism, realism, and modernism. Popular among Little Tokyo's photographers, pictorialism, a style that emphasized beauty and artistry, flourished in Japan during the early twentieth-century and retained widespread popularity until World War II.

Miyatake Tôyô was one of modernism's photography pioneers. He owned a photography studio in the center of Little Tokyo, working as a commercial photographer. He reserved time to create more avant-garde and fine art prints at night. Miyatake was fascinated by light

---

4. See Kerry Ross *Photography for Everyone: The Cultural Lives of Cameras and Consumers in Early Twentieth-Century Japan.* Stanford University Press, 2015.

and shadow and how they interacted. A favorite among dancers, he captured them in motion, mid-dance, rather than posing them. Like Obata Chiura, Miyatake was interned during World War II, but at Manzanar instead of Topaz. Known today primarily for his Manzanar photographs, Miyatake experimented with more abstract images prior to internment. Once interned, he set aside his more conceptual work to document the internees' daily life and the landscape. His photojournalistic approach continued after the war. Working for the *Rafu Shimpo* and other Japanese periodicals, Miyatake photographed visiting Japanese luminaries, local events, and celebrations. He put his fine artwork aside.

Miyatake Tôyô was fourteen-years old in 1909 when he left Kagawa in Shikoku for Los Angeles, where his father owned a confectionary store in Little Tokyo. Like many young Japanese in California—including every artist featured in this book except for Shimizu—he worked in the Central Valley's vineyards and orchards. He wanted to become a painter, but his mother insisted that he would not be able to make a living. Abandoning his initial enthusiasm for painting, he joined Harry Shigeta's photography school when he was twenty years old.

Shigeta had arrived in the United States in 1903, when he was sixteen, and studied art and photography in St. Paul's. After graduating from the Minnesota school, he moved to New York and exhibited his photographs. When he opened his Los Angeles studio and school in 1918, Shigeta had been taking photographs for almost a decade. Photography studios were in high demand in Little Tokyo. Shigeta's photography experience introduced technical skills to his students, teaching composition as well as printing. Photographs were used to stay connected with relatives in Japan and to entice future wives ("picture brides" sent their versions in exchange) to come to California. Photographs were essential for marking special occasions.[5] Shigeta, who also worked as a part-time magician, was

5. Karin Higa, "Little Tokyo betwen the Wars," *Asian American Art: A History, 1850-1970*, edited by Gordon Chang. (Palo Alto: Stanford University Press, 2011.)

skilled at touching up photographs. After he closed his Little Tokyo studio, Shigeta worked in Hollywood applying his skills to movie stills before moving to Chicago, where he became a successful advertising photographer.

As a pictorialist photographer, Shigeta instilled in his students the importance of the printing process as well as how an image could be manipulated in the darkroom. Often using a soft lens for a moody effect, pictorialists manipulated the negative and printing process. Pictorialists were committed to photography as a medium to express beauty. They did not set out to document reality, but to use the camera as an art tool. Spearheaded by Fukuhara Shinzô, who became the founder of Shiseido cosmetics, pictorialism was popular in Japan. Fukuhara studied pharmacology at Columbia University in 1908, when Alfred Stieglitz's 291 Gallery exhibited pictorialists like Alvin Langdon Coburn and Edward Steichen.[6] When Fukuhara returned from Paris to Tokyo in 1913 with his series of atmospheric landscapes taken along the Seine River, he demonstrated how photography could be as expressive as painting. Influenced by Hollywood and cinematography, pictorialism spread among Los Angeles photographers. Edward Weston, an advocate of pictorialism in his early career, announced to the College Women's Club in Los Angeles in 1916 that photography was a form of artistic expression—not for commercial purposes.[7] What defined a pictorialist photo versus a modernist one eventually blurred until the "pictorialist" genre became an all-purpose designation that indicated the image was simply created as art.[8]

When Harry Shigeta sold his studio and school to work in Hollywood film studios, he introduced Miyatake to Edward Weston for further

---

6. Given his proximity to the gallery, childhood interest, and pursuit of photography as a hobby, (his father gave him a camera as a present in 1896), it is highly probable that Fukuhara visited the 291 Gallery.
7. Michael Dawson, "Edward Weston: The Transformation of Fine Art Photography," *LA's Early Moderns: Art/Architecture/Photography.* (Los Angeles, CA: Balcony Press, 2003), 248.
8. Dennis Reed, *Making Waves: Japanese American Photography, 1920-1940.* (Los Angeles, CA: Japanese American National Museum, 2016), 14.

study. Miyatake and other Little Tokyo photographers started visiting Weston's studio in rural Tropico (now part of Glendale) for lessons and to assist him in his darkroom. Shigeta's experience and technique established Miyatake's foundation, but Edward Weston, his subsequent mentor, had even greater influence on Miyatake. At the time, Weston was collaborating with Margrethe Mather, whose aesthetic was inspired by Japanese arts and crafts. Photographs of nudes standing in front of gold screens, hands holding fans, and shadowy figures with simple flower arrangements featured in many of Mather's well-known images from the time. (Mather sought to achieve an "uncluttered Japanese atmosphere" in her home/studio on Bunker Hill, within walking distance to Little Tokyo.)[9] Mather became a frequent judge of *Rafu Shimpo's* photography competitions and attended gallery openings. In addition to Mather and Weston, other artists ventured into the Japanese community to find sources of inspiration. Weston and Mather showed Miyatake their collection of Japanese woodblock prints, which Weston recommended that Miyatake emulate, much as Hamilton Easter Field was doing with Kuniyoshi at the same time. Miyatake later said that he had never seen an *ukiyo-e* print before Weston showed him one.[10]

Like San Francisco, Japanese art continued to capture the imaginations of Angelenos long after it became unfashionable in New York. Photographers like Arthur Kales participated in Japanese Camera Pictorialists of California meetings and visited Miyatake's studio.[11] In 1915, the Los Angeles Museum of History, Science, and Art exhibited 300 Japanese woodblock prints including those by Ando Hiroshige and Kitagawa Utamaro; large numbers of the city's general public attended the show as well as local artists. Compared to artist communities in New York, however, Little Tokyo's artists were isolated within their community. There has never been a "Japantown" in New York that penned in its Japanese immigrants. Whereas Kuniyoshi lived

9. Beth Gates Warren, *Artful Lives : Edward Weston, Margrethe Mather, and the Bohemians of Los Angeles.* Los Angeles: J. Paul Getty Museum, 2011, 95.
10. Dennis Reed, *Japanese Photography in America, 1920-1940* (Los Angeles: Japanese American Cultural & Community Center, 1985), 35.
11. Dennis Reed, *Making Waves*, 49.

in Brooklyn with Jules Pascin and Ishigaki worked in Greenwich Village, Little Tokyo's artists had to actively seek out an international community of artists beyond their borders. There were few modern art schools where Japanese could mingle with non-Japanese like New York's Art Students League. Although a Los Angeles branch of the League was established in 1906, it had not become the nucleus for artists that New York's school was. There was far less spontaneous interaction than New York's art schools, galleries, and artistic networks.

As Obata formed the East West Society in San Francisco to combat ethnic insularity, Little Tokyo's photographers attempted to engage an international coterie of artists. The Japanese Camera Pictorialists of California (JCPC) entered their Los Angeles counterpart's exhibitions. (Although he associated with them, Miyatake never became a member of the Japanese Camera Pictorialist Club.) They entered multiple international salons, studied photo journals like the Royal Photographic Society's *Photographic Journal* and *Film und Foto*, and regularly attended photography exhibitions held in Los Angeles. It was rare to find an international photography journal that did not have a reproduction of an image by a Little Tokyo photographer. Nevertheless, Japanese camera clubs in the United States were comprised of only ethnic Japanese, despite members' efforts to include non-Japanese. With limited success, Dr. Kyo Koike, founder of the Seattle Camera Club, encouraged non-Japanese to join, and regularly extended invitations to the local university to participate in their exhibitions.

Japanese camera clubs were a large and important part of California's art world during the 1920s. Unlike Miyatake, most of Los Angeles' Japanese camera club members did not have commercial photography jobs to support their craft. On weekends, they traveled throughout southern California on photography expeditions. Photographers were interested in both the industrial (tunnels, dams, and bridges) and the bucolic (sheep herds, lily ponds, and coastline) parts of southern California. Their images of Los Angeles in the late 1920s captured the city's utopian idealism and dystopian urbanism; subjects ranged from ocean waves to oil ditches, kimono-clad women playing *shamisen* to dark tunnels eerily lit by car headlights. The hard concrete and steel forms that were built overnight in the fast-growing city loom large in Japanese photographers' work. Pictorialist and modernist, their images paralleled those of Europeans like László Moholy-Nagy and American Karl Struss, whose photographs were exhibited next to theirs at the Los Angeles County Museum of Art's international photography salons.

Miyatake opened his Toyo Studio in 1923 after purchasing the Paris Photo Studio on East 1st street in the heart of Little Tokyo. After struggling for its first few years, Miyatake's studio soon became a Little Tokyo establishment. His wife's joining the studio to manage its accounts helped matters. Since studying with Shigeta and Weston, Miyatake had submitted his photographs to international exhibitions and contests, winning quite a few. His awards helped his reputation in Little Tokyo and his studio attracted customers. Hollywood had a large influence on Los Angeles-based photographers, because many actors, dancers, and performers needed professional portraits. Before and after World War II, a stream of famous Japanese performers, artists, journalists, and businessmen visiting Los Angeles had their portraits taken on East 1st Street at the Miyatake studio.

In the early 1920s, Weston started to move away from pictorialism as a style. His forms became more abstract and printed in high resolution. He started to promote "straight" images that showed how things were and not their idealized versions. Miyatake was working with Weston during his style transition. Miyatake enlisted the Shakudo-sha, a Little Tokyo art group that he co-founded to support Weston's new portfolio of works. Shakudo-sha included photographers, painters, and poets and regularly hosted exhibitions. When Weston returned from a trip to Mexico in 1925, Miyatake enlisted the Shakudo-sha to exhibit Weston's work in Little Tokyo. Unlike his other Los Angeles-based shows, Weston's Shakudo-sha exhibit sold many prints. Weston commented in his journal that even a "laundry worker" purchased 52 dollars-worth of images. (Both Miyatake and the Shakudo-sha declined to take a commission from the sales.) Little Tokyo became the site for two more Weston exhibitions in 1927 and 1931, which were even more profitable than the first.[12]

---

12. Dennis Reed, *Making Waves*, 43.

When dancer Itô Michio arrived in Los Angeles in 1929, he became Miyatake's premier photography subject and source of inspiration. Itô had lived in Paris, London, and New York, where he was friends with the Ishigakis. In Europe, he worked as a celebrated dancer and choreographer and collaborated with Ezra Pound and other modernists on theatrical productions. When Itô left London, he became a star in New York with his Madison Avenue dance studio and Broadway performances. Itô lived on 14th Street, nearby Ishigaki, and was friends with Katayama's group of writers and socialists. By the time he moved to Hollywood, Itô was already a renowned dance celebrity. When he performed in Los Angeles, he hired Miyatake to become his official photographer. The relationship became one of the most significant art collaborations in Miyatake's career. Itô brought to Los Angeles a lifetime of interaction with modernist vanguards in both Europe and New York, a treasure trove of experience that Miyatake had never had the opportunity to encounter.

Born into an elite Tokyo family, Itô moved to Paris in 1911 to study music, but became more interested in dance after seeing Vaslav Nijinsky's performances and Isadora Duncan's groundbreaking choreography.[13] During World War I, he moved to London, where he became a sought after figure for artist and society salons. Interest in Eastern art and philosophies was at its height. When he was introduced to Ezra Pound, he discovered that the poet was reading Ernest Fenollosa's writing on *noh* theater and needed help understanding certain texts. Itô had little experience with *noh* performance, which entails lifelong study, but he consulted with London-based Japanese friends with more experience than he in the art form. The group assisted Pound in his research. One of these friends was the painter, Kume Tamijuro, who created avant-garde Vorticist-like paintings, but who was also cajoled to help Pound interpret Fenollosa's *noh* translations. In 1916 Itô – along with Noguchi Yonejirô–collaborated with Pound's friend, William Butler Yeats, on his *noh*-inspired

---

13. Masayo Duus, *The Life of Isamu Noguchi: Journey without Borders.* (Princeton, NJ: Princeton University Press, 2004), 100.

dramas. Yeats' one-act play, *At the Hawk's Well*, incorporated "*noh*" elements and went on to be a great success.[14] The production sealed Itô's reputation as a creative interpreter of noh and afforded him entre into British society.

In 1916, Itô left London for New York, where he also garnered media attention and audience favor. His English artistic collaborators had moved on from their interest in Japan: Pound, and probably others, had decided that China was "fundamental" and Japan was "not."[15] In New York, Itô continued to perform versions of *noh*, *kabuki*, and *kyogen,* which served as comic relief between more solemn *noh* acts. New Yorkers were still looking to ballet as the preeminent dance form, so Itô's modernist interpretations of Japanese dance were exciting and new. While in New York, Itô met Noguchi Yonejirô's son, Isamu, and became a mentor to him. Itô encouraged the young sculptor to look beyond formal portraiture and seek out modern artistic expression. Noguchi, in turn, created a mask of Itô that scholars claim was the sculptor's first venture into modernism and abstraction.[16]

By the late 1920s, the *Japonisme* fad was still thriving in the west and Itô rode the wave to the Pacific coast in 1929. He became an adviser on Hollywood's productions of "Madame Butterfly" and "No, No Nanette," in which he choreographed "Japanese" dance sequences.[17] His most successful ventures were performing and choreographing large-scale, elaborate productions at the Hollywood Bowl during the 1930s, which Miyatake was charged with documenting. They continued working together on art projects up until World War II. (While Miyatake was taken to Manzanar, Itô spent two years in a Missouri camp before being repatriated to Japan in 1943 on an exchange ship.) Miyatake's photos show Itô in various guises—at times holding a paper umbrella and wearing *geta*, in a tango costume, and

14. Takeishi Midori, *Japanese Elements in Michio Ito's Early Period (1915-1924): Meetings of East and West in the Collaborative Works.* (Gendaitosho, 2006).
15. Letter to John Quinn, 1917.
16. Masayo Duus, *The Life of Isamu Noguchi*, 106.
17. Mary-Jean Cowell, "Michio Ito in Hollywood: Modes and Ironies of Ethnicity." *Dance Chronicle* 24, no. 3 (2001), 263-305.

as a modern expressionist dancer all in black. Miyatake was able to capture Itô's characters and movement, using lighting devices and printing processes that highlighted the dancer's innovations. In a 1931 abstract series, Miyatake showed Itô's movement within a single frame. Itô is unrecognizable; he is reduced to abstract swirls of light against darkness. Soon, Itô recommended other dancers to visit Miyatake, who was able to capture their movement, expression, and form.

When Los Angeles hosted the Olympics in 1932, the *Asahi* newspaper hired Miyatake to take photographs of the Japanese athletes. After years photographing dancers, Miyatake was adept at catching bodies in motion. In addition to straight portraiture, he took action shots of Japanese jumpers clearing the bar or leaping into the sandbox as well as sprinters taking off. His photos would be rushed back by ship to be printed in Japanese newspapers two weeks after the event. In addition to documenting Japanese athletes in action, his photographs captured Little Tokyo's national pride and patriotism as it welcomed the Japanese team. In 1932, the majority of Japanese living in Los Angeles was *issei*, first generation, and their children were still too young to identify as Japanese or American. Miyatake's photographs showed the flag-waving community welcoming the arriving athletes to the San Pedro harbor as well as parades through Little Tokyo. As described by McWilliams, the Olympics further reinforced how Little Tokyo remained a Japanese island on the American continent.

During the early 1930s, Miyatake returned to Japan to visit his father. Miyatake's parents had returned to Japan in 1932, but his father became ill soon after. Like Obata, Miyatake needed to arrange travel fare for his wife, two sons, and a baby. The *Rafu Shimpo* organized an exhibition of Miyatake's photographs and the proceeds helped to raise the fare. While crossing the Pacific, he received word that his father had died. After arriving in Shikoku, Miyatake considered re-settling there and opening a photography studio. He tried for several years, but returned to Los Angeles in 1936 after failing to establish a business.

Upon his return, Miyatake found another space to rent, and the Toyo Studio reopened. His friendship with Itô deepened and helped him financially. Itô introduced Miyatake to Japanese luminaries traveling to Los Angeles, further broadening his network of artists and contacts. As Obata traveled to natural settings to refresh himself as well as find artistic inspiration, Miyatake took his family into the mountains, seaside, and deserts to photograph nature. Weston had advised him to travel to the desert to take photographs, and Miyatake immediately followed his advice, purchasing a car that week. The trips became routine weekend events for the family. Hiroko prepared a picnic lunch and the children played, while Miyatake disappeared into the woods, climbing over rocks and darting through trees to capture his images. Miyatake understood the financial necessity of taking commemorative photographs and portraits at his studio, but he had not yet abandoned photography as a means of artistic expression.[18]

In 1942, members of Little Tokyo's thriving community were rounded up, taken to temporary holding areas, and then scattered across western United States to stay in concentration camps. They shuttered their businesses and homes, amassing enormous financial losses. Kira Hiromu, a member of the Japanese Camera Pictorialists of California, was able to keep his prints and negatives at Little Tokyo's Nishi Honganji temple for the duration of the war, while he was incarcerated at Gila River in Arizona. Most photographers were not as lucky as Kira, who had been selected to participate in the 25th Annual International Salon of the Camera Pictorialists of Los Angeles only days before the attack on Pearl Harbor. During World War II, no Japanese in the United States was allowed to have a camera. (The government had confiscated Kuniyoshi's camera in New York.) Photographers would have to find other ways to make art while incarcerated.

Miyatake was forty-seven years old when he and his family and ten thousand other ethnic Japanese were interned at Manzanar, located two hundred miles away from Los Angeles. The camp was on a former apple orchard, which had died when Owens Valley's water was diverted

---

18. Essay by Archie Miyatake in Miyatake, Atsufumi, Taisuke Fujishima, and Eikoh Hosoe, eds. *Toyo Miyatake Behind the Camera 1923-1979*. (Tokyo: Bungeishunji Co., Ltd., 1984), 8.

to the Los Angeles Aqueduct. Death Valley was to the west and the Eastern Sierras, which were covered in snow for most of the year, were to the east. Freezing in the winter and scorching in the summer, a dramatic, harsh, and spectacularly beautiful landscape surrounded the camp. Sagebrush, rocks, and ancient pines were scattered beyond the barbed wire and watchtowers. It did not take long for internees—some of southern California's master gardeners—to build gardens that utilized available boulders, rocks, brush, and trees.

Life in the 500-acre housing section was an aimless period of waiting. The remaining 5,500 acres comprised a sewage plant, reservoir, guards' living quarters, agricultural fields that supplied the camp with vegetables, and work centers. Internees had no privacy; they were forced to use common showers, toilets, and mess halls, while living with as many as eight people in a single room. Like Obata, Miyatake was resilient (some have credited the stoic and resourceful "Meiji Man" as having a particularly strong backbone), using the time to explore his interests. He joined a "book of the month club" to improve his reading skills, always concerned that he did not have enough formal education.[19] He returned to oil painting to pass the time. He even started playing the saxophone again and established the Manzanar orchestra, which he conducted to perform Beethoven's 5th symphony. Since there were few internees that could drum and they often dropped out of the orchestra, Miyatake let someone else conduct when he played the drums.

After decades pursuing photography as a profession and passion, Miyatake needed to continue taking photographs to introduce an aspect of normalcy into his Manzanar life and, indeed, for his survival. Miyatake could leave his home and studio, but not photography. Aware that this dark chapter needed to be recorded, he smuggled in a lens, film, and film holder to Manzanar and a carpenter helped him build a camera using the lens and scrap wood. Miyatake was friends with one of Manzanar's visiting salesmen, who brought film for him to use.

---

19. Miyatake Atsufumi, Taisuke Fujishima, and Eikoh Hosoe, eds. *Toyo Miyatake Behind the Camera 1923-1979*, (Tokyo: Bungeishunji Co., Ltd., 1984), 8.

Miyatake was no longer interested in experimenting with light and dark, shadows, and abstraction. Instead, he became a documentarian, a witness to the incarceration. Whereas Obata documented daily life at Tanforan and Topaz with brush and paper, Miyatake used his camera to create a visual diary of Manzanar. He had been taking photographs in secret, but the camp director eventually gave Miyatake permission, if a non-Japanese took the actual shot that he set up. This condition was eventually relaxed as authorities (followed by their wives assigned to the task) became bored with Miyatake's laborious process. Although many have credited Miyatake with being the only internee photographer in the camps, there were others as restrictions relaxed over time. Nevertheless, because he smuggled in a lens and constructed a handmade camera, he was probably the first and most consistent photographer (he produced 1,500 images) throughout his confinement.

There are conflicting stories about how Miyatake received this permission, but most accounts somehow lead to Edward Weston. In one interview, Miyatake explained that one of Manzanar's head police guards was interested in photography and a patron of Weston's. Empathizing with Miyatake, who was clearly dispirited, the guard convinced camp director Ralph Merritt to allow Miyatake to take photographs.[20] Other reports claim that Weston, knowing that the loss of his camera would have a dramatic effect on Miyatake, contacted Merritt to ask permission for his old friend to be permitted to use his camera. Furthermore, internees were pushing Merritt to allow photography inside the camp, since families wanted to document weddings, graduation ceremonies, and other events. They also wanted photographs of loved ones, who were gradually leaving. At its peak in 1942, Manzanar housed over 10,000 people and fell to 6,000 by 1944. Many of those allowed to leave were young men and women sent to serve in the Allied war effort in Europe.

Miyatake's landscape photographs show his deep regard for Owens Valley's natural beauty. Like Obata, Miyatake did not abandon

---

20. Miyatake Atsufumi, Taisuke Fujishima, and Eikoh Hosoe, eds. *Toyo Miyatake Behind the Camera 1923-1979*, (Tokyo: Bungeishunji Co., Ltd., 1984), 8.

his aesthetic sensibility or love of nature in his images. Both artists marveled at their camps' dramatic landscape. They endeavored to capture the paradox between bleak, shabby barracks with soaring mountain ranges and high desert sky. Desert colors inspired Obata's imagination, while the sun's light shining through clouds moved Miyatake. On occasion, he photographed the trees and rocks without including the camp, as though the photographs were taken on one of his nature excursions.

Much like Obata's paintings, Miyatake's images were personal, ones that he had elected to capture as an artist and a self-assigned photo-documenter. Once he received permission to photograph, he became bolder with his compositions. One of his most reproduced images of Manzanar shows three boys gazing out from behind barbed wire. The image is unusual, because the WRA did not allow guards, watchtowers, or barbed wire to be photographed by anyone visiting the camps. Miyatake posed the boys and shot them staring from behind barbed wire, indicating that Miyatake must have received permission to take the photo from outside the camp's boundary. Miyatake's photograph is evidence that Manzanar was not merely a benign "relocation center" as the WRA suggested, but a prison in which people were held captive and segregated based solely on their ethnic origin.

Some of his shots expressed an optimistic point of view, earnest attempts to show the internees' willingness to survive the ordeal. He showed cheerleaders practicing routines and portraits of the men's basketball team. In order to document life as it was lived, Miyatake photographed mundane chores, children playing, gardening, funerals, and small business operations. Many of his images are emotionally loaded; for example, he photographed a lone child pedaling a tricycle between the barracks as a dust storm whipped around her. Among those photographers hired by the WRA was Francis Stewart, whose photographs centered on the camp's children. His subjects were cute, smiling, and playful, and avoided the elderly, who were not. As symbols of injustice and innocence, children were frequent photography subjects, but Miyatake's prints show internees exhibiting a range of emotions.

The WRA also hired Dorthea Lange, whose images of the Great Depression had become famous, to document the removal of Japanese from their communities as well as their period of incarceration. Lange's photographs showed the incarceration as tragic and the internees as victims. Although she was sympathetic with the internees' plight, they were most likely skeptical about her, since she was a WRA employee. She was an outsider documenting people overcome by stress, anger, helplessness, and humiliation.[21] A WRA employee or military guard accompanied her as she photographed San Francisco's Japantown, Tanforan Assembly Center, and then Manzanar. Despite the monitoring, her images captured how her employer treated the Japanese: endless lines while internees' bodies and belongings were tagged and surveyed, American flags flying in a dust storm, and dilapidated homes that seemed on the point of collapse. She also included images children playing, reciting the pledge of allegiance, and posing in groups. Lange had been hired to document the "successful" relocation of Japanese, but her photographs are records of abuse. The WRA never made her photographs public until long after the war.

Acting as an independent photographer, Ansel Adams followed Lange to Manzanar in 1943, when he took photos of the camps and internees. Whereas Lange photographed the camp as it was in chaotic disarray, still being built when internees arrived, Adams captured Manzanar after internees had set up welding shops, tilled farmland, and established schools, a newspaper, as well as temple, and a church. He was impressed with the internees' diligence and determination to survive the ordeal and regain normalcy. Adams chose to emphasize the internees' Americanness, depicting nurses on coffee breaks and the *nisei* playing baseball. (Adams was probably unaware that baseball was Japan's most popular sport.) He also photographed the majestic

21. Thy Phu notes Charles Kikuchi's diary entry at Tanforan on April 30, 1942, about a "thing" dressed in slacks taking photos of the elderly, who Kikuchi believed wanted to be left alone. Thy Phu. "The Spaces of Human Confinement: Manzanar Photography and Landscape Ideology." *Journal of Asian American Studies* 11, no. 3 (2008): 337-371. https://muse.jhu.edu/ (accessed March 21, 2017).

mountain and desert landscapes that surrounded Manzanar, which became some of his most collected and reproduced images.

In his self-published book of text and photographs, *Born Free and Equal*, Adams described Manzanar as a "detour on the road of American citizenship," a place "built of shacks and patience." Unlike Lange's photographs of victims, Ansel portrayed internees as heroic and resilient survivors. Lange, a friend of Adams, believed his photographs showing the "triumph of human spirit" in overcoming ordeals to be "shameful" in such a setting. She did not believe his images came from a malicious place, just an "ignorant" one.[22] For his book, which he dedicated "with admiration and respect" to Manzanar camp director Ralph Merritt, Adams wrote captions under portraits that reinforced his message that the U.S. government had incarcerated Americans—not the enemy. Adams showed internees either smiling or looking directly at the camera with confidence. Under one portrait of a grinning Yuri Yamazaki, Adams wrote "An American School Girl." Adams agreed with director Merritt that the camps might not be fair, but they were necessary to secure the country and protect the internees from anti-Japanese violence.[23] According to Adams, there were truly dangerous Japanese enemy aliens: those who had refused to sign the pledge of loyalty, who had reflected the "ideology of Nippon," and *kibei*, who had been educated in Japan and most likely were still under its spell. These individuals, Adams wrote, had been safely rounded up and moved to the Tule Lake Center.[24] He hoped that the "safe" Japanese-Americans would "scatter throughout the country" after being released from the camps rather than stay in "nationalistic groups in towns and rural areas."[25] In other words, it was the island of Little

---

22. Thy Phu, "The Spaces of Human Confinement: Manzanar Photography and Landscape Ideology." *Journal of Asian American Studies* 11, no. 3 (2008): 337-371. https://muse.jhu.edu/ (accessed March 21, 2017).
23. Ansel Adams, *Born Equal and Free: The Story of Loyal Japanese-Americans at Manzanar Relocation Center, Inyo County, CA*, 36.
24. Ansel Adams, *Born Equal and Free*, 40.
25. Ibid, 36.

Tokyo fault that the relocation was necessary.

Adam's photographs also included the Miyatake family, a portrait of Tôyô, and a view of the family inside their barracks. (He did not include the portrait of Miyatake in his book.) The photo that Adams did reproduce of the Miyatake family shows Tôyô overseeing his daughter as she sits at a desk drawing. His youngest son is the only one looking at the camera lens, as mother and eldest brother are fixated on the little girl. Adams' caption for the photo reads simply, "A Manzanar Household," rather than identifying Miyatake as a fellow photographer. The walls of the cramped room are decorated with children's drawings, dolls, and paper flowers, but there is no evidence of Miyatake as an artist.

Compared to photographs by Lange and Adams, Miyatake's photographs are liberated from being forced to take an ideological position about the camp experience. Both Lange and Adams amplified the injustice of the camps, while highlighting the "good" victims. Lange presented victims, Adams showcased heroes, but Miyatake photographed what he lived and saw. They could leave; he could not. Where Adams focused on presenting internees as Americans, Miyatake did not shirk from presenting how Japanese culture was a part of the camp experience. He took photographs of pounding rice (*mochi*) for New Years celebrations, father and son playing *gidayû shamisen*, and Japanese dance (*odori*). He showed Manzanar's fish market with signs written in Japanese script. Sometimes little girls wore kimono for celebrations and other times they wore pinafores; Miyatake shot both. Nor did he feel compelled to erase the "American" elements: cheerleaders, Mickey Mouse decorations, and basketball. Like Obata, this freedom allowed him to take photographs of Manzanar's landscape when it was beautiful (dandelion fields and mountains), and when it was bleak (dust storms, barbed wire, and barracks.) And he took photos of internees as Japanese, American, and Japanese-American.

Manzanar's internees wanted to understand and track the status of the war in the Pacific to know the fate of their Japanese families and friends as well as what turn of events might affect their own fates. In addition to the camera, Miyatake smuggled a radio into the camp.[26] A friend rebuilt the radio so that it could receive Japanese shortwave broadcasting about the war's status. Miyatake's wife, Hiroko, wrote down the reports every night and distributed them to camp *issei* leaders throughout Manzanar. Camp director Merritt became aware of the radio and Hiroko's reports. According to Miyatake, Merritt was seemingly indifferent saying, "It's natural that Japanese would believe news from Japan about its victories and be happy about it." Miyatake saw Merritt's reaction as magnanimous toward the internees. Likely, the radio confirmed Merritt's belief that the internees supported the Japanese military and their incarceration was justified. It is more likely, however, that the internees wanted to be informed about their families' status and their fate as prisoners if the war was won on either side.

On August 15, 1945, internees gathered around the shortwave radio to hear that Japan surrendered. Miyatake described some men crying out loud at the news, while others "hid their tears."[27] Hearing about Japan's surrender must have been deeply emotional and conflicting. Hibi Matasusaburô, Obata's friend and replacement at the Topaz Art School, painted a watercolor on August 15 to commemorate the event. In the painting, the silhouette of a figure faces the sunset. On the back of the painting, Hibi wrote that his "heart was heavy," with the knowledge that the Japanese empire had "collapsed." Hibi lamented the loss of the empire's "perfect record" for its mythical 2,600-year history:

> In spite of their exclamations of "Death, if not victory!" our compatriots in Japan were unable to prevail against the might of the atomic bomb and have unconditionally surrendered in obedience to the Imperial Command. This very day, the setting sun in the clear western sky reflects the sorrowful downfall of the Empire of Japan. There is nothing left for us but to face the skies of our fatherland and weep.[28]

---

26. Miyatake Atsufumi, *Tôyô Miyatake Behind the Camera 1923-1979*, 8.
27. Ibid.
28. Hibi Hisako, *Peaceful Painter: Memoirs of an Issei Woman Artist*, (Berkeley: Heyday Books, 2004), 57.

Perhaps because they lived as captive enemy aliens throughout the war, artists like Hibi and Miyatake did not voice a hope for fascist Japan's defeat as Kuniyoshi and Ishigaki did. Hibi's art reviews and correspondence in previous decades noted no particular allegiance to the Japanese nation, but locked in Japanese desert ghettos, his connection to Japan seemed to have deepened. Miyatake chose to stay until after August 15 to document Manzanar's final days. One of his images was of hands cutting barbed wire with scissors. The last Manzanar internees left in November, unsure where their next home would be.

(Opposite): Miyatake Tôyô and Itô Michio at the Hollywood Bowl, Los Angeles, California, 1937.

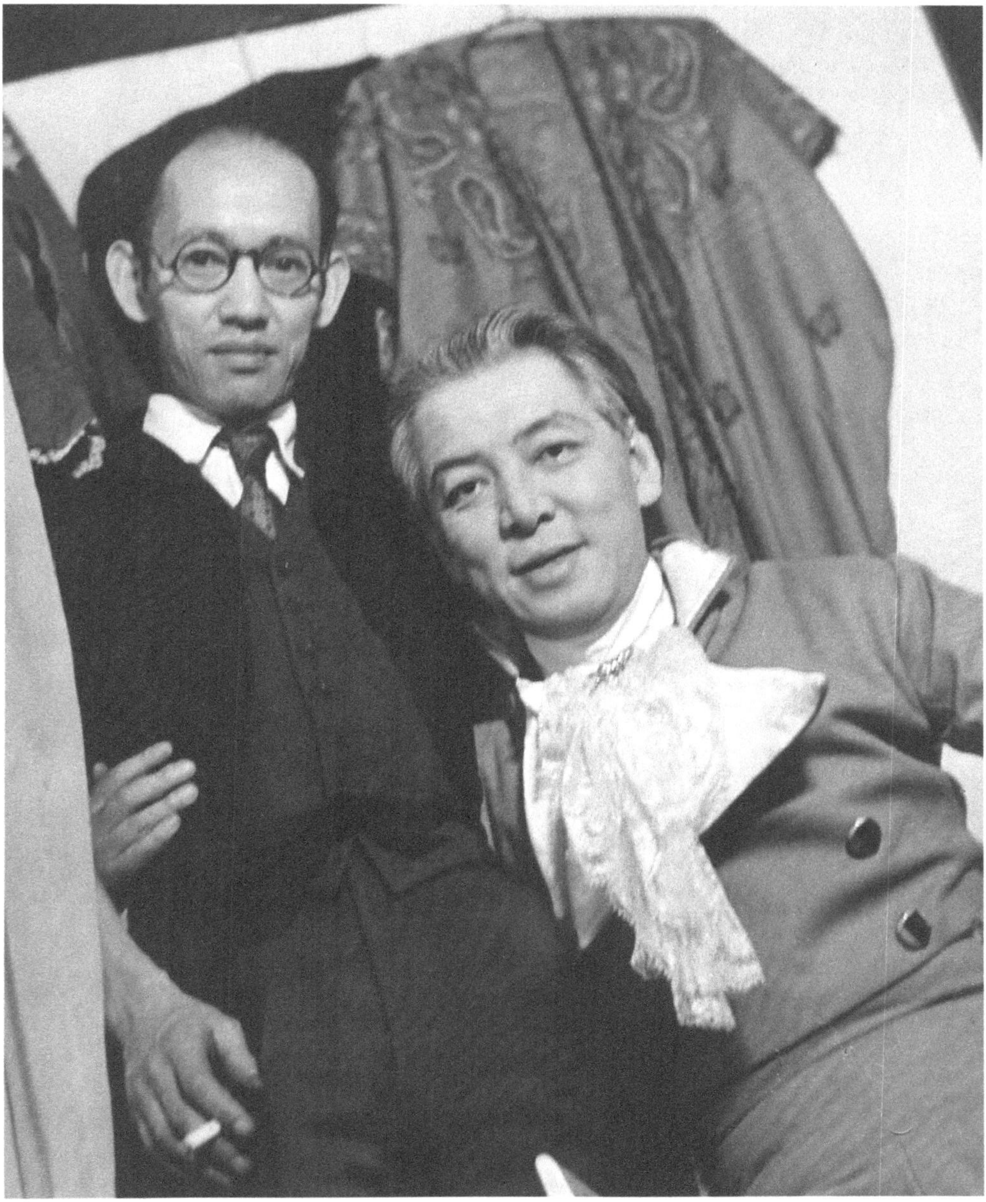

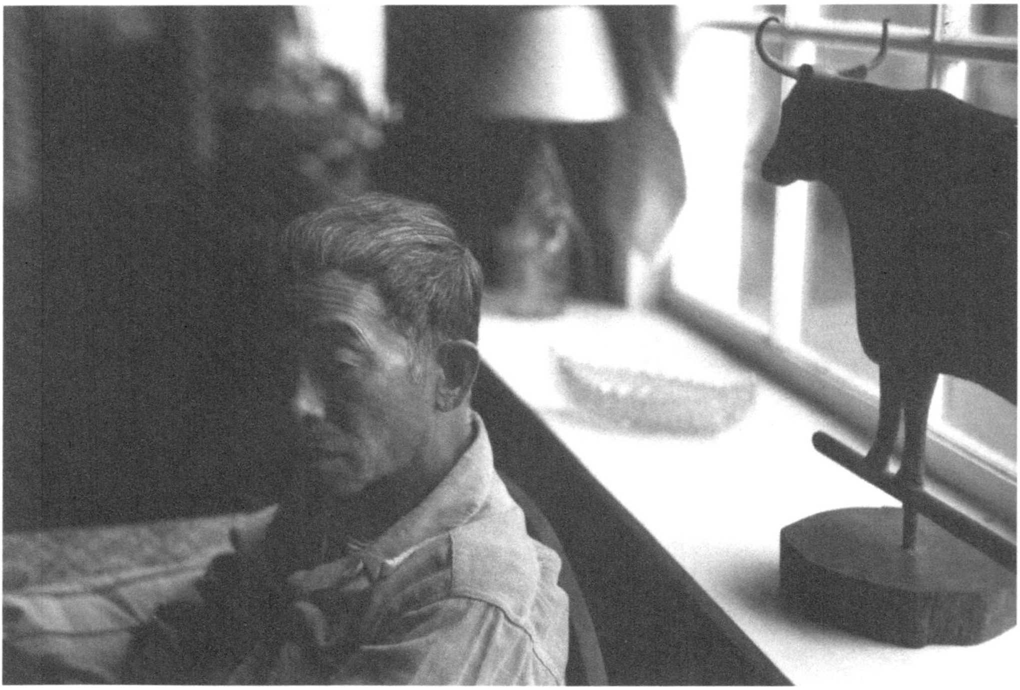

Kuniyoshi Yasuo by Adrian Siegel, ca. 1950. (Rosalie Berkowitz collection of photographs, 1927-1950). Archives of American Art, Smithsonian Institution.

Conclusion

What Is Un-American Art?

As **their lives and careers intersected and diverged prior to** World War II, so did the artists' postwar fates. By November 1945, all Japanese internees had moved out of the concentration camps to rebuild lives in Little Tokyo, Japantown, and beyond. Many Japanese returned to find their homes occupied, businesses vanished, and zero assets or support to rebuild their lives. Admitting that the government's decision to incarcerate ethnic Japanese was based on "race prejudice, war hysteria, and a failure of political leadership," President Ronald Reagan signed into law the Civil Liberties Act of 1988, apologizing for the internment on behalf of the United States government. It was not until 1952, seven years after their release from camps, when Japanese-born, *issei*, could become naturalized citizens.

During the Occupation, the victorious Allied powers prosecuted war criminals and dismantled bureaucracies that had reinforced Japan's war effort. Initially, former New Deal administrators stationed in Japan encouraged a free press and open elections. Socialists formed political parties, unions increased in influence and membership, and demonstrators marched through the streets. Its occupiers feared, however, that they had allowed Japan to swing too far to the left. On the global stage, communism replaced fascism as the West's ideological enemy and American occupiers became less concerned with Japan's democratic progress. No longer Enemy Number One, Japan was being rebuilt as a counter to communism under the aegis of the United States. As in the 1947 Marshall Plan for Germany, the United States poured resources into Japan to rapidly rebuild from the rubble and ash, so it could form a bulwark against the Soviet Union. When the Chinese Communist Party was victorious over the Nationalists and the Soviet Union tested its first nuclear device in 1949, Americans "reversed course" in Japan: claims to war reparations were abandoned, and efforts to dissolve the *zaibatsu*—business conglomerates—were eased. War criminals and gangsters were released from prison to combat the Japan Communist Party. Previously purged politicians and bureaucrats returned to Nagata-cho and Kasumigaseki to reclaim their seats. The Korean War, which occurred during the final years of the Allied Occupation, jump-started Japan's economic recovery and ushered in an era of high-speed growth. The United States ultimately regretted the inclusion of Article 9 in the Japanese Constitution, which renounced war as a mean to settle international disputes. Hoping a rearmed Japan could check communism in East Asia, the Americans spent decades trying to revise the constitution, but had to settle for using Japanese territory for permanent U.S. military bases. After a seven-year military occupation, three years longer than actual combat, the United States and Japan became Cold War allies.

Changing relations between the Japanese and the United States governments played a role in the artists' postwar fates. The tectonic shift in geopolitical alliances following World War II transformed the art world. As the United States assumed a leadership position for the West, the art capital moved from Paris to New York. While newly liberated leftists, intellectuals, and artists in Japan found themselves once again the targets of a Red Purge, U.S. government agencies trained its crosshairs on domestic actors suspected of leftism. Those people who had been active in communist circles prior to the war, had merely attended a rally or two, or were friends with someone who was a leftist, were persecuted. The government paid careful attention to New York's artists, who were suspect for their leftist sympathies due to their prewar and wartime activities. Fearful of being targeted by the government as leftists, artists adopted content and stylistic devices that were politically neutral. Social realism, associated with communism, was replaced with abstract expressionism, which seemed free of political ideology.

As it had during the Meiji era, the West once again looked to Japan as a cultural beacon, an aesthetic ideal, rather than a military or economic power. Part of declawing Japan meant celebrating those artists who used traditional motifs, Buddhist philosophy, or other historic relics. There was a renewed art-for-export industry as Occupying forces brought home *netsuke*, porcelain, and fans as souvenirs rather than Japanese flags or swords captured on the battlefield. Once again, Japan became an aesthetic, recalling Oscar Wilde's impression that the country was "pure invention." Japanese calligraphy, Zen philosophy, *wabi-sabi*, and other Japanese touchstones suited a new generation of artists: abstract expressionists, the Beat Generation, and consumers of Eastern religions. Those artists like Kuniyoshi and Ishigaki, who painted desert landscapes and muscular arms wielding hammers, would have to adjust to these new trends or fade into obscurity and irrelevance.

There were World War II Japanese casualties who did not die in battle, but from trauma and grief on the home islands. Shimizu Toshi died during the last days of the war, exhausted, debilitated, and heartbroken from the loss of his son, who died on a ship in the Pacific Ocean. Shimizu's lifelong friend Nakayama Iwata, who lived in Kobe and became one of Japan's most revered and innovative modernist photographers when he returned from Paris, died from alcoholism not long after. Unlike Shimizu, he never engaged politically, instead retreating to alcohol and his Ashiya-based photography studio, which was populated by an international coterie of dancers and fellow bar flies. Before he died, Nakayama took a series of photographs documenting Kobe after the aerial bombings, creating a record of devastation unlike any of his previous works.

Since the 1990s, Tokyo's Photographic Art Museum and Ashiya-based museums regularly exhibit Nakayama. Despite being a contemporary of Man Ray's, Nakayama's name is wholly unknown outside of Japan's photography circles. Similarly, Tochigi Prefectural

Museum has been dedicated to exhibiting Shimizu's paintings, reproducing his work in catalogs, writing his biography, and reprinting his meticulously kept diaries, which have been windows into the artist and his experience. These artists' hometown institutions have largely been responsible for maintaining their legacy. Partly because of this localization, their international roles have been lost.

When scholars grapple with the legacy of Japan's imperial war illustrators, Shimizu's experience is always included in their accounts. I am not the only writer confounded by Shimizu's (and Fujita Tsuguharu's) seeming withdrawal from cosmopolitan humanism and interest in diversity in favor of militarism and fascism. For Shimzu and Fujita, who heralded from the higher classes, art might have been emblematic of their positions as cultural elites rather than a means to serve a humanist impulse. Shimizu's prewar artwork should be appreciated and preserved as documents of a sensitive artist capturing foreign lands and people, but it should also be regarded as evidence that a cosmopolitan experience does not preclude nationalist tendencies. Unlike Ishigaki and Kuniyoshi, who were dedicated to celebrating borderless humanism, Shimizu's early conversion to Japan's militarist and expansionist ambitions reveals that he was more of an art world mercenary, whose choices were opportunistic rather than idealistic.

Those artists who remained in the United States during the war fared better than Shimizu, but they also faced unanticipated challenges. Kuniyoshi Yasuo, Ishigaki Eitarô, Obata Chiura, and Miyatake Tôyô physically survived the war, but their interior lives were transformed. Kuniyoshi Yasuo continued to teach at the Art Students League, exhibit in galleries and museums, and win awards. Nevertheless, his journals from the time reveal that he was deeply affected—and frightened by—the new world order. Ishigaki and Ayako survived World War II, but not McCarthyism, which targeted their socialist ideology and resulted in their forced return to Japan in 1952. After they returned to Berkeley from St. Louis, Obata and Haruko restarted their lives from zero. Miyatake Tôyô returned to Little Tokyo to continue his documentation of Japanese-American lives and visiting Japanese celebrities for local newspapers. However, he abandoned his artistic experiments done in the middle of the night at his Little Tokyo studio.

Kuniyoshi Yasuo

As the United States ascended to its superpower position, so did its art world. Kuniyoshi, however, was unconvinced that there was an "American Renaissance" in painting. "When I see people here buying pictures . . . the way they buy radios and electric refrigerators, then I will believe the 'American renaissance' is really at hand."[1] Some critics referred to Kuniyoshi as "America's favorite Japanese" and others patronized him as one of the Manhattan-Woodstock world's "pets."[2] However, only a few understood the psychic pain Kuniyoshi endured. One of the clippings from his scrapbook described his World War II paintings as an "accumulation of sadness," but his postwar canvases also showed anxiety and emotional strain.[3]

Kuniyoshi's mood was dark during the final days of the war, even when it was clear that the Allied forces would be triumphant. In 1945 he painted a headless horse figure—a carousel horse—that reflected his pessimism. "Headless Horse Who Wants to Jump" (1945) is nightmarish: a decapitated horse hopelessly claws at the air as it rears up on its hind legs. The canvas' stark desert setting had become a prominent background for most of his paintings from this time. At the horse's feet was Kuniyoshi's OWI commissioned "Torture" poster, discarded among other litter. Japan had already surrendered by the time Kuniyoshi finished "Headless Horse," but his painting was not celebratory, nor did

1. "Portrait of the Artist," *New World Telegram*, February 23, 1940. Scrapbook of printed materials relating to Yasuo Kuniyoshi, 1934-1945. "Yasuo Kuniyoshi Papers, 1921-1993," Smithsonian Archives of American Art.
2. Rosamund Frost, "Kuniyoshi, American of Two Decades," *The Art News*, May 15, 1942, Scrapbook of printed materials relating to Yasuo Kuniyoshi, 1934-1945. "Yasuo Kuniyoshi Papers, 1921-1993." "Smithsonian Archives of American Art. Party." Scrapbook of printed materials relating to Yasuo Kuniyoshi, 1934-1945. "Yasuo Kuniyoshi Papers, 1921-1993."
3. Scrapbook of printed materials relating to Yasuo Kuniyoshi, 1934-1945. "Yasuo Kuniyoshi Papers, 1921-1993," Smithsonian Archives of American Art.

it signal an optimistic or peaceful future. Kuniyoshi was skeptical that fascism had been defeated, writing after the war:

> In spite of our great victory, our enemies' destructive ideology has not been conquered and as long as its evils persists we must be on guard. Today, those of us who paint and who have prospered through the encouragement and recognition accorded us by museums, schools, organizations, and individuals, have a two-fold responsibility. First, we must be prepared to defend our own freedom as artists. Second, and most important of all, in spite of the grave threats looming all over the world, we must hold firmly with all those who believe in and encourage freedom of expression and democratic principles, so that—for them and with them—we may continue to create a great American art.[4]

Kuniyoshi sensed that fascism's "destructive ideology" persisted despite the Allied victory. He also feared that similar threats existed from within the Allied cause. Stating that artists had a responsibility to be watchful against censorship, he reminded fellow artists that they must remain vigilant to protect freedom of expression. Kuniyoshi was convinced that the world was plagued by "looming threats" and that artists had an ongoing responsibility to protect each other.[5]

The transfer of the art world's center from Paris to New York following the war benefited Kuniyoshi. He had been frustrated by the art community's fixation on Europe, so he applauded the "awakening" of American support for domestic institutions. Nevertheless, he did not approve of the chauvinism at the heart of American regionalist painting, which had remained popular since the 1930s. He lambasted painter Thomas Hart Benton for his call for a pure American art, saying that "the injection of foreign influences has regenerated and enriched all cultures." He added that "People say they want a purely American art, but what I want to know is what is *un-American* art?"[6]

---

4. "Yasuo Kuniyoshi Papers, 1921-1993," Smithsonian Archives of American Art.
5. Ibid.
6. Elsie McIlroy, "Yasuo Kuniyoshi—The Fist and the Shadow of the Fist (1948? date unknown)," "Yasuo Kuniyoshi Papers, 1921-1993." Smithsonian Archives of American Art.

(Kuniyoshi's emphasis.) He wrote that all art works are "colored by (their) immediate environment," where and when they are created, regardless of the artist's nationality. Likewise, Kuniyoshi's friend, Stuart Davis, who had an early interest in abstract art but found little support during the social realist era, was concerned about the "mountain of 'Americanism' in art propaganda," which he believed isolated American artists.[7] In the years after the war, when influential critics like Clement Greenberg claimed abstract expressionism as particularly American in spirit and execution, artists abandoned Regionalism for abstraction. Davis was then celebrated as one of its native pioneers. Kuniyoshi, however, never embraced abstract expressionism, choosing instead to explore new expressionist modes through representation.

Kuniyoshi soon realized that the "democratic freedoms" he had broadcast to the Japanese literati during the war had limits in the United States, despite its propaganda. His paintings were targets of criticism in the 1946 State Department-sponsored exhibition held at New York's Metropolitan Museum, called "Advancing American Art." Originally planned to tour Europe and Latin America, conservative politicians criticized the show, arguing that federal money should not be spent on expressionist and abstract works that countered their image of traditional American painting. The Hearst papers also denounced the participating artists as leftist radicals.[8] Many editorials dismissed the paintings as "ugly or absurd" and created by a "lunatic fringe."[9] Suspicious of federal money for the arts, conservative Republican congressmen led by Senator Joseph McCarthy attacked the project as un-American and invaded by "foreign" interests.[10] President Harry Truman entered the debate, specifically reacting to Kuniyoshi's "Circus

7. *The Artist in America*. Introduction by Lloyd Goodrich. Compiled by The Editors of Art in America. New York: W. W. Norton & Company, 1967, 184.
8. David M. Sokol, "The Founding of Artists Equity Association after World War II," *Archives of American Art Journal* 39 (1999).
9. Taylor D. Littleton and Maltby Sykes, *Advancing American Art: Painting, Politics, and Cultural Confrontation at Mid-Century.* (Tuscaloosa. University of Alabama Press, 1989), 27.
10. David M. Sokol, "The Founding of Artists Equity Association After World War II," 20.

Girl Resting" saying, "If that is art, then I'm a Hottentot."[11] Under fire, the exhibition was cut short and the War Assets Association sold the works in 1948 at public auction. (When Kuniyoshi's paintings were displayed in Moscow in 1963 as part of a contemporary American art show, the Soviets did not care for his works either. The *New York Times* printed a photograph of Nikita Khruschev laughing at Kuniyoshi's 1950 painting of a clown wearing a mask, accompanied by a quote saying that it looked as though it had been painted by a "monkey.")[12]

In 1947, nine New York-based artists came together to form the Artists Equity Association (AEA) to support American artists after the war. Founded at the Woodstock Art Colony, the group elected Kuniyoshi as their first president, who went on to serve two terms. Following the "Advancing American Art" exhibition debacle, artists felt they needed an organization to represent them as well as to promote sales of their paintings. Distancing themselves from institutions like the prewar John Reed Club and the American Artists Congress, the AEA expressed an early commitment to avoid politics. It refused to take a stand on any controversial issues. Artist Equity member Henry Schnakenberg met museum and gallery individuals to convince them that the AEA did not have a political platform. He wrote to Kuniyoshi in 1948 stating that to combat the conservative political attacks on the AEA, they would have to present themselves as an a-political group. Kuniyoshi responded by saying that he understood how "ruthless" artist groups with ideological causes could be. However, if members' economic welfare was assured, artists would "be careful and not dare use Equity (AEA) as a front organization" for political activities.[13] Leftist artists retreated from the AEA. Although he had been proud of his political involvement during the 1930s and admonished artists to be tireless in their fight against censorship, Kuniyoshi distanced himself from political movements during the postwar years.

11. Taylor D. Littleton, Advancing American Art, 55.
12. John Canaday, *New York Times*, 1964.
13. David M. Sokol, "The Founding of Artists Equity Association After World War II," 26.

Even as conservative politicians targeted him for ridicule, Kuniyoshi's exhibition record accelerated and his peers celebrated him. In 1948 the Whitney Museum of American Art selected Kuniyoshi for its first solo exhibition of a living artist, prompting many interviews in newspapers and art journals. The Whitney show included 85 paintings as well as 33 drawings and lithographs lent by private collectors and museums. In 1952 the American Federation of Arts chose Kuniyoshi as one of the artists to represent the United States at the Venice Biennale, along with his old colleagues and friends, Alexander Calder—who won first prize for sculpture—Stuart Davis, and Edward Hopper. Reviews for both exhibitions were positive. While critic Stuart Peterson echoed foreign critics, who identified Hopper as "authentically American," he also praised Kuniyoshi paintings as a "feast for the eyes"[14] Howard Devree characterized Kuniyoshi's decades of work as "unusually consistent."[15] A few years before, Devree had noted a few changes when he described Kuniyoshi's early paintings as a combination of folk art with "something oriental" and intersected by modernism.[16] He noted that as the years passed, Kuniyoshi's colors became richer, tones darker, and there was more emotional expression.

Kuniyoshi submitted "Koi Nobori," a painting of a large flying carp seen on the Boy's Day holiday in Japan, to the Metropolitan Museum in 1949. The painting was one of the few direct references to Japanese culture in Kuniyoshi's portfolio. And, yet, the painting is also a paradox: whereas Boy's Day is celebrated on May 5, Kuniyoshi painted "July 4," the date of American Independence, on the canvas. He used a bright palette, and the figures seem joyful, perhaps suggesting that Kuniyoshi's confidence had returned. During the last phase of his

---

14. Stuart Peterson, "Art Survey by Nations: Moderns Are Compared in Big Italian Show," *New York Times*, July 20, 1952.
15. Howard Devree, "Kuniyoshi and Davis as Seen in Venice," *New York Times*, December 14, 1952.
16. Howard Devree, "Kuniyoshi, 1921-1947: Whitney Museum Opens its Retrospective Show."

artistic career, Kuniyoshi rejected the brown-and-gray palette of the Depression and war years for the vibrant reds, oranges, and pinks seen in "Koi Nobori." His compositions also became more abstract. According to scholar Alexandra Munroe, Kuniyoshi was keenly aware of the shift in the American art world from realism and socialist art works to abstract and surrealist works after the war. Paintings like "Koi Nobori" might have reflected a better mood as well as a willingness to find a place in the postwar New York art world.[17]

In 1952, the law barring Japanese from becoming United States citizens was abolished. Kuniyoshi immediately applied for citizenship, but he died in 1953 before his paperwork could be processed. According to Sara Mazo Kuniyoshi, he was in the planning stages of having a retrospective of his work at the National Museum of Modern Art in Tokyo before he died. She helped to arrange for the show to be held in March and April of 1954. Katherine Schmidt and her second husband, Irvine, along with Mazo, were at Kuniyoshi's hospital bedside as he struggled with painful stomach cancer. Schmidt recounted that just before Kuniyoshi died, he called them to share some whiskey with him and to say good-bye.[18]

Japan paid attention to Kuniyoshi when he visited in 1931, when he died in 1953, and during his 1954 exhibition at the National Museum of Modern Art in Tokyo. Attendance at the show (over 25,000 visitors) exceeded expectations, given that he was almost completely unknown.[19] For the next two decades, however, Kuniyoshi was largely ignored in Japan. This changed starting in the high-velocity economic growth era, when the Japanese art world claimed Kuniyoshi as one of its own, despite his life and career spent in the United States. When the old

---

17. Alexandra Munroe, "The War Years and Their Aftermath, 1940-1953," *Yasuo Kuniyoshi: tanjô 100nen kinen—nyû yôku no yûshû* (Tokyo: Tokyo Teien Art Museum, December 1989).
18. "Oral history interview with Katherine Schmidt, December 8-15, 1969." Smithsonian Archives of American Art.
19. Hideo Tomiyama, "Yasuo Kuniyoshi and his Native Country, Japan," *Yasuo Kuniyoshi, 1889-1935: A Retrospective Exhibition*. (Austin, TX: University Art Museum, 1975), 57.

Downtown Gallery sold its collection, it launched a buying spree—a "Kuniyoshi Boom"—in Japan that made the price of his work skyrocket in the marketplace.[20] Since then, Kuniyoshi's work has been far more regularly exhibited in Japan than in the United States, as Japanese museums and collectors possess a large portion of his paintings. From the 1970s through the 2000s, Japanese art journal and book publishers highlighted Kuniyoshi's career with multiple reproductions of his work that spanned his career. Often Kuniyoshi's art is considered in the context of his Japanese contemporaries active in the United States. like Ishigaki Eitarô, Shimizu Toshi, and Noda Hideo. They are generally categorized as *nikkei*, of Japanese origin living in the Americas, but they are always claimed as part of Japan's history and heritage.

Identifying Kuniyoshi and his art as being either Japanese or American has been central to the discourse about his work and his life. Kuniyoshi, too, wrote on the subject regularly, stating in the beginnings of an autobiography: "Being a stranger in a strange country is very difficult and hard to get along. All through my life I never expected anything without giving, but I felt much more so in this country. Whether I was born to fight to get it. I never thought anything could be had easily and therefore my attitude has always been to fight to get it."[21] He recalled being on a subway with someone from out of town who was unsure about which direction the subway was headed. The man asked another subway rider, but he did not know either. When Kuniyoshi volunteered the information, the man was "flabbergasted" that Kuniyoshi could speak to him in English and knew his way around New York. The experience, Kuniyoshi said, made him feel proud, but also very sad.

Ishigaki understood that Kuniyoshi always struggled to find his place. When Kuniyoshi died in 1953, Ishigaki had already returned to Japan the previous year. Reading the news of Kunioyshi's death "shocked" Ishigaki. Soon after, he memorialized Kuniyoshi for the

---

20. Hideo Tomiyama, "Yasuo Kuniyoshi and his Native Country, Japan," 57.
21. Yasuo Kuniyoshi, "Preliminary Notes for an Autobiography, 1944," *Yasuo Kuniyoshi Papers: 1921-1993*, Smithsonian Archives of American Art.

influential Japanese art journal *Geijutsu Shinchô*. He quoted American newspapers that described Kuniyoshi as one of the "greatest American artists."[22] Ishigaki grappled with ideas of Kuniyoshi's identity, writing:

> Since Kuniyoshi Yasuo studied in America, worked in America, and painted images with the American life as his subject, there is no doubt that he was an American artist. Although he was someone who had come to live in America for nearly half a century, he probably still had something Japanese about him. He was a Japanese, so it was necessary for him to make more of an effort. He had deeper hardships and worries and he was forced to struggle more."[23]

Ishigaki's understanding of Kuniyoshi's position in the global art world pointed to his existential condition: Kuniyoshi was an American artist who faced the hardships and struggles of a Japanese living in the United States.

In a 1969 interview, Katherine Schmidt also claimed that Kuniyoshi had always maintained a "fundamental Japanese point of view," although he had been "Americanized" in some ways.[24] When the interviewer pressed her to identify this particularly Japanese perspective, she recounted that Kuniyoshi told her that Japanese women always walked three steps behind men. Schmidt thought of herself as too "irrepressible" to concede to such norms and, thus, his anecdote confirmed to her why she chose not to join Kuniyoshi when he returned in 1931. She did not say, however, if Kuniyoshi expected the same behavior from her that he had observed while in Tokyo. He almost certainly did not. Still, it is clear from her retelling of Kuniyoshi's characterization of Japanese society that Schmidt, at least, understood Kuniyoshi as a part of Japan.

In 1942, Kuniyoshi participated in a letter exchange program with a school in Grand Rapids, Michigan, where students were studying his

---

22. Ishigaki Eitarô, "Kuniyoshi no gyôseki," *Geijutsu Shinchô*, (July 1953), 60-63.
23. Ibid.
24. Oral history interview with Katherine Schmidt, December 8-15, 1969. Smithsonian Archives of American Art.

art. One student inquired about his Japanese heritage, but Kuniyoshi replied by writing about his admiration of democracy in the United States instead. His handwritten version of the letter shows several paragraphs describing the hardships he experienced in life, but he crossed these sections out. He eventually sent a typewritten version of the letter without any mention of his struggles. However, Kuniyoshi, included one biographical note for the students: he was not able to become a citizen, despite his many years in the United States and his deep love for the country. Denied citizenship and legal rights, categorized as an enemy alien, Kuniyoshi's *person* was never American, despite his inclusion in American art exhibitions. Assigning him a Japanese-American category posthumously cannot erase his personal history and struggles.

Ishigaki Eitarô

Once Ishigaki returned to Japan in 1953, he stopped painting altogether. He never became a member of the *gadan*. He and Ayako moved to the Tokyo neighborhood, where the artist Yanase Masamu's family lived. One of the founders of the avant-garde artist group, MAVO, Yanase had been killed in an air raid that struck Shinjuku in May of 1945. His family gave Yanase's easel to Ishigaki, and he did some small works that he never exhibited. Ishigaki never again did a full-size painting.

However, Ishigaki stayed engaged with the art world as an observer and critic. Ishigaki regularly wrote essays for art journals about his colleagues in New York in addition to some reviews of Japanese art shows that he visited. Writing about his impressions of the Nika-kai exhibition he viewed in 1953:

> Since this was my first time to see a Japanese art exhibition, I was deeply interested and waited for the fall art season to begin . . . I especially wanted to see the Nikakai, which (I thought) had held on to old traditions. Japanese artists in America spoke of their dealings with the Nikakai exhibition, so I went on September 1 when it opened. I wandered around the show once and saw

> each art group that was assembled. It was not all monotonous and there were paintings of interest, but I felt like I was seeing an American exhibition. I was extremely disappointed. It was because I did not expect an American art exhibition, or a French art exhibition. I was thinking that I wanted paintings that had Japan as the subject by Japanese living in Japan."[25]

After forty-two years in the United States, with little exposure to the Japanese modern art world, Ishigaki expected to see the Japan that he understood and remembered. Judging from his disappointed reaction to modern Japanese art, Ishigaki's idea of Japanese aesthetics might have been frozen in the early 1900s when he left for the United States.

Ishigaki's participation in Japanese politics was tepid compared to his activities in New York. Upon arrival in Japan in 1952, he joined the Tokyo May Day protests. Ayako noted that "Bloody May Day," as it would be later called due to the state's violent suppression of the communist-led protest, was exciting for Ishigaki. Apart from this event, Ayako shared little comment from Ishigaki on Japan's politics.[26] Later that year, Margaret Sanger, his friend from New York, arrived in Japan as a guest of the *Mainichi* newspaper to lecture on birth control. Although they had not seen each other for thirty years, Ayako reported that they were both pleased to meet again in Tokyo. Since Ishigaki did not write about politics, our window into his activism is limited to Ayako's accounts. After years of persecution in New York, Ayako might have shied away from bringing attention to their political activities.

Ishigaki chose to tout Kuniyoshi's career rather than his own. He wrote many articles about Kuniyoshi's career and art philosophy. Ishigaki declared, "Japan must research, care for, and respect (Kuniyoshi's) paintings. For the Japanese, knowing an international artist born in Japan is more important than knowing Picasso or

25. Ishigaki Ayako, *Ai ni tsuite*, 221.
26. Only a few days after Japan's independence was restored, many of the May Day protestors targeted American personnel and jeeps, holding banners saying "Yankee Go Home!" Anti-riot police killed two protestors and wounded more than 400 in the protest that marched from the Meiji Jingu Shrine to the Imperial Palace grounds.

Matisse."[27] Ishigaki often referred to Kuniyoshi as a "genius," writing about him as an artist as well as his strength of character. He became an early advocate for Japanese art circles' claiming Kuniyoshi as one of their own, rather than leaving him to the Americans. Yet his disappointment that Kuniyoshi was virtually unknown in Japan may have mirrored a disappointment in his own lack of recognition. Unlike Kuniyoshi, who many considered to be an "American artist," critics categorized Ishigaki as a "Japanese artist raised in the United States."[28] Though his paintings were steeped in United States history and the social realism common among American artists of his time, his persistent identification as a Japanese artist might derive from the fact that Ishigaki's work never received the recognition in the United States museums and media that Kuniyoshi's did.

The location where an artist died had some impact on which nation seized his legacy. Having returned to Japan with his canvases, his entire collection is now housed in Japanese museums and nowhere to be found in the United States. Ishigaki died in Tokyo in 1958 at the age of sixty-four. Ayako claimed that he never recovered his health after the war. Whether it was his distress over the loss of family members, alienation from the New York postwar art world, or being forced out of his home of over forty years, Ishigaki's artistic life had ended years before his death. Later interest in Kuniyoshi's life and career generated some interest in both Shimizu and Ishigaki's as a kind of residual effect. After he died, the *gadan* considered Ishigaki's legacy, like Shimizu Toshi, as a Japanese artist who lived and worked in the United States. As a member of New York's Japanese prewar art group, Ishigaki has been lauded for his early struggles in a strange land as well as his liberal and international creative associations with the Art Students League, the John Reed Club, and other groups. Like Kuniyoshi and Shimizu, Ishigaki has been understood as a Japanese representative of a cosmopolitan artistic coterie.

---

27. Ishigaki Ayako, *Ai ni tsuite*.
28. "Amerikan doriimu ni moketa Nihonjin gakatachi," *Geijutsu shinchô*, (October 1995).

Ishigaki's star was later eclipsed by his wife's fame as a writer and journalist. She used her renown to crusade on behalf of her husband's career and legacy. Whereas Sara Mazo Kuniyoshi promoted her husband's work in Japan and the United States, Ayako focused exclusively on Japan. She, too, left New York with bitter feelings. Ayako often wrote about her husband's life and work, conducting interviews with NHK (Japan's public broadcasting company), writing memoirs, and opening a museum in Taiji, Wakayama, dedicated to Ishigaki's works.

In an essay written in the mid 1960s, Kimura Shigeo reflected on Ishigaki's influence on the course of modern Japanese art.[29] He had first seen Ishigaki's paintings in the 1930s and again in a little-known art club that had formed around Ishigaki when he returned to Tokyo in the 1950s called the Ten-ten-kai. (Though the club's participants encouraged him to participate, Ishigaki ultimately declined.)[30] Kimura concluded that Ishigaki's work said less about the Japanese art world, than it did about modern American art. What Kimura found significant was that a Japanese artist was able to reveal the contradictions in American society and the "inequities in its capitalist system." He surmised that only an outsider could hold up a mirror to America's darkest moments. Many Japanese artists were still going to Europe and the United States in the decades after the war, but many of them did not return to Japan as previous generations had done. It was artists like Ishigaki, Kimura wrote, who first provided a point of view, expression, and technique that revealed the realities of American life. Kimura explained that Japan's "complex" (*konpurekkusu*) about American art meant that it would favor the European art world. However, artists like Ishigaki provided a window from which to see and understand the United States.

Kimura's statement that Ishigaki had special insight into American injustice was accurate, but it was not only because he was a Japanese

---

29. Kimura Shigeo, "Ishigaki Eitarô," *Bijutsu Gurafu* 14, no. 16, (1983).
30. In 1955, Okamoto Toki invited him to show some of his works with other Tokyo artists. He suggested forming a group called the Ten Ten-kai that centered around Ishigaki. Although he participated in their exhibitions, he did not create any new works to display, and the group dissolved shortly after his death. Ishigaki Ayako, *Ai ni tsuite*, 221-228.

"outsider." Ishigaki's point of view was grounded in humanism and his lifelong interest in socialism. Because of his past working as a laborer and lifelong financial struggle, Ishigaki had experience that extended beyond art circles. He was less tied to Japan—or the United States—than to a global struggle for equality and peace: his paintings of Cuban slave revolts and killings of Chinese civilians were of a piece with his paintings of a lynching in the South or the urban scene on New York's 14th Street. Nevertheless, Kimura's assessment of Ishigaki's success as an artist in terms of his "outsider" status does recognize the way in which being unfettered by national identity can serve an artist's work. In the case of Ishigaki, his life and politics were instilled with internationalism; the United States was merely a base of operation.

Obata Chiura

Obata and Haruko returned to Berkeley at the end of the war to resume his teaching position at the university. Like the rest of the Japanese community, they had lost everything they established—their home and gallery—before the war. UC Berkeley hosted an exhibition of his wartime paintings. His prewar paintings had been carefully stored and protected on the campus throughout the war. Although he retired from teaching in 1954, he wrote numerous books on brush painting techniques and *sumi* paintings. He joined the San Francisco Art Association and the Sierra Club. Obata went fishing throughout California, Montana, and Wyoming, always wanting to "follow the trout and salmon."[31] They devoted their post-Topaz lives to activities that they loved and gave them serenity.

Obata was never conflicted about his Japanese identity. He told a Japanese interviewer that after experiencing a tea ceremony in Kyoto when he was seventeen, drinking tea and performing a tea ceremony had affected his life, art, and interests.[32] Obata unselfconsciously

31. Chiura Obata: An Oral History. The University of California at Los Angeles Special Collections Library. Japanese American History Project. Tape 2.
32. Ibid.

revered Japanese sports (archery, judo) as well as flower viewing (*hanami*) and moon viewing (*tsukimi*).[33] He regularly interacted with non-Japanese, but according to his granddaughter and biographer, Kimi Kodani Hill, Obata stopped speaking in English in his later years. After he retired, he resolved to return to Japan in 1954 to visit his parents' grave. A Japanese travel agency encouraged him to use the opportunity to conduct a tour with American visitors. Obata and Haruko established a series of "cultural exchange" tours to improve relations between Japan and the United States, saying that preventing future wars required that the countries have a "better understanding."[34] The tours were carefully choreographed, so that American visitors saw a highly aestheticized version of Japan. He did take them, however, to Hiroshima in 1954, when survivors were still not comfortable seeing American faces. More frequently, they took visitors to view antique Japanese arts and crafts, temples and shrines, gardens, and architectural landmarks that had survived the wartime bombings.

The tours were also a way for Obata to relearn and re-appreciate Japan. While acknowledging that Mt. Fuji had become something of a cliché, Obata stressed that the mountain was a "symbol of peace" and as Japan's paternal guardian.[35] He spoke fondly of seeing how well-behaved school children in naval uniforms behaved with their teacher. He enjoyed eating Japanese food and finding out what the Americans would or would not eat. Always interested in Japanese women's hair, he was chagrined to find that many Japanese were dyeing their hair red and perming it. He also questioned why Japanese department stores displayed mannequins of Western women. He spoke admiringly of how hard the Japanese worked and the fact that women were the "biggest driving force that made it possible for Japan to make a comeback after the war."

Although raised as a Buddhist and having lived at a Methodist church upon arriving in San Francisco, Obata's religion was "Great

33. Chiura Obata: An Oral History.
34. Ibid.
35. Ibid.

Nature." The blessing of nature, he said, was his God. Because he found power in nature, he claimed not to need religion.[36] He found his church when he went hiking at Mono Lake, Yosemite's Half Dome, and even the desert surrounding Topaz. This faith in nature as a source of solace helped immeasurably during his internment. Years after the war, he recalled for an interviewer, "In between (the Rocky Mountains and Topaz Mountain), the rising sun in the morning and the sunset [are] calm." He found a "profound gratitude for these things" that gave him the feeling that he had not been "abandoned" during the internment.[37] Because he had gone to Topaz, he could realize that beauty also exists in the "enormous bleakness" of the desert. His ultimate fear was that Americans, living in a land rich in natural resources, did not respect nature as a blessing. After his postwar trips, seeing the landscape under construction and dams in its rivers, Obata feared the same for Japan.

While at Topaz, Obata found a canal that had been built by Mormons over one hundred years before the start of World War II. He discovered—to his delight—that there were fish living in the canal. Obata recalled that he had joked with the camp's director that he had found both a Japanese and German species of carp—an Axis alliance in the Utah desert.[38] Nature, for Obata, was a constant source of joy and appreciation.

Tôyô Miyatake

After World War II, Little Tokyo became a way station for Japanese visiting the United States. San Francisco had been the primary point of entry prior to the war, but the development of Long Beach harbor increased traffic into Los Angeles. Visiting Japanese did not need to speak English or even leave "Japan" when they stayed in Little Tokyo. Like San Francisco's Japantown, Little Tokyo was a Japanese outpost,

36. Chiura Obata: An Oral History.
37. The interview was given in Japanese, but Obata referred to the "rising sun" in English. Chiura Obata: "An Oral History." The University of California at Los Angeles Special Collections Library. Japanese American History Project. Tape 2.
38. Chiura Obata: An Oral History.

where they could stay at the Miyako Hotel, eat at Kawafuku, and read the *Rafu Shinpo* to catch up on the latest news in Tokyo. First generation Japanese and their offspring ran the stores that sold *mochi* rice, *Asahi Kamera* magazine, and Japanese wine. Miyatake Tôyô was the local media's primary photographer, documenting visiting Japanese luminaries as well as Little Tokyo events. Fujiwara Yoshie, who was the director of Japan's leading opera house, insisted that members of his company stop at Miyatake's studio before boarding a ship back to Japan.

Although artists incarcerated during World War II continued to paint, photograph, and even exhibit works in the camps, their art and lives would forever be marked by the internment experience. After his release from Manzanar in 1945, Miyatake returned to Little Tokyo and reopened his portrait studio with his son Archie. Although he had participated in international photography groups before the war, Miyatake's activities became focused on the Japanese community, where he served as an ambassador of sorts for visiting Japanese. Unlike Arnold Genthe's photographs of Chinatown, a white photographer taking photos of the exotic for white viewers, Miyatake's documentation of Little Tokyo was as a member of the community. Miyatake became a leading figure in the Little Tokyo community, serving as Grand Marshal in the annual Nisei parade, photographing visiting Japanese actors and politicians for the *Rafu Shinpo*, and meeting members of the Japanese imperial family when they visited Los Angeles. Hollywood actors continued to create a demand for new portraits and Miyatake's skills were highly sought after. Suzuki Denmei, a Japanese star who traveled to Los Angeles to act in movies, stated that "Miyatake himself seeped into his portraits."[39] He was freed from the barbed wire surrounding the Japanese community in 1945, but Miyatake Tôyô did not stray far from the Japanese-American community after being released.

---

39. Essay by Suzuki Denmei in Miyatake, Atsufumi, Taisuke Fujishima, and Eikoh Hosoe, eds. *Toyo Miyatake Behind the Camera 1923-1979*. (Tokyo: Bungeishunji Co., Ltd., 1984), 191.

Miyatake stopped taking fine art photographs, however. There are probably several reasons for this. First, he was extremely busy with commissioned photographs and managing the studio. He became Little Tokyo's official documenter: family portraits, parades, visiting Japanese celebrities and dignitaries, including the imperial family, athletic events, weddings and banquets, were captured on film. Miyatake was also older and had less energy. He could no longer stay up into the wee hours once his studio was closed to experiment with his images. Furthermore, Itô Michio, his creative collaborator, was no longer in Los Angeles. Although he visited Los Angeles and ensured a steady flow of customers for Miyatake's studio, the pair no longer worked together on new, creative projects.

The postwar fortunes of Obata, Kuniyoshi, Ishigaki, Shimizu, and Miyatake are instructive. Obata's family members were resourceful and effective in protecting his work, but his contribution is somewhat subsumed in the wartime internment experience of Japanese Americans. In the early 1990s, a beautiful book with his art and letters created during his 1927 trip to Yosemite was published introducing Obata's landscapes to a wider audience.[40] Scholars of the Japanese concentration camp experience during World War II pay more attention to Miyatake's depictions of life in Manzanar than his equally great contribution to the history of modernist photography prior to the war. Both Obata and Miyatake emerged from the camps devoted to building bridges between their Japanese-American communities, Anglo-Americans, and the Japanese government, and less dedicated to pioneering new forms of modern art expression.

Alone among these artists, Kuniyoshi has received by far the most attention from United States scholarship, but primarily as an

40. *Obata's Yosemite: The Art and Letters of Chiura Obata from his Trip to the High Sierra in 1927*. Reprint of letters and journal entries. Essays by Janice T. Driesbach and Susan Landauer. Yosemite National Park, CA: Yosemite Association, 1993.

important Asian-American artist. As the Museum of Modern Art recognized in 1929, his art was American and did not require qualified, "hyphenated" designation, so the category seems to be limiting. At the same time, Kuniyoshi was keenly aware that he was forever a Japanese national until he could become a U.S. citizen. Proud of their local hero, collectors from his hometown prefecture of Okayama, purchased much of Kuniyoshi's work. Japanese museums exhibit Kuniyoshi's art in rooms designated for "modern Japanese artists," hosted his 100-year anniversary exhibition, and regularly publish biographies on his life and art.

Virtually nothing has been written about Ishigaki or Shimizu in English; their paintings, too, have been relocated to Japanese museums in their home prefectures, Wakayama and Tochigi respectively. Ishigaki sometimes appears as a footnote in scholarly works on American leftist art movements as a founding member of the John Reed Club. That his studio was used for its inaugural meeting is dismissed. It is perhaps no surprise that Shimizu is completely unknown in the United States, since he left early and none of his works are in American collections. Still, he exemplifies how cosmopolitan and inclusive the New York art world was prior to World War II, and he also shows how life as a cosmopolite does not prevent one from rising to a nationalist cause and supporting a war of aggression.

These five artists are only a few examples selected from hundreds who traveled from Japan to the United States during the interwar period. These representative stories will—hopefully—instigate not only further investigation into their lives and work, but into other U.S.-based Japanese artists, whose stories are worthy of being in the art history record.

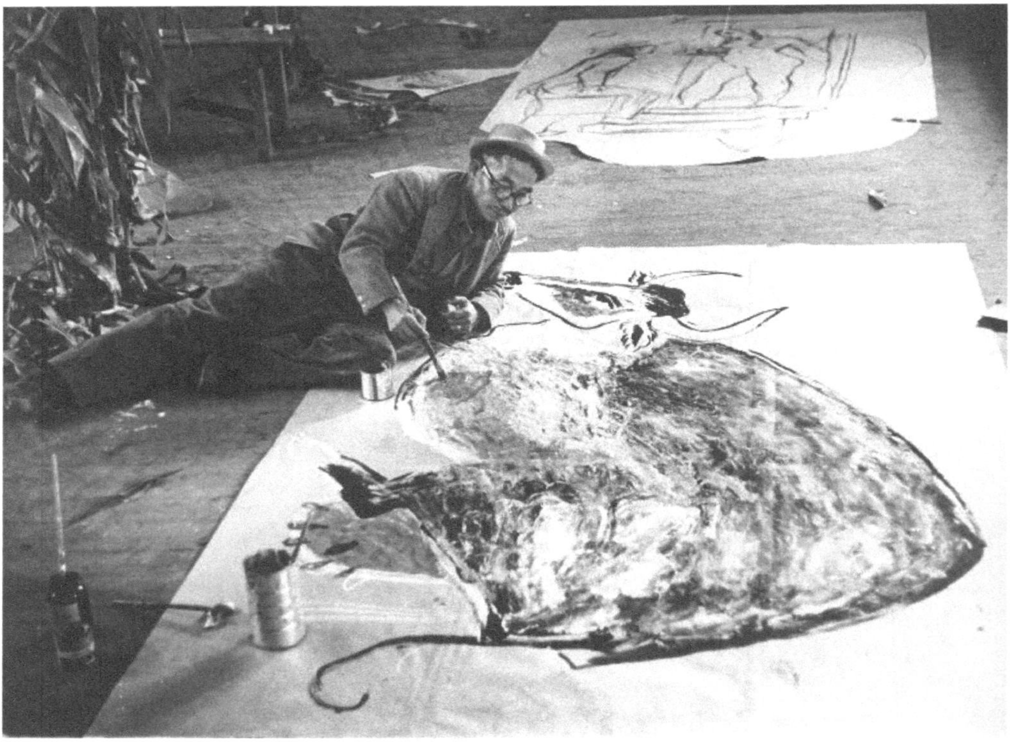

Kuniyoshi Yasuo painting, 1945. Yasuo Kuniyoshi papers, 1906-2016. Archives of American Art, Smithsonian Institution.

Bibliography

Archives and Collections

Tokyo Metropolitan Museum of Photography

Museum of Contemporary Art, Tokyo

JCII Library, Tokyo

National Research Institute for Cultural Properties, (Tobunken), Tokyo

Japanese American National Museum, Los Angeles

Los Angeles County Museum of Art

Art Students League, New York

Fine Arts Museums Archives, San Francisco

Asian American Art Project, Stanford University

Gannett, Lewis, 1891-1966. Papers (Harvard University)
  Fujita Jido Papers, 1936-1937

Hayward Historical Society, Hayward, California

Inventory of the Chuzo Tamotsu Papers, 1924-1975: Center for Southwest Research, General Library, University of New Mexico

Smithsonian Institution, Archives of American Art
  Yasuo Kuniyoshi papers
  Tanaka Yasushi – correspondence with Frederic C. Torrey, art dealer in San Francisco, 1915-1924
  Wood and Adelaide Lawson Gaylor papers, 1866- (Includes information about Kuniyoshi, Salons of America, etc.)

Smithsonian Institution Research Information System (Includes letters and archives of conversations with Kuniyoshi Yasuo)

Robert Laurent Papers, 1869-1973 (Includes correspondence with Kuniyoshi Yasuo)

Oral History Interview with Katherine Schmidt 1969, December 8 – 15, Archives of American Art, Smithsonian Institution

Oral History Interview with Peggy Bacon, 1973, Archives of American Art, Smithsonian Institution

Japanese American History Archives, San Francisco

Henry Sugimoto Papers

Miyatake Toyo, oral interview, JANM oral history program

University of Washington Libraries, Special Collections

Dr. Kyo Koike papers

San Francisco Art Institute Archives

SF Museum of Art Collection, East West Art Society Folder, 1922

Collection of the Japanese American History Archives, San Francisco

University of California, Los Angeles, Special Collections

Hibi (George Matsusaburô) Papers, 1893-1972 (painter)

Nishimura (Yoshio) Papers, 1875-1947 (socialist and journalist)

Yoneda Papers, 1928-1970

Obata (Chiura) Papers, 1965

Ashiya Municipal Museum

Nakayama Iwata Research Center

Wakayama Prefectural Museum

Ishigaki Eitarô Papers – Ishigaki Eitarô memorial museum archives

Bulletins, 1996, 1997

Periodicals: Newspapers, Magazines and Journals

The American Annual of Photography, (1928)

American Photography, (1927)

The Art Digest, (1930)

Art Front, (1936)

The Art News, (1924-1925)

Arts Weekly, (1932)

Asahi Kamera, (1920-1939)

Asahi Shinbun, (1958-1959)

Atorie (Atelier), (1924-1950)

Bijutsu Gurafu, (1970-1983)
Bijutsu Shincho, (1952)
Bijutsu shinron, (1931)
Bijutsu Techô, (1949-1980)
Bi no Kuni, (1925-1932)
Boston Globe
Bulletin of Photography, (1897-1915)
Camera, (December 1950)
Camera Craft
Chûô Bijutsu, (1927-1936)
Creative Art
Daily News, (1938)
Daily Worker, (1936-1938)
Fototaimusu, (1929-1933)
Geijutsu Shinchô, (1995)
Kashû Mainichi (1933)
Kindai Bijutsu Kenkyû, (1959)
Los Angeles Express, (1919)
Los Angeles Herald, (1895)
Los Angeles Times, (1916-1949)
Mainichi Shimbun, (1950)
Mizue みづゑ, (1920-1983)
Modern Photography (The Special Autumn Number of "The Studio"), (1931)
Nanpo Gashin, (1942)
New Yorker, (1928)
New York Herald – Tribune, (1924-1927)
The New York Times, (1910-1948)
The New York Times Magazine, 1926
New York Post, (1936-1938)
New York World-Telegram, (1937)
Nihon Dokusho Shinbun, (1959)
Parnassus, Volumes 1-13, (1929-1941)
Pasadena Daily News, (1903-1912)
Pictorial Photography in America, (1929)

Pilotis, Hyogo Prefecture Museum of Contemporary Art News, (1987-1993)
Rafu Shinpo, (Los Angeles Japanese Daily News), (1928-1936)
Sansai, (1973-1974)
Shashin Saron, (1934-1935)
Shashin Geijutsu, (1921)
Shashin Geppô, (1895-1940)
Time, (1938)
Tokyo Nichi-nichi Shinbun-sha, (1931)
Tokyo Taimuzu, (1951)
Toshin Shimbun, (1931)
Vanity Fair, (1931)
The Year's Photography, Royal Photographic Society Publication, (1929-1933)
Yomiuri Shinbun, (1958-1969)

PRIMARY SOURCES

Anderson, Antony.
"Of Art and Artists: A Son of Nippon with Originality." *Los Angeles Times*, (December 16, 1923).
"Art News from Laguna. Art Talent Among the Local Japanese." *Los Angeles Times*. (December 21, 1930).

Arishima Ikuma.
"Sekai to shite no Kuniyoshi Yasuo gahaku." *Tôkyo Nichi-nichi shinbun* (November 13, 1931).
"Hajimete Kuniyoshi-kun ni atte." Zaigai nihon sakka no shôkai. *Chûô Bijutsu Fukkô* (June 1, 1934).

Arima Ineko. "Kari no shukushu (Noda Hideo)." *Geijutsu Shinchô* 221, (May 1968).

Benjamin, Ruth L. "Japanese Painters in America." *Parnassus*. 7, no. 1 (October 1935).

Blair, Dorothy. "Hiroshi Yoshida, 1876-1950." *Artibus Asiae*. Artibus Asiaei, 14, no. 1-2 (1951).

Brook, Alexander. "Yasuo Kuniyoshi – A Tribute." *Yasuo Kuniyoshi, 1889-1935: A Retrospective Exhibition*. Austin, TX: University Art Museum. (1975).

Bulliet, C. J. "On Trying to Smile in Front of Kuniyoshi's Babies." *Chicago Evening Post*, (May 3, 1927).

Burrows, Carlyle. "Waifs of the W.P.A and Other Artists." *New York Herald Tribune*. (July 25, 1937).

"Photography in Japan." (English) *Camera*. (April 1946).

Canaday, John. "A Couple of Americans. (Yasuo Kuniyoshi and Charles Sheeler)." *The New York Times* (January 10, 1965).

Cummings, Paul. "The Art Students League. Part II." *Archives of American Art Journal*. 13, no. 2, (1973).

Devree, Howard.

"A Score of Art Shows: Sculpture, Oils, Watercolors, and Work in Black-and-White in Current Openings. (Ishigaki Eitarô Review)." *New York Times* (March 15, 1936).

"On the Local Calendar." *New York Times* (September 19, 1937).

"Kuniyoshi: 1921-1947; Whitney Museum Opens Its Retrospective Show." *The New York Times* (March 28, 1948).

"Davis and Kuniyoshi as Seen in Venice." *The New York Times* (December 14, 1952).

Duroc, Margaret. "Critique from the Left." *Art Front* (January, 1936).

Eglington, Guy. "Salons of America Open with a Bang." *The Art News* (October 24, 192).

Endo Chiyuki. "Hiko-san." *Nihon to Amerika* (February 1957).

Ezaki Masanori. "Kitagawa Tamiji." *Geijutsu Shincho* (November 1958).

Fenollosa, Ernest. *Epochs of Chinese and Japanese Art: an outline history of East Asiatic design*. London: William Heinemann Limited (1912).

Fujioka, Noboru. "Kuniyoshi Yasuo-kun no danmen." Zaigai nihon sakka no shôkai. *Chûô Bijutsu Fukkô* (June 1, 1934).

Fujishima, Taisuke. "Shakin-ka tamashii. (Miyatake Tôyô Shashin-ka: Miyatake Tôyô no sekai. Renzu ga toraeta ninngennno kiroku. 50-nen no nichibei kôryû-shi." *Bungei shunjû* (1980).

Fukuhara, Shinzô.

Shashin o kataru. Tokyo: Musashi shobo, 1943.

Shashin geijutsu. Tokyo: Musashi shobo, 1943.

Musashino fubutsu shashinshû. Osaka: Seibunsha, January 1943.

Hawai fûkei. Tokyo: Nihon shashin-kai, 1937.

The Old Town of Matsue. Tokyo: Japan Photographic Society, 1935.

"Nihon shashin no sûsei no fu-naiyô no keikô." *Nihon shashin nenkan Taisho 13 – 14 nen. Dai-ichi nenpan*. Tokyo: Asahi shinbun-sha. 1925.

"Shashin-dô." *Asahi Kamera*. (April 1926).

Hikari to sono kaicho. Tokyo: Shashin geijutsusha shuppan, 1923.
"Shashin no shin-shimei." (September 1922).
"Watashi no shashin geijutsu ni tai suru kenkai." *Taisho-ki no toshi sanshakusha-tachi – shashin geijutsu no jidai.* Photography Art 1921-1924. Shieseido and Shoto Art Museum, 1998.
"Shashin no shinshimei – shôzen." Reprinted. Oshima, Hiroshi editor. *Sairoku: shashin-ron. 1921-1965*. Tokyo Metropolitan Museum of Photography. Tankosha, 1999.

Foujioka Noboru. "Whistler and Japanese Art." *Kashu Mainichi.* (April 2, 1933).

Genauer, Emily. "Oriental Artists Exhibit." *New York World-Telegram*. (September 18, 1937).

Goodrich, Lloyd.
Yasuo Kuniyoshi. Published for the Whitney Museum of American Art. 1948.
"Lloyd Goorich Reminisces. Part II. *Archives of American Art Journal.* 3, no. 1 (1983).

Hailey, Gene. Editor *California Art Research* Reprinted in 1987 by Ellen Schwarz. Originally Published by Works Progress Administration. San Francisco, CA 1936-1937.

Hartmann, Sadakichi. *Japanese Art*. London: Putnam, 1904.

Hayakawa, Sessue. *Zen Showed Me the Way . . . to Peace, Happiness, and Tranquility*. Indianapolis: Bobbs-Merrill, 1960.

Hibi, George Matsusaburo. Art criticism articles. *Shinsekai Asahi, (*August 9, 1927).

Hibi, Hisako. *Peaceful Painter: Memoirs of an Issei Woman Artist*. Berkeley: Heyday Books, 2004.

Horino Masao.
Kamera me tetsu kôsei, 1930-1931. Tokyo: Kokushokankokai.
Gendai shashin geijutsuron. Tokyo: Yumanishobo. (Orig. 1930).

Hosoe Eikô. "Jidai no dokyumento. Dance." Shashin-ka: Miyatake Tôyô no sekai. Renzu ga toraeta ninngennno kiroku. 50-nen no nichibei kôryû-shi." *Bungei shunjû*. (1980).

Ishigaki Ayako.
Restless Wave. (Penname Matsui Haru.) New York: Modern Age Books, 1940.
"Zaibei Nihonjin gaka no seikatsu – Watashi no oto no yokogao." "A Japanese Artist's Life in America: My Husband's Profile." *Atelier* 258. (June 1948).

"Watashi no shinkon jidai: Amerika no hôrôki." *Shûkan Asahi Bessatsu*. (December 10, 1956).
"Nijûhachi nen no ai no fûsetsu." *Fujin kôron* 485. (September 1957).
"Ai wa tokoshie ni: Naki oto Eitarô ni sasagu." *Shûkan Asahi Bessatsu*. (February 28, 1958).
"Whipping" *Sekai* 301. (December 1970).
An interview with Ayako Ishigaki: About Democratic Art in America and about Eitaro Ishigaki. *Bijutsu Undo* 89, (April 1971).
"Ishigaki Eitarô: Nichibei futatsu no kokka no hazama o hyumanizumu no gaka to shite ikinuku." *Jinbutsu showa-shi* 8*: hyôhaku no shôgai*. Tokyo: Chikumashobo, 1975.
"Noda Hideo no mihapyô sakuhin." *Mizue* 867, (June 1977).
"Watashi to Ishigaki Eitarô." *NHK Nichiyô bijutsukan*. (December 6, 1977).
"Ishigaki Eitarô to Kuniyoshi Yasuo." *Gendai no me*. 333 Tokyo: Kindaibijutsu-kyokai, 1982.
Umi o watatta ai no gaka: Ishigaki Eitarô no shôgai. Tokyo: Ochanomizu-shobo. 1988.
Ishigaki Ayako nikki (Shita/Ue). Tokyo: Iwanami Shoten, 1996.

Ishigaki, Eitarô.
"Young Japanese Artist Finds Strange Contrasts in American Men and Women: Eitaro Ishigaki Marvels That Women Are So Much More Cultured and Better Educated Than Opposite Sex Members." (Interview with Ishigaki Eitarô.) *Evening Telegram New York*. (November 4, 1922).
"Iro-toridori na bijutsu-ten: hôjin shuppinsha jûroku nin hatsuratsu na seiki tsuyoi shikisai no shigeki to kosei o daitan ni jiyû ni hôsha shite." (Review of the 9th Independent Artists' Association Exhibition, *Japanese Times*, (March 11, 1925).
"Sôzoku gasshuku: Dokuritsu bijutsu-ten zakkan." (Review of the 13th Annual Independent Artists' Association Exhibition.) *Japan Taimuzu*. (March 13, 1929).
"Message of Ishigaki." *The Art Digest*. (May 15, 1940).
"Amerika bijutsu no ayumi." *Bijutsu Techo* 49. (October 1951).
"Amerika garo kara mita nikaten – hoshii Nihonteki na kaori, seikatsu yôshiki to no chôwa mo." *Tokyo Taimuzu* (September 8, 1951).
"Amerika ega-ten." *Minami Nihon Shinbun*. (January 30, 1952).
"Zaibei Nihonjin gaka no seikatsu-hô." *Geijutsu Shincho* (May 3-5, 1952).
"Purofessa Kuniyoshi." *Geijutsu Shincho* (September 3-9, 1952).
"40 Years' Wandering in America." *Chuo Koron* 67. (7-10,12-14)

June-September 1952; November – December, 1952. *Chuo Koron* 70, 9. September, 1952. (Reprinted in *Ai ni tsuite no kokuhaku; otoko to shite onna to shite*).

"Kuniyoshi no gyôseki." *Geijutsu Shinchô*. (July 1953).

"Horeisho-gai nanajûsan banchi." *Chûô Kôron*. (September 1955).

"Katayama Sen sôde." *Meiji bunka zenshû geppô*. (October 25, 1955).

"Mukashi no nakamatachi – Jon Ri-do kurabu." *Geijutsu techo: tokushû Mekishiko no bijutsu*. (October 1955).

Jenks, Anne L. and Thomas M. Messer. *Contemporary Painters of Japanese Origin in America*. Boston: Institute of Contemporary Art, 1958.

Jewell, Edward Alden.

"Kuniyoshi, In New One-Man Exhibit at Downtown Gallery Shows Considerable Progress." *The New York Times*. (February 8, 1933).

"Art Under A Democracy: Annual of American Artists Congress Raises Some Far-Reaching Questions (Ishigaki Eitarô)." *The New York Times*, (May 8, 1938).

"New Artists Group in First Exhibition: Japanese-American Unit Offers Painting and Sculpture at the Riverside Museum." *The New York Times*, (May 27, 1949).

Kainen, Jacob.

"Eitaro Ishigaki." *Daily Worker*, New York. (March 18, 1936).

"The Art World Dismissed WPA Chinese and Japanese Artists Express Unity in Paintings at ACA Gallery." *Daily Worker, New York*. (September 18, 1937).

Kakefuda, Isao. "Ôtaguro Moto-o, Kakefuda Isao, Fukuhara Shinzô: Geijutsu shashin tenrankai." *Shashin geijutsu 1-4*. September, 1921.

Kamei, Takeshi. *Nihon shashinshi e no shogen*. Kyoto: Tankosha, 1997.

Kamiya Yukio. "Watashi to Kitagawa Tamiji." *E* (July 1984).

Kanamaru, Shigene.

Shashin geijutsu. Tokyo: Asahi shinbunsha, 1979.

Shinkô shashin no tsukurikata. Tokyo: Genkô-sha, 1932.

Kaneko, Yoshio. "Yasuo Kuniyoshi no koto." *Bijutsu Shinron*, 6-12, 1931.

Kato, Taizo. Review of Shakudosha exhibition. *Rafu Shimpo*, (June 23, 1923).

Kimura, Ihee.

Four Japanese Painters: Taikan Yokoyama, Gyokudo Kawai, Shoen Uemura, Kiyokata Kaburaki / with reproductions and remarks by the artists. 49 Leica photographs by Kimura Ihee. Japan Photo Service, 1939.

Japan through a Leica: 100 Glimpses, Scenery, Life and Art. Tokyo: Kokushokankokai, 2006.

Kimura, Shigeo.

"Ishigaki Eitarô." *Bijutsu Gurafu* 14-6. (August 1965). Reprinted in August 1983.

"Ishigaki Eitarô–Suron, Ben Shan, Mashu to soshiaru shiin ha no nihon no gakatachi: Ishigaki Eitarô, Shimizu Toshi, Noda Hideo, Kuniyoshi Yasuo," *Bijutsu Gurafu* 2, (August 1983).

King, Ray. "Japanese Painter Ishigaki Portrays Chinese Struggle." *Daily Worker, New York*. (May 16, 1940).

Kira, Hiromu. "Why I Am a Pictorialist Photographer." *Photo-era Magazine*. (May 1930).

Kitagawa, Tamiji.

"Mekishiko gakatachi." *Bijutsu techo*. (April 1953).

Kitagawa Tamiji bijutsu kyôikuronshû. Sofusha, 1998.

Kiyama, Henry (Yoshitaka). *The Four Immigrants Manga: A Japanese Experience in San Francisco, 1904-1924*. Translated by Frederik L. Schodt. Berkeley: Stone Bridge Press, 1997.

Klein, Jerome.

"First One-man Show by Eitaro Ishigaki." *The New York Sun*. (March 14, 1936).

"Chinese Artists Join Japanese in WPA Job Protest." *New York Post* (Art Comment) (September 18, 1937).

"Democracy Aided by World Figures at Art Congress." *New York Post*, (December 18, 1937).

Kojima Usui. "Sôkô pureshideo bijutsukan ni chinretsu saretaru ukiyo-e." *Mizue*, (August 1921).

Kojima Zenzaburô. "Kuniyoshi Yasuo-shi kotenhyô." *Tokyo Asahi Shinbun*, (November 20, 1931).

Kôtoku Yukie. "Oji Shusui no omoide." *Chûô Kôron*. (April 1933).

Kubo Sadajiro.

"Zakuro o motu onna." *Geijutsu shinchô* 7-2, (February 1956).

"Hômon Kitagawa Tamiji." *Bijutsu Techo* (April 1957).

"Kitagawa to no 20 nen." *Geijutsu shinchô* 9-11, (November 1958).

"Kitagawa Tamiji no hekiga no shigoto." *Mizue* (February 1960).

"History of the Sufferings of the Japanese Citizens. *Hokubei nihonjin no shûyôjo: kiroku kaiga*. Editors: Henry Sugimoto Kubo Sadajiro. Tokyo: Sobunsha. (April 1981).

Kitagawa Tamiji: Bijutsu no sekai 1. Sobunsha, 1984.
Nihon no hanga sakkatachi: Bijutsu no sekai 5. Tokyo: Sobunsha, 1987.

Kuniyoshi Yasuo.
"Art and Artists in Japan." *Arts Weekly*. (April 23, 1932).
"East to West." *Magazine of Art*. (February 1940).
Yasuo Kuniyoshi. New York: American Artists Group, Monograph (no. 11 1945).
"Geijutsu no sekai ni tsuite." "On the World of Art." *Bijutsu Techo*, (July 1949).
Archives of American Art. Letter. General Correspondence 1941-1962, 1971-189, undated; Box 1, Folder 2.
"Civilization Beseiged." Archives of American Art. No Date.

Kusama Yayoi, Laura Hoptman and Akira Tatehata. *Love Forever: Yayoi Kusama in New York, 1958-1968*. Los Angeles: Los Angeles County Museum of Art, 1998.

Laurent, Robert. "Memories of Yas." *College Art Journal*, 13, no. 1, (Autumn 1953).

L, J. "Ishigaki: Cosmopolite and Contemporary." *Art News*. (May 11, 1940).

Louisgarde. "Yasushi Tanaka at Devambez." *Paris Review*. From the Smithsonian Institute archives. Yasushi Tanaka letters to Frederic C. Torrey, 1913-1924. Archives of American Art.

Maedako Hiroichiro (Koichiro).
"Santô senkyaku." *Gendai Nihon bungaku zenshû* (77). *Maedakô Hiroichirô, Fujimori Seikichi, Tokunaga Sunao, Murayama Tomoyoshi shu*. Tokyo: Chikumashobo, 1957.
"Akai basha." *Gendai Nihon bungaku zenshû* (77). *Maedakô Hiroichirô, Fujimori Seikichi, Tokunaga Sunao, Murayama Tomoyoshi shu*. Tokyo: Chikumashobo, 1957.
"Semuga." *Gendai Nihon bungaku zenshû* (77). *Maedakô Hiroichirô, Fujimori Seikichi, Tokunaga Sunao, Murayama Tomoyoshi shu*. Tokyo: Chikumashobo, 1957.

Markino Yoshio.
A Japanese Artist in London. Illustrations by Yoshio Markino. Philadelphia: George W. Jacobs & Co. Publishers. 1910.
My Recollections and Reflections. London: Chatto and Windus, 1913.

Matsuyama Shisui.
Geijutsu shashin to kôzu. Jitsugyô no nihon sha, 1922.
Shashin no ichi nichi. Tokyo: ARS Arusu, 1923.

McBride, Henry.
“Review of Yasuo Kuniyoshi exhibition.” *The New York Herald*, (January 8, 1922).
“Review of Yasuo Kuniyoshi exhibition. *The New York Herald*, (January 3, 1924).
“The Palette Knife.” *Creative Art: An Illustrated Magazine of Fine and Applied Art.* (January 1930, February 1930).

Meixner, Mary. “Kuniyoshi Talks with Students.” *College Art Journal*, 13, no. 1 (Autumn 1953).

Millier, Arthur.
“Japanese Artist Paints in Occident.” *Los Angeles Times*, (November 21, 1926).
“Japanese Artist Returns.” *Los Angeles Times,* (November 7, 1926).
“City’s Japanese Show Art.” *Los Angeles Times*, (December 29, 1929).

Mitchell, Louise. “The Fight for Negro Liberation: Eitaro Ishigaki, Well Known Anti-Fascist Japanese Artist, Answers Slurs Against Murals in Harlem Court.” *Daily Worker, New York.* (April 5, 1938).

Miyasaka Masaru. “Nika-kai. (Shimizu Toshi).” *Mizue.* (October 1927).

Miyatake Toyo.
A Life in Photography: The Recollections of Toyo Miyatake. With Enid H. Douglas. Claremont, CA: Oral History Program, Claremont Graduate School, 1978.
Shashin-ka: Miyatake Toyo no sekai – renzu ga toraeta ningen no kiroku 50nen no nichibei kôryû-shi. Tokyo: Bungeishunjushin-sha, 1980.
Miyatake Tôyô no shashin 1923-1979. Tokyo: Bungeshunju, 1984.

Moriguchi Tari. “Nikakai egahyô.” *Mizue,* (October 1938).

Mori Yoshitarô. *Saishin jitsuyô shashinjutsu kôwa.* Tokyo: Maruzen, (July 1920 and February 1923).

Mori Yoshitarô and Kaye Shimojima. *Annual of Japan Photographic Art, 1935-1936.* Shashin Shino-sha.

Murayama Tomoyoshi. “Shashin no atarashii kinô.” Oshima, Hiroshi editor. *Sairoku: shashin-ron. 1921-1965.* Tokyo Metropolitan Museum of Photography. Tankosha, 1999.

Nagai Kafû. *American Stories.* Translated by Mitsuko Iriye. New York: Columbia University Press, 2000.

Nakai Masakazu.
“Kabe.” *Kôga*, 1, no. 3 (1932).
“Utsusu.” *Kôga*, 1, no. 4 (1932).

Bigaku nyûmon. Tokyo: Asahi shinbun-sha, 1975, 1991.

Nakano Tomiko. "Chichi no omoide." *Shimizu Toshi ten*. Musashino Cultural Center, 1991.

Nakayama Iwata.

"Tabi no omoide shashin-shû – Supein yo! Doko e iku!" *Asahi Kamera* (November 1937).

"Nakayama Iwata chojutsu shô." Reprinted in *Hikari no modanizumu: Nakayama Iwata shashinshû*. Heibôsha: 1987.

Nakayama Masako.

"Kaisô – Nakayama Iwata." *Pilotis* 56. Hyôgo kenritsu kindai bijutsukan nyûsu. (July 1985).

Haikara ni 92 sai – shashinka Nakayama Iwata to ikite. Tokyo: Kawadeshoboshinsha. 1987.

"Zutto, Iwata no soba ni ite." *Hikari no dandizumu: Nakayama Iwata shashinshû 1895-1949*. Tokyo: Heibonsha 1987.

Nanpô Gashin: Daitô-a Sensô. Rikugun bijutsu kyôkai. (September 1942).

Naoki Tomojirô. *Takagi Haisui den*. Tokyo: Daihizen sha. 1941.

Neuhaus, Eugen. *The Galleries of the Exposition: A Critical Review of the Paintings, Statuary and the Graphic Arts in the Palace of Fine Arts at the Panama-Pacific International Exposition*. San Francisco: Paul Elder and Co., 1915.

Newhall, Nancy, editor. *The Daybooks of Edward Weston, Volume II. California*. Center for Creative Photography, University of Arizona. 1981.

Noda Hideo.

"Saikin Amerika bijutsukai no jôsei." *Atorie* May 1935.

"Gendai hekiga no riron to hôhô." *Atorie* July 1936.

"Saikin beikoku bijutsukai no dôkô." *Atorie* January 1937.

"Hiranonimasu Boshu." *Mizue*. February 1938.

Obata Chiura.

"How Painting Is Taught in Japan." The Argus. April 1928.

Obata's Yosemite: The Art and Letters of Chiura Obata from his Trip to the High Sierra in 1927. Reprint of letters and journal entries. Essays by Janice T. Driesbach and Susan Landauer. Yosemite National Park, CA: Yosemite Association, 1993.

An Oral History (California Asian American Artists biographical survey information, SC 0929. Stanford University Archives, Stanford, CA).

Okakura Tenshin.
The Ideals of the East, With Special Reference to Japan. Vermont: C. E. Tuttle Company, 1970.
"Modern Art from a Japanese Point of View," *The International Quarterly*, 11. New York: Fox, Duffield, and Company, 1905.

Okamoto Tarô.
Kuroi taiyô. Tokyo: Kôdansha, 1980.
Nihon no dentô. Tokyo: Kobunsha, 2005.

Okamoto Toki.
Puroretaria bijutsu to ha nani ka? Tokyo: Atorie-sha, 1930.
Nihon puroretaria bijutsu-shi. Tokyo: Zokeisha, 1967.

Omura Bunji. "Japanese Artists Born in America Excel Many in Nippon, Experts Say." *The Japanese American Review.* New York, (August 9, 1941).

Orozco, José Clemente. *The Artist in New York: Letters to Jean Charlot, 1925-1929.* University of Texas Press, 1974.

Otani Isao. *Tanin no kuni, jibun no kuni: nikei amerikajin ozakike sandai no kiroku.* Tokyo: Kadokawashoten, 1983.

Pach, Walter. *Queer Thing, Painting: Forty Years in the World of Art.* Tomlin Press, 2014.

Phillips, Duncan. "2nd Annual Exhibition of the Washington Independent." (Review of Kuniyoshi Yasuo exhibition.) *The Arts.* (April 1928).

Price, Claire. "A Talk With Yoshio Markino in His Attic Studio." *The New York Times.* (August 5, 1928).

Saisho Tokuji. "Robato Henri no ga ni tsuite." *Mizue: Ôbei no gendai gaka.* (January 1922).

Sawa Hajime. "Nikakai hyô." *Bijutsu.* (October 1937).

Sekai shashin zenshû: 3 Amerika. Tokyo: Heibonsha. 1958.

Sekikawa Sakio. *Yumeji no tegami.* Tokyo: Kodansha. 1985.

Shimizu Akira. "Edowado Suteiken no hito to geijutsu." *Kôga*, 1, no. 4 (1932).

Shimizu Kashin. *Wind of Spring: A Book of Poems.* Introduction by Edith Daley. Illustrations by Obata Chiura. San Francisco: Beishin Press. 1923.

Shimizu Toshi.
"Beikoku etching kai keni. John Sloan." *Chûô Bijutsu* 153 (August 1928).
"Yasuo Kuniyoshi-kun." *Mizue* 322 1931.
"Kuniyoshi Yasuo-kun o kataru." Zaigai nihon sakka no shôkai. *Chûô Bijutsu Fukkô.* (June 1, 1934).
"Watashi no koto. Kyôkai no koto." *Dokuritsu Bijutsu jûnen kinen gashû. Asahi shinbunsha.* (March 1940).

*Nanpô jûgungashin.*Kokusai johosha shuppanbu, (October 1943).
"Shimizu Toshi nikki. 1924" (Repinted in *Shimizu Toshi ten* Musashino Culutral Center, 1991.
Shimizu Toshi: Tochigi kenritsu bijutsukan shôzo. Utsunomiya: Tochigi kenritsu bijutsukan, 2007.

Shirey, David. "Japanese Step Up Quest for Art in the U.S.; Preference for Impressionists Fancy for Foujita Open Own Museums." The New York Times. January 24, 1973.

Statler, Oliver. *Modern Japanese Prints: An Art Reborn.* Vermont & Tokyo: Charles A. Tuttle, 1956.

Suzuki Yasunori. "Shimizu-kun no geijutsu." *Dokuritsu bijutsu.* Volume 9. Dokuritsu bijutsu kyôkai. Kensetsusha. 1933.

Taguchi Shôgo. "Shimizu Toshi-shi kotenhyô." *Mizue* (June, 1937).

Takamura Kango. *Hariuddo ni ikiru.* 1988.

Takamura Kôtarô. Translated by Hiroaki Sato. *A Brief History of Imbecility: Poetry and Prose of Takamura Kôtarô.* Honolulu: University of Hawaii Press, 1992.

Tanaka Masao. "Nakayama Iwata sakuhin: omoide no meisaku arubamu no. 4." *Camera.* (December 1950).

Tani Jôji.
Meriken jappu shôbai ôrai. Tokyo: Shakai shiso-sha, 1975.
"The Shanghaied Man." *The Columbia Anthology of Modern Japanese Literature: Volume 1: From Restoration to Occupation, 1868-1945.* New York: Columbia University Press, 2005.
Tekisasu mushuku / Kiki. Misuzu Shobo. 2003.

Tateishi Tetsuomi.
Ishigaki Eitarô. Tokyo: Bijutsu shuppansha, 1959.
"Aru natsu no netsui omoide: Ishigaki Eitarô to no deai." *NHK Nichiyô bijutsukan* 6. (December 1977).

Terada Takeo.
"Eitaro Ishigaki." *Miru 4. The News of the National Museum of Modern Art, Kyoto.* (September 1967).
"Noda Hideo no kaisô." *Bijutsu techo.* (April 1953).
"Noda Hideo no omoide." *Beijutsu Gurafu 25-4.* (March 1976 and reprinted in August 1983).

Tilney, F. C. "American Work at the London Exhibitions." *American Photography* 21, 1927.

Tower, Grace Hortense.
"In And Out of Some Pasadena Studios: What the Artists Are Doing with Palette and Brush. T. Aoki." *Pasadena Daily News.* (July 28, 1906).
"Hand Painted Rooms Fad of Society Women." *The Pasadena Daily News.* (February 9, 1907).

Von Wigand, Charmion. "Ishigaki's Two Traditions." *New Masses.* (April 28, 1936).

Watanabe Kôzô. "Nikakai o miru." *Bijutsu.* (October 1937).

Wilder, Marshall P. "Smiling 'Round the World. Number 5 – In Japan." *Boston Daily Globe.* (March 8, 1908).

Yabe Nobutoshi. *Fukuhara Shinzô.* Tokyo: Shieseido. 1970.

Yanagi Ryô.
"Burboo Kuniyoshi." *Atelier* 8-12. 1931.
"Eko-ru do Pari no genjitsu." *Kôga*, 1, no. 4 (1932).

Yoshida, Hiroshi.
Yoshida Hiroshi zen mokuhan gashû. Tokyo: Abe shuppan, 1989.
Yoshida Hiroshi ten: kindai fukeiga no kyoshô seishin to jojô. Fukuoka-shi bijutsukan, 1996.

Zigrosser, Carl. "Contemporary American Artists: The Prints of Yasuo Kuniyoshi." *Parnassus.* Volume 12, Number 2. February, 1940.

Secondary Sources

Ajioka Yoshihito. "Kuniyoshi Yasuo shoden." *Kuniyoshi Yasu: tokubetsu-ten.* Fukutake Collection, Shibuya kuritsu shôtô bijutsukan, 1987.

Ando Terumi. "Genichiro Inokuma: Circa his 'Sea and Women' Period." *Inokuma Genichirô kaiko-ten.* A Retrospective Exhibition of Genichiro. Inokuma. Marugame Genichiro Inokuma Museum of Contemporary Art. Marugame, Kagawa, November 2003 – February 2004.

Aoki Fukiko. "Natori Yônosuke to 'Raifu' no jidai." *Amerika 1937: Natori Yônosuke shashin-shû.* Tokyo: Kodansha, 1992.

Aoki Shigeru. "Fudôsha no Yoshida Hiroshi." *Yoshida Hiroshi ten. Kindai fûkei no kyoshô. Seishin to jojô." A Master of Modern Landscape Painting: Yoshida Hiroshi Exhibition. Refreshingly Original and Lyrical.* Fukuoka Art Museum, October 26-November 24, 1996.

Asano Toru.
"Amerika jidai no Shimizu Toshi." and "Ishigaki Eitarô." *Amerika ni mananda Nihon no gakatachi: Kuniyoshi, Shimizu, Ishigaki, Noda to*

Amerikan shiin ega. Japanese Artists Who Studied in U.S.A. and the American Scene. Exhibitions in Tokyo at the National Museum of Modern Art, July 24-September 5, 1982 and Kyoto at the National Museum of Modern Art, September 14-October 11, 1982.

Ashton, Dore. *Noguchi East and Wes*t. New York: Knopf, 1992.

Azuma Eiichiro. *Between Two Empires: Race, History, and Transnationalism in Japanese America*. Oxford and New York: Oxford University Press, 2005.

Bahr, Ehrhard. *Weimar on the Pacific: German Exile Culture in Los Angeles and the Crisis of Modernism*. Berkeley and Los Angeles: University of California Press, 2007.

Barnhisel, Greg. "Perspectives USA and the Cultural Cold War: Modernism in Service of the State." *Modernism/Modernity*. 14. (November 2007).

Becker, Howard S. *Art Worlds*, University of California Press, 2008.

Bernstein, Sheri. "Selling California, 1900-1920." "Contested Eden, 1920-1940." *Made in California: Art, Image, and Identity, 1900-2000*. Los Angeles County Museum of Art University of California Press, 2001.

Birnbaum, Phyllis. *Glory in a Line: A Life of Foujita, the Artist Caught Between East & West*. New York: Faber and Faber, 2006.

Bolger, Doreen. "Hamilton Easter Field and His Contribution to American Modernism." *American Art Journal*, 20, no. 2, (1988).

Boorstin, Daniel J. "Introduction: The Immigrants Vision." Exhibition catalog. *The Golden Door: Artist-Immigrants of America, 1876-1976*. Hirshorn Museum and Sculpture Garden, Smithsonian Institution, 1976.

Bunnell, Peter C. *Camera Work: a Centennial Celebration*. Langhorn, PA: Photo Review, 2003.

Caldwell, Helen. *Michio Ito: The Dancer and His Dances*. Berkeley: University of California Press, 1977.

Casanova, Pascale. *The World Republic of Letters*. Cambridge, MA: Harvard University Press, 2004.

Chang, Gordon H., Mark Dean Johnson, and Paul J. Karlstrom, editors. *Asian American Art: A History, 1850-1970*. Palo Alto: Stanford University Press, 2008.

Chisolm, Lawrence A. *Fenollosa: The Far East and American Culture*. New Haven and London: Yale University Press, 1963.

Clark, John. *Modern Asian Art*. Honolulu: University of Hawaii Press, 1998.

Clayton, Virginia Tuttle. "Picturing a 'Usable Past'," *Drawing on America's Past: Folk Art, Modernism, and the Index of American Design*. Edited by Ulrike Mills, National Gallery of Art, Washington, 2002.

Cohen, Milton A. *Movement, Manifesto, Melee, the Modernist Group 1900-1914*. Lanham, MD: Lexington Books, 2004.

Coke, Van Deren. *Avant Garde Photography in Germany 1919-1939*. New York: Pantheon Books, 1982.

Conant, Ellen P., Editor. *Challenging Past and Present: The Metamorphosis of 19th Century Japanese Art*. Honolulu: University of Hawaii Press, 2006.

Crunden, Robert M. *Body and Soul: The Making of American Modernism*. New York: Basic Books, 2000.

Davis, Mike.

City of Quartz: Excavating the Future in Los Angeles. London: Vintage Books, 1992.

Ecology of Fear: Los Angeles and the Imagination of Disaster. London:" Vintage Books, 1998.

Dawson, Mike. "South of Point Lobos." *LA's Early Moderns: Art/Architecture/Photography* Los Angeles: Balcony Press, 2003.

Denning, Michael. *The Cultural Front: The Laboring of American Culture in the Twentieth Century*. London and New York: Verso, 1998.

Dower, John. "Introduction," *A Century of Japanese Photography*. New York: Pantheon Books, 1980.

Duus, Masayo. *The Life of Isamu Noguchi: Journey without Borders*. Princeton: Princeton University Press, 2004.

Ellis, George R. "Filling a Room With Small Triangular stones." *Inokuma Genichirô kaiko-ten*. A Retrospective Exhibition of Genichiro Inokuma. Marugame Genichiro Inokuma Museum of Contemporary Art. Marugame, Kagawa. (November 2003 – February 2004).

Fowler, Josephine. *Japanese and Chinese Immigrant Activists: Organizing in American and International Communist Movements, 1919-1933*. New Brunswick, NJ: Rutgers University Press, 2007.

Fujihara Sadao. "Bijutsu-shigaku to kokusaishugi: 1920nendai no bijutsushika no kokusaiteki seikô to sono imi." *Bijutsu Forum 21*, 9. Daigo Shobô, (Winter 2004).

Genjo Masayoshi. "Tenrankai tanpyô – (Kyoto bijutsu) – shinseisaku shunju Kyoto Nihon gaten, panriaru shunju Shimotori Yukihiko kinsakuten." *Sansai* 288 (June 1972).

Gluck, Carol. *Japan's Modern Myths: Ideology in the Late Meiji Period.* Princeton: Princeton University Press, 1985.

Greene, Vivien. "Aestheticism and Japan: The Cult of the Orient," *The Third Mind: American Artists Contemplate Asia, 1860-1960.* New York: Guggenheim Museum, 2009.

Griffin, Roger. "Modernity, Modernism, and Fascism. A Mazeway 'Resynthesis'." *Modernism/modernity.* 15, no. 1, (January 2008).

Guilbault, Serge. *How New York Stole the Idea of Modern Art: Abstract Expressionism, Freedom, and the Cold War.* Translated by Arthur Goldhammer. University of Chicago Press, 2004.

Hakutani Yoshinobu. "Father and Son: A Conversation with Isamu Noguchi," *Journal of Modern Literature* 17, no. 1, (Summer 1990).

Harootunian, Harry.

Overcome by Modernity: History, Culture, and Community in Interwar Japan. Princeton: Princeton University Press, 2000.

"Postwar America and the Aura of Asia," *The Third Mind: American Artists Contemplate Asia 1850-1969* New York: Guggenheim Museum, 2009.

Harvey, David. *The Urban Experience.* Baltimore and London: The Johns Hopkins University Press,1989.

Hayashi Kiichirô. "Tanaka Yasushi to sono shuhen – Amerika to Furansu de manande gaka." *Tanaka Yasushi o megutte.* Seibu – The Contemporary Gallery, 1986.

Hemingway, Andrew. *Artists on the Left: American Artists and the Communist Movement, 1926-1956.* New Haven: Yale University Press, 2002.

Heyman, Therese. "Encouraging the Artistic Impulse: The Second Generation, 1890-1925." *Watkins to Weston: 101 Years of California Photography, 1849-1950.* Santa Barbara Muesum of Art, 1992.

Higa, Karin.

"Hidden in Plain Sight: Little Tokyo Between the Wars." *Asian/American/Modern Art: Shifting Currents, 1900-1970.* Fine Arts Museums of San Francisco. University of California Press, 2008.

Living in Color: The Art of Hideo Date. Berkeley: Heyday Boosk, 2001.

The View from Within: Japanese American Art from the Internment Camps, 1942-1945. Los Angeles: UCLA Wright Art Gallery, 1992.

"Some Thoughts on National and Cultural Identity: Art by Contemporary Japanese and Japanese American Artists." *Art Journal* 55, no. 3, (Autumn 1996).

Hijikata Teiichi.

"Shimizu Toshi no hito to sakuhin." *Shimizu Toshi gashû*. Nichidô shuppan, 1975.

"'Gendai no yoga' to 'Fyûzan'." *Hijikata Teiichi chosakushû 7, Kindai Nihon no gaka-ron II. Tokyo*: Heibonsha, 1976. Originally printed in *Hon no techo*, 1961.

"Inshoshugi ikô." *Hijikata Teiichi chosakushû 7, Kindai Nihon no gaka-ron II.* Tokyo: Heibonsha, 1976. Originally printed in *Sekai bijutsu zenshû. Dai 25 maki, Nihon IV.* Heibonsha, 1951.

"Fujita Tsuguharu no koto." *Hijikata Teiichi chosakushû 8, Kindai Nihon no gakaron 3*. Heibonsha, 1976. Originally printed in *Sansai*, (March, 1968).

Hill, Kimi Kodani. *Chiura Obata's Topaz Moon: Art of the Internment.* Introduction by Timothy Anglin Burgard. Berkeley: Heyday Books, 2000.

Hirano Chieko. "One Aspect of Modernism in America – Meyer Schapiro and Abstract Expressionism." *Nijuseiki kaiga no shintairiku nyû yôku sukuru: porokku, de kuningu soshite genzai. Founders and Heirs of the New York School.* Tokyo: Yomiuri shinbunsha, 1997.

Hirayama Mikiko. "Ishii Hakutei on the History of Japanese Painting." *Art Journal* 55, no. 3. Japan 1868-1945: Art Architecture, and National Identity, (Autumn 1996).

Hiyane Teruo. "Rafu no jidai: Miyagi Kôfu to Nanka Seishun Gunzô." *Shin Okinawa Bungaku* 81, (1991).

Honma Masayoshi. "Tanaka Yasushi no koto." *Tanaka Yasushi o megutte.* Seibu – The Contemporary Gallery, 1986.

Hosley, William. *The Japan Idea: Art and Life in Victorian America.* Hartford, Connecticut: Wadsworth Atheneum, 1990.

Hoston, Germaine. "Marxism and Japanese Expansionism: Takahashi Kamekichi and the Theory of "Petty Imperialism." *Journal of Japanese Studies* 10, no. 1, (Winter 1984).

Ichida Koji. *Nyû Yôku kaiga hattenshi.* Tokyo: Doyoubijutsusha, 1990.

Ichikawa Masanori.

"*Kuniyoshi Yasuo o tôjite mita Amerikaha no mondaiten.*" *Amerika ni mananda Nihon no gakatachi: Kuniyoshi, Shimizu, Ishigaki, Noda to Amerikan shiin ega. Japanese Artists Who Studied in U.S.A. and the American Scene.* Exhibitions in Tokyo at the National Museum of Modern Art, July 24-September 5, 1982 and Kyoto at the National Museum of Modern Art, September 14-October 11, 1982.

"Amerika dansô – tenrankai hoi." *Gendai no me.* 333. (August 1982).

"Kuniyoshi Yasuo no geijutsu – uchi naru kokkyô." *Kuniyoshi Yasuo ten. Amerika to nihon, futatsu no sekai no aida de."* National Museum of Modern Art, Tokyo, 2004.

Ichioka Yuji.

"Japanese Immigrant Nationalism: The Issei and the Sino-Japanese War, 1937-1941." *California History* 69, no. 3, (Fall 1990).

The Issei: the First Generation of Japanese immigrants, 1885 – 1924. New York: Free Press London, 1988.

"A Buried Past: Early Issei Socialists and the Japanese Community." *Amerasia Journal* 1, no. 2, (July 1971).

Igarashi Yoshikuni. "The Bomb, Hirohito, and History: The Foundational Narrative of Postwar Relations between Japan and the United States." *Bodies of Memory: Narratives of War in Postwar Japanese Culture, 1945-1970.* Princeton: Princeton University Press, 2000.

Iizawa Kôtarô.

Fotogurafuazu. Photographers. Tokyo: Sakuhin-sha, 1996.

Nakayama Iwata: Nihon no shashinka 7. Tokyo: Iwanami shoten, 1998.

"Hikari no dandizumu – Nakayama Iwata no kiseki." *Hikari no dandizumu: Nakayama Iwata shashinshû 1895-1949.* Tokyo: Heibonsha, 1987.

"Mou hitori no Nojima Yasuzo." *Nojima Yasuzo: Nihon no shashinka 4.* Tokyo: Iwanami shoten, 1998.

" 'Hikari no shi' o motomete." *Fukuhara Shinzô to Fukuhara Rosô: Nihon no shashinka 3.* Tokyo: Iwanami shoten, 1998.

" 'Geijutsushin' no ôgon jidai." *Takayama Masataka to Taisho pikutoriarizumu: Nihon no shashinka 5.* Tokyo: Iwanami shoten, 1998.

Shashin ni kaere – Kôga – no jidai. Tokyo: Heibonsha, 1988.

Watanabe Yoshio: Nihon no shashinka 13. Iwanami Shoten, 1997.

Horino Masao: Nihon no shashinka 12. Tokyo: Iwanami shoten, 1997.

Zohô–toshi no shisen: Nihon no shashin 1920-1930 nendai. Heibonsha, 2005.

Imaizumi Atsuo.

"Kuniyoshi Yasuo no kyôshû." *Geijutsu Shinchô* 5, 1954.

"Shimotori Yukihiko gahaku." *E* 170. (April 1970).

Imamichi Tomonobu. *Bi ni tsuite.* Tokyo: Kodansha, 1973.

Ina Nobuo. *Shashin ni kaere: ina nobuo shashin ronshû.* Tokyo: Heibonsha, 2005.

Inaga Shigemi. "Gaka no ryûgaku: Aoyama Yoshioshi ni ukagau. 1920 nendai Furansu taizai no hitokusari." *Bijutsu Forum 21*, 9, Daigo Shobô. (Winter 2004).

Inoue Chôzaburô. "Minshû no ga – Shimizu Toshi." *Bijutsu Gurafu* 2, August 1983.

Ishii Ayako. "Fukuhara Shinzô Fûkei no taiji to taiwa; Fukuhara Roso Ki mama na sanposha no mesashino yukue." *Nihon no shashinka 3: Fukuhara Shinzô to Fukuhara Roso.* Edited by Iizawa Kotaro. Tokyo: Iwanami, 1997.

Ishikawa Kô. *Furanku to yobareta otoko.* Tokyo: Jôhô Center Shuppan Kyoku, 1993.

Ito, Johnson, Mark Dean. "Uncovering Asian American Art in San Francisco, 1850-1940." *Asian/American/Modern Art: Shifting Currents, 1900-1970.* Fine Arts Museums of San Francisco. University of California Press, 2008.

Itô Kyô. *Yoshida Hiroshi.* Tokyo: Daiichi hoki shuppan. 1989.

Itsumi Kumi. *Okina Kyuin to imin shakai: 1907-1924. Zaibei jûhachinen no kiseki.* Tokyo: Benseishuppan, 2002.

Iwasaki Yoshikazu.

"Shimizu Toshi no kiseki." *Mizue,* 817. (April 1973).

"Tokai seikatsu-sha no yûshû – Noda Hideo no sobyô." *Mizue,* 760, (May 1968).

"Amerika ni okeru Shimizu Toshi." *Shimizu Toshi ten.* Musashino Cultural Center, 1991.

Jameson, Frederic. *The Modernist Papers.* New York, London: Verso, 2004.

Johnson, Chalmers. *An Instance of Treason: Ozaki Hotsumi and the Sorge Spy Ring.* Stanford, CA: Stanford University Press, 1964.

Kanbayashi Akatsuki. "Kôtoku Shûsui no Oi." *Shinchô,* 72. (March 1, 1980).

Kanbayashi Tsunemichi. *Kindai Nihon "bigaku" no tanjô.* Kodansha, 2006.

Kaneko Ryuichi. "Japanese Photography in the Twentieth Century." *Modern Photography in Japan 1915-1940.* The Friends of Photography, San Francisco, 2001.

Karatani Kôjin. "Japan as Museum: Okakura Tenshin and Ernest Fenollosa." *Japanese Art after 1945: Scream Against the Sky.* New York: Harry Abrams, 1994.

Kashiro Yukiko. "Beyond an Alliance of Color: The African American Impact on Modern Japan," *positions* 11, no. 1, (Spring 2003).

Kawakami Mari. "Gaikoku ni zairyû shite kyôiku suru koto." *Bijutsu Forum 21* 9, Daigo Shobô, (Winter 2004).

Kijima Shunseuki. "Inokuma Genichirô to nyû yôku." *Inokuma Genichirô kaiko-ten.* A Retrospective Exhibition of Genichiro. Inokuma.

Marugame Genichiro Inokuma Museum of Contemporary Art. Marugame, Kagawa. November 2003 – February 2004.

Kikuchi Akiko. "Ishigaki Eitarô: -Machi- no ikutsu ka no gimon." *Bijutsu Gurafu*. (August 1983).

Kim, Elaine H., Margo Machida, and Sharon Mizota editors. *Fresh Talk/ Daring Gazes: Conversations on Asian American Art*. Berkeley: University of California Press, 2001.

Kim, Kristine. *Henry Sugimoto: Painting an American Experience*. Los Angeles: Japanese American National Museum. Berkeley: Heyday Books, 2001.

Kimura Rinkichi. *Me ga nai jigazo: Gaka Kotoku Yukie no shôgai*. Miyoshikikaku, 2001.

Kitaoka, Shinichi. "Kiyoshi Kiyosawa in the United States – His Writings for the San Francisco *Shinsekai*" *The Japanese Journal of American Studies*, no. 3, 1989.

Kubo Ikuko. "Yashiro Yukio to amerika junkai: nihon kobijutsu tenrankai 1953." *Kindai gasetu 12*. Meiji bijutsu gakaikan, 2003.

Kubo Sadajirô. "Zaibei 60nen Henry Sugimoto." *Geijutsu Shinchô* 367, (July 1980).

Kuboshima Seiichirô.

Uddosutoku no mori kara. Tokyo: Nishida shoten, 1995.

Hyôhaku: Nikkei gaka Noda Hideo no shôgai. Tokyo: Shinchosha, 1990.

Noda Hideo soshite Tamotsu Chuzo: hekiga kikyo kinenten, 1992

"Noda Hideo no gagyô to shôgai." *Noda Hideo gashû*. Tokyo: Heibôsha, 1987.

"Beikoku – Noda Hideo kinenkan no koto." *Aato Toppu*. 96 17-6, (December 1986).

Noda Hideo sukecchibukku: amerika de mituketa nijû no shôhin ni miru, Nikkei gaka no shôzô. Tokyo: Yayoishobo, 1985.

"Usui Bunpei-shi ganmei na e." *Mizue* 926, (March 1983).

"Noda Hideo to Ishigaki Eitarô." *Gendai no me* 333. Tokyo: Kindaibijutsu-kyokai, 1982.

"Amerika ni Noda Hideo o otte." *Geijutsu Shinchô* 327. (March 1977).

Kumada Tsukasa. "Rondon no seishun: zengo Shirataki Ikunosuke, Minami Kunzô, Tomimoto Kenkichi no ryûgaku jidai o chûshin ni." *Rondon no seishun: zengo tenzuroku*. Fukuyama bijutsukan, 1990.

Kuraya Mika.

"Yasuo Nojima's Eye for Photography." *Alfred Stieglitz and Nojima Yasuzo*. Exhibition catalog. Tokyo: National Museum of Modern Art, 1997.

"Kuniyoshi Yasuo no fushigi na kûkan." *Kuniyoshi Yasuo-ten. Amerika to nihon, futatsu no sekai no aida de.* The National Museum of Modern Art, Tokyo, 2004.

Kusaka Shirô and Okabe Masayuki. *Takehisa Yumeji: Ai to kanashimi no shijin gaka.* Tokyo: Gakushû Kenkyûsha, 1995.

Kuwabara Sumio.
"Kuniyoshi o unda jôken." *Geijutsu Techo.* October 1975.
Bijutsu ronshû: Amerika-hen. Chusekisha, 1996.

Lee, Anthony W. *Picturing Chinatown: Art and Orientalism in San Francisco.* Berkeley and Los Angeles: University of California Press, 2001.

Lee, Shelley Sang-Hee. "Good American Subjects Done through Japanese Eyes: Race, Nationality and the Seattle Camera Club, 1924-1929." *Pacific Northwest Quarterly* 96, no. 1, (Winter 2004-2005).

Leja, Michael. "Modernism's Subjects in the United States." *Art Journal*, 55, no. 2, (Summer 1996).

Levin, Gail. "Between Two Worlds: Folk Culture, Identity, and the American Art of Yasuo Kuniyoshi." *Archives of American Art Journal.* Volume 43, Number 34. Smithsonian Institute, 2003.

Littleton, Taylor D. and Maltby Sykes. *Advancing American Art: Painting, Politics, and Cultural Confrontation at Mid-Century.* University of Alabama Press, 1989.

Lubowsky, Susan. "From Naivete to Maturity: 1906-1939." *Yasuo Kuniyoshi: tanjô 100nen kinen – nyû yôku no yûshû.* Tokyo Teien Art Museum, (December 1989).

Machida, Margo. Asia/America: Identities in Contemporary Asian American Art. New York: The Asia Societies Galleries, 1994.

Marquardt, Virginia Hagelstein. "'New Masses' and John Reed Club Artists, 1926-1936: Evolution of Ideology, Subject Matter and Style." *Journal of Decorative and Propaganda Arts* 12, (Spring 1989).

Masuda Rei.
"Nakayama Iwata to Kobe ni tsuite." *Art Ramble* 2, (March 20, 2004).
"Alfred Stieglitz and the Eminence of his Straight Photography." *Alfred Stieglitz and Nojima Yasuzo.* Exhibition catalog. Tokyo: National Museum of Modern Art, 1997.

Matsume Shôkô. "Kaette kita Urashima Tarô gaka – Shimizu Toshi shoron." *Kôzô.* (Reprint.) (March 8, 1989).

Matsumoto Fumihisa. *Amerika no shôsuha geijutsu katachi: tabunka shakai no jitsugen o yume mite.* Tokyo: Akashishoten, (October 2001).

Matsumoto, Valerie J. "Pioneers, Renegades, and Visionaries: Asian American Women Artists in California, 1880s-1960s." *Asian American Art: A History, 1850-1970*. Stanford: Stanford University Press, 2008.

McCabe, Cynthis Jaffee. "A Century of Artist-Immigrants." *The Golden Door: Artist Immigrants of America, 1876-1976*. Exhibition catalog. Washington: Smithsonian Institute Press, 1976.

McWilliams, Carey. *Southern California: An Island on the Land*. Peregrine Smith Books, 1946, 1973.

Mellow, James R. *Walker Evans*. New York: Basic Books, 1999.

Michaels, Leonard, David Read, and Raquel Sherr, editors. *West of the West: Imagining California, A Collection*. Harper Perennial, 1989.

Minemura Toshiaki. "Bijutsu ni okeru modanizumu to iu koto." *Modanizumu no jidai. The Age of Modernism*. Exhibition Catalog. Tokyo Metropolitan Museum of Photography, 1995.

Mitsuda Yuri.

"Nojima Yasuzô: Geijutsu no tame ni." *Nojima Yasuzo: Nihon no shashinka 4*. Tokyo: Iwanami shoten, 1998.

"Fukuhara Shinzô no 'geijutsu' no imi." *Fukuhara Shinzô to Fukuhara Rosô: Nihon no shashinka 3*. Tokyo: Iwanami shoten, 1998.

Nakayama Iwata: Nihon no shashinka 7. Tokyo: Iwanami shoten, 1998.

"'Shashin Geijutsu' – Photography Art Radical and Nostalgic." *Shashin geijutsu no jidai*. Shiseido, 1998.

Miyake Shôtarô. "Kawashima Riichirô no sekai." *Aato*. 18-2, 1970.

Miyamoto Takaaki. "Eikinzu (Eakins) to Okiifu (O'Keefe): futari no amerikajin gaka." *Bijutsu Forum 21*, 9, Daigo Shobô, (Winter 2004).

Miyatake Atsufumi, Taisuke Fujishima, and Eikoh Hosoe, eds. *Toyo Miyatake Behind the Camera 1923-1979*. Tokyo: Bungeishunji Co., Ltd., 1984.

Mizuno Takashi. "Saitama no yôgaka tenbyô – Tanaka Yasushi." *Pari – Nihon – Mekishiko-ten zuroku – Tokushima-kenritsu bijutsukan*. 1992.

Moholy-Nagy, Laszlo. *Vision in Motion*. Chicago: Paul Theobald, 1938. Reprinted in *Twentieth Century Art Theory: Urbanism, Politics, and Mass Culture*. Editors Richard Hertz and Norman M. Klein. Prentice Hall, 1990.

Montgomery, Harper. "Carlos Merida and the Mobility of Modernism: A Mayan Cosmopolitan Moves to Mexico City," *The Art Bulletin*, 98, no. 4, 2016.

Monroe, Robert D. "Light and Shade: Pictorial Photography in Seattle, 1920-1940, and the Seattle Camera Club." *Turning Shadows into Light: Art and Culture of the Northwest's Early Asian/Pacific Community*. Young Pine Press, 1982.

Mori Hitoshi. "Haru-moya ka shûsui ka – Tosa kikô kara." *Issun*. 16, (October 2003).

Morita Naruo. *Sensô to geijutsu: jûgun sakka gakatachi no senchû to sengo*. Sankei shinbun shuppan, 2007.

Morse, Marcia. *Legacy: Facets of Island Modernism*. Honolulu: Honolulu Academy of Arts, 2001.

Motoe Kunio. "Hideo Noda or the Unfinished 'Bridge.'" *Japanese Artists who Studied in the USA and the American Scene*. Catalog. National Museum of Modern Art, Tokyo, 1982.

Munro, Eleanor. *Originals: American Women Artists*. Simon & Schuster, Inc., New York, 1979.

Munroe, Alexandra.

"American Art and the East: An Exhibition Proposal." *Asian Art History: In the Twenty-First Century*. Clark Studies in the Visual Arts. Edited by Vishakha N. Desai. Distributed by Yale University Press, 2007.

Japanese Art After 1945: Scream Against the Sky. New York: Harry N. Abrams, 1994.

"The War Years and Their Aftermath, 1940-1953." *Yasuo Kuniyoshi: tanjô 100nen kinen – nyû yôku no yûshû*. Tokyo Teien Art Museum, (December 1989).

Murata Masahiro. "Kitagawa Tamiji no ega – Mekishiko jidai wo chûshin ni." *Kitagawa Tamiji ten*. Nagoya: Kitagwa tamiji jikko iinkai. Aichi-ken bijutsukan, (November, 1996).

Myers, Jane and Tom Wolf. *The Shores of a Dream: Yasuo Kuniyoshi's Early Work in America*. Amon Carter Museum, Fort Worth TX, 1996.

Nagayama Takiko. "Ishikawa Toraji, Yoshida Hiroshi, Nakagawa Hachirô gajô." *Koriyama Municipal Museum Bulletin*, (March 31, 1999).

Nakada Sachiko. *Maedakô Hiroichirô ni okeru "Amerika"*. Tokyo: Kokusho, 2000.

Nakahara Yûsuke. "Ishigaki Eitarô: shucho to tsuyosa no e." *Nihon Dokusho Shinbun*, (December 7, 1959).

Nakajima Tokuhiro.

"Fujita Tsuguharu to Nakayama Iwata." *Pilotis: Hyogo Prefecture Museum of Contemporary Art News*, 62, 1987.

"Toshi no shashinka. Nakayama Iwata – sono shirarezaru ichimen."

Shirarezaru Nakayama Iwata. Hyogo Prefecture Modern Art Museum, 1989.

"Isamu Noguchi to Nakayama Iwata, 1927 Pari de deai." *Miru: Kyoto kokuritsu kindai bijutsukan nyusu,* 300, 1992.

"Nakayma to Supein: 1926 nen to natsu no taiken." *Pilotis: Hyogo Prefecture Museum of Contemporary Art News* 88, 1993.

Nakamura Shinichirô. "Modan toshi no miryoku: 1930 nen zengo no Tokyo to watashi." *Taiyô*, 1987.

Nakane Kazuko. "Facing the Pacific: Asian American Artists in Seattle, 1900-1970." *Asian/American/Modern Art: Shifting Currents, 1900-1970*. Fine Arts Museums of San Francisco. University of California Press, 2008.

Ngai, Mae M.

Impossible Subjects: Illegal Aliens and the Making of Modern America. Princeton University Press, 2004.

"Birthright Citizenship and the Alien Citizen." *Fordham Law Review*. Volume 75, 2007.

Nishimaki Isamu. "Gai no seiyô bijutu juyô to sono nihon ryûgaku." *Bijutsu Forum 21* 9, Daigo Shobô, (Winter 2004).

Noda Utarô. "Iwamura Toru gojûnennki." *Gakuto* 63, no. 12. Maruzen, 1966.

Nomoto Ippei. *Miyagi Yotoku: imin seinen gaka no hikari to kage*. Naha, Japan: Okinawa Taimususha, 1997.

Ogura Tadao.

"Hikisakareta kyôshû: Kuniyoshi no kunô to eikô." *Bijutsu Techô* 27, no. 399, (October 1975).

"Kuniyoshi Yasuo no hito to geijutsu – Amerika to Nihon." *Kuniyoshi Yasuo: tokubetsu-ten*. Fukutake Collection. Shibuya kuritsu shôtô bijutsukan, 1987.

Ôi Kenji. Geijutsu-teki ryôshin no jikaku no toki. *Amerikan- shin no Nihonjin gakatachi-ten*. Nerima kuritsu bijutsukan, 1995.

Oka Yoshiaki. "Nikki ni miru: Shimizu Toshi taiô soshite kikoku ato no kiseki." Okawa Museum.

Okabe Masayuki.

"Miotoshi to sarete ita tobei gakatachi." *Geijustu Shincho*, October 1995.

"Gakatachi no shin-sekai – Nichibei bijutsu kyôryû-shi." *Amerika ni ikita Nikkeijin gakatachi: kibô to kunô no hanseki 1896-1945. Japanese and Japanese American Painters in the United States: A Half Century of Hope and Suffering 1896-1945*. Edited by Tokyo Metropolitan

Teien Art Museum. Co-edited by Ayako Ishii. Translated by Kikuko Ogawa. Bijutsu Shuppan Design Center, 1995.

Okada Yasuo. "The Japanese Image of the American West." *The Western Historical Quarterly* 19, no. 2, (May 1988).

Okamoto Kaneko. "Maboroshi no yôgaka: Kobayashi Senko." *Kobayashi Senko tenzuroku.* Hiroshima: Hiroshima Municipal Museum of Art, 1984.

Okawa Eiji. "Shimizu Toshi ten ni tuite." *Shimizu Toshi ten.* Musashino Cultural Center, 1991.

Ôkubo Mamoru. *Yume wa ônabara o koete: ima yomigaeru yôgaka Ishii Kôfû no kiseki.* Matsudo: Bijutsu no tosho miyoshi kikaku, 2001.

Ôkubo Shizuo.

Tanaka Yasushi: The Painter Who Worked in Seattle and Paris. Saitama: Museum of Modern Art, 1997.

"Gaka – Tanaka Yasushi o saguru tabi o rinkaku." *Shikaro: Museum of Art, Saitama News.* 40, 1992.

"Tanaka Yasushi: Pari to Shiatoru. Kisoteki shiryô no shûchû hatasu." The Japan Association of Art Museums, 34, (April 1992).

Omi, Michael and Howard Winant. *Racial Formation in the United States from the 1960s to the 1990s.* New York: Routledge, 1994.

Oshima Hiroshi, editor. *Sairoku: shashin-ron. 1921-1965.* Tokyo Metropolitan Museum of Photography. Tankosha, 1999.

Ota Yasuto. "Kindai Nihon bijutsuka retsuden 74 Shimizu Toshi." *Bijutsu Techô* 733, (November 1996).

Ôtaguro Motoo. "Shashin shôron" *Taisho-ki no toshi sanshakusha-tachi – shashin geijutsu no jidai.* Photography Art 1921-1924. Shieseido and Shoto Art Museum, 1998.

Otake Akiko. "Imintachi no Amerika." *Gendai no me.* 333. (August 1982).

Ôtsuji Kiyoji. "Fainda-no shinbime: Nakayama Iwata mobo no kansei." *Taiyô,* no. 13, (1987).

Ozaki Hotsuki. "Mikan no gaka: Miyagi Yotoku no baai." Paper presented at the 50th Anniversary of the Sorge Incident, 1990.

Ozaki Masato. "Tamotsu Chûzô." *Bijutsu Techo* 665. (February 1993).

Ozawa Yoshio.

Hishô to kaiki: Kuniyoshi Yasuo no seiyô to tôyô. Okayama: Nihon bunkyo shuppan, (July 1996).

Yasuo Kuniyoshi: neo-Amerikan aatisuto nokiseki. Okayama City: Fukutake shoten, 1991.

Kuniyoshi Yasuo: genmu to saikan. Fukutake bunko, 1991.

"Amerika ni 'kishû' sareta nikkeijin gaka." *Geijutsu Shincho,* (October 1995).

"Kuniyoshi Yasuo o meguru Nihonjin – Usui Bunpei hoka." *Geijutsu Shinchô* 310, (October 1975).

Palmquist, Peter E. "Asian American Photographers on the Pacific Frontier, 1850-1930." *With New Eyes: Toward an Asian American Art History.* San Francisco: San Francisco State University, 1995.

Patterson, Anita. *Race, American Literature, and Transnational Modernisms.* Cambridge University Press, 2008.

Peterson, Christian A.

After the Photo-Secession, American Pictorial Photography, 1910-1955: Minneapolis Institute of Arts & W. W. Norton & Company, 1997.

"Harry K. Shigeta of Chicago" (JANM) *History of Photography* 22, no. 2, (Summer 1998).

Phu, Thy. "The Spaces of Human Confinement: Manzanar Photography and Landscape Ideology." *Journal of Asian American Studies* 11, no. 3 (2008).

Raynor, Vivian. "Art: War Cartoons of Kuniyoshi." *The New York Times*, (January 18, 1980).

Reed, Dennis.

Japanese Photography in America, 1920-1940. Japanese American Cultural & Community Center. Los Angeles, CA 1985.

Pictorialism in California; Photographs 1900-1940. The J. Paul Getty Museum and the Henry E. Huntington Library and Art Gallery, 1994.

Riehlman, Franklin, Tom Wolf and Bruce Weber. *Yasuo Kuniyoshi: Artist as Photographer.* Annendale-on-Hduson, New York and West Palm Beach: Norton Gallery and School of Art, 1983.

Robinson, Greg and Elena Tajima Creef editors. *Mine Okubo: Following Her Own Road.* Seattle: University of Washington Press, 2008.

Roe, JoAnn. *Frank Matsura – Frontier Photographer.* Seattle: Madrona Publisher Inc., 1981.

Sakamoto Tetsuo. "Tanaka Yasushi – Shirazaru kyôdo isai." *Gifu-kenritsu bijutsukan shozô meihinten zuroku, Saitama kenritsu kindai bijutsukan.* 1985.

Satô Dôshin. "Koritsu shita 'Nihon bunmei' to ryûgaku." *Bijutsu Forum 21* 9, Daigo Shobô, (Winter, 2004).

Sawa Hajime. "Ben Shan no shi." *Bijutsu Gurafu*, August 1983.

Sawada, Mitziko. *Tokyo Life, New York Dreams: Urban Japanese Visions of America, 1890-1924*. Berkeley and Los Angeles: University of California Press, 1996.

Sawatari, Kiyoko. "Innovational Adaptations: Contacts Between Japanese and Western Artists in Yokohama, 1859-1899." Ellen P. Conant, editor. *Challenging Past and Present: The Metamorphosis of 19th Century Japanese Art*. Honolulu: University of Hawaii Press, 2006.

Seidensticker, Edward. *Tokyo Rising: the city since the great earthquake*. Cambridge, MA: Harvard University Press, 1991.

Seki Akio. "Obata Chiura no tôbei ni kansuru – shiron." *Japanese and Japanese American Painters in the United States: A Half Century of Hope and Suffering 1896-1945*. Edited by Tokyo Metropolitan Teien Art Museum. Co-edited by Ayako Ishii. Translated by Kikuko Ogawa. Bijutsu Shuppan Design Center, 1995.

Shimojima Tetsurô.

Amerika kokka hangyakuzai. Tokyo: Kodansha, 1993.

Samurai to Kariforunia: Ikyô no Nihon gaka Obata Chiura. Tokyo: Shogakukan, 2000.

"Hideo Kobashigawa: A Biographical History," Hideo Kobashigawa: A Retrospective. Naha, 2000.

Simmel, Georg. "The Metropolis and Mental Life." From *The Sociology of Georg Simmel. Excerpt in Art in Theory 1900-2000: An Anthology of Changing Ideas*. Edited by Charles Harrison and Paul Wood. Blackwell Publishing, 2006.

Sivard, Susan. "The State Department 'Advancing American Art' Exhibition of 1946 and the Advance of American Art," *Arts Magazine* (April 1984).

Sokol, David M. "The Founding of Artists Equity Association after World War II." *Archives of American Art Journal* 39, no. 1-2, (1999).

South, Will. Marian Yoshiki-Kovinick, and Julia Armstrong-Totten. *A Seed of Modernism: The Art Students League of Los Angeles, 1906-1953*. Berkley: Heyday Books, 2008.

Sunouchi Tôru. "Ki magure bijutsukan: Kaku no gotoku ni shite iki kaku no gotoku shisu. (Kotoku Yukie)" *Geijutsu Shincho. 33-2*. February 1982.

Starr, Kevin. *The Dream Endures: California Enters the 1940s*. Oxford University Press, 1994.

Stillinger, Elizabeth. "From Attics, Sheds, and Secondhand Shops: Collecting Folk Art in America, 1880-1940," *Drawing on America's Past: Folk Art, Modernism, and the Index of American Design*. Edited by Ulrike Mills, National Gallery of Art, Washington, 2002.

Sugimura Hiroya. "Toshi Shimizu Shôgai to gagyô." *Shimizu Toshi ten. Shimizu Toshi Retrospective Exhibition*. Tochigi Prefectural Museum of Fine Arts, November 1996-January 1997.

Sullivan, Michael. *The Meeting of Eastern and Western Art*. New York: New York Graphics Society, 1973.

Tajika Kenzo. "Tenrankaihyô: Terada Takeo, Iwafune Shûzô, Hayakawa Gikô kaku-koten." *Sansai* 245, (June 1969).

Tajima Natsuko. "Nôshômusho kaigai jitsugyo renshûsei to wagakuni no bijutsukai." *Bijutsu Forum 21,* 9. Daigo Shobô, Winter, 2004.

Takagi Shigenori. "Shirataki Ikunosuke no Minami Kunzô ate shokan." *Hiroshima kenritsu bijutsukan kenkyû kiyô*. Number 1. (March 31, 1994).

Takashina Shûji. *Nihon kindai bijutsushi-ron*. Chikuma geibunsho. 2006.

Takeyama Hirohiko. "Kazoku no shôzô – Shimizu Toshi no shikaku sekai." *Musashino no ibukiten – 13 sakka sakuhin no genfûkei zuroku: Musashino Cultural Center*. 1994.

Taki Teizô. "Geiein zatsujiki: Kindai bijutu hihyô no genson – Iwamura Toru no koto." *Bijutsu no mado*. (July 1992).

Takumi Hideo. "Shimizu Toshi nenpu." *Shimizu Toshi gashû*. Nichidô shuppan, 1975.

Tamura Norio and Shiramizu Shigehiko editors. *Beikoku shoki no Nihongo shinbun*. Tokyo: Keisoshobo, 1986.

Tanaka Yukito. "Saitama no gakatachi to gendai e no iriguchi." *Paris/Japan/ Mexico: The Selected Works*. The Museum of Modern Art, Saitama, 1992.

Tchen, John Kuo Wei. "Believing is Seeing: Transforming Orientalism and the Occidental Gaze." *Asia/America: Identities in Contemporary Asian American Art*. The Asia Society Galleries, New York. New York: The New Press, 1996.

Terada Chiharu. "Kindai kyoshô no meisaku-ten: Terada Takeo-ten, Nakamura Naondo-ten, Yoshida Kiyoshi-ten, Amaharashi kaiten, Nihon no shiki-ten). *Tôkyô Shinbun* (Evening edition). 6-7, 1974.

Tomii, Reiko. "Border-Crossings: A Preface to the Exhibition." *Making a Home: Japanese Contemporary Artists in New York*. Japan Society, New York. 2007.

Tomiyama Hideo. "Bôkyô no gaka - Kuniyoshi Yasuo: sono shôgai wo tsuranuita hyûmanizumu." *Nihon no meiga* 41. Tokyo: Kodansha, 1974.

Tsukasa Osamu. *Sensô to bijutsu*. Tokyo: Iwanami shoten, 1992.

Tsurutani Hisashi. *Yumeji no mita Amerika*. Tokyo: Shin Jinbutsu orai-sha, 1997.

Tsutakawa, Mayumi, editor. *They Painted from Their Hearts: Pioneer Asian American Artists.* Seattle: Wing Luke Asian Museum/University of Washington Press, 1994.

Uchiyama Takeo. "Faraway and Close to Home." *Kuniyoshi Yasuo ten: Tanjô 100 nenkinen Nyû Yôku no yûshû.* Tokyo Metropolitan Teien Art Museum, 1989.

Uemura Takachiyo.

"Rearizumu kentô: atarashii rearizumu." *Atelier.* January, 1938.

"Ishigaki Eitarô isakuten." *Bijutsu Techô* 152, (January 1959) and *Mizue* 644, (January 1959).

Ueno Kenji. "Shimizu Toshi-ten." *Bijutsu Techô* 467, (July 1980).

Unno Hiroshi.

"Moving Man." *Bijutsu Techo.* (September 1979).

"Shimizu Toshi: shoku modan sutairu saihô." *Aato* 92, (Autumn 1980).

"Kuniyoshi Yasuo: shoku modan stairu saihô." *Aato* 93, (Winter 1980).

"Shimizu Toshi ten." *Bijutsu Techô* 468, (August 1980).

"Modan sutairu saihô 4: Tanaka Yasushi." *Aato,* (Summer 1981).

Modan toshi Tokyo: Nihon no 1920 nendai. Tokyo: Chukoron-sha, 1988.

Inbô to gensô no dai-ajia. Heibonsha, 2005.

Ushiroshoji Masahiro. "Senjika no ryûgakusei – kindai nihon to tai no bijutu kôryû." *Bijutsu Forum 21,* 9. Daigo Shobô, (Winter 2004).

Wang, ShiPu. "Japan against Japan: U.S. Propaganda and Yasuo Kuniyoshi's Identity Crisis." *American Art* 22, no. 1, (Spring 2008).

Wattles, Miriam. "The 1909 Ryûto and the Aesthetics of Affectivity." *Art Journal* 55, no. 3, (Autumn 1996).

Weisberg, Gabriel P. "Japonisme: The Commercialization of an Opportunity." *Japonisme Comes to America: The Japanese Impact on the Graphic Arts 1876-1925.* Harry N. Abrams Inc., 1990.

Weisenfeld, Gennifer.

Mavo: Japanese Artists and the Avant-Garde 1905-1931. University of California Press, 2002.

"Touring Japan-as-Museum: NIPPON and Other Japanese Imperialist Travelogues." *positions: east asia cultures critique. positions* 8, no. 3, (Winter 2000).

Weschler, Jeffrey. *Asian Traditions / Modern Expressions: Asian American Artists and Abstraction, 1945-1970.* New York: Harry N. Abrams, 1977.

Wilson, Robert A. and Bill Hosokawa. *East to America: A History of the Japanese in the United States.* New York: William Morrow and Company, Inc., 1980.

Winther-Tamaki, Bert.

Art in the Encounter of Nations: Japanese and American Artists in the Early Postwar Years. University of Hawaii Press, 2001.

"Emobdiment/Disembodiment: Japanese Painting during the Fifteen-Year War." *Monumenta Nipponica* 52, no. 2, (Summer 1997).

Wolf, Tom. "The Tip of the Iceberg: Early Asian American Artists in New York." *Asian/American/Modern Art: Shifting Currents, 1900-1970.* Fine Arts Museums of San Francisco. University of California Press, 2008.

Yaguchi Kunio.

"Tokushû Shimizu Toshi – Shimizu Toshi, sono hyôdenteki shiron." *Sansai* 315, (March 1974).

"Shimizu Toshi nenpu." *Shimizu Toshi gashû.* Nichidô shuppan, 1975.

Yamada Chisaburô. Editor. *Dialogue in Art: Japan and the West.* Essays by Giulio C. Argan, Gordon Washburn, Takashina Shûji, Kawazoe Noboru. Interviews with Kenzô Tange, Isamu Noguchi, Okada Kenzô, Mark Tobey, Morita Shiryû. Tokyo: Kodansha International, 1976.

Yamada Katsumi. Editor. *Shashinka: Fukuhara Shinzô no shoshin 1883-1948.* Tokyo: Shiseido, 2005.

Yamaguchi Taiji.

"Kuniyoshi Yasuo no uma to shojo." *Bijutsu undôshi kenkyûkai nyusu.* Club for Action History, New Letter, (April 28, 2002).

Amerika bijutsu to Kuniyoshi Yasuo: kaitakusha no kiseki. Tokyo: Nihon hôsô shuppan kyôkai, (March 2004).

"Kuniyoshi Yasuo: Amerika no kibô o ikita kunou no gaka." *Tokushû: Bi no kaihô to jiyû o Kuniyoshi Yasuo. Hana Bijutsukan* 99, (February 2009).

Yamanashi Emiko. "Nakagawa Hachirô no ikita Nihon kindai yoga-kai." *Nakagawa Hachirô to sono jidai tenzuroku.* Aichi-ken ritsu bijutsukan, 1999.

Yamazaki Hitoshi. "Garô' no tanjô. Ôtsuka Ginjirô to Kobe no modanizumu." *Art Ramble* 3, Hyogo Prefectural Museum of Art, (June 2004).

Yanagiwa Hideyuki. "Kitagawa Riichirô – 1920 nendai – Pari to Tokyo musubumono." *1920 nendai no Pari yori ten – Kitagawa, Gontcharova, Larionov – Dai 6 Shiseido Gallery to sono atisutotachi zuroku.* March 1995.

Yang, Alice. *Why Asia? Contemporary Asian and Asian American Art.* New York: New York University Press, 1998.

Yasunaga Kôichi.

Yoshida Hiroshi shiryôshû: meiji yoga shinshiryô. Fukuoka: Fukuokashi bunka geijutsu shinkozaidan, 2007.

"Yoshida Hiroshi: Hito to geijutsu." *Yoshida Hiroshi: Zen mokuhan gashû.* Abe Publishing Limited, 1987, 2008.

"Yoshida Hiroshi no Amerika ni gyôseki to ashiato." *Kashima bijutsu zaidan nenpô.* 1991.

Yasugi Masahiro.

"Ishigaki Eitarô no Amerika – aru tobei gaka no shôgai." *Amerika no naka no Nihon – Ishigaki Eitarô to senzen no tobei gakatachi."* Wakayama: The Museum of Modern Art, Wakayama, 1997.

"Kenkyû nôto: Hamaji Seimatsu Amerika jidai no ashiato o ta dotte." *Wakayama kenritsu bijutsukan nyûsu* 17, (June 1, 1998).

Yiengpruksawan, Mimi Hall. "Kawabata Ryûshi and the Emptying of the Modern." *Archives of Asian Art* 46, 1993.

Yoshii Tadashi. "Ben Shan no geijutsu." *Bijutsu Gurafu* (August 1983).

Yoshiki-Kovinick, Marian. "The Art Students League of Los Angeles: A Japanese American Connection." *A Seed of Modernism: The Art Students League of Los Angeles, 1906-1953.* Pasadena Museum of Art. Berkeley: Heyday Books, 2008.

Yui Shoichi. "Shimizu Toshi to ano koro New York jazu shin." *Shimizu ten.* Musashino Cultural Center, 1991.

Exhibition Catalogs

Alfred Stieglitz and Nojima Yasuzo. Exhibition catalog. Tokyo: National Museum of Modern Art, 1997.

Amerika ni ikita Nikkeijin gakatachi: kibô to kunô no hanseki 1896-1945. Japanese and Japanese American Painters in the United States: A Half Century of Hope and Suffering 1896-1945. Edited by Tokyo Metropolitan Teien Art Museum. Co-edited by Ayako Ishii. Translated by Kikuko Ogawa. Bijutsu Shuppan Design Center, 1995.

Amerika ni watatta bijutsukatachi-ten. Nagano-ken Shinano bijutsukan, 1990.

Amerika no naka no Nihon – Ishigaki Eitarô to senzen no tobei gakatachi." Exhibition catalog. Wakayama: The Museum of Modern Art, Wakayama, 1997.

Amerikan shiin no nihonjin gakatachi ten: Shimizu Toshie, Kuniyoshi Yasuo, Ishigaki Eitarô, Kitagawa Tamiji, Noda Hideo. Tokyo: Nerima Art Museum, 1995.

Andersen, Irene Poon, Mark Johnson, Dawn Nakanishi, Diane Tani. *With New Eyes: Toward an Asian American Art History in the West.* San Francisco: Art Department Gallery, San Francisco State University, 1995.

Asian/American/Modern Art: Shifting Currents, 1900-1970. Fine Arts Museums of San Francisco. University of California Press, 2008.

Barron, Stephanie and Sheri Bernstein, Illene Susan Fort editors. *Made in California: Art, Image, and Identity, 1900-2000.* Los Angeles County Museum of Art, University of California Press, 2000.

Brown, Michael D. *Views from Asian California, 1920-1965.* San Francisco: Michael D. Brown, 1992.

Chew, Ron. "Foreward." *They Painted from Their Hearts: Pioneer Asian American Artists.* Seattle: Wing Luke Asian Museum, 1994.

Contemporary Painters of Japanese Origin in America 1958. Catalog by Thomas M. Messer and Anne L. Jenks. New York: The Japan Society, 1958.

Dai-ikkai Nihon shashinkai tenrankai. July 1925.

Dokuritsu bijutsuten jûnen kinen gashû. Asahi shibun-sha, 1940.

East West Art Society Second Exhibition in San Francisco Museum of Art, 1922.

Edward Weston in Los Angeles, exhibition catalog. J. Paul Getty Museum and the Huntington Library, 1986-1987.

Foujioka Noboru: Special Exhibition of Works. Nippon Club, April 19-27, 1924. Smithsonian Institute Archives.

Gilbert, Jeffrey. "Nojima Yasuzo and his Contemporaries: One Aspect of Modern Japanese Photography and Paintings." Tokyo: Shoto Museum of Art, 1991.

The Golden Door: Artist-Immigrants of America, 1876-1976. Hirshorn Museum and Sculpture Garden, Smithsonian Institution, 1976.

*Harry K. Shigeta: Life and Photograp*hs. Exhibition catalog. Ueda City: Ueda City Museum of History, 2003.

Ishigaki Eitarô-ten Catalog. Tokyo: Shibuya-ku ritsu shôtô bijutsukan, 1988.

Hosley, William. *The Japan Idea: Art and Life in Victorian America.* Hartford, Connecticut: Wadsworth Atheneum. 1990. Exhibition from October 21 to December 30, 1990.

Japonisme Comes to America: The Impact on the Graphic Arts, 1876-1925.

Kitagawa Tamiji hanga-ten: daisankai toyotashi shûzo bijutsuhinten. Toyota: Toyotashi bijutsu shuzo bijutsuten, October 1991.

Kitagawa Tamiji ten. Nagoya: Kitagwa tamiji jikko iinkai. Aichi-ken bijutsukan, November 1996.

Kômoto, Shinji. *Nojima Yasuzo and his Contemporaries: One Aspect of Modern Japanese Photography and Paintings*. Tokyo: Shoto Museum of Art, 1991.

Koyama Shotaro to "Sho ha bijutsu narasu" no jidai: meiji shin kokka ni moeru atsuki riso aburae vs. nihonga soshite "sho". Nagaoka: Niigata-kenritsu kindai bijutsukan, October 2002.

Kuniyoshi Yasuo: tokubetsu-ten. Fukutake Collection. Shibuya kuritsu shôtô bijutsukan, 1987.

Los Angeles Oriental Artists' Group. Exhibition Catalog. At Japanese American National Museum.

Mekishiko no bijutsu 1920-1950 ten katarogu: Nihonjin Mekishiko ijû 100 shûnen kinen. Asahikawa, 1998.

Modanizumu no jidai. The Age of Modernism. Exhibition Catalog. Tokyo Metropolitan Museum of Photography, 1995.

Munroe, Alexandra. *Japanese Art After 1945: Scream Against the Sky*. New York: Harry N. Abrams, 1994.

Nakagawa Hachirô to sono jidai tenzuroku. Aichi-ken ritsu bijutsukan, 1999.

The New Japanese Painting and Sculpture. Essay by William S. Lieberman. New York: The Museum of Modern Art, 1966.

Noda Hideo soshite Tamotsu Chuzo: hekiga kikyo kinenten Exhibition catalog, Kumamoto kenritsu bijutsukan, 1992.

1920-1930 nendai–Rapusodi in pari: Tanaka Yasushi o meguru gakatachi. (*Rhapsody in Paris: Tanaka Yasushi and his contemporaries in Paris.*) Saitama kenritsu kindai bijutsukan, 1988.

Paris/Japan/Mexico. The Selected works; The Museum of Modern Art, Saitama. May-June, 1992.

Rondon no seishun: zengo tenzuroku. Fukuyama bijutsukan, 1990.

Shaku-do-sha Art Exhibition. Exhibition catalog, June 15-28 1923

Shimizu Toshi ten. Musashino shimin bunka kaikan, 1991.

Shimizu Toshi ten. Shimizu Toshi Retrospective Exhibition. November 1996-January 1997. Tochigi Prefectural Museum of Fine Arts.

Shimizu Toshi: Works from the Collection of Tochigi Prefectural Museum of Fine Arts. Shimizu Toshi: tochigi kenritsu bijutsukan shozo. Utsunomiya: Tochigi kenritsu bijutsukan, 2007.

Sugimura Hiroya. *Shimizu Toshi Retrospective Exhibition.* Exhibition catalog. Tochigi Prefectural Museum, 1996.

Japanese Artists who Studied in the USA and the American Scene. Catalog. National Museum of Modern Art, Tokyo, 1982.

Amerika no naka no Nihon: Ishigaki Eitarô to senzen no tobei gakatachi. Wakayama kenritsu kinndai bijutsukan hen, 1997.

Usui Bunpei ten katarogu. Fuji terebi gyararii. (1973).

Taiheiyô o koeta Nihon no gakatachi ten: Amerika ni mananda 18nin. Hiroshima kenritsu bijutsukan, 1987

Kuniyoshi Yasuo ten: Nyû yôku no yûshû. Tokyo: Nihon terebi hosomo, 1989.

Noda Hideo soshite Tamotsu Chûzô: hekiga kikyô kinenten. Kumamoto: Kumamoto kenritsu bijutsukan, April 1992.

Watts, Jennifer A. "Moving in Place: Los Angeles in Photographs." *This Side of Paradise: Body and Landscape in Los Angeles Photographs.* The Huntington Library, Art Collections, and Botanical Gardens. New York: Merrell, 2008.

With New Eyes: Toward an Asian American Art History in the West. San Francisco: San Francisco State University Art Gallery, 1995.

Yasuo Kuniyoshi, 1889-1935: A Retrospective Exhibition. Austin, TX: University Art Museum, 1975.

Yasuo Kuniyoshi: tanjô 100nen kinen – nyû yôku no yûshû. Tokyo Teien Art Museum, December, 1989.

Yoshida Fujio ten zuroku. (Yukio Fujio: A Painter of Radiance.) Tokyo: Fuchûshibijutsukan, 2002.

Yoshida Hiroshi ten. Kindai fûkei no kyoshô. Seishin to jojô." A Master of Modern Landscape Painting: Yoshida Hiroshi Exhibition. Refreshingly Original and Lyrical. Fukuoka Art Museum, October 26-November 24, 1996.

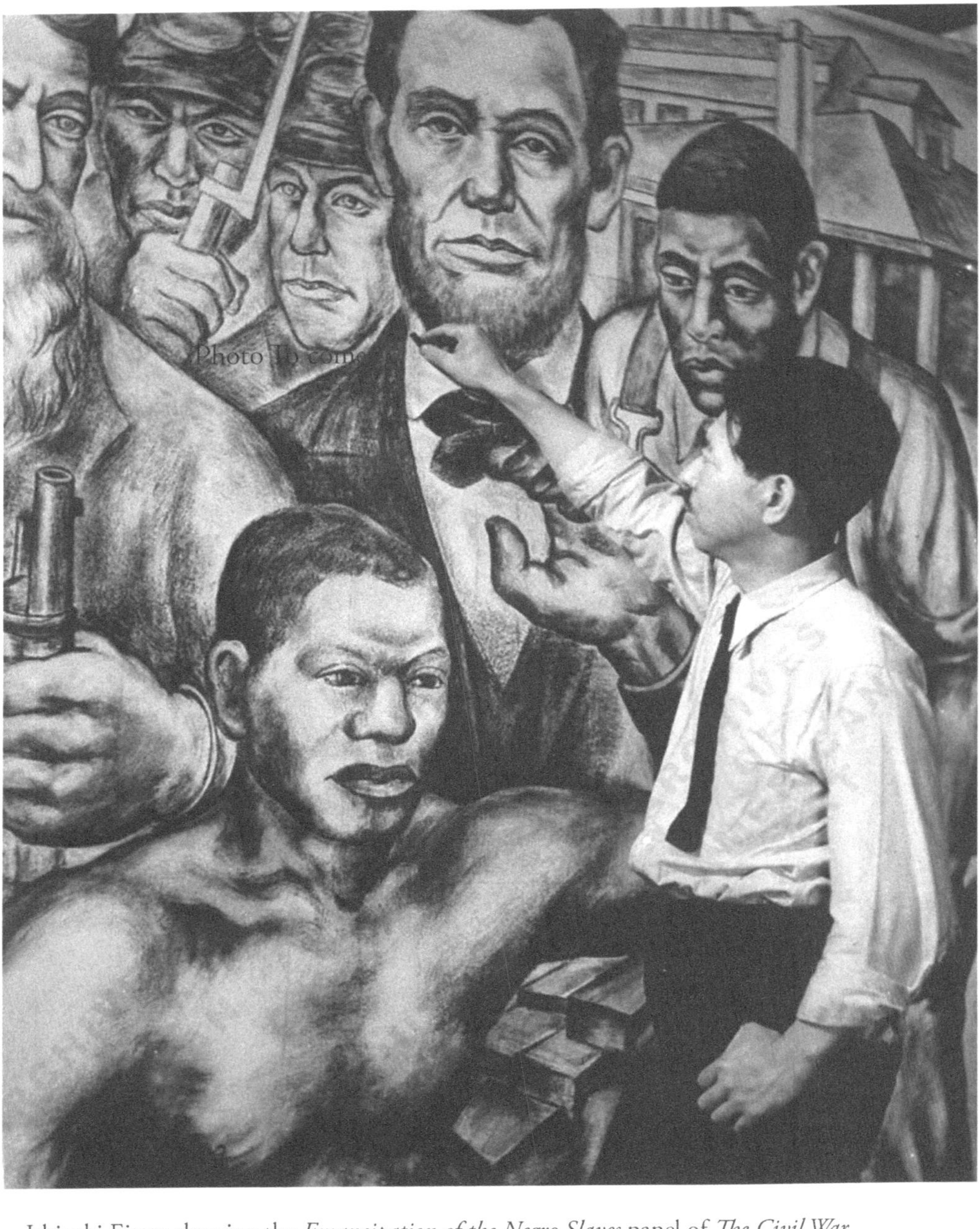

Ishigaki Eitaro drawing the *Emancipation of the Negro Slaves* panel of *The Civil War* mural at the Harlem Courthouse in New York, circa 1937. Federal Art Project.

Index

Note: *n* after page numbers refers to a footnote number. (For example, 112n7 references page 112, footnote number 7.) An italic page number with an *i* following, indicates a photograph. **Color Plate** references art works or photographs that are in the center of the book, found in pages 138-161.

F

G

H

I

L

N

O

P

R

T

U

V

About the Author

Born in Lihue, Kauai in 1973, Ramona Handel-Bajema was raised in San Francisco, California. A lifelong writer and historian of modern Japan, Ramona is currently a lecturer at Columbia University in New York.

Following the 2011 triple disaster in Japan, Ramona worked in disaster relief in northeastern Japan and wrote about the region's recovery. Her next project is on the seminal artist, Okamoto Taro.